P9-CKF-076

The Glass Ocean

Also by

Beatriz Williams, Lauren Willig, and Karen White

The Forgotten Room

Beatriz Williams

The Summer Wives

Cocoa Beach

A Certain Age

Along the Infinite Sea

The Secret Life of Violet Grant

A Hundred Summers

Lauren Willig

The English Wife

The Other Daughter

That Summer

The Ashford Affair

The Pink Carnation Series

Karen White

Dreams of Falling

The Night the Lights Went Out

Flight Patterns

The Sound of Glass

A Long Time Gone

The Tradd Street Series

The Glass Ocean

A Novel

BEATRIZ WILLIAMS,
LAUREN WILLIG,
AND KAREN WHITE

wm
WILLIAM MORROW
An Imprint of HarperCollins*Publishers*

This book is a work of fiction. References to real people, events, establishments, organizations, or locales are intended only to provide a sense of authenticity, and are used fictitiously. All other characters, and all incidents and dialogue, are drawn from the authors' imagination and are not to be construed as real.

HarperCollins books may be purchased for educational, business, or sales promotional use. For information, please email the Special Markets Department at SPsales@harpercollins.com.

FIRST EDITION

Designed by Bonni Leon-Berman

Library of Congress Cataloging-in-Publication Data has been applied for.

ISBN 978-0-06-264245-5

18 19 20 21 22 LSC 10 9 8 7 6 5 4 3 2 1

To the victims and survivors of the final voyage of RMS Lusitania

and those who loved them

The Glass Ocean

CHAPTER 1

Sarah

New York City
May 2013

THE EVENING HAD turned blue and soft, the way New York does in May, and I decided to walk to the book club and save the bus fare. According to Mimi's Facebook message, the group was gathering at her apartment on Park Avenue, deep inside the plummy center of the Seventies—at least thirty minutes from my place on Riverside Drive—but I didn't mind. I was a New Yorker, I could walk all day. Anyway, a brisk hike (so I told myself, scrolling through the Mimi message chain for the millionth time that afternoon) would settle my nerves.

I allowed myself plenty of time to get ready so I wouldn't arrive late. Lateness was unprofessional, Mom used to tell me, dressed in her ladylike suit and smelling of Youth Dew and good manners. Select your outfit the night before, leave ten minutes early. All good advice. I'd already laid out a pair of indigo skinny jeans and a silk blouse, and I only changed my mind about the blouse twice. My favorite wedges, because they loaned me a few necessary inches without trading off my ability to walk. Collar necklace, hair in ponytail. You know, just the right kind of casual, threw-this-on-without-thinking elegance to set those Park Avenue yummy mummies back on their Louboutins.

The necklace itched my collarbone. I undid the ponytail, redid it. Changed necklace. Grabbed Kate Spade tote and tied Hermès scarf to handle. Took off scarf. Started to tie it back on and stopped, because the whole scarf-on-handbag look was kind of aspirational, wasn't it? Or was I overthinking again? Checked my phone and realized I should have left five minutes ago.

So off I went, sprinting, as usual, across the Upper West Side and Central Park, lungs burning, ankles wobbling, while the softball games wound up noisily and the lovers met after work, hand in hand, heading for wine bars and tapas, for apartments and takeout. When I wasn't in a hurry, when I was just strolling or even sitting on a bench, eating a hot dog with ketchup and mustard but no onion, I liked to study them, my fellow New Yorkers. I liked to pick someone out from the crowd, some man in a suit, loosening his tie, checking his watch. I tried to divine his life, his history, the peculiar secrets hidden in his past. Mom used to tell this story about the dinner parties they once had, before Dad left, and how I used to peek through the banister when I was supposed to be sleeping and watch the guests, and how in the morning I would bombard her with questions about them, who was married to whom, who did what for a living, who came from where and had how many siblings. And I used to think this story of hers was true. I used to think I was born for my career.

Now I wasn't so sure. Not anymore, not while I galloped past Belvedere Castle, dodging baby strollers; not while the smell of Central Park filled my mouth, warm green leaves and hot dog stands, car exhaust and pavement stained with urine. The great metropolitan outdoors. On my left, the gray-beige spike of Cleopatra's Needle loomed up, cornered by about a dozen tourists brandishing their selfie sticks, and the sight of them seized me with panic. I accelerated to a jog, then back to a speedwalk. When I burst through the gap to the horns and shouts of Fifth Avenue, I paused to check my phone and realized the panic I'd felt was genuine instinct: I'd misjudged the walking time. I was already eleven minutes late. All the other women would've arrived by now. Probably figured I'd flaked and felt pity for me. Upper East Side housewives always had their act together, checklists every morning neatly checked off by bedtime, and they couldn't understand those who daydreamed and lost track of time, whose brains and lives could not be contained inside straight, organized lines.

Mimi hadn't mentioned the cross street in her message, just the address on Park Avenue that suggested Seventies. I plunged across Fifth, weaving between two tour buses and into the path of an oncoming taxi. The driver laid on the horn. I reached the curb and dashed down Seventy-Ninth Street to Madison, waited for a gap in traffic, crossed Madison and tore east toward Park. A dogwalker blocked the sidewalk with six or seven pooches, ranging in size from a gray-and-white Havanese to an Irish wolfhound who belonged anywhere in the world except New York City. The Havanese lunged toward me like an old friend—I had this thing with dogs—and I thought, maybe I should be a dogwalker, maybe that's my calling. Not this. Running down a sidewalk to a book club meeting, hoping I wasn't too late for the hors d'oeuvres. I was counting on those hors d'oeuvres. Mimi probably catered from Yura or someplace equally exquisite. Checked phone. Fourteen minutes late.

Of course the building was all the way between Seventy-Second and Seventy-First. I counted down the numbers on the long green awnings, passed doorman after doorman, finally found the right digits. Checked them against Mimi's message, just to be sure. When I looked up, a doorman in a sober black suit was staring at me. I straightened my back the way Mom used to make me and said, "Hi there? I'm here for the book club? Mimi Balfour? 8B? Sorry, I'm a little late!" Bright smile.

He smiled back, kind of sympathetic, hired help to hired help, and pulled open the bronze-grilled door. "Elevator's right ahead," he said.

I guess I should mention that I don't *know* Mimi Balfour, not personally. We've never met. She sent me a message on my Facebook author page, explaining that her book club was reading *Small Potatoes* in May, she noticed I was a New Yorker from my bio, would I mind meeting with them.

It was the kind of self-assured message that assumed my acceptance; opposite to the messages and emails I received from book clubs in the months after *Small Potatoes* was first published, when you couldn't turn on the *Today* show or *The View* or *Live with Kelly and Michael* without watching me hold forth—brimming with wit and importance, taking Joy's fascination and Michael's flirtation for granted—about the Irish potato famine like I might break out in Gaelic any second. Remember those emails? The deference, the *how busy you must be*, the *adored your book so much*, the *forever grateful*. I passed them all on to my publicist, who picked out a few lucky winners and sent the rest my regrets and a helpful list of articles and interviews. No more than twice a month, I told her then. I just can't fit any more into my schedule.

As the elevator rose slowly toward Mimi's floor—how I loved old Candela buildings and their small, dignified lifts—I tried to recall the last time I visited a book club. A year ago, maybe. No. Longer. That group in Greenpoint, in the tiny apartment that smelled of cat food. There was a blizzard, and they canceled the meeting without bothering to tell me, so I turned up while the woman and her roommate were binge-watching *House of Cards* on the sofa with their cats. To her credit, she apologized. She'd just assumed no author in her right mind would venture out in that snowstorm. Made me some hot chocolate, offered me stale Tostitos, and asked what I was writing next. My favorite question. By the time I left, the subways had shut down, and I had to walk all the way back home in a pair of too-short Uggs, across the Williamsburg Bridge to Manhattan, crosstown and uptown while the snow bit my cheeks and piled on the sidewalks. Good times. How could I forget a night like that?

I stared at the bronze arrow, inching its way around the arc, and I told myself Mimi would be nothing like the cat food lady. There would be hors d'oeuvres for my empty stomach, wine for my empty soul. They would drench me with their enthusiasm for *Small Potatoes*. Everybody loved the book, once they read it. The trouble was, five years out from publication, not a lot of people did. Long ago were the days of that Boston school district that ordered *Small Potatoes* for the entire seventh grade and asked me to speak at the middle school assembly.

Floor six, floor seven. I rehearsed a few key bits from my stump speech in my head. That riff about the sheep always got a laugh.

Floor eight. The doors of the elevator parted, revealing a small cream-and-gold foyer. To the left, 8A. To the right, 8B. Only two apartments per floor in a building like this. Mimi's husband was probably an investment banker or a hedge fund manager. Maybe a partner at one of those white-shoe corporate law firms. Wouldn't that be nice, to have someone else worry about making all the money that kept you alive? I'd once had a fling with a hedgie. He was in his late thirties and stinking rich, a mathematical genius with a crass sense of humor, and also sort of handsome in a skinny, electric, thin-lipped way. That was a few months after *Small Potatoes* came out, when my celebrity writer cachet briefly eclipsed my Irish freckles and too-curly reddish-brown hair. Dinners at Daniel, sex at his sleek Tribeca loft, private cars taking us everywhere. I'd broken it off when I discovered he was also having flings with a couple of twenty-year-old Victoria's Secret models, but maybe that was a rash decision, after all. I stepped forward and knocked on the door to 8B. Checked my phone a last time before sliding it into my tote. Nineteen minutes late.

The door opened. I half-expected a uniformed maid, but a tall, skinny, sharp-boned blonde stood before me, wearing white jeans, holding a glass of white wine, still giggling over some joke left behind.

I held out my hand. "Mimi? I'm so sorry—"

"Oh, *hi*! I'm Jen. Mimi's in the living room. Are you *Sarah*? Oh my *God*, you look *nothing* like your author photo!"

"Sadly, you can't take the makeup artist home with you," I said, my standard answer. "I'm so sorry I—"

"Come on back," she said, turning away. "Everyone's dying to meet you."

I realized, as I stepped after Jen into a massive paneled gallery painted in tasteful dove gray, that my silk blouse—bought during the days of plenty—was sticking to my skin. That I was still sweating from the mad dash across Manhattan, that my hair was wet at the temples, that my lungs were sucking wind. That my stomach was actually growling. I hadn't eaten since breakfast. Figured I'd be feasting tonight, so why not save a few dollars? I lifted my hand and wiped the sleeve of my cardigan against the sides of my face, along the skin above my upper lip. Jen's back wove in front of me, the bumps of her spine just visible underneath her snug navy tank. Her arms swung, improbably sleek. Probably a team of vigilant stylists kept every follicle on Jen's body under immaculate control. Blond, thick, shining hair growing rampant on top and absolutely, positively, *nowhere* else.

The foyer opened into a formal-yet-contemporary living room, shades of gray accented in crimson, containing a pair of opposing sofas and a flock of chairs in coordinating upholstery, all of them occupied by straight-haired women in skeletal white jeans identical to Jen's. Jen stepped aside and gestured to me with her wineglass. "I brought the *author*!" she trilled, and I realized she was already half-drunk, and I thought, For God's sake, how much wine could you possibly drink in twenty minutes?

I waved my hand a little. "Hi, everyone! I'm so sorry—"

A woman rose from the left-hand sofa, a brunette in a turquoise trapeze top, anticipating summer. "Sarah! I'm Mimi. Wow, you look *nothing* like your author photo!"

Jen screeched, "I know, right? That's what I said!"

"Sorry, I'm just a lip gloss and mascara girl in real life. And again, I apologize for being so late—"

Mimi checked her watch. "Oh my gosh, is it past seven *already*? Girls, we've been chatting for an hour and a *half*!"

Everybody laughed. On the coffee table lay a few trays of elegant tidbits. I spotted Lilliputian cheeseburgers crowned by single tiny sesame seeds, ceviche, some kind of bruschetta, guacamole furrowed by tracks from the blue corn tortilla chips in a bowl alongside. Glasses of white wine perched between fingers, and a Filipino woman in a uniform was refilling them methodically from a chilled bottle.

"I'll bet you're dying for a glass of wine, right?" said Mimi. "Angel, could you pour a glass for Miss Blake? And you can take all this back in the kitchen. You're not hungry, are you, Sarah?"

"Actually—"

"Just bring out the cupcakes, Angel. And the wine for Miss Blake." Mimi turned back to me and waved at a strange, high-backed wooden chair at the far end of the coffee table, painted in silver. "Sit! Omigod! This *book*! So amazing."

I tottered to the silver chair and sank on the seat. Allowed my tote to slide to the floor. Before me, Angel scurried around the table, lifting trays of beautiful, untouched food. I started to reach for a miniature cheeseburger, but she went by too quickly, and I converted the gesture into a sleeve adjustment. "Thanks," I said. "It came out of some research I did for my thesis—"

"What I loved," Mimi said, "were all the stories of the Irish women immigrating to America. That really resonated with me. I'm totally Irish on my mother's side. My great-grandmother was a maid, can you believe it?"

"Domestic service was one of the few occupations open to women and girls who—"

"Wait, your great-grandmother was a *maid*? *Meems*! I had no *idea*!" one of the women said.

"I *know*, right? To some family on the Upper East Side. I wish I knew where. Wouldn't it be *crazy* if she worked in *this* building?" Mimi tossed her hair over her shoulder. "Anyway. Go on, Sarah."

"Um. So there I was in Dublin on this research grant, seven or eight years ago, and I actually wasn't studying the potato famine at all. I was researching the absentee landlords—Englishmen, basically, whose families had been granted land in Ireland, but they never lived there at all, just took all the rents from the tenant farmers and hired estate managers to oversee—thanks so much." I snatched the glass of wine from Angel and sipped. The eyes of the women around me had taken on a polite, glassy sheen. Jen reached for her iPhone and skidded her thumb in quick strokes across the screen. I swallowed the wine and hurried on. "Anyway, blah blah, I came across this archive—"

"So when you're doing your research," one woman said, "do you ever, like, come across stuff that nobody else has seen? Or something really valuable, like a painting or whatever from a famous artist that was, like, lost or something?"

"Um, not exactly. It's more like—"

"Oh, I totally saw something like that on a TV show once! It was like a da Vinci or like Michelangelo or something."

"*Yes*! I saw that, too! And I was like, wow, that dealer could have totally screwed that guy over, like bought the painting for five bucks or whatever—"

"Wait!" Mimi held up her hand, palm out, like she was trying to stop traffic. "Girls. Come on. The author's talking. So you were getting your master's, right? What subject?"

"Doctorate, actually. History."

"Oh, obvs!" She laughed. "Where did you go to school again, Sarah? Somewhere in New York, right?"

"Columbia. It's in my bio? On the back of the book?" I looked around the room and realized, for the first time, that not one single copy of *Small Potatoes* lay on any of Mimi's expensive surfaces. "Um, I don't know if anyone brought a copy with them—"

"Oh, I've got it right here." Mimi set down her wine and picked up an iPad from the side table at her left. "Hold on a sec. Ugh. Messages. Did anyone else bring their iPad?"

"I've got it on my phone," said Jen.

"Can you open the file and find Sarah's bio? I have to answer this."

Mimi burrowed into her iPad and Jen swiped away on her phone. I swished my wine and said, "It doesn't matter, really. Long story short, I was at grad school, doctorate program in history, went to Dublin for a semester and found—"

"Oh, here it is!" said Jen. She stood up and handed me her phone. "Here, read it out for us."

I took the phone and looked down at the screen. "It's kind of blurred, isn't it?"

"Yeah, sorry about that. Mimi found this awesome website so we could all download it for free."

I looked up and stared at Jen's bright, smooth face. The upholstery behind her was some kind of gray-toned leopard print with a furry texture, like a real hide, stretched over a delicate Louis XVI frame painted in the same silver as my own chair. I found myself wondering if it was a reproduction or an antique, if Mimi and her interior designer had actually gone and refinished a genuine Louis XVI chair in silver paint.

The words looped in my head. *Download it for free.* Cheerful, triumphant. *Download it for free!* What a freaking bargain.

"I'm sorry," I said. "She found *what?*"

"That website. Meems, what was the name again? Bongo or something?"

Mimi looked up from her iPad. "What are we talking about?"

"That website where you found Sarah's book."

"Oh," she said. "Bingo. Haven't you heard of it? It's like an online library. You can download almost anything for free. It's *amazing*."

My hands were shaking. I set down Jen's phone, and then I set down the wineglass next to it. Without a coaster.

"You mean a pirate site," I said.

"Oh God, no! I would never. It's an online library."

"That's what they call it. But they're just stealing. They're fencing stolen goods. Easy to do with electronic copies."

"No. That's not true." Mimi's voice rose a little. Sharpened a little. "Libraries lend out e-books."

"Real libraries do. They buy them from the publisher. Sites like Bingo just upload unauthorized copies to sell advertising or put cookies on your phone or whatever else. They're pirates."

There was a small, shrill silence. I lifted my wineglass and took a long drink, even though my fingers were trembling so badly, I knew everyone could see the vibration.

"Well," said Mimi. "It's not like it matters. I mean, the book's been out for years and everything, it's like public domain."

I put down the wineglass and picked up my tote bag. "So I don't have time to lecture you about copyright law or anything. Basically, if publishers don't get paid, authors don't get paid. That's kind of how it works."

"Oh, come on," said Mimi. "You got paid for this book."

"Not as much as you think. Definitely not as much as your husband gets paid to short derivatives or whatever he does that buys all this stuff." I waved my hand at the walls. "And you know, fine, maybe it's not the big sellers who suffer. It's the midlist authors, the great names you never hear of, where every sale counts. . . . What am I saying? You don't care. None of you actually cares. Sitting here in your palaces in the sky. You never had to earn a penny of your own. Why the hell should you care about royalties?" I climbed out of my silver chair and hoisted my tote bag over my shoulder. "It's about a dollar a book, by the way. Paid out every six months. So I walked all the way over here, gave up an evening of my life, and even if every single one of you had actually bought a legitimate copy, I would have earned about a dozen bucks for my trouble. Twelve dollars and a glass of cheap wine. I'll see myself out."

I turned and marched back across the living room, tripping on the last chair leg. Angel stood frozen in awe, holding a tray of two-bite cupcakes and a chilled bottle of Pinot Gris. My armpits dripped; my heart thudded so hard I felt dizzy. As I opened the door, I heard somebody's voice carry down the gallery.

"What a *bitch*!"

I considered holding up my middle finger. But I didn't. My mom would have been proud, if she were still lucid enough to understand.

I took the crosstown bus back home and made some mac and cheese from the box. Told myself that was okay because it was organic boxed mac and cheese. Told myself that at least they hadn't gotten around to asking me what I was working on for my next book. Plopped on the sofa and toed off my wedges and picked up the remote. I had a few shows queued up on the DVR. Some history, some true crime. I told myself I'd be working, actually, because you never knew where your next book idea might come from. You never knew when inspiration might strike.

Oh, the things you tell yourself.

I switched on the TV and picked up my bowl of mac and cheese. From across the room, inside my tote bag, my phone started ringing. An outraged Mimi, probably. If I were lucky, she'd call Page Six or something. No such thing as bad publicity, right? Some intern would contact me to ask for details. Small Potatoes *author Sarah Blake melts down at Park Avenue book club . . . Sarah, whatever happened to all that movie talk around* Small Potatoes *. . . ? Sarah, what are you working on now . . . ?*

A year after *Small Potatoes* came out, my editor took me to lunch and asked about my ideas. I said I was thinking about Queen Victoria's children. She frowned and said what about a racehorse, like Seabiscuit or Secretariat, only another one, obviously. She was sure there were more famous racehorses out there. I said I'd look into it. Then she called up six months later and said she wanted me to write the next *Boys on the Boat,* maybe like an America's Cup team made up of hardscrabble youths from Minnesota. Then it was World War Two. World War Two was red-hot. Some scrappy bilingual girl working for the French Resistance. Or what about Coco Chanel? The Lindbergh baby? I said I thought those were all pretty well covered already. I wanted something new. I said the story would find me when it was ready.

She hadn't called since. My agent stopped replying to my emails personally. The foreign translation deals dried up. The movie people didn't pick up the option after all. The royalty checks shrank and shrank.

Don't get me wrong. There was a lot of money that first year, or at least a lot of money by the standard of what I was used to: daughter of a divorced mother and an absentee father, grad student living on financial aid and ramen noodles. But I spent it all. I had to. Not on myself. Well, not most of it.

The phone rang again. I thought, Maybe it's not Mimi or Page Six. Maybe it's Mom.

The images on the screen shifted and flashed. I couldn't even remember what I was watching. I set aside the mac and cheese and rose to fetch my tote from the hall stand. My feet ached. Even my favorite wedges had their limits. My legs ached, my head ached. I rummaged in the tote and drew out my phone, just as the call went to voice mail.

Not Mom. The care home. They'd already left two messages.

I didn't bother listening. I just swiped the notification and pressed *redial.*

For the past four years, Mom had been living a few blocks away—hence my tiny studio here on Riverside Drive, which was not my natural habitat—in a small, private care home for Alzheimer's patients. She started showing symptoms when she was only fifty-six, and it progressed pretty quickly from there. I won't bore you with the details. Long story short, I moved her into Riverside Haven about the time *Small Potatoes* went from hardcover into trade paperback, and sold the adorable Carnegie Hill one-bedroom I'd bought a year earlier in order to fund her care. The place had dedicated therapists for each patient, private rooms, views of the river. Nothing was too good for my mother, who raised me by herself after Dad split when I was four. Sure, it was expensive, but I figured I'd just write another book, right? Another blockbuster work of narrative nonfiction. No problem.

"Riverside Haven, can you hold, please?"

"No, wait—"

The hold music started. I sank back on the sofa and stared at the mac and cheese, which had begun to congeal. Turned my head toward the hall closet instead. The door. The doorknob. What lay behind it, singing like a siren. A siren I'd done my best to ignore for four long years.

"Riverside Haven, can I help you?"

"Hi! It's Sarah Blake. You were trying to reach me? Is Mom okay?"

"Oh, hello, Miss Blake. Diana Carr here. No, your mother's just fine. She's had a quiet day. I didn't mean to scare you. I just wanted to speak to you about last month's invoice."

When I finished speaking to Diana Carr—yes, I understood how many months in arrears I was, I understood that Riverside Haven would do its best not to have to resort to eviction—I set my phone down next to the bowl of congealed macaroni and went to the hall closet. Opened the door and rose on my toes. Found the small wooden trunk and dragged it from the shelf. The smell of dust filled my head, dustiness and mustiness and old wood, and above it all a slight hint of Youth Dew, even though I had removed this chest from my mother's apartment four years ago. I placed it carefully on the coffee table, squaring the edges, and sat on my knees and stared at the lid.

ANNIE HOULIHAN
593 Lorimer Street
Brooklyn, New York

I had opened this chest once before, when I was about ten or eleven. My mother found me in her closet, lifting out the contents, and that was the only time in my life she ever screamed at me. Slammed down the lid and sent me to my room. When she was calm again, she took me to the sofa and tucked me under her warm, soft arm. *That was your great-grandmother's chest*, she said. *With all your great-grandfather's things in it. All they found on him when they pulled his body out of the water. The Cunard company sent it back to her in a parcel, and she wouldn't even look at it. She had your grandmother pack everything into a chest and promise never to open it. She said it was his tomb. So you are never to open that chest again, do you hear me? Never again.*

I'd obeyed my mother, because what else could I do? I knew the story of my great-grandmother and great-grandfather, how they left Ireland together in search of a new life, how my great-grandfather Patrick had worked as a steward for the Cunard Line while my great-grandmother Annie raised five children in a small upstairs apartment in Brooklyn, saving up to buy a house of their own.

But I also knew what lay in that chest. I'd seen it with my own eyes, before Mom slammed down the lid. And my curious brain never could let it go. Never could erase that knowledge from my head, or banish the questions those objects raised. Because, my God, what a story they told.

And I was just born that way. Mom said so herself.

So maybe Mom would forgive me for what I was about to do. Maybe she would shake her head and understand, because I was Sarah, her daughter, and I was born to wonder and to dig for answers. Maybe she and my grandmother and my great-grandmother would absolve me for breaking my word, because I was at the end of the road, nowhere else to go, and I wasn't doing it for myself, not entirely. I was doing it for Mom. I was doing it for that invoice lying in the drawer of my bedside table. For the voice in my head that said, *This is the story, the story that wants to find you. No other story.*

I lifted the lid.

The hinges creaked. The smell of brine filled the air. Brine and wool and wood. I closed my eyes and breathed it in, and then I reached inside with two hands and pulled out the little bundle.

Just a few things. All that remained on his body when they pulled him from the sea, ninety-nine years ago. His white steward's uniform, stained dark at the collar and the right arm, so stiff it crackled under my fingertips. An oilskin pouch, containing an envelope with *Mr. Robert Langford, Stateroom B-38* typed on the back, and a series of numbers and letters written in black ink along the other side.

A few coins, minted by the United States Treasury in the early years of the century.

A silver pocket watch, slightly tarnished at the seams.

And a first-class luncheon menu from RMS *Lusitania*, dated Thursday, the sixth of May, 1915, on the back of which was scribbled the following message, the ink smeared with moisture and barely legible.

No more betrayals. Meet me B-deck prom starboard side.

CHAPTER 2

Caroline

New York City
Friday, April 30, 1915

Caroline Telfair Hochstetter stood at her opened bedroom window facing Fifth Avenue, the cool breeze attempting to rip the curtains out of her tightly clutched fists. She was freezing—as usual—but the feeling of claustrophobia, never far away, had latched on to her with clawlike fingers from the moment her maid, Jones, had awakened her with the breakfast tray and a reminder that they needed to finish packing for their departure to England the following day.

Once more, she breathed in a lungful of air hoping, just once, that she could pretend she was back home in Savannah, with the dulcet tones and dropped consonants of her fellow natives falling softly on her ears, and a breeze carrying the beloved scent of the salt marshes that surrounded the city brushing her skin and lifting her hair like a mother's hand. Instead she coughed on the fumes from the congestion of motor-cars and buses below, feeling so far from home that she could have been on the moon and not seen her surroundings as more alien.

"Ma'am?"

Caroline glanced over her shoulder to see her new maid, Martha Jones, standing at the dressing room door, balancing a tray holding a crystal glass and a decanter of claret.

Jones was a recent hire following the rather quick departure of Caroline's previous lady's maid, whose only reason for leaving had been that her circumstances had changed for the better. Happily, Caroline had not been without a maid for long. Jones had been the first to appear on her doorstep as soon as the employment advertisement had appeared in the paper. She'd come with an impressive list of references and talents, including a self-professed genius with a hair tong, and Caroline had immediately hired her without interviewing any other candidate. She'd no time to waste, after all, as her trip across the Atlantic was to commence the following week. Caroline had told herself she'd been lucky, and had quickly brushed aside any reservations she might have had about her new lady's maid.

"I beg your pardon, ma'am. My last mistress was a society hostess in San Francisco and always asked for a glass or two of claret while I dressed her hair before a party. I hope you don't mind me being so forward." She placed the tray on the dressing table, making room amid the hairpins and brushes.

Caroline smiled gratefully, closing the window. "I do believe you're a lifesaver, Jones." She sat down and allowed the maid to pour her a generous glass of claret before taking a long sip. "Yes, a definite lifesaver."

Jones smiled, their eyes meeting in the mirror. "Just doing my job, ma'am. Now, let's see to your hair. Unless you have a preference, I had an idea for an evening style I saw in the American *Vogue* last month that I believe would look simply stunning on you—not that you need any enhancements, that's for sure."

Caroline looked at the maid's reflection, wondering if Jones was trying to ingratiate herself to her new employer of if she really was the consummate lady's maid, always equipped with the right tools and the right flattery. Jones smiled benignly, her rather plain face and doughy figure emanating a no-nonsense aura of confidence and ability.

Feeling magnanimous after another long sip of her claret, Caroline said, "You're the expert, Jones. Why don't you have fun with it?" She stared at her reflection as her maid deftly unbraided the large plait that lay over her shoulder, allowing the thick, dark brown waves to cascade down her back.

The color matched her eyes, and Caroline smiled to herself, recalling how her mother had said she'd wanted to name her Susan, like the black-eyed Susans that grew in the pine forests near their Savannah home. But her father had insisted on the name Caroline and, as in all things concerning her father, her mother had capitulated.

The room was silent as Caroline's hair was deftly coaxed into curls and rolls that nature had never intended. Only the ever-present noise of the busy street outside and the sound of scurrying servants intruded, even these getting quieter and quieter as Caroline sipped her wine, her thoughts twisting and turning along well-worn paths.

She hadn't wanted to have this party, a great extravagant affair orchestrated by her husband, Gilbert, who thought this would be a marvelous opportunity for all of the first-class passengers embarking the following day on Cunard's great liner *Lusitania* to get better acquainted.

Her fingers tightened on the stem of her glass. Caroline was well aware that the party was just another excuse for Gilbert to show off his wealth in the face of old money, as if his generosity and benevolence could ever erase the fact that his money was crisp and shiny, having been earned by Gilbert himself from the steel mills of Gilbert's home state of Pennsylvania.

She wanted to tell him that there was no need for him to prove himself to these people, that their opinions didn't matter. That what did matter was that she loved him because of who he was. Not because he was the founder and president of Hochstetter Iron & Steel, but because he'd known poverty and through hard work, brains, and persistence had become the man she'd fallen in love with. Yet that had been the subject of their first fight. The first of many in their four-year marriage.

A knock sounded on the dressing room door just as Jones put down the comb and hair tongs. "Come in," Caroline called out.

Gilbert stepped into the room, immediately dwarfing it. He was taller than most men, his shoulders broader and filling out his expertly tailored dinner jacket in a way that made Caroline want to run her hands down his arms to absorb some of their strength. Because she needed it now. The wine had given her the courage to try one last time. "Please leave us for a moment, Jones. Just ten minutes and then you can help me into my gown."

The maid bowed her head before leaving, quietly shutting the door behind her so that Caroline barely heard it latch.

Caroline met Gilbert's bright blue eyes with her own, the wine doing nothing to calm the tightening in her chest as she regarded him. His blond hair had been combed back and oiled, making him look years younger—perhaps in an effort to make him appear closer to Caroline's own age of twenty-four. His hands were held stiffly behind his back as he smiled awkwardly at her, unsure of what he should say.

Taking advantage of the situation, Caroline spoke first. "I beg of you, Gilbert. Please. Let's not go to England now. It's not safe to cross the Atlantic. You know this—we have both been reading the papers. So many ships have been sunk by German U-boats. And not just cargo ships, but passenger ships, too. The Germans don't seem to care as long as they torpedo something."

He didn't move. "We've already been through this, Caroline. Not going is not an option. I've already made an appointment with an antiquities dealer in London and he is expecting us."

Caroline stood, grateful for the wine that seemed to be working as a barrier between her anger and her voice. "But why now? Are you so desperate for money that you must sell something so precious to me? I had to read in the paper that your government contracts to make barbwire were a boon to your business, but other than that I'm in the dark about our finances. You tell me nothing of your business affairs so I don't know how desperate you might be. Maybe if you confide in me . . ."

"No. I will not burden you with my business affairs. When I married you, I promised your mother that I would keep you in the manner to which you deserve. I will never go back on that promise."

"But why that manuscript? And why now? Surely you know how special it is to me?"

He stiffened. "I do know. But an unpublished Johann Strauss waltz is worth a considerable amount of money. As I have only just become aware of its real value, I feel the need to investigate it further. I know this sounds impulsive to you, but may I remind you that I have built an empire on these sorts of feelings and impulses."

Caroline sat back down in the dressing table chair. "It was your wedding gift to me," she said softly. "Even if it were worth no more than a penny, I would cherish it with all of my heart."

His eyes met hers again, blue and inscrutable. That inscrutability was what made him a successful businessman. And a sometimes horrible husband. He brought his hands in front of him, showing her a square, black velvet box. "I thought this might make you happy."

She felt nothing as she reached for the box. He was always buying her baubles, great, big, expensive, gaudy baubles that she secretly hated and never wore, preferring her great-grandmother's heirloom pearls at her throat instead. Not that Gilbert noticed enough to stop.

She opened the lid and stared at the diamond tiara inside, not knowing what to say.

"I thought you could wear it tonight. So everyone could see that you're my queen."

It was when he spoke such naïve thoughts that Caroline loved her husband most. Yet she still couldn't envision putting the diamond tiara on her head to be paraded about downstairs. She could only imagine what their guests would say behind their backs.

"It's lovely. Thank you. But Jones has already done my hair. I'll have her pack the tiara so that perhaps I can wear it on the ship."

She saw a flash of disappointment in his eyes. *Good.* She felt guilty for the thought, but only until she remembered what they'd been arguing about. She stood again to face him, feeling slightly wobbly on her feet. She put her hands on his arms, her fingers only able to reach halfway around them. "Please, Gilbert. I will never ask you for anything else. But please don't make us take this journey. I don't have a good feeling about it."

"There is nothing to be afraid of, Caroline. The Royal Navy will give us an escort when we are in international waters. And besides, the Germans wouldn't dare torpedo a ship carrying American citizens. The last thing they want is to encourage American involvement in the war." He paused, as if trying to find a way to make his next words more palatable before apparently giving up. "My decision has been made," he said brusquely, pulling away from her. "Our guests will be arriving shortly. May I suggest you wear the ruby necklace I gave you for your last birthday?" With a stiff bow, he left, the door shutting loudly behind him.

A half hour later, Caroline stood next to Gilbert receiving their guests, wearing her great-grandmother's pearls. Gilbert appeared not to have noticed, too caught up in playing lord of the manor and gracious host. He bade everyone to enjoy themselves and to make themselves comfortable, although Caroline was quite sure the latter would be impossible.

She found the French Renaissance monstrosity, in its enviable location on the corner of Fifth Avenue and Sixty-First Street, cold and foreign with its Italian marble, Tudor paneling, and gilded extravagance. It was too different from the Greek Revival home of her childhood, a place of creaking wide-plank pine floors and wraparound porches filled with rocking chairs and flowers that spilled over the edges of their pots like rainbows. When Gilbert had presented her with the house as a first-anniversary gift, she'd wanted to love it because he wanted her to. But try as she might, she could only shiver inside its lofty opulence and wonder how long it would take before it felt like home.

She greeted their guests, aware of their scrutiny, feeling not a little like one of the caged animals at the Central Park menagerie where Gilbert had taken her earlier in their marriage. Caroline realized that since she was a Southerner, people were eager to meet her, to ask her what she thought of the recent heat wave, and to hear her pronounce certain words. She'd been uncomfortable at first, until she'd felt Gilbert's gentle touch on her back, on her arm, encouraging her. Reminding her that he was nearby.

That's how it had started between them, all those years ago when she'd been in finishing school in Philadelphia with his younger sister and her best friend, Claire. Although Caroline's father had been a Telfair of the Savannah Telfairs, it was an impoverished branch and her widowed mother, Mrs. Annelise Telfair, had sold a rare Chippendale sideboard to send her daughter to the best finishing school money could buy, and to meet the sort of people Annelise envisioned her daughter hobnobbing with as an adult.

And so Caroline had, but not in the way her mother thought. As an only child and knowing no one at the school, Caroline had been quickly befriended by Claire Hochstetter. New money, as Annelise had sniffed with derision, when Caroline had introduced her to Claire and her brother Gilbert on one of Annelise's rare visits up north. With only her mother to claim as family, her father having died in a riding accident when Caroline was a little girl, Caroline had been lonely and aloof, a rudderless boat until Claire had introduced her to Gilbert. He was the type of person who dominated a room just by being in it, who took charge of any situation, who was quiet and smart, his size alone making him a beacon of strength and protection not only for Claire, but for Caroline as well.

She looked at her husband now, admiring his size and strength, and wondered when things between them had changed. But maybe that wasn't right at all. Nothing really *had* changed. He still treated her as a rare and precious object that needed his protection. Even though they'd been married for four years, he still saw her that way. Not as a wife or lover, but as a rare bird in a gilded cage.

He looked down at her and smiled, and it was the smile she'd first fallen in love with, making her heart stutter inside her chest. Maybe this trip was a way for him to take them both away from the pressure of their busy lives in New York. A way to reconcile. Perhaps a chance to conceive the child they both so desperately wanted.

The massive front doors closed behind them as the orchestra began to play. She looked up at her husband and smiled back, to let him know that she would go willingly. That she'd understood his purpose for this trip. That it was for both of them. "Dance with me," she said.

Gilbert was no longer looking at her, but at a small group of men on the far side of the room, near the door to his study. They appeared to be waiting for something, and when her husband nodded in their direction, Caroline understood they were waiting for him.

"I can't, my darling. I have urgent business I need to attend to before we depart tomorrow." He leaned down to briefly kiss her cheek. "Enjoy yourself." He walked away from her, the clicking of his heels against the marble floor seeming louder than the music coming from the orchestra.

She wondered if it was the wine that made her feel so close to tears as she quickly ran to the music room, her one refuge in the large mansion. Her Mason & Hamlin grand piano had been brought up from Savannah for her, and every time she sat down to play was like visiting an old friend. It was the one thing that calmed her, the one thing that helped her feel not so alone in a city and house full of strangers.

A single lamp was lit on the chest between the tall windows, but Caroline didn't need to see. She sat down on the familiar bench and removed her long white gloves before placing her hands on the ivory keys, the cool touch of them an immediate panacea to her mood. Without thinking, her fingers began to dance over the keys, the haunting melody of a Chopin nocturne singing out in the darkened room, her voice where she had none.

Something soft and warm settled itself on her shoulders, and she startled, lifting her fingers from the keys.

"Don't stop. You have such a gift for music."

She looked up at the familiar voice and smiled with relief. "Robert Langford! What on earth are you doing here?"

"From the looks of it, making sure you don't die of pneumonia. Is the house always so cold?"

"Sadly, yes." She patted the seat on the bench next to her and he obliged. She didn't stop to think of the propriety—or impropriety—of it. They'd known each other for years—ever since he'd held her hair out of her face as she'd vomited into the rosebushes at Hamilton Talmadge's garden party. The incident was her greatest embarrassment and his biggest secret. Not that he'd ever ask for payment. It had been the year she'd been sent to finishing school, the episode no doubt being one of the reasons Annelise had decided Caroline had needed it. At the time, Robert had been visiting the Talmadges in Savannah. Although British and aristocratic, he was from an untitled family and unlikely to inherit anything more than a leaky roof, as Caroline's mother had made clear. Annelise had bigger plans for her only child.

Not that Caroline had been interested. Her humiliation had been so intense that she hadn't found the courage to speak to Robert until their third meeting, at a ball celebrating her engagement to Gilbert.

"It's good to see you," she said, meaning it. "How is it that you never change? You're still that handsome young man who saved my reputation and dignity all those years ago."

"And you're as beautiful as ever," he said softly. His eyes reflected the light from the lamp, obscuring his expression.

"And you're as much of a flatterer as you've always been."

He put his hand on his heart. "I only speak the truth. How is it that some women become more and more beautiful with age? You must sell your secret. I understand there's at least one actress on board the *Lusitania*—I'm sure she'll be interested."

Caroline laughed. "I'll keep that in mind. So, what on earth are you doing here?"

"Same reason you are, I suspect," he said with a disarming grin. "I'm sailing on *Lusitania*. Family affairs that require my attention across the Pond, I'm afraid. Probably more scolding from my father regarding my unfortunate choice of journalism as a career. But why are you going? In case you're not aware, there's a war going on."

"I know," she said, drawing nearer to him for warmth. "My husband is looking to sell a rare piece of music—an unfinished waltz by Johann Strauss."

"Really? That's rather an important piece of music, I'd say."

"It is. Which is why he's looking to sell it." She began plucking the middle C key with her index finger, her long, white digits unadorned by any of the rings Gilbert had given her except for the plain gold band on her left hand.

"And you're not happy about it." It wasn't a question.

Caroline shook her head. "I don't understand why this particular object, and why now. Gilbert believes I should be protected from anything unpleasant and therefore won't confide in me. I'm baffled, I'm afraid, but don't have any options."

He grinned, his teeth white against the darkness of the room. "At least you'll have me. We'll keep each other cheered up while on board. That's something to look forward to, isn't it?"

She returned his smile. "It is. And I'm rather embarrassed to say how relieved I am to know this now. I won't dread boarding that ship quite as much tomorrow."

He studied her for a moment, suddenly serious. "I'd love to see the manuscript—if it's not too much of a bother."

"Do you still play?" she asked.

He appeared to have been taken off guard by her redirection. Smiling quickly, he said, "Of course." He placed both of his hands next to hers on the keyboard. "Do you know 'The Celebrated Chop Waltz'?"

In response she began playing the bass part of the duet while he immediately joined in with his part on the upper register of the piano. It soon became a race, with each of them playing faster and faster until they both collapsed in giggles as their hands came crashing down on the keyboard.

He was watching her with an odd gleam in his eyes that she wasn't completely sure was a trick of the dim lamplight. She sobered quickly, realizing how close they were sitting, how near his face was to hers, and how she didn't blame the wine for wanting him to get closer.

A burst of laughter from somewhere outside the door brought her to her senses and she immediately stood. "If you're serious about seeing the manuscript, I have it in here. I was being childish and took it from my jewelry safe this morning and hid it in the piano bench. I was hoping Gilbert wouldn't look for it before we left tomorrow and assume it was packed with my jewelry. But even I know that he's not one to overlook details."

Robert stood and lifted the lid of the bench, revealing an oilskin pouch bound with leather ties. "May I?" he asked.

Caroline nodded as Robert pulled out the pouch and slowly lowered the lid. Carefully, he unwound the leather ties then slid out the almost parchment thin papers with amber-colored musical notes covering the hand-drawn staff lines of the treble and bass clefs. Notations written in the composer's native German were scribbled in the margins.

"This is remarkable," Robert said, his words saying the right thing, but their intonation saying something else entirely. "I can see why you wouldn't want to let this go." He turned to her. "Do you know what these words in the margins say?"

"I don't speak German, and Gilbert wasn't keen on the idea of me showing this to anyone who might. It's very valuable."

"Of course." He studied the piece for a moment, a frown contracting his brows. "Have you played it?"

She took the sheets and placed them on the music stand of the piano before reseating herself on the bench, and began to play. Even though it was dark, she didn't miss any notes. She'd played the piece enough times that her fingers remembered where to fall, her mind remembering the picture journey in her head that led her from one note to the next. For a moment she forgot where she was, and who she was with, until she'd finished and Robert was clapping.

"Stunning," he said. "Simply stunning." And when she looked at him, she wasn't completely sure if he was referring to the music.

"Thank you," she said. "Although now I'm sad once more, knowing I'll most likely never have another chance to play this again." She carefully placed the music into the pouch then stuck it back in the piano bench, reminding herself to return it to her jewelry safe before they left the following morning. It was easier than waiting for Gilbert to ask her for it, as he surely would.

"May I get you some champagne to lift your spirits?" he asked just as the orchestra began to play a tune that made Caroline's feet itch to dance again and her to remember that Robert was a wonderful dancer.

"No, but you could dance with me." As she slid her hands back into her gloves, she had a brief thought of Gilbert, heading to his study with those men, and hoped he'd step out long enough to see her dancing with someone else. With Robert, her old friend, handsome, accommodating, fun, and familiar. And who she imagined seemed to be looking at her in the same way Gilbert once had.

He smiled. "That would be my pleasure," he said, taking her hand and leading her from the music room while Caroline tried to pretend it was the claret that made her feel the warmth of his touch right down to her feet, which had already begun to move in step with the music.

CHAPTER 3

Tess

New York City
Friday, April 30, 1915

"YOU, THERE! MOVE along!"

Music and light spilled from the open doors of the Hochstetter house, but the invitation they provided was an illusion. Police manned the cordons that kept the hoi polloi, their breath misting in the cold night air, a safe distance from New York's aristocracy. Modern motor-cars and old-fashioned barouches inched their way along Fifth Avenue, the smell of horse manure vying with the scent of hothouse flowers out of season, Paris perfumes, and Lyons silks. The crowd pressed closer with each new arrival—a Whitney! a Vanderbilt!—only to be pushed back again by the police, every inch hard won and just as quickly lost.

Tess Schaff wiggled her way up to the barricade, weaving between the sightseers and the avid members of the press scribbling in their notebooks, recording this one's jewels and that one's dress. A flashbulb exploded in front of Tess's eyes, wreathing her with rainbows. Tess bit off a curse. She couldn't afford to lose any of her senses tonight, thank you very much. Not when this was the biggest job of her career.

Not to mention, please God, the last job of her career.

Blinking away the last of the glare, she tugged at the nearest policeman's arm, pressing against his side just a little. Just enough.

"Do a girl a favor, will you?" And then, as he frowned down at her, with a quick laugh, "Not that kind of favor! I'm with the staff from Delmonico's. The restaurant? I was meant to be here an hour ago, but . . . I had to come in on the El from Brooklyn and there was a breakdown near Canarsie."

Tess had no idea whether there had been a breakdown near Canarsie or not. But it was the sort of thing that might have happened. One of the first pieces of wisdom she had learned at her sister's knee: *Truth is a poor second to a convincing lie.*

Ginny had also taught her how to produce the same card from the pack nine times out of ten, how to lie without breaking a sweat, and how to kick a man where it hurt and run like hell. She was hoping that last skill wouldn't come into play tonight.

"Aww," the policeman began.

Tess shivered dramatically, rubbing her arms to draw attention to the tight-fitting sleeves of her uniform: black dress, white pinny. Was anything less calculated to raise suspicion? She was coal in Newcastle, a marble tile on a hall floor, a feather on a hat, as commonplace as that. She did her best to exude "commonplace," which was made easier when you had muddy blond hair and mid-brown eyes, the opposite of memorable. She was pretty enough, she knew, with the rounded curves and cheeky charm of a girl on a billboard inviting you to enjoy the seaside. They were the sort of looks that invited a man to try his luck with a wink and a grin, but nothing that stood out of the ordinary, nothing that lingered in the mind after the moment had gone. At least, she hoped not.

Tess turned up the charm, a hand pressed artlessly against her breast. "Please, you can't imagine . . . I can't lose this job, I can't."

More true than he knew.

A commotion at the other end of the line made the policeman swerve. "You! Back!"

Tess took the opportunity to say, "If you please—I'll just nip right in . . ."

The policeman was already moving elsewhere, muttering under his breath about the pay not being enough. "All right, all right—servants' entrance is around to the left. And don't let me catch you loitering about."

"No, sir. Thank you, sir." Tess was through the cordon before he could think better of it, invisible in her servant's costume, just another menial bustling hither and thither.

That was the idea, at any rate.

The biggest job of our lives, that was what Ginny had told her. *Enough to keep you for life.*

No, Tess had said. She was done. Finished. That last job they'd done, she'd been as near to caught as made no difference. There was a price on her head. Well, on the head she'd been wearing at the time. They'd dyed her hair black for that one. She'd been South American money, the daughter of a wealthy cattle rancher looking to add to Daddy's art collection. It was a heist they'd played a dozen times before. Some time with the picture to "examine" it. Maybe even a few girlish sketches.

Never big pieces, always small ones. Miniatures, tiny triptychs. Once even a few pages from a medieval book of hours. It had been hell coming by the right pigments for that one, the crushed lapis lazuli and the gold leaf. But Ginny had arranged it. Ginny always arranged it.

What's the harm? Ginny would say, sounding so like their father. *Yours look as good as the original. They'll never know the difference.*

And they hadn't. Until that last switch, when something—Tess flinched at the memory of it—something had gone wrong. She'd made a mistake. It had been a miniature, attributed to Holbein. More complex than usual. Tiny, delicate brushstrokes, miniature jewels glimmering on the neck of a sixteenth-century beauty. Rubies. And she'd painted sapphires.

Don't think about that. Don't. The police were looking for Assumpta de los Argentes y Gutierrez, swathed in furs and dripping in paste jewels, not Tess Schaff in a black uniform and white pinny.

But she kept her head down all the same as she hurried around the side of the house. Her hair still felt rough where she'd washed out the dye. A thin film of gray had clung to her cheeks and neck and back, refusing to rinse out. It had taken hours of scrubbing with carbolic before she'd removed the stain of it, and even now, Tess felt like she could feel it on herself, that shadow of deception upon deception, lie upon lie, as though the corruption from her soul had grafted itself upon her skin for all to see.

Ginny had snorted at the notion. *If you want to go clean, go clean. Don't make a drama out of it. But first . . .*

But first.

Most New York townhouses had a service entrance in the front, a half-flight of steps down. But not the Hochstetter house. It sprawled over four lots, a vast French Renaissance pile, the pale stone glowing in the electric streetlights, adorned with an abundance of tracery and the odd gargoyle. A service entrance would have ruined the façade, made too obvious the labor required to keep the great house running. The staff entrance was around the back, where it couldn't bother anyone.

We don't bother anyone, that's what her father had always said. Never mind that the nostrums he peddled were compounded of turpentine and red pepper, mutton fat and mineral oil. By the end, Tess suspected he half-believed his own claims, that he had spent months in the desert learning the tribal secret of snake oil from a Hopi medicine man, when instead he was a German immigrant who had failed as a pharmacist, lost his wife, and, if Tess was being honest, his mind as well.

Sometimes, he would be Zaro the Magnificent, an opulent silk scarf wrapped around his balding pate, peddling pearls in vinegar—otherwise known as vinegar in vinegar. A town over he would be Spitting Snake, an honorary member of an apocryphal tribe, having borne his daughters with him through territories unknown to other white men. Anything but Jacob Schaff, anything but the man he had been.

Dimly, Tess remembered a time when their mother had been with them, when she had played waltzes on the small upright piano her father had hauled with them from Hell's Kitchen to Kansas. Until her mother died and the music ended. Tess couldn't play; she had, she had been told, a tin ear. It wasn't that she didn't appreciate music. She just couldn't produce it, any more than Ginny could replicate the shades of a sunset or the curl of a lip. Her skill with a brush was a talent, yes, but one that had brought her more sorrow than joy, from the day her father had caught her sketching a dragonfly on the windowsill and decided her quick fingers might be put to more practical use.

Better to sing as her mother could, lieder from the old country, softly, piano and voice blending in perfect harmony.

Tess could hear music now, the notes of a waltz, a waltz like her mother used to play, sweet and sad all at once. For a moment, she thought she could hear her mother's voice, singing in German.

She probably ought to have eaten something today, shouldn't she? Her stomach had been too unsettled to cram down more than a hard roll, and here she was, hearing music that wasn't.

Except it was. That was no phantom tune, beneath the more strident tones of the orchestra. It was a waltz, played on a piano with a far more resonant tone than her mother's. Tess didn't know much about musical instruments—being too small to secret in a pocket, they hadn't figured largely in her felonious past—but she could tell that this one was the very Rembrandt of its tribe, its tone rich and sweet even through the leaded-glass panes of the faux-medieval window. Through the gothic arches of the window, Tess could see a woman as rich as the sound, sitting at a piano bench, her fingers drawing forth wonder. Her dark hair was coiled in the latest style, as sleek as the wood of the piano. Pearls shimmered in restrained opulence at her neck.

But what really made the scene was the man, his body bent toward the lady's as he reached over to turn a page, leanly muscled beneath his evening clothes, his hair slicked away from a side parting, revealing a thin, interesting face, all bones and shadows.

Tess wanted to paint him. She wanted to paint all of it: the fall of lamplight on the piano, the music on the stand, the woman's slender neck bent over the keys. But most of all, she wanted to paint him. The music wrapped around Tess like an enchantment, stoking longings she hadn't known she had, a longing to be inside that well-lit room, as perfect as a doll's house, with that man, that man, leaning toward her with that same predatory grace, restraint and hunger all mixed together written in every line of his body.

Damp tracked down her cheek. A tear.

Tess dashed it away. A fool, that was what she was being. *We're not like other people*, that's what her father had always told them. *Why would you want to be like everyone else? Pah, cattle.*

Maybe it was a lie. Maybe they could have been like other people, Tess thought rebelliously. Maybe her father could have worked behind the counter of a shop and Tess might have learned to play the piano. Never that well and never in a room so elegant, but enough that some man might have come calling and leaned over her to turn the pages and laughed with her as this man was laughing now, the mood breaking, changing, as they plunged together into something fast and clamorsome, hands moving together across the black and white keys, bumping into one another, making a game of it.

Enough. Tess shook herself out of it. Even if they'd been like other people, she wouldn't have been like that, like Caroline Hochstetter. She recognized the woman from the pictures Ginny had cut out of *Town Topics*: the former Miss Caroline Telfair, pampered Southern belle with a pedigree that went back to God. Or, at least, to three or four Founding Fathers.

Tess felt a shiver of unease. This wasn't part of the plan. Mrs. Hochstetter would be in the ballroom, that's what Ginny had instructed her. Out of the way. *She'll be busy with her guests, you'll have a clear field, I promise.*

Never mind. Ginny couldn't control the movement of the tides—or spoiled society matrons. Grimly, Tess set her back to the music room window and stomped toward the servants' entrance. If Caroline Hochstetter was sparking with a swain in the music room, it meant she wasn't in her rooms, and from Tess's point of view, that was all that mattered.

The kitchen was just as Ginny had described it, not one room but several, all busy with people bustling about. Through a door, Tess could see some of the upstairs servants taking their ease, sitting over tea, or something stronger, in the upper servants' hall. Tess felt the tightness in her chest ease slightly. In this, at least, Ginny had been right. Mrs. Hochstetter's lady's maid was firmly ensconced in one of the heavy oak chairs, her profile to Tess.

"You! Take this." A superior-looking sort of man in a starched shirtfront thrust a tray into Tess's hands, champagne glasses jangling. "Ballroom."

Damn. Well, she could always abandon it somewhere along the way. Tess tried not to buckle under the weight of the tray, not silver plate, judging from the heft, and most certainly too big to stash beneath her apron.

We've bigger fish to fry, honey. She could almost hear Ginny's voice. *What's a tray to this?*

What, indeed? Ginny was in it for the money, but Tess had demanded more, had refused to act until she had assurance of it: a new life, in a new land. Papers, passage, everything she needed to start fresh. Tessa Fairweather. She'd picked the name herself, based on another of her sister's maxims: *Keep it close to the truth.* She could be this woman, this Tessa. She knew she could. Twenty-four and unscathed, returning home to England after a failed attempt to make her fortune in the new world.

After all, Tess knew everything there was to know about failed fortunes.

Are you sure you want this? Ginny had demanded, when she'd named her conditions. *You might not have noticed, but there's a war on over there.*

The sarcasm, Tess knew, came from concern. Concern and hurt. It hadn't been easy for Ginny, at fourteen, being saddled with a four-year-old and a father whose every scheme was crazier than the last. Ginny had cooked, cleaned, stolen, lied, helped their father when necessary, stood up to him when she'd dared. She'd done whatever was needed to keep Tess safe, and Tess knew she saw this development as a personal betrayal. In Ginny's eyes, she was still looking out for Tess, still keeping her safe.

Even if keeping her safe meant keeping her just one step away from being taken up by the law.

Tess had seen Sing Sing. She didn't want to go there. But that was where they were headed if they stayed on their current course. The world had changed over the last twenty years, grown smaller. You couldn't pull a scam in one town and escape with impunity to the next: the telegram wires clacked, electric lights lit the night, and papers poured with abundance from the presses in every town, news traveling from place to place with the speed of a brushfire. The day of the traveling con man was done. At least for them.

"Come with me," Tess had urged. "We'll—oh, I don't know. We'll open a seaside stall. I'll paint miniatures on seashells and you'll sell them."

"To the gulls?" Ginny had snorted. "Never mind that. I've bigger plans."

Just like their father. "Don't plan too big, Ginny."

"You just concentrate on the job. I'll take care of the rest." There had been a look on Ginny's face, a look that reminded Tess of their father when he had promised them that this was the next sure thing—which it wasn't. Not ever. "Don't fret, honey. This will be the easiest job you'll ever have."

Ginny had a strange idea of what constituted "easy."

Tess hoisted the tray up in the air and weaved her way through the throng of menials, out through the green baize door, into a marble hall easily the size of the entire town where Tess had been born. You could herd cattle in that hall and still have room left over for a dry goods store and a saloon.

Arches led off the hall into varied delights: a Moorish smoking room; the lush dense plants of a conservatory; the music room, the doors open now, the piano still. Tess frowned over her burden of bubbly. Where had Mrs. Hochstetter gone?

Tess bobbed and weaved through the guests, proffering her tray at random. Let them deplete her stock; it would give her an excuse to find the servants' stair, *just returning to the kitchen, that was all, lost my way* . . . But first she had to find Caroline Hochstetter. If she'd gone up to her room, the whole game was up.

The ballroom had been decked with a fantasy of palm fronds that tickled Tess's nose and blocked her view. The undulating dancers reminded Tess of a kaleidoscope she'd begged for as a child. It had seemed so pretty at first, all those little pieces swirling from one pattern to another, but it had given her a headache when she'd looked too long, trying, always trying, to find that moment of stillness, for the pattern to fix itself into something safe and sure.

Or, in this case, a woman in rose silk, draped and beaded. Surely that should be easy enough to spot? It took a moment, but Tess finally found her, dancing with a man with a monocle and moustache, his uniform stiff with assorted orders.

Keeping her eyes on Mrs. Hochstetter, Tess sidled sideways. A man, obviously the worse for drink, lurched into Tess's path. Tess swerved—and bumped into something hard and warm, sending the last glass of champagne on her tray flying up and over, sparkling liquid cascading over the immaculate evening attire of the man who had grabbed her shoulders to keep her from falling.

For a moment, all Tess could do was gape. She'd soaked him, soaked him through, from his white tie to his ebony studs.

Inconspicuous. She prided herself on being inconspicuous. And now—

"Are you all right?" His voice was like chocolate. English chocolate. Rich, but with a hint of bitter. Tess lifted her stricken eyes to his face, and found herself looking into the eyes of the man who had been with Caroline Hochstetter in the music room.

"I'm so sorry, so sorry. Er, it's that sorry, I am." Tess hastily improvised a brogue, backing away. Irish. She could be Irish. The swells thought all servants were Irish, just another Bridget or Mary. "I'll just be after getting you a cloth, so I shall. Don't step in that!"

Shards of crystal festooned the ground, like Cinderella's slipper come to grief. Tess stooped and began scooping the fragments onto her tray with more haste than discretion.

"Wait." The man's hand snagged her wrist. "You've cut yourself."

"'S nothing," Tess mumbled. He wasn't supposed to be behaving like this, this man. He ought to be berating her, threatening to report her, demanding restitution for the clothes that cost more than a laborer's wage. It was easier to rob them when you could despise them. "Please, don't. Don't be after troubling yourself."

"It's no trouble." Deftly, the man produced a handkerchief from his pocket and bound up her wrist. He smelled of cologne and fresh linen, whisky and spilled champagne. Tess's head reeled with it.

"Are you—is it a doctor, you are?"

"No, a newspaperman." Tess could hear the amusement in his voice. He gave the linen a twist, rising easily to his feet. "But one does pick up a useful skill or two along the way. As well as a bit of ink on the cuffs."

An undertone there, but Tess didn't have time to figure it out. Lunging to her feet, she backed away, the tray under her arm. "Thank 'ee. Thank 'ee kindly, sir. I'll fetch a cloth, sir. Won't be a moment, sir—"

His handkerchief marked her hand like a brand. Tess twitched it away, discarding it with the tray on a small table beneath a potted palm. Stupid to feel a pang of regret. What was she planning to do, sleep with it beneath her pillow? Just because the man had been human enough to spare a kind word for a menial didn't mean she should begin embroidering linens.

There. A barely perceptible line in the paneling marked the entrance to the servants' stair, just where it had been on the plans Tess had studied. Tess slipped through, drawing it shut behind her, closing out the light, the music, the sounds of revelry.

That man wouldn't be able to return to the dancing, soaked with champagne like that. Petty to feel glad for it. Especially since she was unlikely ever to see the man again, whoever he was. Tomorrow, God willing and the crick don't rise, she would be setting sail on the *Lusitania*, with new documents, a new identity.

Two floors up, Ginny had said. Family bedrooms were on the third floor. And by bedrooms, she meant suites, composed of a sitting room, bedroom, and dressing room. The master and mistress slept not just in separate rooms, but in separate kingdoms, each with their own staff.

Third door to the left. There it was: Caroline Hochstetter's dressing room, but it wasn't empty. A woman jumped up as Tess entered, her filmy drapes agitating unattractively around her spare frame.

"Really! Is it too much to ask for a moment of peace in this nest of parvenus?" The woman glared at her and Tess felt her hands go very cold as she recognized her. Margery Schuyler, to whom Ginny had sold a Franz Marc painting. Or, rather, a Tennessee Schaff copy of a Franz Marc painting.

Tess ducked her head. "Beg pardon, ma'am," she mumbled. She'd been German for that one. An ex-mistress of the great artist, all brassy hair and German accent. Margery Schuyler had lapped it up, loving her brush with the louche, wanting to know what it was like to be, ahem, painted by the great man. Given that he painted mostly animals, and those in distorted shapes and colors, Tess had not found the question flattering. But she was used to art collectors who thought they knew more than they did. They made the best marks. "Only family upstairs. That was what we was told."

Margery Schuyler sniffed, although whether it was with scorn or from the permanent drip at the end of her rather long nose, Tess couldn't tell. "I was just leaving."

She swept past Tess in what might have been a grand manner if she hadn't tripped on one of her own drapes before slamming the door behind her.

Darn, darn, darn. Just what she needed. Not that anyone remembered a maid, but Tess doubted either guests or staff were meant to be up here. And if Margery Schuyler chose to complain . . .

Fear made some people clumsy. For Tess, it was the opposite. The world slowed, everything deliberate, precise, colors clearer, edges sharper. The dressing table bristled with crystal bottles with jeweled stoppers, garish and new, the only discordant object a well-worn silver brush set adorned with an entwined *C* and *T.*

She won't keep it in the safe, Ginny had said. *There's a drawer in the dressing table, a secret drawer. Press the right spot and it will spring open.*

Tess's sister had made no secret of her contempt for people who held their valuables so lightly. Why, they were practically begging to have them stolen. *We're doing them a favor,* that's what her father would have said.

Her father, who had a remarkable talent for remaking the world to his own imaginings.

He'd been an honest crook in his way.

But what did that make her? And Ginny? Tess had been feeling uneasy about Ginny recently, uneasy about all of it.

A slight pressure and the drawer popped open, just as Ginny had promised. Absurdly easy. Too easy. The drawer was crammed with velvet boxes emblazoned with jewelers' insignia from New York, Boston, Philadelphia, Charleston, London, Paris. The wealth of nations bundled into a drawer, emeralds jumbled with sapphires, rubies sneering at garnets. Tess's artist's eye lingered longingly on a pair of earrings made to resemble butterflies, the iridescent wings a miracle of the jeweler's art, tiny chips of gems blending together into a harmonious whole. Ginny would have noted the wealth of the stones, but Tess felt drunk on the craftsmanship of it, the care taken in putting the pieces together.

Reluctantly, she set aside a diamond pavé cat, arching its back, its ruby tongue caught between tiny fangs. It wasn't the jewels she was after, not this time.

"Nothing too difficult," Ginny had said, with an arch of her brow. "Sheet music. It's not even that old. You could copy it in your sleep."

"How long is it?" Tess had asked with trepidation.

"Just a few pages, that's all."

"Wouldn't it be in the music room?"

"Not this. She'll keep it close. It's the only copy. An unfinished waltz by Strauss." Ginny's voice had turned wheedling. "You don't even have to make the swap. Just transcribe it exactly. My client is willing to take the copy—so long as it's a perfect copy. It's the music and the composer's notes he wants. He doesn't need the page the great man touched. Although it might earn us a premium."

Tess scrabbled though the jewel boxes, looking for the music. It would be in a flat, leather portfolio, that's what Ginny had said. Behind her, the clock on the mantel ticked, every sound a warning. Another minute lost.

Another. Margery Schuyler was downstairs by now, might be complaining to her hosts about the insolent maid who had rousted her from her rest. Tess dug beneath the diamond tiara, the parure of emeralds. She checked every box, felt every lining.

Nothing.

Torn between anger and fear, Tess rocked back on her heels, setting the boxes back in their places with trembling hands, each one just so.

The manuscript wasn't there.

She would have to find it on the ship. The *Lusitania*.

CHAPTER 4

Sarah

London
May 2013

ONE THING I knew about John Langford: he was a man of habit. Each morning at half past seven, he emerged from his flat on Westbourne Grove, set his teeth curtly against the photographers waiting outside, and darted down the sidewalk (the "pavement," as they called it here) to the Tube station.

On Monday it was the Circle line from Notting Hill Gate; on Tuesday he joined the Hammersmith and City line at Ladbroke Grove. Today he cruised back over to Notting Hill Gate, but rather than turning for the Circle and District lines, he plunged right down the steep escalators to the Central line, cruising nimbly past the queue of standers on the right while the photographers piled up at the top, vying for precedence. Luckily, I wasn't encumbered by either professional competition or camera equipment. I darted down the empty stairs that ran between the escalators, checking my phone like I was any old City worker late for her job on the trading desk, and stepped onto the eastbound train at the instant the doors slid shut. Kept my eyes fixed studiously on the easyJet advertisements at the top while the train lurched forward and rattled down the tracks, slammed to a stop at each station, lurched forward again, repeat. Just as the other passengers began to stir, recognizing at last the man who actually stood in their midst, sliding hands into pockets for iPhone cameras and fifteen glorious minutes of social media fame, John stepped off the train. Today, it was the Oxford Circus station, and I lost him on the escalators.

But not to worry. Like I said, John was a man of habit, and when I emerged into the drizzly, commercial bustle of Oxford Street, I knew I had only to look around for the nearest Costa Coffee shop. There it was, just a few steps away down Argyll Street.

Another thing about John Langford: for all his pedigree, he was a man of the people.

He was also tall, significantly tall, almost six and a half feet, which made him easy to spot inside the warm, java-scented air. He wore an American-style baseball cap awkwardly over his dark blond hair, but you couldn't mistake him. Long and lean; sharp, large nose; naked chin floating above the bearded hipsters. His scarred brown Barbour coat and green Wellington boots made you imagine he was just grabbing a coffee before he zoomed off in a Range Rover to stalk deer in Scotland or somewhere. He waited patiently in line, keeping his head bowed in fascination at the glass display case crowded with the pastries, and his collar up around his clenched jaw.

For the past three mornings, I'd followed John Langford on a Costa Coffee tour of London. A different branch each day, but the same routine. As soon as the paparazzi tracked him down, he stood up politely and left, heading back home, or else to the British Museum or the National Portrait Gallery: some sacred, patriotic place where photographers couldn't follow. Usually he had time to finish his coffee before they found him. Actually, I had to admire him for going out at all. In his place, I would've stayed home in my flat, ordering curry takeouts and avoiding windows until the whole sordid affair blew over. But not John. He refused to be caged. He stalked outside defiantly. He made the photographers hustle for their shots.

I wanted to ask him why. I wanted to sit down and pepper him with questions, to find out what had really happened with his wife and the Russian oligarch, to discover what fascinating quality of British bloody-mindedness drove him to strike out every morning at half past seven for a very public latte somewhere in the capital. But I hadn't yet dared to approach him. Just ordered my own coffee and sat down along the bar, while John quietly read the newspaper—yes, an actual print newspaper, two of them, the *Daily Telegraph* followed by the *Guardian*, getting both sides of the story—and kept his head down until somebody inevitably pulled out an iPhone and tipped off the paps, and he moved on to seek refuge in a cultural institution. Monday passed, Tuesday, and still I held back. I was sizing him up, I told myself. Figuring out the best angle of attack. John Langford was a disgraced politician in the middle of the year's biggest, juiciest scandal; I couldn't just walk up to him and introduce myself while he stared ruminatively at the Holbein portrait of Henry VIII. He was vulnerable. He was defensive. This was going to require care, tact, diligence. All the investigative skill I possessed.

On the other hand. Today was Wednesday, and I'd already squandered four whole days of the two weeks I'd allotted myself to write this book proposal before I headed back to New York. Not just because I couldn't be away from my mother any longer, but because my groaning Mastercard could only just stretch to afford my shoddy hotel in Shepherd's Bush.

The milk steamer started up with a wet, violent noise. Behind me, the door opened. *Now or never. Make your move, Sarah. He's the last customer in line for exactly three more seconds.*

I drew in a thick, sweet breath and stepped forward, just ahead of the new arrival, to slip in line behind Langford.

Up close, he was bigger than I thought. His height made him seem narrower than he really was; when you stood next to him, you realized his shoulders and back were actually broad enough to hide behind, like huddling in the shelter of a Stonehenge monolith. I was five foot seven, and I couldn't see the top of his shoulder. I told myself this was a good thing. I wanted to remain inconspicuous, right? Didn't want him to notice me hovering there at his elbow, following his gaze along the rows of giant muffins and croissants as the line inched forward. The sounds went on around us, the chatter and laughter, the calling of orders, the frothing of milk and the high-pitched whir of grinding beans. My heart beat hard; the cold, light sensation of adrenaline moved through my veins. The last customer moved away, and John stepped in front of the register.

"Large americano, please. Extra hot."

I hadn't actually heard his voice before, except on YouTube clips. He was more resonant in real life, more baritone, which made sense given the size of his chest. And he drank americano. That was interesting. Was he lactose intolerant or did he simply prefer his coffee black? He never added milk afterward, just a brief shake of sugar. (Real sugar, not artificial sweetener.) I watched his hands as he counted out pound coins from his pocket—real money, not plastic—and said something to the counter attendant that I couldn't quite hear. Then he stepped away to join the pickup queue, and I moved into place.

"I'll have a large americano, please. Um, extra hot."

The attendant lifted her eyebrows and scribbled on the cup, while I dug into my wallet for my Mastercard. "That's all right," she said. "Chap ahead of you already paid."

My hand froze on the leather. "What did you say?"

She nodded to the pickup counter. "Chap ahead of you. Picked up your bill, right?"

"Are you kidding me?"

The attendant was young, with pale skin and crimson streaks in her dark hair. She leaned forward over the register and said, woman to woman, "I reckon you're well in there, miss."

I considered walking right out, do not pass Go, do not collect your coffee and look John Langford in the eye. Then I reminded myself I had a job to do. The stakes were high. That pound and a half saved on coffee? Actually meant something.

I moved to the pickup queue, remaining a careful few feet away from John's sturdy shoulder. He didn't seem to notice me. Maybe he did this kind of thing all the time, maybe these little acts of random generosity were all part of his routine, not some menacing attempt to rattle the woman who was trailing him. Noblesse oblige and all that. Somebody ahead of us picked up a flat white. Another received a caramel macchiato. Just the two of us left now, pretending not to notice each other. My face was hot, and not because of the heat rising from the espresso machine.

The barista set a cup on the counter. "Large americano, extra hot," he called out.

Here we go.

I reached forward and snatched the cup.

"I beg your pardon," said John Langford, "I believe that's mine."

"Pretty sure it's mine. Large americano, extra hot?"

"I see. What a coincidence. That's precisely what I ordered."

"Oh, gosh. Is it? So sorry. Here you go. I'll just wait for the next one."

"No, please. Take it."

"No, really." I pushed the drink toward his waxed-leather chest.

"Look," he said, in a hushed voice, holding his arms rigid at his sides, "I don't know what kind of game you're playing, but I'm not talking to any journalists at the moment, so you're wasting your time."

I opened my mouth to say that I didn't know what he was talking about, but as I did so, I looked into his face for the first time. The *true* first time: not the images I'd Googled on my laptop, not the YouTube clips, not the sidelong glances at his turned-away features. Eye to eye, nose to nose. Well, nose to sternum, to be precise. But you know what I mean. Like the rest of him, his face was lean and bony, in square proportions, too grim and too spare for beauty. His hazel eyes were narrowed and cold, and I couldn't look away from them.

"It's not what you think," I said lamely.

The next customer joined us. "Large americano, extra hot," said the barista, setting another cup on the counter. John reached out his long arm and took the coffee. "Have a good morning," he said, turning away, and I grabbed his elbow in desperation.

Langford jerked back in shock, like I'd punched him in the nose.

"I'm sorry." I dropped my hand. "It's not about the—the thing you're going through. The scandal. It's something else."

"The hell it is. Would you mind leaving me alone to nurse my coffee and my dignity, or is that too much to ask?"

"Please. Just five minutes."

"I'm afraid not."

The customers in line were starting to shoot curious glances our way. I maneuvered myself between them and Langford, as if my five and a half feet could somehow shield his six and a half feet from view. He scowled at me and put his hand on his baseball cap, the way you do when you want to run your fingers through your hair, but forgot you're wearing a hat. Thwarted, the hand went to the brim instead, and pulled it lower on his forehead.

"Look," I said. "It's not about your wife. It's about your great-grandfather. It's about *Lusitania*."

Langford made a startled movement, spilling his extra-hot coffee through the mouth hole onto his hand. He swore and sucked the drops away. "*What* did you say?"

"RMS *Lusitania*. My great-grandfather was on that ship the day it sank, and so was yours. Robert Langford. The spy novelist?"

"I know who my great-grandfather was!" he snapped. He lifted his other wrist and checked his watch. Who wore a watch anymore, in the age of smartphones? John Langford did. Stainless steel and chunky. The kind that was probably waterproof to fifty meters.

I leaned forward. "Listen to me. I have some information I think you might find—"

"Five minutes," he said. "And you do all the talking."

We sat in the corner nearest the door, looking out over the tiny, pedestrianized corridor of Argyll Street toward Bond Street, where the whizzing motorbikes, the black taxis, the small white delivery vans, all maneuvered around each other in a delicate, noisy ballet. I sipped my coffee and choked. "If I get up for milk and sugar, does that count against my five minutes?" I asked.

"Yes."

I scuttled to the counter and splashed in milk, tossed in sugar, grabbed a stirring stick. When I returned, Langford regarded me with an expression that plainly disapproved of my decadence.

"Four minutes and forty-five seconds," he said. "Go."

"All right." I set down the coffee and reached inside my tote bag. "Here."

"What's this?"

"It's a watch, obviously. My great-grandfather's watch. His name was Patrick Houlihan. He was a steward in the first-class section; he'd worked aboard *Lusitania* almost from her launching. The Cunard company sent this back to my great-grandmother after they found his body, along with his uniform and everything he had on him at the time of the sinking. See how it stopped at two thirty-six? That's when he hit the water. I don't think he could swim."

Langford set down the watch in the middle of the table. The silver flashed back a bit of light from the bright lamps overhead. "I'm sorry for your loss," he said blandly. "But I don't see what this has to do with my great-grandfather, other than the fact that they were both on the ship, among thousands."

"So turn it over."

"I don't have time for games, Miss—?"

"Sarah. Sarah Blake."

"Miss Blake." He checked his own watch. "And neither do you, it seems."

"All right, all right." I picked up the silver pocket watch and turned it over. "Look, on the back. It's inscribed. *To Patrick, a small token of my grateful esteem, R.H.L.*"

Langford squinted at the lettering, which I held up helpfully before his eyes. He wasn't inclined to touch the watch itself. Kept his right hand firmly around his coffee cup, and his left hand atop his leg. "I'm sorry. I don't see what you're getting at."

"Those are your great-grandfather's initials! Robert Horatio Langford."

"Or anyone else with those initials. It's a coincidence, nothing more."

"Coincidence? It's a pretty big coincidence, wouldn't you say? Especially when taken together with these." I reached back into my tote bag and drew out the oilskin pouch and the luncheon menu. "Also found on Patrick's body, which means he had them in the pockets of his uniform when the torpedo struck at ten minutes past two o'clock on the afternoon of May seventh. Just look what's in this pouch. This *waterproof* pouch, I might add, which means someone wanted to make sure it survived the sinking."

"It's an envelope," Langford said, a little distastefully.

"Specifically, it's an envelope from the Marconi radio room, addressed to one Robert Langford, Stateroom B-38. Pretty sure *that's* not a coincidence, right? And somebody's written a message on the other side, a message that doesn't make any sense unless, say, you're writing in some kind of cipher."

"Oh, for Christ's sake! You bloody Americans and your conspiracies. What exactly are you trying to imply, Miss Blake? That my great-grandfather was some kind of secret agent? Maybe had something to do with the sinking of the ship?"

"Now that's interesting. What makes you say that?"

He held up a finger. "Don't even think about it."

"Think what?"

"Think you're going to trap me. Idiots have been cooking up conspiracies about *Lusitania* from the moment it went under. Wasn't *my* idea."

"Fair enough," I said, "but take a look at this. The luncheon menu. The note on the back. *No more betrayals. Meet me B-deck prom starboard side.*"

"Yes?"

"Come on, Langford. You know the torpedo struck right after lunch on the starboard side."

"Robert Langford's name isn't anywhere on that menu."

"No. But it was found on my great-grandfather's body. So something funny was going on, maybe something more than just funny, and I want to get to the bottom of all this. I *need* to get to the bottom of this. I need to find out what really happened. I need to find out if Patrick Houlihan was a good guy, was a traitor, was none of the above."

"Why?"

"What do you mean, *why*? Because it's the truth."

"And you want to profit from it. You're a journalist."

"What makes you say that?"

He was drinking from his coffee cup. He set it down, and at last he smiled at me. It wasn't a nice smile. "I can smell it on you," he said. "It smells like money."

I sat back in my chair and started shoving the articles back into my tote bag. "Well, you're wrong. I'm not a journalist. I'm a historian. I'm writing a book."

"So I'm not wrong. You *are* in it for the money."

"Okay, fine. Yes. I have to earn a living, unlike *you*, Mr. Langford, with your handy-dandy family fortune and your God-given privilege. But I also happen to think there's a story here that needs to be told, even if it means finding out my ancestor was a traitor and a murderer, because the truth *matters*, okay? The truth sets you free."

Langford took another drink of his coffee and checked his watch. "Oh, look. It seems your time is up, Miss Blake."

"Are you serious? That's it?"

"I'm perfectly serious. I don't like to waste my time, especially not with money-grubbing Americans eager to rewrite history. Nor can I quite shake the notion that your intentions aren't so honorable as you insist. Given the circumstances."

"That," I said, "is about the most stupid, prejudiced, asinine thing I've heard in—in *forever*. You don't even know me."

"I don't need to know you. I know your type. You damned journalists, ripping apart people's lives for the sake of sensation. The truth? You don't give a toss for the truth. Just your grubby paychecks." Langford's eyes shifted to a point over my right shoulder. He gathered up his laptop bag and his coffee and rose from the chair, so immediately tall I found myself addressing his waist. "Just as I thought," he said.

I turned around to follow his gaze and saw a pair of men—no, three—barging through the doorway, cameras in hand. Langford drew down his cap and swept past me, shoulders hunched, while the men shouted questions at him, overcoming the noise of the espresso machines. As if the room had plunged into some kind of war zone.

I jumped up and tried to follow, but the cameras got in the way. I shouted, "Please! I'm at the Camelot Hotel in Shepherd's Bush! Just—*please*!"

Langford turned his head over his shoulder. "This conversation is over," he said, and he pushed the door open and turned left down Argyll Street, around the corner to Bond Street, dodging past a motorbike to hail a black cab that had just come conveniently to rest by the curb, the way it always did for men like him.

By the time the photographers stumbled back out after him, the taxi had zoomed away, leaving nothing behind except the faint smell of exhaust, filtered through a modern catalytic converter.

I walked back to the hotel, taking my time. For one thing, I loved London, and for another thing, the Tube was expensive. The drizzle had lifted, and the sky lost some of its dreariness as I tracked my way back down Oxford Street, looking wistfully in the shop windows, and ambled through Hyde Park. As I crossed into Kensington Gardens, the clouds parted, and the sunlight briefly poured in around me, making the trees sparkle. I took off my coat. My empty stomach expanded to fill my entire torso, until I was one big yawning void of hunger. The coffee had long gone. Somewhere along Notting Hill Gate, I found a Gregg's and bought a tuna mayonnaise sandwich and a yogurt smoothie, which didn't much help. The sky closed again when I reached the hotel. A few raindrops pattered against my sleeves.

Nice omen, I thought. Thanks.

Among its pitifully few virtues, the Camelot did have Wi-Fi. I found a seat along the empty bar—another Camelot virtue, an on-premises liquor license—and opened my laptop. I was working on the proposal for my *Lusitania* book, which I'd tentatively titled *Small Chance: How an Irish Steward and a British Aristocrat Conspired to* Bring *Hurl America Into the First World War*, in the wild hope that my current working theory would prove true. Into this proposal I'd already inserted considerable background on the Langford family—*Each generation had its own impact on British history, from the Edwardian spymaster to the postwar statesman*—based on everything I'd Googled during the past week, and the suitcase full of books I'd brought with me on the airplane. But I needed more. I needed original sources. I needed private documents. I needed things I could only get from a Langford descendant.

A Langford descendant who liked me.

A Langford descendant who wasn't mired in a scandal of his own.

A Langford descendant who wasn't a complete and utter wanker.

I glanced at the battered clock above the bar—one thirty in the afternoon—and considered pouring myself a drink from the array of bottles on the shelves. The bar didn't officially open until five, and I needed alcohol *now*. The room was unlit, the bottles dusky and promising in the dull glow from the small, rain-splattered window overlooking the basement steps. I listened for the sound of footsteps creaking upstairs in the lobby, but there was nothing. All the guests were out enjoying London. Just me and the clerk in the office, and she wasn't going to leave her post and venture down here, was she?

Besides, I'd charge it to my room.

I disengaged my legs from the stool and walked softly around the end of the bar. I'd never stood behind one before. It felt strangely powerful, like I owned everything on the shelves and the cabinets, like I could decide who drank and who did not. Normally I sided on Team Grapes, with preference for something bubbly or else something red, but when I bent to examine the paltry vino collection underneath the bar, I decided I was better off upstairs. "Upstairs" meaning the vodka lined up in tantalizing profusion above my head.

Or gin. I was in London, I was a historian. I should drink gin.

I pulled a glass from one shelf and a bottle of Beefeater from another. What was the proper proportion of gin to tonic? Who knew. Who cared. I filled the glass halfway and found the tonic on tap. Sipped. Coughed. It was strong, extremely strong. On the other hand, I needed strong.

I sipped again, and that was more tolerable. Funny how your mouth and stomach adjust themselves to suit the occasion. I finished the glass and turned to pour another.

"As long as you're serving," said a voice behind me, "make it two."

I whipped around to find the tall figure of John Langford filling the doorway, head bent slightly under the lintel to avoid concussion. A sense of giddy wonder started in my chest, spreading outward into my belly and my arms and legs. Or maybe that was the gin. The gin spreading outward. I leaned back against the counter to save myself from collapsing and waved the bottle, which remained in my hand.

"It's going to cost you," I said, and I was proud of the fact that my words neither slurred nor shook.

"I more or less expected that." He stepped forward into the room and swung his extensive frame atop the stool next to my laptop. "I came to apologize."

"I more or less expected that, too. Gin and tonic all right for you?"

"Yes. And no, you didn't expect me to apologize. You thought I was a complete wanker. I could see it in your eyes."

"The way you could sniff my money-grubbing ways?"

"Look, I'm sorry. You've caught me at rather a bad moment, I'm afraid. Not that it's any excuse for bad manners."

I set down the gin and tonic on the counter in front of him. "Cheers. To bad manners."

He lifted the glass, clinked it against mine, and tilted his head for a drink.

"Ah," he said. "Now that's better. I like a woman who pours a strong G-and-T."

"You might say I needed it. I had a really crappy morning."

"Did you really? Some run-in with one of those arrogant English blokes?"

I shrugged. "Yeah. He was kind of my last hope, you know? I'm trying to write this book, this second book I've been trying to figure out for five or six years, because I'm all tapped out from my first book, and my mom has Alzheimer's, and—and—I'm sorry." I turned away and started to pour another drink.

"A real sob story, is it?"

"Yes." I sniffed. "Anyway, it's not your problem. You've got enough on your plate."

There was no answer. I heard the soft sound of his glass coming to rest on the counter. I wondered if my laptop had gone to sleep, or if the book proposal still lay bright and open on the screen, a few feet away from John Langford's sharp hazel eyes.

"I bought your book," he said. "*Small Potatoes*. Went into Waterstones after I escaped and found the last copy on the shelf. Read the first few chapters. It's quite good."

"Gosh. Thanks."

"I did sense a certain amount of antipathy toward English aristocrats and their careless, high-handed ways."

"Hey, I'm Irish. What can I say?"

"You see, that's another funny thing about you Americans. I mean, you *personally*, Sarah Blake, are not an Irish citizen. Your family's lived in America for generations now. You spout all this seductive, patriotic rubbish about melting pots and so on. And yet you still wear your shamrock badge of Irishness."

I turned around. He wasn't looking at my screen, thank God, and it occurred to me that he probably wouldn't, even if he could. His face was much softer now than in the coffee shop, almost handsome. He'd taken off his coat, revealing a worn green sweater over a collared shirt, and his thick shoulders hunched a little around his drink. He watched me steadily, with great interest, like an anthropologist studying a member of an unknown tribe. Which was probably pretty close to the truth.

I stepped forward and leaned my elbows on the counter, a foot or two away from him. "So are you going to hold it against me?"

"Your Irishness? No. Your Americanness? Maybe."

"What exactly have you got against Americans? I mean, it seems to me your biggest problem speaks Russian, at the moment."

He lifted the glass. "Touché."

"So you'll help me? At least let me take a look at the family papers?"

"Miss Blake, do you realize that nobody has *ever* been allowed to look at the family papers? That we've refused every single request, over the years, by journalists and historians and money-grubbing Americans to peek inside the Langford vault?"

"I realize that. I was hoping you might make an exception."

Langford glanced at my laptop. Reached over and closed the lid, as if shutting himself off from temptation. He'd almost finished his drink. I wrapped my fingers around his glass and made to pour another, but he stopped me. Put his hand over mine. For a second, I thought he was making a move, but when I looked at his face it was anything but amorous. Dark and stormy, and not with lust. With something else. Some other storm.

"You have to promise me one thing," he said.

"Anything. Almost anything."

"You have to promise me you won't—"

A flash of light exploded in the room, followed by another. We snapped our heads toward the doorway, which was blocked by a tangle of jostling arms and legs and a series of bright, irregular starbursts, like the Fourth of July.

CHAPTER 5

Caroline

New York City
Saturday, May 1, 1915

CAROLINE BLINKED FROM the flash of a camera as their driver stopped near the terminal at Cunard's Pier 54. He held open the door of the Rolls-Royce as Gilbert took her hand and helped her out of the car. She hoped her mother would see the photograph. Annelise would pretend to be embarrassed to have Caroline's face appear in a newspaper, but secretly she'd be proud that her daughter had reached such a high echelon of society. It had been Annelise's dream since Caroline was a baby, if not Caroline's.

But she'd dressed the part today, with Jones's help, who assured her that Caroline would be the most fashionable lady on the entire ship. Caroline appreciated Jones's straightforward nature and the way she'd begun to anticipate Caroline's needs. Jones had already selected the entire outfit and had it steamed and waiting in her dressing room before Caroline had even awakened. Jones was on her way to making herself indispensable, and Caroline felt grateful and even optimistic. Perhaps she wouldn't be as lonely on this voyage as she'd originally feared.

She wore a pale cream traveling dress with a waist-length fur-covered shawl and long dolman-style sleeves. Her brown and cream button boots with pointed toes hurt her feet, but Jones said they were necessary to complete the perfection of her outfit. At least the large straw hat she wore, a pretty one with a wide wired brim trimmed with striped ribbon and a feather, was comfortable. It also allowed her to hide her face with a tip of her head whenever a camera was pointed in her direction.

A motion-picture camera had been set up just outside the entrance to the terminal, capturing the images of passengers as they moved in and out of view. Caroline dipped her head, an unwilling subject, recalling something Robert had told her once about the series of stories he'd written about the Indian situation out west. How many of the natives were unwilling to have their images captured on film, afraid their spirits would be held captive there forever. Caroline clung to Gilbert's arm as he led her toward the looming black hull of the great ship, the word LUSITANIA emblazoned on the side in white block lettering, trying to shake the image of her spirit frozen in sepia for all time.

She forced a smile as they moved forward, reminding herself that she and Gilbert were embarking together, sharing what she was sure would be a new beginning for them. She tried not to think about Robert and the night before, or how warm his hand had been on her back as they'd danced. She told herself that she'd been wishing her partner was Gilbert, dancing with her instead of locked away in a smoky study with business associates. That it had been her husband looking at her with eyes that burned. Yet when Caroline saw the arm her hand rested upon now, she was surprised to see the large muscled forearm of her husband, and not the lean, elegant arm of Robert Langford. Yes, she told herself as she forced another smile and tilted her head back to look into Gilbert's face, this was a new beginning for them. She was sure of it.

They nodded and smiled at their new acquaintances from the party the night before, commenting on the weather and the general excitement of boarding such a luxurious liner, a star of the Cunard fleet. The recent heat wave was already a memory, with heavy clouds and a drop in temperature that allowed the boarding passengers to wear their heavy coats. Porters bustled about, taking trunks and luggage from arriving vehicles and moving them into the vast ship and myriad corridors before storing them safely in the cabins and staterooms.

Jones, traveling separately with their luggage, had disappeared and presumably would already be unpacking by the time they'd reached their Regal Suite—one of only two on the ship, and the only suites to contain two bedrooms, upon which Gilbert had insisted. As at home, they had separate bedrooms, due to Gilbert being afraid that his size would interrupt her sleeping. Despite her reassurance that it wasn't necessary for the trip, and that Alfred Vanderbilt had reserved a smaller, one-bedroom Parlor Suite, Gilbert had pressed his point and, as usual, Caroline had capitulated.

She could only imagine how much it had cost, but when she'd tried to tell Gilbert that she would be perfectly happy to spend the voyage in a less opulent and less expensive suite, he'd simply patted her hand and told her that she wasn't to worry about their finances. She'd bristled at his dismissal, and had wanted to argue, but then realized that she couldn't. She knew absolutely nothing about their finances, and she had no one to blame for that except herself.

Caroline held a scented handkerchief—supplied by the ever-helpful Jones—to her nose. The briny scent of the water mixed with the odors of too many bodies crammed together seemed to congeal with the dark smoke belching forth from the funnels of the ship. She took a deep breath through the fine linen of the handkerchief, silently congratulating herself on her astute judgment in the hiring of her new lady's maid.

"Are you all right, darling?" Gilbert leaned toward her, his look of concern calming her, reassuring her that they were of like mind about the journey.

She tilted her head to look up at him. "How could I not be?"

He met her eyes for a long moment, filling her with hope and warmth. He pressed his hand against hers as it lay on his arm, then escorted her up the ramp and to the Promenade Deck, where porters and stewards bustled around directing people and luggage to their proper places. A middle-aged gentleman, dressed in the smart white uniform of a steward, introduced himself as Patrick Houlihan, who had been assigned to their stateroom and would make himself available to them for the journey. He had the ruddy complexion of a redhead, his nose and cheeks deeply freckled from exposure to the elements. He was small-statured, and spoke with a lilting Irish accent, reminding her of what a leprechaun might look like if they were real. Except instead of having a jolly sparkle, his green eyes were sharp and piercing, making Caroline believe that this was a man who missed nothing.

"I'd be happy to take you to your rooms and see you settled now," he offered.

Gilbert said, "I'm sure Mrs. Hochstetter needs a rest, but if you could direct me to the smoking room . . ."

"I don't need a rest," Caroline said, not meeting her husband's gaze. "I'm afraid I'm far too excited to close my eyes. I'd like to walk around for a little bit."

Mr. Houlihan bowed his head, his hands clasped in front of him. "Then I will check back with you later." He looked at Gilbert, who had pulled out his gold watch for the third time since reaching the pier.

"One more hour until we depart, yes?" Gilbert didn't smile.

"I'm afraid not, sir. There's been a slight delay, but rest assured that Captain Turner will do all he can to make up for lost time. The *Lusitania* is a fast ship. One of the fastest, sir."

Gilbert frowned down at his watch before tucking it back into his waistcoat. "That's why we're here."

Mr. Houlihan bowed again then walked away as Caroline nestled her hand again into the crook of Gilbert's elbow. After a brief hesitation, he started walking, moving them slowly around the Promenade Deck. It was the place to see and be seen, as ladies and gentlemen paraded up and down, looking out toward the harbor and open sea, the gulls shrieking at them all as they prepared to say goodbye to New York.

They passed a man in a resplendent navy blue uniform complete with gold braid and shiny brass buttons. He wasn't overly tall or necessarily handsome, but the uniform made him appear to be both. Even without an introduction, she knew him to be their captain, William Turner. He'd been invited to their party but had sent his regrets. This hadn't surprised Caroline as she'd been told that Captain Turner wasn't prone to enjoying social occasions either on or off his ship. Which was really fine with her, as long as he knew how to safely navigate *Lusitania* across the Atlantic.

He was speaking with none other than Alfred Vanderbilt, who'd made an appearance at the Hochstetters' party the previous evening. Caroline and Gilbert nodded, but continued walking as the other two seemed deep in conversation about something important, the captain speaking in reassuring tones.

"What do you think they're discussing?" Caroline asked her husband as they continued to walk along the promenade. When he didn't answer, she looked up at him and saw that his thoughts were elsewhere. He distractedly patted the breast pocket of his overcoat as he'd done about one hundred times since they'd left the house that morning. It was where he kept the Strauss music sheets, carefully stored in their oilskin pouch.

"Gilbert?" she said, a little more loudly.

He looked startled to find her walking next to him. "Yes?"

"I was wondering what the captain and Mr. Vanderbilt were discussing. It seems to be a serious matter."

He looked back to where the two gentlemen were still talking, a small frown on his lips. Patting her hand gently, he said, "Nothing for you to worry about, my dear. Nothing for you to worry about at all."

She opened her mouth to let him know that she was much stronger than he thought, and if there was something bothering him, about his business, or this voyage, or even if his shoes were too tight, she wanted to know. Because she loved him, and what affected him affected her. But they'd had that argument too many times already, and walking the deck of the *Lusitania*, surrounded by so many people, was not the time nor the place to bring it up again. *Later,* she told herself. Later, when they were alone in their stateroom, perhaps over tea, she would bring it up again.

They continued to walk until the shrill of a woman's voice near the railing caused Caroline to stop. She glanced around until she recognized the owner of the voice. Of course, the outrageously large hat with an excess of peacock feathers would have identified Prunella Schuyler even if she'd been silent instead of in a heated conversation with her well-known adversary, her very disagreeable sister-in-law Margery Schuyler. Both were grand dames of Manhattan society, but Caroline made a point of avoiding them, owing in part to their vindictive gossiping and also because they disapproved of Gilbert and his new money. Which only made Gilbert try even harder to ingratiate himself into their world.

Caroline tried to reverse their steps but they'd already been spotted and Gilbert was removing his hat to greet them. "No, Gilbert, please don't stop. They are such vexations. . . ."

But he was already speaking to them. "Mrs. Schuyler. Miss Schuyler. How lovely to see you both." He made a point of kissing their gloved hands while both women stared stonily at him.

Knowing it was too late to escape, Caroline greeted them both, doing her best not to focus on the unattractive sore in the corner of Margery's mouth. "I hope you're feeling better, Miss Schuyler."

The woman looked at her, not understanding.

"You left our party early because you were taken ill. I hope you're feeling better."

Margery didn't even pretend to be mortified at being caught in a lie. "I'm feeling quite well, thank you."

Gilbert touched Caroline's shoulder. "I'll leave you in the good company of these fine women, dear. I'm headed to the smoking room."

"But . . ." she started, but he'd already begun to walk away, unaware of her fantasy of them waving goodbye to New York together, then retiring to her bedroom as the ship sailed out into the Hudson River on its way to the Atlantic.

Prunella gave Caroline a tight smile, her upper lip pulled over her slightly protruding front teeth. "I was just telling Margery about my brilliant stepson, Phillip. He's at Harvard Law now, you know. He will be quite the catch, I'm sure. Brilliant, handsome, and the Schuyler name. We'll have to be very careful about whom he marries. Blood will tell."

Margery's watery blue eyes had taken on a glassy cast, as if she'd been listening to Prunella wax poetic about Phillip since they'd boarded the ship. Apparently eager to change the subject, she said, "There will be a talent night here on board Thursday evening. Isn't that exciting? My late father, God rest his soul, loved my singing voice and always asked for me to sing at our parties."

"Wasn't he deaf in one ear?" Prunella asked, her face serious.

Ignoring her sister-in-law, Margery continued, "I think the talent evening will be the perfect place to showcase my singing voice. I just need to find someone to accompany me on the piano."

Both eyes turned to her and for a brief moment, Caroline contemplated throwing herself over the railing.

A twisted grin settled on Prunella's face. "You play the piano, don't you, Mrs. Hochstetter?"

"Ah, yes, I do, but—"

"Perfect," Margery said. "And rumor has it that you have a rare Strauss waltz with you here on the ship. Perhaps I shall sing it and you may accompany me."

Caroline blinked. "Actually, there are no lyrics. Waltzes rarely do . . ."

Margery frowned at Caroline. "Don't be such a defeatist. I'm quite quick with the pen and can create my own. I'll just need to see the waltz so that I can match the lyrics to the melody."

Caroline looked about for a means of escape, trying not to look dejected when she found none. "I'm afraid that's impossible. It's very rare, and my husband is very protective of it. He will have it under lock and key for the duration of the voyage."

"Hrmph. I find that very unacceptable," Margery said, her lips pressed together in disapproval. "Regardless, before I will agree to perform with you, you will need to audition, to make sure you're up to standard. There's nothing more terrible than an accompanist who is not of the caliber of the vocalist. I'll have my maid contact you with a time and place. Which stateroom are you in?"

"B-48 and 50—the portside Regal Suite. Although, I'm not sure if—"

Margery was already speaking over her. "Do you have any medical knowledge, Mrs. Hochstetter? I have this pesky sore on my mouth, and I'm not quite sure how to get rid of it."

Caroline looked with longing at the railing just as a male voice sounded behind her. "Mrs. Hochstetter. Ladies. What a lovely surprise."

Caroline turned around to find Robert Langford, looking darkly handsome in a black wool overcoat, and his chestnut hair, unencumbered by a hat, blowing in the wind and lending him a boyish air. He smiled at the older ladies, and Caroline was fairly sure that Margery—a spinster in her late thirties at least, with a dour face and sallow complexion—actually blushed.

Caroline made the introductions, trying not to show her relief at his sudden presence. He bowed his head to the two older ladies. "I apologize for the intrusion, but Mr. Hochstetter has sent me to find his wife and return her to his side. Will you please excuse us?"

They said their goodbyes and walked away down the promenade. "Did Gilbert really send you to find me?" She hated the eagerness in her voice.

"No, I'm sorry. It's just that I saw you with those two ladies and I was concerned at the look you kept giving the railing. As if you'd prefer to be on the other side of it."

"Was it that obvious?" she asked, holding her gloved hand to her mouth.

"Only to those of us who know you well," he said. His face was serious as he regarded her, making something odd happen to her breathing. But then he smiled, and they both laughed and the moment was forgotten.

"I'd be happy to escort you to your stateroom if you'd tell me where."

"We're in the portside Regal Suite on B-deck, but I'm not ready to go down yet."

"What a lovely coincidence. I'm also on B-deck. A smaller cabin, alas, but still first-class. And I've been told I have a porthole so I at least have a view. Are you up here until we head out to sea, then?" he asked.

She nodded. "I was hoping Gilbert would want to do the same, but apparently he found the lure of the smoking room to be more appealing."

"I couldn't imagine," Robert said, keeping his gaze ahead of him. "Perhaps he was looking for someone with whom to discuss this morning's news."

"News?"

He gave her a quick glance as if judging whether or not she was strong enough to hear it, and then deciding that she was. "Yes. The German embassy put a warning in most major newspapers warning passengers that the *Lusitania* is a British ship and that Germany is at war with Britain. And that travelers sailing in the war zone on a ship of Great Britain or her allies do so at their own risk."

She stopped and he stopped, too. "Should we be afraid?"

"It's wartime, Caroline. We should all be afraid. But Captain Turner is assuring passengers that *Lusitania* is too fast for a German U-boat to track long enough to launch a torpedo. We will also be given a naval escort as soon as we reach international waters." He smiled gently. "Does that make you feel better?"

Lifting her chin, she said, "Yes, thank you. And thank you for sharing the news with me. I'm sure Gilbert doesn't think I should be burdened with it."

Robert didn't say anything but continued to walk around the deck with her. She studied his profile, remembering something he'd said to her about his reason for going home to England. "You said you had family business to attend. Do I dare hope it's to reconcile with your father?"

He looked away from her, but not before she saw the shadows in his eyes. "One could certainly hope, but that's not why. It's a little more . . . complicated. All completely boring, I assure you, which is the only reason why I'm not sharing every excruciating detail with you. Boring but necessary, I'm afraid. At least it gives me a reason to be on board this ship with you."

They were approaching an area where games had been set up and a large number of children, escorted by what appeared to be an army of nannies, were busy playing hopscotch, jumping rope, and pushing wooden toys. Caroline stopped, watching a little girl of about three with unruly blond curls that had escaped an enormous bow on top of her head. She clutched a ragged teddy bear as she jumped with sturdy legs on the hopscotch board, unable, or not caring, to avoid the lines.

"She's adorable, isn't she?"

Caroline nodded, unsure if she could trust her voice.

"I'm surprised you don't have children of your own," Robert said. "I always pictured you as a mother."

She waited a moment to force a smile before turning back to Robert. "Me, too. We're hopeful it will happen. It would be our greatest joy to have children."

"It will happen, Caroline. I'm sure of it. Just as I'm sure you'll be a wonderful mother."

"Mr. Langford, Mrs. Hochstetter."

They both turned to see Patrick Houlihan, the steward, approaching with what appeared to be two telegrams clutched in his hands. "I beg your pardon. But I have a telegram for each of you." He handed one to Robert and one to Caroline, then bowed to them both before hurrying away.

Assuming Robert would be as eager to read his as she was to read hers, she ripped it open, smiling as she saw it was from her mother, then sobering as she read the rest. She glanced up at Robert. He was looking at his own unopened telegram, his fingers stiff against the paper.

"Aren't you going to open it?" Caroline asked.

He shook his head. "No, I don't think I will." He indicated hers. "Good news, I hope?"

She considered her answer. "I suppose so. Our mutual friend, Hamilton Talmadge, of the infamous garden party incident, has apparently saved my mother from ruin. He has purchased our family home and will be allowing my mother to live in it for the rest of her life for a penny a year."

"Nice chap."

"I suppose so. He's a widower now, you know. He's a bit too young for my mother, otherwise I think they'd make a lovely match. But at least Mama won't have to worry about her finances anymore."

She could tell Robert wasn't really listening, staring instead at his own unopened telegram. "Please open it," Caroline said. "I could leave if you'd like some privacy."

His eyes met hers. "It's from my father," he said bluntly.

"Then you should definitely open it."

"Should I?" Their gazes held before Robert turned abruptly and walked toward the railing. He held the telegram suspended over the water for a long moment as if undecided.

"Don't!" she shouted, moving toward him. She thought of her own beloved father, his memory faded like fabric left out in the sun, yet the imprint of his love and devotion as permanent as the stars.

He ripped a corner of the telegram, clutching both pieces. Caroline held her breath. If she had just one letter from her father, just one . . . "Don't!" she said again, louder.

"Why?" he asked. "I already know what's in it. He cabled me yesterday telling me to stay in New York. Touching, isn't it? How eager my father is to keep an ocean between us?"

Caroline watched as Robert was suddenly surrounded by a throng of people moving to starboard holding large white handkerchiefs in preparation for the ship's departure. Everyone seemed dressed in shades of black and gray, giving the impression of unsettled ghosts.

"Because he's still your father," she said over the din, unsure if he'd heard her.

He must have because he turned back to her, but not before the ripped corner of the telegram was torn from his hand by a strong gust. He clutched what remained of the telegram with one hand but shifted his gaze to watch the errant piece of paper. It sailed on the blustery wind, twisting and looping on its descent toward the grasping waves of the harbor as the great ship's funnels belched black smoke into the pewter sky, and the gulls continued to scream.

CHAPTER 6

Tess

New York City
Saturday, May 1, 1915

WOULD THOSE BLASTED birds never shut up?

Tess slipped through the door from the promenade, letting the wind slam it shut behind her. That was better. The promenade was crammed with hanky-wielding travelers and their well-wishers, everyone jammed up against the rails, waving at the shore for all they were worth. The society reporters were making their rounds, cozying up to the swells; children were running back and forth, jamming hoops into unprotected ankles; and, above it all, the gulls circled like vultures with a head cold.

It wasn't the crowds Tess minded. Crowds were good. Crowds were a place you could lose yourself. It was the incessant rock, rock, rocking of the ship, even at anchor, and that tang of salt in the air. Salt and something vaguely fishy.

The closest Tess had come to the sea was the swan boats in Central Park.

Deep breaths. Tess leaned back against the white wainscoting of the wall and breathed in starch and soap with a soupçon of coal smoke. Even here, even on B-deck, where the Vanderbilts slept in state, they couldn't keep out the stench of the fuel that made the ship run.

But it was more bearable. It was certainly more bearable.

It was quieter in here than outside, but nearly as busy. Servants bustled about, making sure their masters' belongings were settled. Porters staggered beneath vast bouquets of flowers, delivering farewell trophies to the proper suites. Tess clutched her battered carpetbag to her chest and tried to look suitably lost, which wasn't as hard as she'd feared, since she was.

Find me on B-deck, Ginny had told her. *By the parlor suites.*

Well, here she was, incongruous in her navy serge traveling suit from Gimbels ($10.75, with belt), a poor, lost wanderer from the second-class lounge, just looking to find her way to the stairs down to E-deck. Never mind that the staircase was smack in the middle of the second-class lounge, and clearly marked, at that. What American girl wouldn't want a glimpse of the luxury of her betters?

Oh, wait. She wasn't meant to be American. She was Tessa Fairweather, from Devon. Where, apparently, they made some special sort of cream and had something to do with Sir Francis Drake. Ordinarily, Tess researched her roles better than this, but Ginny had sprung this one on her. One week's notice and here she was, on this floating palace, planning a light bit of major felony and personal reinvention.

Tess craned her neck, scanning the busy servants, the porters with their bundles. *Damn it, Ginny. Where are you?*

It felt like she spent a lot of time hunting down Ginny these days.

It would, Tess thought sourly, have made it a great deal easier had Ginny simply given her the cabin number. But, no. For her own safety, she wasn't to know Ginny's whereabouts on the ship. Which wasn't really so much for her safety as for Ginny's convenience. Ginny didn't want her showing up and declaring the game was off. Ginny could sense cold feet the way a gull could scent . . . what did gulls scent? Seaweed? Fish? Passengers with particularly elaborate hats?

Despite herself, Tess couldn't help grinning. Her fingers twitched to sketch the image: a seagull diving into Mrs. Prunella Schuyler's elaborate headgear.

Perhaps that was what she ought to do when she got to England: offer up her skills to the papers. *Need a spot of light libel via scurrilous sketch?* She could draw the Kaiser in compromising positions to prove her bona fides.

England. Now there was a sobering thought. Only seven days to complete her assignment, all of it while the world—ugh—swayed beneath her as it was swaying now.

By the watch pinned to her chest, it had now been ten minutes. *Look for me at the first blast of the ship's horn,* Ginny had said, but that blasted horn had blasted and blasted and blasted again, and Tess's sister was nowhere to be seen.

Casually, just another inquisitive passenger, Tess sidled past the great wrought iron grille of the lifts, toward the Regal Suites. These weren't just cabins; they were complexes, a whole wilderness of rooms around a private hall. The one on the left, that was the Hochstetter domain. A redheaded porter strutted into the narrow enclosure, bearing roses. Tess followed behind. She caught a glimpse of a lavishly appointed parlor, the figured carpet half-hidden by trunks and bags.

Did one of those contain the musical manuscript?

Tess edged a bit closer, only to find herself hailed by a loud voice from behind. "Move along, now." It was a passing porter, his arms full of boxes. "This ain't a free show."

"No need for that," Tess retorted, hefting her carpetbag. "I was just looking for the lifts, I was. Show a girl the way?"

The porter paused long enough to give her Gimbels couture a quick once-over. "Try the stairs, love," he tossed back over his shoulder. "First-class only."

Somehow, Tess doubted that he referred to the likes of Mrs. Hochstetter and Mrs. Schuyler as "love."

She'd have to go now, she knew. Having been reprimanded once, she couldn't stay on. But she couldn't help pausing for one last look, like a glimpse into a fairy tale kingdom, the walls embellished with wreaths of gold that glittered in the light of the lamps. This was the world of Caroline Hochstetter, a world so far beyond Tess's reach, it might have been in another universe entirely.

"It's in the style of the Petit Trianon."

The man had been so quiet, she'd hardly heard him approach. Tess didn't have to feign her start of surprise; the hard part was hiding her recognition. It was the man she'd seen playing piano with Mrs. Hochstetter. He leaned casually against the white wainscoting, his eyes on Tess.

"Marie Antoinette's country cottage," he added helpfully, when Tess failed to respond. "She was Queen of France. For a time."

"I—er." Tess swallowed the comment about cake that came to mind, and said, belligerently, "I was just looking for a way to E-deck."

"It's not through the Regal Suite," said the man dryly. To Tess's surprise, he unfolded himself from the wall, offering her an arm. "Let me show you the way to the lifts."

"Didn't you hear? They're first-class only." Tess hid her confusion in a show of indignation. Ignoring the outstretched arm, she stomped ahead on her own. "Don't want me soiling their fine marble floors."

"The elevators aren't marble. They're mahogany. Marble would be a bit heavy for the purpose." The man made no attempt to hide his amusement. He strolled beside her, for all the world as though they were having a promenade on the deck. Which, Tess realized, had the effect of moving her neatly away from the Hochstetter suite. "Have we met before?"

"You say that to all the girls?" Tess scoffed, adding a bit of Cockney to her voice. She was meant to be English, after all. "Don't seem likely, do it? You're too grand for the likes of me."

Blast it. She'd meant to discourage him, instead she'd intrigued him. He stopped in front of the elaborate wrought iron cage that contained the lifts, looking down at her with the light of challenge in his eye. "I'm hardly so grand as all that—and I rarely forget a face."

"Well, then." Tess gathered her wits. A bit of cheek went a long way as a distraction. She cocked her hip and raised her chin. "If you've a glass slipper in one of those pockets of yours, I won't say no to being Cinderella."

"I'm afraid I'm no prince." Removing his leather glove, the man extended a hand. "Robert Langford."

Thankful for the cotton gloves that hid the healing scab on her palm,

Tess held out her own. Not that he'd remember a maid with a cut palm, but still. "Tessa Fairweather."

Langford's hand closed around hers. "I know a few Fairweathers back home in Devonshire. Perhaps you're related."

"It's a very common name," Tess babbled. At least, that's what the man who had drawn up her papers had assured her. "Now if you'll excuse me, I'd best be getting to my cabin before the others bag the best beds."

"Your family?" There was something about the way Robert Langford looked at you that made you feel like the only person in the world, Tess thought. Last night, she would have given anything to be the recipient of that single-minded attention. Not so much right now.

"No." Tess backed away. There were stairs to the side of the lifts. She could just take the stairs. If she could only get to them. "Bunkmates. They pack us four to a room in second. I'm going home to me family, if that's what you mean. Back to me old mum."

"In . . . ?"

Where was she meant to be from again? "Devon," Tess supplied. "In Devon."

"Devon?" Mr. Langford's brows quirked. "Now there's a coincidence. Whereabouts?"

"Coincidence?" At the end of the corner, Tess spied Ginny, who cast her a look of deep annoyance and then disappeared again. As if this were her fault. "It's a small village, you'll hardly have heard of it. I hardly remember it myself, it's been ever so long."

"Try me. You'll find I know the neighborhood rather well." With difficulty, Tess brought her attention back to Mr. Langford, who was looking at her as though she were an outré naturalist's specimen.

"Do you?" Tess asked weakly, holding her carpetbag with both hands. "It's beautiful country, isn't it?"

"Not everyone agrees, but I think so." Mr. Langford favored her with a smile that did strange things to the backs of her knees. "Are you quite sure you aren't any relation to my Fairweathers? My family seat is in

Devon. Just west of Ashprington. Where did you say your village was again?"

"Nowhere near your *family seat*," Tess tossed back. "Sure you're not a prince and all?"

Mr. Langford held his hands wide. "Sorry, fresh out of glass slippers. I must say," he added lazily, "yours is quite the most, er, piquant Devon accent I've ever encountered. Is it unique to your village?"

Damn, damn, damn. She would have to encounter the one man on the boat actually from Devon. So much for Ginny's assurances that it was suitably remote. Usually, Tess did her own research, made up her own background. But this had been a rush job. A rush job and a lucrative one. Between the two, Ginny hadn't left Tess a lot of time to ask questions.

"I've moved about a bit," Tess said airily, moving toward the stairs. "Haven't been home since I was little more than an infant. I expect my own mother will hardly know me."

"Hmm," said Mr. Langford.

One step, and then another. Tess did her best to look as though she weren't running away, even if she was. Again. "Well, it's been lovely and all, but my bunk calls. Bon voyage to you, or whatever it is those Frenchies say."

"Miss Fairweather?" Just when she'd thought she was safe. Four steps down and his voice stopped her, and a very nice voice it was, too, like Guinness, velvet and bitter.

"Yes?" she demanded pertly. "Decided you can't live without me?"

Mr. Langford smiled crookedly. "Weren't you going to take the lift?"

"And have that porter toss me out on me ear?" Tess waggled her fingers in the vicinity of Mr. Langford's knees. It would have made a much better exit if she were going up the stairs, rather than down, but you worked with the material you got. As knees went, it wasn't a bad view. "Nice to make your acquaintance. I doubt I'll be seeing you again."

"I wouldn't be so sure of that, Miss Fairweather." His voice followed her down the stairs, carrying either a warning or a promise. "Like a bad penny, I tend to turn up."

It was very clearly meant to be a last line. She was well away now, below the sight of his shoes. But Tess couldn't resist calling back, "Oh, if there's money in it, then . . ."

His startled laugh echoed down the stairs. In a softer voice, he called, "Bon voyage, Cinderella."

The click of his heels on the marble tiles told her he was gone.

Renewing her grip on her carpetbag, Tess marched down the stairs, a crooked grin on her lips and a glow in her cheeks. By any account, that had been an unmitigated disaster. She'd utterly failed in her masquerade and been caught suspiciously close to the Hochstetter suite. The only solution, she knew, was to stay well away from Robert Langford for the duration of the voyage.

Unless he made good his promise to turn up like a bad penny.

Tess wrinkled her nose at herself. She'd better hope he didn't, she told herself sternly. That was a complication she didn't need. And if she'd been lurking near the Hochstetter suite, why, then, he had, too.

Tess gave a snort. Not much question there. At least, not if the other night was any indication.

They'd looked good together, Caroline Hochstetter and Robert Langford. Both of them first-class all the way.

Tess's carpetbag weighed heavy on her wrist, heavier than it had a moment ago. It was a long way down to E-deck. And wasn't that always the way? Well, it was up to Ginny now to find her. Tess spared a moment to hope Ginny wouldn't. But that was foolish. She had her papers, yes, and her ticket, but she wouldn't get far in England without the money that had been promised her for copying the Strauss piece. Unless, Tess thought wryly, she turned thief for real and made off with some of that jewelry Mrs. Hochstetter left lying about. Just one of those gems would set her up for years.

And make her something she didn't want to be.

Oh, and forgery was that much better? Somehow, forgery had always felt cleaner than outright stealing, as if she were leaving them something of herself in return. And if they didn't realize they were missing it, how could it hurt them? That was what Ginny had insisted, and Tess had tried to believe it. If they didn't care enough to realize they had a copy, then they didn't deserve to own it in the first place.

Enough. After this voyage, she'd be out of it.

Bon voyage, Cinderella, Robert Langford had called after her.

A fresh start. Maybe not with a glass slipper—or a silver spoon—but a fresh start all the same. She'd make her own mistakes this time around, thank you very much.

Tess stumbled off the last step into the hall of E-deck, tasteful, but less grand than B-deck. Third-class on one end, second-class on the other, with a smattering of first-class cabins in the center, the smaller kind, not like the grand Parlor Suite she'd glimpsed through the door upstairs. Those were only to be found upstairs, not down.

Tess gave a tentative knock at the door of her own cabin, and then pushed it open. "Hello? This is E-22, isn't it?"

"Home, sweet home!" chirped a woman who was swinging her legs from one of the top bunks. Her dark hair had been swept into an exuberant chignon, the front puffing out a good three inches. A jaunty bow marked the high neck of her blouse. "For the next five days, that is. Not bad, is it?"

The woman's gesture encompassed the red brocade coverlets and the yellow silk curtains that would screen off the beds at night, but had been looped up for day, as opulent as anything Tess had seen upstairs.

"Not bad at all," agreed Tess. "I wasn't expecting silk."

The cabin was small, but the materials were rich. The wood of the massive dressing stand that stood between the bunks had a rich hue to it, and the china basins and ewers were far nicer than anything Tess had ever used at home.

"Well, it *is* the *Lusitania*. I was supposed to be on the *Cameronia*, but it got commandeered by the British navy this morning, so they transferred me over here. That's your bed," Tess's new friend added, pointing at the bunk across from hers. "Hope you're not afraid of heights!"

"Ha-ha," said Tess, since some answer seemed to be required.

The woman on the bunk below looked pained, but pointedly carried on with the letter she was writing, her nose at an angle that indicated she had no idea how these riffraff had come to be in her cabin.

"I'm Mary Kate Kelly," continued the girl with the pompadour, "and that's Nellie Garber"—the letter writer's shoulders stiffened—"and, well, we're not quite sure what *her* name is."

Her appeared to be the woman lodged in the bunk beneath Tess, her fair hair elaborately braided and wrapped around her head in an old-fashioned style. Her clothes were equally unfashionable, of heavy wool with embroidery that had never seen the inside of a shop.

"Haven't you asked her?" said Tess, intrigued despite herself.

"Oh, she doesn't speak a word of English," said Mary Kate confidingly. "I think she's Norwegian? Or Swedish? Something like that."

"Hello," said Tess, and smiled determinedly at her bunkmate, who gave a shy smile back and then dropped her head again.

"So," said Mary Kate, giving a bounce on the bunk that made Nellie glare. "What brings you on board?"

"Oh, I'm going home to Devon," said Tess. After that encounter with Robert Langford, it seemed a good idea to practice her story a bit. She heaved her carpetbag onto her bunk and waved her hand in a deprecating gesture. "Well, it doesn't feel much like home anymore. I've been living in the States since I was five. There were seven of us at home, and I had an aunt here. You know how it is."

Mary Kate nodded understandingly. "I was a mere babe in arms when we came over. I've lived my whole life in Brooklyn," she said proudly.

"What brings you back, then?"

Mary Kate winked. "A man, of course. What else?" She dug a picture out of her pocket, displaying a man with a cap pulled low over his forehead. "That's my fiancé, Liam. He got called home to join up, so here I am!"

"That's awfully brave of you," said Tess, handing the photo back.

Mary Kate grinned. "Braver to leave him on his own over there with all those French girls! This way I'll be nearby when he has leave. His mother grew up with my mother," she added, as though that explained everything. She lowered her voice. "Speaking of being brave, did you hear?"

"Hear what?" Tess began unpacking her things, putting her comb and brush on her shelf on the large dressing table that stood between the bunks.

Mary Kate glanced over her shoulder, as though the very walls had ears. "About *the Germans*."

"I hear there are a great many of them in Germany," said Tess. Including her own ancestors, although once her mother had died, her father had stopped speaking German at home. It was Ginny to whom her mother had told the old fairy tales in the old language and sung the old songs, leaving Tess to hear them at secondhand, in English.

"No, silly. The ones on the ship! They caught them this morning. I heard it from one of the firemen—he knows my Liam. They say they've got them all chained up in the brig."

Tess gave her head a quick shake. "Got who?"

"The Germans! Jimmy—the one that's friends with my Liam—he says they're here to sink the ship. Can you believe it?"

"No," said Nellie succinctly from the bottom bunk. "It's pure sensational nonsense. For the weak-minded. No one is sinking anything."

"Then why are there three Germans in the brig, Miss Know-It-All?" demanded Mary Kate. "I hear they mean to take over the Marconi room and signal our position to U-boats!"

"Then it's a good thing they're in the brig, isn't it?" said Tess, in a conciliatory tone. "They can't do much signaling from there."

"Yes, but"—Mary Kate's eyes glowed with the excitement of it—"what if there are more? Why, any one of us could be an enemy agent!"

"Only if they mean to talk us to death," muttered Nellie, and pressed so hard on her pen that the nib snapped.

"You can't deny they mean to sink us!" retorted Mary Kate. "Why, they said so in the paper this morning! *Everyone* is talking about it."

"Talking about what?" The door cracked open to reveal one of the second-class stewards, his arms laden with parcels. "Afternoon, ladies."

"The Germans," said Mary Kate, with a superior look down at Nellie.

"Now don't you be worrying about those," said the steward soothingly. "We've the British navy watching after us, so we have. Now, which of you lovely lasses would be Miss Garber?"

There was a letter and a basket of rock cakes for Mary Kate and a staggering pile of parcels for Nellie, cards and chocolates, roses, gloves, and silk stockings.

"Merciful mother of God," said Mary Kate, staring with frank appreciation at the pile of packages. "Is it your birthday?"

Nellie daintily set down a card on the pile. "I am simply fortunate in my friends."

"Well, lucky you, then," said Mary Kate. "Rock cake, anyone?"

Tess had expected the steward to go, but, instead, he looked to her. "Miss Fairweather?"

"Yes?" She half-expected to be booted off the boat already.

The piece of paper he handed her was just a single sheet, folded and sealed. "This is for you."

"Thank you." Tess fished in her purse and found a coin for the steward. "For your troubles."

"Aren't you going to open it?" Mary Kate craned to see over Tess's shoulder. "Your young man?"

"No." Tess didn't need to open it to know who it was from. Or what it would be about. "My sister."

"Oh," said Mary Kate, losing interest. "That's nice."

Overhead, the great horn sounded and the ship lurched forward. Tess grabbed at the side of the bunk to keep herself from staggering as the great boat began to move. Her stomach heaved in time with the motion.

"Yes," gasped Tess. "Isn't it? Pardon me—I believe that's my basin."

Ginny would just have to wait.

CHAPTER 7

Sarah

Devon, England
May 2013

JOHN LANGFORD GLANCED warily in my direction and asked if I was feeling carsick.

"Not at all," I said, which was true. It wasn't the car that was making me sick; it was the quantity of Beefeater gin I'd drunk earlier that afternoon, behind the bar of the Camelot Hotel. My head seemed to be stuck on sideways, and my stomach had lost its connection to the planet's gravitational field. The motorway, undulating like a gray ribbon around the green Devon hills, had no end in sight. "I just had this idea that England was a lot smaller. We've been driving for hours."

"We can stop for coffee if you want."

For an instant, coffee sounded perfect. Until it didn't.

"No, thanks. I can stick it out. We *are* almost there, right?"

John checked his watch. "About half an hour, I guess. I rang ahead to the housekeeper. She'll have something ready for us when we get there."

"A housekeeper. Must be nice."

"It's not what you're thinking. She's been with us since before I was born. She must be eighty years old at least. So be kind."

"What do you mean, 'kind'? I'm always kind."

"You'll see what I mean when we get there." He reached for the climate-control knob and turned it to the left. "Here. That should help. You can roll down the window if you like."

"I told you, I'm not carsick."

"Sarah. When I said 'carsick'? I meant 'hungover.'"

"You know, that's the thing about you Brits. You never say what you really mean."

"We call it being polite. I know you Americans struggle with the concept."

"We're just honest, that's all. Frank. Call a spade a spade."

"All right. I'll start again." He cleared his throat. "Why, Sarah. You're not hungover, are you?"

"Hungover? Why, yes, John. Yes, I am hungover. I drank my own body weight in gin four hours ago, on an empty stomach, and you're just lucky I'm not barfing all over this gorgeous Range Rover leather."

"'Barfing'?"

"Sorry, I don't know the Cockney rhyming slang for 'vomit.'"

"Wallace and Gromit," he said helpfully. "If you give me a few seconds' warning, I can pull over."

"Thank you, John. I will do that." I closed my eyes and leaned my head back against the headrest. John and Sarah, I thought. At least we were John and Sarah now. That was a start, wasn't it? "You don't actually live in Langford Hall with only one housekeeper, do you?" I asked.

"Actually, the family moved out of the hall years ago, when my grandfather died. Taxes. We deeded the building to the National Trust and soon realized that a house isn't really a home when you've got busloads of tourists traipsing through the drawing room at all hours. So my grandmother decamped for the Dower House."

"Your grandfather. That would be Robert's son, right? The politician?"

He hesitated. "Yes."

"Do you remember him?"

"No. He married a bit late, because of the war, and then the cancer got him in the sixties."

"I'm sorry."

John shrugged. "One of those things. I wasn't around to miss him. Now, of course . . ."

"Now . . . what?"

He checked the mirror. His knuckles were large and white as they gripped the steering wheel. "Nothing."

I glanced at the side of his face, which had turned heavy again—mouth clenched, brow stern. The landscape blurred past his head, green and hilly, a patchwork of farms and woods. We were headed to the Langford family seat, in a village called Ashprington somewhere near the coast, although I suspected the journey had less to do with John's generous desire to help out an unknown historian than his emphatic desire to escape the paparazzi. In the morning papers—if not today's *Evening Standard*—there would appear grainy, guilty photographs of the two of us, sharing intimate drinks in a grubby basement bar in Shepherd's Bush in the middle of the day. John Langford and a Mystery Brunette. We'd ducked into my room to escape the flashbulbs and the lenses, and John had cast an appalled gaze about the peeling walls and suggested—chivalrously, probably, and also a little recklessly thanks to the gin and the adrenaline—that we might as well head down to Devon to start our research.

Our research? I'd asked, sort of doubtful.

He'd looked me in the eye and asked if I had a better plan, perhaps?

Well, I didn't have a better plan, and as I returned my stare out the window to the left, and the distant, occasional glitter of the English Channel between the southern hills, I figured that John Langford probably didn't have one, either. When your wife was caught by a *Daily Mail* photographer leaving the One Hyde Park residence of a Russian oligarch at four in the morning, and it just so happened that oligarch was a close crony of the Russian president, and you found yourself resigning your Parliament seat as fast as you could say "Profumo" amid a fusillade of flashbulbs and shouted questions that continued, without relief, for nearly a fortnight . . . well, you really weren't looking past surviving the next hour or two. You just existed.

You saw the excuse to flee the capital for a few days with a destitute American stalker—possibly unhinged, possibly fraudulent—and you took it.

What did you have to lose, after all?

"How old is the house?" I asked. "Langford Hall, I mean."

"I'm surprised you have to ask. Shouldn't you know all this already?"

"Just trying to change the subject. Since you obviously don't want to talk about anything personal."

John cleared his throat. "The house, as you probably well know, was completed in 1799, by my great-great-great-great-grandfather James Langford."

"The admiral, right?"

"Yes. Came from a line of prosperous shipbuilders, joined the Royal Navy as a midshipman when he was twelve or thirteen. Made post captain by the time he was twenty-two. He was a damned fine sailor and a decent battle tactician, but he had one excellent quality that set him above the rest."

"What's that?"

"Luck," John said. "In 1786, our man was out charting the Pacific and stumbled on the Manila galleon, which had lost its escort in a storm. Of course he snapped it right up. One of the greatest prizes ever. I believe it was carrying something in the neighborhood of a million in specie, besides another million or so in cocoa and spices and that sort of thing. That's Spanish dollars, of course," he added, after a second's thought. "In pounds sterling, the total was closer to half a million. In any case, he had a proper three-eighths share, because his orders came directly from the Admiralty, so his fortune was made. All hail the noble custom of prize money. To his credit, he didn't resign his commission straightaway."

"Just married an earl's daughter and bought an estate near the sea."

He cast me a sidelong look. "Aha. I knew you'd done your research. Well, here we Langfords are, anyway. Gentlemen and politicians, thanks to Admiral Langford's cheeky luck in the Pacific. Just think how it all might have turned out if the wind had come from the wrong quarter that day."

"Chaos theory. The beating of a butterfly's wings—"

"And I wouldn't be here today." He said it almost wistfully.

I wrapped my hands around my knees. John Langford drove a Range Rover, yes, but it was ten years old at least, and the leather seats were worn to a comfortable softness. The interior smelled strongly of dogs and wet wool, almost (but not quite) overcoming the scent that belonged to John himself—his soap or his shaving cream, maybe, sweet and clean. I knew it was John because I'd smelled it earlier, when I was leaning across the bar in Shepherd's Bush, pouring him a gin and tonic. A faint scent, of course. He wasn't the kind of guy who wore cologne. You only smelled it when you were close enough. When he let you.

"What about Robert, though?" I said. "He wasn't a statesman."

"Not in the least. He was a right charming rascal, though. The family rebel. Not that I blame him. He had the original British lion for a father, an Eminent Victorian with the whiskers to prove it. Sir Peregrine Langford. There was another son, you know. Robert's older brother. He drowned when Robert was quite young, eight or nine. Some kind of boating accident. The way I heard it, James was trying to save Robert, who had gotten into trouble—that was Robert's specialty, apparently, getting into trouble—and ended up drowning himself instead, poor chap."

"Oh my God. Are you serious? That wasn't in any of the stuff I read."

"The family kept it quiet. We're exceptionally good at that sort of thing. Well, we *used* to be, at any rate. I think the official line was that he died of pneumonia or something. The truth was, they pulled him out of the water and he died a day or two later. Apparently James was a brilliant fellow, the perfect golden-haired Edwardian Adonis. Head boy, wrote poetry in Latin and captained the cricket, that sort of thing. His mother died a year later, probably of grief, and his father never really forgave Robert for any of it."

"What a bastard."

"Not much in the way of grief counseling back then." John nodded to a passing road sign. "Nearly there. Next junction."

"Look, the sun's coming out!"

"It always does, around here," he said, changing lanes. "That's how I know I'm almost home."

I couldn't help noticing the way the late afternoon sunshine touched John's hair as we made our way up the gravel drive toward the Dower House. This was partly because he walked a half-step ahead of me, eating up the ground with his long legs, and partly because the flash of pure gold did something strange to my breath. In the next instant, he turned his head and slowed his stride, like he'd only just remembered my existence.

"Sorry." He took my duffel bag from my hand. "Didn't realize how eager I was to be home."

"I don't blame you. It's beautiful."

"Ah. You might want to hold your opinion until you see it up close."

I squinted at the rectangle of elegant Georgian bricks ahead, which glinted a brilliant red-brown in the same languorous sunshine that gilded John's hair, and saw only the kind of settled, symmetrical beauty that screamed—or rather, sang softly—*English country house, circa 1800*. Three stories tucked under a hipped, dormered roof. Sash windows, twelve panes each, evenly spaced on either side of the front door. A row of boxwoods, in need of a trimming. Gravel drive, in need of a raking. Behind us, a garage that had once been a stable, containing the Range Rover in a space that had once been a box stall. Could it get any more perfect, really? Maybe in an hour or so, when the sun began to set. But not much.

Naturally, the door was unlocked. John reached past me, turned the knob, and pushed it open, releasing a heavenly smell of dust and old wood and beeswax. "Mrs. Finch!" he called out. "I'm home!"

There was a huge, damp silence, the kind of quiet you only encounter inside an old house where nobody lives. I stepped over the threshold into a square foyer, paved in checkerboard marble, chipped at the corners. A small stone fireplace lay empty in the corner. Twelve feet above our heads, the acanthus plasterwork ran riot around the perimeter of the ceiling, but the decoration was otherwise spare. Just a couple of stately Victorian portraits frowning down in obvious disapproval. Or else indigestion.

"Sorry," said John. "She's a little deaf. Just go straight through and turn left past the staircase. She's probably in the kitchen. With luck, she'll have the kettle on."

I marched obediently through the doorway into the hall, where a handsome, curved staircase wound up to the second floor and a pair of doors stood closed on either side, leading probably to the drawing room and dining room, or maybe the library, if I knew my Georgian floor plans. At the end of the staircase, I turned left down another hall, narrower, and found myself standing on the brink of an enormous kitchen, last renovated around the middle of the previous century.

"Mrs. Finch!" John shouted again. "We're here!"

"Johnnie?" came a floral English voice, echoing strangely in the room before me, as if belonging to a ghost.

I took another step, turned left again, and tripped over something that turned out to be one of a pair of stainless steel dog bowls, sitting before a cupboard adorned in peeling paint the color of green apples. Ahead of me, a gargantuan yellow Aga dominated the wall, flanked by more cupboards. I turned back toward a large wooden island and, beyond it, a round table inside a nook of French windows, overlooking the gardens. By the table stood a gray-haired lady in a dress of pale blue, covered by a pinafore apron. She squinted at me and reached for the broom that rested against the wall to her right.

"You!" she snapped, lifting the broom. "Out of my kitchen!"

"But—"

She whacked me around the kneecaps. "Go on! The likes of you!" *Whack.* "Didn't I say you wasn't welcome here?" *Whack.* "Go on! Out! Powdering your pretty nose on my nice clean pastry board." *Whack.* "Breaking my poor boy's heart—"

She raised the broom to whack me again. John grabbed the handle just in time. Though I wasn't looking at him, I had the idea that his chest was shaking with laughter.

"Mrs. Finch! You must stop!"

"I'll stop when I want! What are you thinking, you muddle-headed boy, bringing that tart back in my kitchen—"

"Mrs. Finch! For God's sake! It's not Callie!"

"What's that?"

"Not Callie!" he boomed.

She squinted at me from behind a pair of thick, old-fashioned spectacles. "You're not Callie."

"Who's Callie?"

"My ex-wife," John said dryly, putting the broom away in a cupboard.

"Oh," I said. "Calliope. Callie. I get it."

"I'm terribly sorry," Mrs. Finch said, though she didn't sound that contrite. In fact, she sounded a little proud of herself. The demented force of her onslaught had driven me back against the Aga, and the housekeeper now stepped back and reviewed my defeated figure with an air of satisfaction. I didn't have the heart to tell her that I'd only fallen back out of a sense of chivalry. She stood about an inch over five feet, and probably weighed less than the broom. Her silver hair frizzled out of what she'd intended, no doubt, to be a very strict, very neat bun at the back of her head. John, returning to her side, loomed over her like a tree. She tilted her head back to meet his gaze and demanded, "If she's not Callie, then who is she?"

"She's a friend," he said.

She clasped her hands. "Ooh, Johnnie! A girlfriend!"

"No! A *friend*. A historian. She's come to look at some papers."

Mrs. Finch looked back at me in utter bewilderment. Her pale eyes were so large behind the glasses, she might have been a Disney princess. A very old Disney princess. Behind me, a kettle whistled. She made no sign of having heard it.

"Um, Mrs. Finch?" I stepped aside. "The kettle?"

"The what, dear?"

John cupped his hands around his mouth. "The kettle!"

"Yes! I'm making tea. She does drink tea, doesn't she?"

I turned around, lifted the kettle from the hot plate, and closed the lid. "When I have to," I said.

"So I know I promised to be kind and everything," I said, heaping sugar into my tea from a dainty porcelain sugar bowl, "but isn't she a little—well—"

"Deaf? Blind? All those things." He sighed. "I just can't let her go. For one thing, I'd have to find somebody else. For another thing, we've always had Finches at Langford House. We have an old saying—Are you all right?"

I ran for the sink and spat out the tea. "Salt!" I gasped.

"Salt?"

"In the sugar bowl."

He dipped his fingertip in the bowl and tasted it. "Christ."

"It's okay. Just kind of took me by surprise." I straightened away from the sink—a great big bathtub of a farmhouse basin—and walked back to the round table, where we sat with the tea things between us.

"You don't have to finish it," John said.

"I wasn't going to, believe me. Just pour it out and try again."

"No, let me." He rose from his chair and took my cup to the sink. Turned on the tap and rinsed it out. I watched his back curiously as he performed these chores, trying to reconcile this domesticated figure with the eloquent, passionate John Langford I'd seen on one of those YouTube videos, holding forth with tremendous authority during Prime Minister's Questions about the failings of the NHS emergency services during the winter flu season. Now he was disgraced, defeated, and yet he didn't look like either of those things. He looked tired. Resigned, maybe. But still upright. His shoulders still straight. He turned back to me and frowned. "I'm not sure where we're going to find any sugar, however."

"That's okay. I can do without. The cake's sweet enough."

He flashed a smile that hit me right in the stomach. "You're a good sport, Sarah."

"We Americans mostly are, when you get to know us."

"Right." He handed me my teacup and sat back down. The smile lingered a little, just at the corner of his mouth. "He married an American, you know. Robert Langford. The great love story."

"Are you serious? She was *American*? I didn't read that anywhere. I mean, I knew he married sometime after the ship went down, but I couldn't even find the date."

"They kept it hushed, the two of them. Just a registry office, no notice in the papers. I've always suspected there must have been some kind of scandal involved."

"Why do you say that?"

He leaned his forehead into his palm and trawled his fingers through his hair. His other hand idled around the handle of his teacup. "Can you imagine Robert Langford marrying for any other reason? Anyway, the story goes, they fell madly in love after they were rescued together. Although inevitably there must have been more to it than that. Nobody falls in love in an instant."

I smiled and spoke without thinking. "Don't they? I mean, she *was* an American."

For an instant, our eyes held. There was a brief, electric connection, like when you put a pair of wires together and set off a spark, and for the space of that second I forgot my own name.

Then John's smile disappeared, leaving his face even more plain and harsh than before. He kept his eyes fixed on mine and said grimly, "Not in my experience, no."

I examined the tiny, beautiful streaks of gold around his pupils, and all at once I realized what I'd just said. My face—*damn you, fair Irish skin!*—went aflame, and if I could have shrunk like Alice and dived into my teacup, I'd have eaten any mushroom on the planet. And I don't even like mushrooms.

John sighed, slung back the rest of his tea, and reached for the pot. "So. Feeling any better yet?"

"Feeling better?"

"Your—*ahem*—carsickness, Sarah?"

"Oh! No. I mean, yes. A lot, actually. All that nice fresh air. I think I can even smell the sea from here." I looked out the window, grateful for the excuse, and saw a long green lawn stretched toward a copse of trees. In the distance, to the left, I could just glimpse the magnificent pale corner of Langford Hall.

"Torquay's only a few miles away," he said.

"Torquay? Like in *Fawlty Towers*?"

"The very one. Loads of beaches, if that's your thing. Also Blackpool, except in the other direction. The big house overlooks the river Dart. I used to keep a scull in the boathouse, back when I was living here. Before I got married."

"What about the dogs?" I asked. "They must like the beaches."

"Dogs?"

I nodded to the bowls by the doorway.

"Oh. That's Walnut. Last of the Langford whippets. Callie took him with her when she left."

"*What?* She took your *dog*?"

He shrugged. "Her therapist said she needed an animal for emotional support."

"What about you? Don't you get any emotional support?"

"That's not the point, Sarah." He set down his cup and rose from the table. "If you're finished, we should probably get to work."

"Get to work? Now?"

"Why not? Or have you got anything better to do?"

"I guess not." I stuffed the last of the apple cake into my mouth. "What are we doing?"

"You shouldn't talk with your mouth full." He took the tea things and brought them to the sink. "But since you ask, we're headed down to the folly."

I swallowed. "Folly? Aren't we already there?"

"Very funny." He turned around and leaned against the counter, crossing his arms, making me feel as if I were undergoing some kind of examination in a subject I didn't understand. Maybe John felt it, too. His face, already grim, squished into a frown. "I can't believe I'm doing this," he muttered.

"Doing what? Helping me?"

"Nobody's been down there for years, except Mrs. Finch and her broom. God knows what we're going to find."

My fingers froze around the teacup. My heart went *thud* against my ribs. I stared at John's enormous figure propped against the edge of the sink. His head, struck by sunshine. His arms crossed over his chest, his legs crossed at the ankles. Everything crossed, not about to allow a single thing inside.

"Say that again," I whispered.

"Say what again?"

I put the teacup in the saucer. Picked up the saucer and the pretty china plate with the scalloped edges that held my cake crumbs. Made my way over to the glowering figure of John Langford and set all that ancient, beautiful porcelain in the sink behind him, trying not to let everything tumble from my trembling fingers. *"Nobody's been down there for years,"* I repeated. "I mean, you do realize I'm a historian, right?"

"So you claim."

"God knows what we're going to find." I held up my hands. "Look at me."

"You're shaking."

"Yes, I'm shaking. So could you please tell me exactly what you're talking about? Where the hell is this *down there* of yours?"

"I told you. The folly, out there in the garden, past the copse." He gestured with his hand. "Sort of a summerhouse. The admiral had it built as an observatory, and his son turned it into a shelter for picnics and things, but Robert used it as his study."

"His study? You mean he didn't work in the main house?"

"No. He liked to write by himself, where no one could disturb him. So he had the old folly fixed up with a desk and shelves and a place to sleep. He'd disappear in there for days. It's where he wrote all his books and kept all his papers."

"And these papers," I said slowly, staring at the V of John's cashmere sweater, trying to keep my voice under control. "These papers. They're still there? Nobody has ever gone through them?"

"Not a soul. We weren't allowed."

I looked up. "Why not?"

He gazed down into my face, still frowning, but I had the feeling he wasn't really looking at me. He was looking *through* me, almost, or maybe not looking at anything at all. Maybe just lost somewhere inside his own head. Either way, it wasn't giving him much pleasure. The lines of his face deepened. His hazel eyes seemed to darken, as if a shadow had just passed over his brow. If I didn't know better, I'd have thought somebody was causing him pain.

"Because," he said at last, in a voice that surprised me by its softness. "After Robert died, my great-grandmother locked it up. She let the roses die outside, the ones she'd planted herself. She loved him so much, I guess she couldn't bear to go near that room again."

CHAPTER 8

Caroline

At Sea
Sunday, May 2, 1915

THE FIRST THING Caroline noticed upon waking in her stateroom the following morning was the scent of roses. For a moment she forgot she was on a ship, crossing the vast Atlantic and far beyond the sight of land. The scent made her think of her mother in her garden in Savannah, her attention to her prized roses rivaled only by her devotion to her daughter. The bouquet had been waiting in her stateroom when she'd arrived, yet in the bustle of settling in and getting changed for dinner the previous evening, she'd forgotten to thank Gilbert.

Although the sky outside appeared leaden, light poured in from the three portholes on the opposite side of the room from her brass bed, the curtains having been opened and tied back to allow in the day. She sat up and blinked, realizing Jones must have already been in the room, Caroline's outfit for the day carefully laid out on the second bed beneath the portholes. She sniffed again, smelling the roses, and could that be . . . ?

"Coffee, ma'am?" Jones appeared in the doorway leading into the suite's private corridor, holding a tray with a silver coffeepot and a single cup and saucer, along with sugar and cream dispensers in what Caroline was already recognizing as the *Lusitania* china. With its distinctive cobalt-and-white floral design, it was hard to miss. "I know how you like your coffee first thing."

Caroline smiled. "Oh, Jones, you're a lifesaver! I was afraid that all I'd be able to find on this British ship would be tea."

Jones settled the tray on the small table next to the washstand by the rose bouquet, then picked up Caroline's dressing gown from the foot of her bed and helped her slip her arms into it. The maid returned to the tray and poured the rich brew into a cup before measuring out exactly the right amount of sugar and cream that Caroline liked. She'd only had to be told once, the first time—the true mark of a lady's maid.

"This is *Lusitania*, ma'am," Jones said. "I expect if you wanted a giraffe they'd be able to accommodate you." A hint of a smile lifted the corner of the maid's mouth, softening the usual stern features. "And with all these Americans on board, there'd most likely be a mutiny if coffee wasn't available."

Caroline accepted the proffered cup and took a grateful sip. "I think you might be right."

"Patrick is asking what you'd like for breakfast, ma'am. There's already enough food in the dining room to feed an army, but he wants to make sure he has your favorites. I told him you usually took only coffee and toast in bed, but he wanted me to make sure." She pressed her already thin lips together to show her disapproval.

"Patrick?" Caroline asked, her head still foggy from sleep, her coffee cup still almost full.

"The steward, ma'am. You met him yesterday. Irish." She said this last word with the same inflection one might use when saying "insect."

Caroline remembered the redhead with the jovial smile and serious eyes. "Yes, of course. I remember." She took another sip of coffee, feeling her brain starting to awaken. "Perhaps Gilbert and I can share breakfast in the dining room while on board. He's usually gone by the time I'm dressed in the morning in New York, so this will be a nice change. Please tell Patrick that I will eat whatever Gilbert is having—as long as it includes poached eggs." She smiled up at the maid, then watched as Jones left the room to notify the steward and promised to be back shortly to help Caroline dress.

Despite the sheer size of the ship and multiple assurances from Gilbert that she wouldn't even be able to tell she was on water, she felt herself sway, feeling a little like when she'd had too much champagne. Or when she discovered a new piece of piano music that took hold of her. But she knew she was on a ship. Knew because of the distant yet distinct odor of burning fuel. With the large funnels on top of the ship billowing out black smoke, she supposed it was inevitable. She took another sip of coffee, sniffing deeply and hoping she'd get used to the acrid scent of whatever powered the ship so that she wouldn't notice it anymore.

At least she knew she wouldn't get seasick. Growing up by the water in Savannah, she'd spent many hours on a sailboat with her various male cousins, plying the waves of the Atlantic off the Georgia coast, learning how to swim, fish, and sail along with the best of them. Until the age of twelve, when her mother had said it was time to start acting like a lady and to stay out of the sun to protect her skin. Caroline still missed the water. And the sun.

She slipped from her bed, ignoring her slippers and feeling the plush carpet beneath her feet as she padded to the tray to pour more coffee, admiring the East India satinwood paneling (according to Gilbert) and the delicate moldings and plasterwork on the cornices and ceilings. Her least favorite parts of the suite were the overabundance of tiny painted raised floral motifs that decorated most of the walls along with garish gilt-braided trim that, again, according to Gilbert, were meant to be a nod to Marie Antoinette's Petite Trianon. It was exactly Gilbert's style and Caroline was glad because she wanted him to be happy. She just hoped that she'd grow used to the décor along with the scent of fuel or she was quite sure she'd develop a bad case of seasickness.

There was a soft knock on the opened door and a gentle cough, making her turn to see her husband standing in the doorway. Her heart warmed at the way he filled the space, at the way the light made his blond hair shine. And the way he wore his custom-tailored jacket as if he'd been born to wear fine clothes instead of actually being the son of a coal miner.

She placed her cup on the table then rushed toward him. "Good morning, darling. And thank you for the roses." She stood on her tiptoes to kiss his lips, but he turned from her at the last moment so that she only touched his soft, shaven cheek, which smelled vaguely of shaving cream and his musky cologne that she loved.

"Roses? I didn't send any. It must be from Cunard as a thank you. I half-expected roses in every room for what I paid for this suite."

Shoving down her disappointment, she kept her fingers laced around his neck, loving the solid feel of him. Reaching up again, she kissed his neck, right below his jaw in the place she knew he liked. "I thought you'd come to my room last night." She kissed him again, nibbling gently at the soft skin. "I missed you."

He reached behind his neck and gently pulled her hands away, keeping them clasped in his. "Please, Caroline. The servants might see."

"It's only Jones since you refuse to have a valet." She tugged on his hand to pull him into the room, feeling her rising desire.

But Gilbert stayed where he was, and looked behind her to where her tousled bed sat, inviting. "The beds are so small," he said. "I didn't want to make you uncomfortable."

She lowered her voice, aware of Jones somewhere in the suite. "How are we ever going to have a child if we sleep apart?"

She could tell she was making him uncomfortable, but it needed to be said.

His lids lowered, his pale lashes dark at the roots. "It's been four years, Caroline. I think we need to resign ourselves to the fact . . ."

She put her finger over his lips, not wanting him to voice her own fears, believing somehow that to say it out loud might make it true. "Don't," she whispered. She pressed herself closer. "Besides, what we do in our marriage bed doesn't have to be all about making a family."

He stepped back, his cheeks ruddy with embarrassment. "I don't know what to think when you talk that way. I wasn't . . ." He stopped, his eyes apologetic. "You're so refined. And when you act . . . like that, it makes me think that my coarser upbringing has somehow rubbed off on you like so much coal dust."

She dropped her hands from around his neck, not willing to have this conversation again. Despite her reassurances that her need for her husband had nothing to do with his upbringing, the argument never changed. Moving back, she felt her knees hit the side of her bed and she sat, needing to put distance between them. Instead of the crushing disappointment she'd expected, all she could feel now was a growing, burning anger. Keeping her gaze focused on the middle porthole window, she said with a level voice, "Will you be attending Sunday services with me this morning?"

Gilbert cleared his throat. "I'm afraid not. I've business to attend. I'm sure Prunella and Margery Schuyler would be happy to accompany you. Would you like me to have Patrick pass a note to them to let them know you'll be joining them?"

She couldn't look at him. "No. That won't be necessary." She stared at the first sharp stabs of rain as the drops hurled themselves at the glass, sensing each icy needle piercing her skin. She was only vaguely aware of Gilbert kissing the top of her head and then exiting, his footsteps silent on the thick carpet as if he'd never been there at all.

Caroline managed to make her way from her suite to the lifts to take her up to A-deck and the main lounge, where Captain Turner would be delivering church services. She was barely aware of where she was or whom she passed, inordinately grateful for the black-and-white marble tile pattern of the floor surrounding the lifts so she could focus on it instead of her thoughts, which roiled in her head much like the waves outside.

"A penny for your thoughts?"

Caroline looked up, startled at the male voice so close to her ear. "Robert," she said, feeling an immediate lifting of her spirits. "It's so good to see you." She surprised herself by how much she meant it. "Are you going to the church services?"

He raised a decidedly wicked eyebrow. "Why? Do you think I'm in need of saving?"

"We all need saving, Robert," she said softly. Making an effort to clear her mind of her earlier conversation with Gilbert, she smiled brightly. "That's where I'm headed."

He held out his arm. "Then I will be more than happy to escort you."

She put her hand on his arm, feeling the warmth of him even through his jacket sleeve and her glove. He began leading her toward the lift, but she pulled back. "Let's take the stairs. It's only one flight, and I'm in need of a bit of exercise to clear my head."

He didn't ask her why, having known her long enough to expect that she would tell him when she was ready. She liked that about him, liked that he'd cared enough to understand this about her. Lifting her skirts slightly with her left hand, she found herself leaning against his arm more than necessary, feeling like a lost child on a cold night in search of a fire.

The lounge, with its barrel-vaulted skylight and stained glass windows that each represented one month of the year, was already filling with people. They stopped, looking around for seats, Caroline taking a moment to admire the elegant Georgian style of the room with its walls festooned with inlaid mahogany panels, and the floor covered with a thick jade-green carpet containing a yellow floral pattern. They moved toward one of the two fireplaces in the room, both tall and towering, made of green marble with enameled panels. Gilbert would love it.

Caroline only nodded toward acquaintances, not wanting to stop and chat and have to explain why Gilbert wasn't with her, and why Robert was. He was too handsome and self-assured to be introduced simply as a friend. Because, if she were being honest with herself, she wasn't exactly sure what their relationship actually was.

Robert directed her toward two seats. As he held her chair for her to sit, he spoke softly in her ear. "Did you receive the roses I sent?"

She was so surprised she couldn't speak for a moment, and then Captain

Turner began the service so that she was forced to keep her questions to herself. She spent the rest of the service acutely aware of Robert sitting next to her, of his beautiful tenor voice as they sang "For Those in Peril on the Sea," and of his arm brushing hers as he held her hymnal.

They were silent afterward as they followed the crowd out of the main lounge, finding themselves walking down the Saloon Promenade toward the Verandah Café. "Would you like some tea?" Robert asked.

Caroline nodded, still unsure of what she should say, thinking of a thousand things and rejecting them all before they reached her tongue. She'd prefer coffee, but doubted she'd be able to taste anything so it didn't matter. They were seated at a small table for two, surrounded by ivy, trellises, and wickerwork, and for a moment Caroline could almost believe she was at home in her own garden. They talked about the weather and fellow passengers while they waited for their tea to be poured, then stared at each other for a long moment.

"You sent me the roses?" Caroline finally asked.

Robert nodded. "At your party, you seemed so sad, and not looking forward to the voyage. And I remembered how much you loved roses. The first time I ever met you was in a rose garden." His eyes twinkled as they both remembered the circumstance. "I thought they might lighten your spirits a bit."

"They did," she said, impulsively reaching over and placing her hand on top of his. Their eyes met as heat sparked between them, holding just for a moment before Caroline quickly withdrew. She sat back in her chair, concentrating on putting the right amount of sugar and milk in her tea, watching the liquid gently sway inside her cup.

"How are you holding up in the rough weather?" he asked, returning to a safe topic of conversation.

"I've barely noticed it," she said, taking a sip. "I suppose I'm made of sturdier stuff, despite what other people might think."

He waited in silence for a moment, to see if she'd say more. When she didn't, he said, "I'm assuming you've heard about the three Germans held in custody on board?"

"No, I haven't. Is it something I should be worried about?"

"I don't think so. I think the mere fact that we caught them before any damage could be done is good enough reason to not be alarmed. But I wanted to let you know. So that you'd be . . . vigilant."

"I hadn't heard, so thank you. Gilbert doesn't believe in upsetting me, but I think it's best we are all aware of possible dangers. Especially on board this ship. Do you think there might be more spies on the ship?"

He didn't answer right away. "I suppose anything is possible. This is wartime, after all. But if we all agree to be diligent and alert, I would expect if there are more spies, they will be found out before any harm can be done."

Caroline found herself relaxing, despite the less-than-reassuring news. Maybe it was because it was coming from Robert that she felt safe. "Thank you, Robert. I appreciate your frankness." She sat up. "Perhaps you would allow me to be just as frank?"

"Of course." He continued with his casual air, but she detected a hardening in his eyes.

"You should open the telegram from your father."

His expression didn't change. "What makes you think I haven't?"

She allowed herself a small smile. "Because I know you too well. You always like to have the upper hand. And by not reading your father's telegram, you have all the power still."

His eyes narrowed slightly. "Is that so?" Leaning forward, he said, "What if I told you that my father, despite his heroic public image, isn't quite the man he would lead you to believe?"

Caroline recalled the stories of his brother's drowning, of how Robert's father had blamed him, and how the news had all but killed his mother. But she also knew how important her last remaining family member was to her, and how an estrangement would wound her deeply and permanently.

"I won't pry into your family matters, Robert. But I do know that your father is all you have left, and it is my belief that you should do whatever you can to make amends with him. He won't be in your life forever, you know."

"I'll take that under advisement." Almost imperceptibly, his gaze traveled down to her lips, bringing to mind the electric moment her hand had touched his, and making them both aware of all the dangers that might be lurking. His eyes met hers again and she thought that perhaps she'd only imagined it.

When they were done, he led her outside to the Saloon Promenade. The driving rain had mercifully stopped, but the pregnant clouds lay low and swollen, promising more rain. Three nannies marched past them in a desperate attempt to run off some of the pent-up energy of their various charges, forced earlier to stay inside due to the inclement weather. One nanny fell back to lift a little girl with blond curls—the same little girl Caroline had seen the day before, still clutching her teddy bear—who'd stopped walking to stare at Robert and Caroline.

"Come along, Alice. It's not polite to stare."

The children disappeared down the promenade, leaving the two of them alone. The rough seas were keeping many passengers in their beds, near their basins, giving the decks a nearly abandoned air. Caroline turned back to Robert to comment, her smile quickly fading at the serious expression on his face.

"Why are you so sad?" he asked quietly.

She opened her mouth to reply just as a large swell hit the ship, causing Caroline to lose her footing and slam into Robert. His feet remained steady as his arms went around her and even after the danger had passed, he didn't release her. She tilted her head toward him, so close she could see the green flecks in his eyes. Could see the softness of his lips and the dark stubble that was already beginning to show on his cheeks. Could smell the spicy maleness of him that had nothing to do with soap or cologne. It was simply *Robert*. The man she'd known for years, the person she always searched for at parties. The man who'd thought to send her roses because he thought she'd seemed sad.

Without thinking, she pressed her lips to his and all the lights in her world dimmed for one brief moment before becoming startlingly bright. Their mouths fit together perfectly, the touch of skin on skin feeling as if it were the first time she'd ever experienced the sensation. His arms tightened around her and she was glad, quite certain her knees couldn't support her without them.

The sound of a distant bell brought her back to reality, reminding her where she was. And with whom. She stepped backward and Robert released her, his eyes mirroring the confusion she felt. Caroline pressed her fingers against her lips. "What have we done?"

He continued to stare at her without speaking, his silence as clear an answer as if he'd shouted.

"We shouldn't have done that," she said, trying to evoke a response that would make her feel better.

Robert stepped back, his eyes never leaving hers. "Do you really mean that?" He gave her a short bow, then left her alone with her thoughts and guilt. She stood like that for several moments, gathering her breath, preparing herself to return to her cabin as if nothing untoward had happened, only church services in the lounge and tea in the café.

She turned to head back inside and spotted a lone figure of a man standing next to the engine hatch leaning on the railing, staring out to sea. With a start she realized it was Gilbert and her heart began to race, wondering how long he'd been there. And what he might have seen. She stood still, waiting for him to acknowledge her, to fling accusations at her. Instead, he drew back from the railing and began walking down the promenade away from her, in the opposite direction Robert had taken.

Caroline waited for a solid fifteen minutes, despite the chill wind and her frozen fingers and toes, long enough for her heart to settle and her blood to resume its usual pace as she remembered the kiss and wondered what Gilbert had been doing by himself on the promenade. Then she made her way back to her cabin to lie down, the scent of the roses rotting in stagnant water a just punishment for her transgression.

CHAPTER 9

Tess

At Sea
Sunday, May 2, 1915

THE BLOOMS IN the dining room were beautiful, but Tess could smell the rot beneath the roses.

"Have you ever seen anything like it?" demanded Mary Kate, stopping in awe at the threshold of the second-class dining room. Large pillars stretched to the delicately frescoed ceiling, where a round colonnade opened up onto a second-story balcony. Palm fronds decked the room, some reaching nearly to the ceiling.

"Splendid," said Tess weakly. She was sure it was all very grand, but those palms were making her feel distinctly hemmed in. And the smell of the flowers—they looked pretty enough, to be sure, but there was something cloying about them, something that got in Tess's nose and made her stomach churn.

"Well, we won't have any trouble finding a place," said Mary Kate cheerfully, half-pulling Tess toward one of the long tables. The dining room was sparsely occupied; with the seas choppy, Tess wasn't the only one suffering from seasickness. "You'll see, a bit of food and you'll feel right as rain."

"What's so right about rain?" protested Tess, but Mary Kate ignored her, plopping down into one of the red velvet–upholstered chairs. The ship rocked, all but throwing Tess into her seat.

She should have stayed in the cabin. Except Nellie was in the cabin, in command of the basin. *It will be like living in luxury*, Ginny had said. *Everyone loves a sea voyage*, Ginny had said. Ha. If they'd been meant to go on the sea, God would have given them fins, Tess thought darkly.

She had missed her rendezvous with Ginny last night. Second-class promenade, nine o'clock. But at nine o'clock, Tess had been curled up in a ball on her bunk, whimpering into her pillow, and what she'd felt about Ginny and her schemes wasn't fit to be printed. What was the prospect of a fortune compared to a patch of dry land? She wanted to be in New York—Chicago—Kansas City—anywhere, just so long as it didn't rock beneath her feet as the dining room was rocking now, sending the water in the jugs sloshing to and fro. Tess couldn't stop watching it. Back and forth, slopping almost to the top and then down again, hypnotic and revolting.

"*Puree soubise*—I'm not sure what that is, but it sounds grand, doesn't it?—and then there's salmon trout in Dutch sauce—I wonder what's Dutch about it? Oooh, and then there's braised veal." Mary Kate had seized on the menu with its Cunard logo and was reading it with what seemed to Tess to be ghoulish relish. She turned to Tess inquisitively. "Unless you're going to have the steak and kidney pudding? There's roast turkey or corned tongue, but those just don't sound as fancy, do they, Miss Fairweather?"

"It sounds lovely," Tess croaked. It sounded horrible. "Is that my water? I just need a sip of water."

"Do you know you've turned quite green?" said Mary Kate with interest. "Why, I remember the time Liam took me boating—not that it was a boat like this—and—"

"'Scuse me," Tess gasped, and shoved her chair back from the table, nearly bumping into an affronted waiter. If she heard yet another tale of Liam the Great, she really would be ill.

Mary Kate sprung up from her own chair. "Do you need—?"

Tess flapped a hand at her without looking back. "No. Enjoy your"—her throat twisted on the word—"food."

And she fled the room, pursued by the scent of braised veal.

Air. That was what she needed. Air. But the stairs led up to the well above the dining saloon, and the smell of mashed turnips and steak and kidney pie followed her, wafting through the opening. Tables had been set up in the upper foyer to accommodate the overflow of second-class passengers. None was occupied by diners, but a group of gentlemen had established themselves over a game of cards, reeking of smoke and laughing too loudly. Someone was pounding the keys of the upright piano in the corner, while another man crooned the words of the popular ballad: "*Can't you hear me calling, Caroline . . . It's my heart a-calling thine . . .*"

Tess hastily fell on the first door she found, pushing against the wind that was holding it closed.

"*I'm wishing I could kiss you, Caroline . . .*"

Air at last! But Tess tripped over a skipping rope and nearly fell, catching at a deck chair as the starchy English voice of a nanny intoned, "Now, Beatrice, what did I tell you? You mustn't leave your things lying about."

She was surrounded by a sea of children, dozens of them, all on Shelter Deck being herded to their own lunch in the special children's dining room: girls in starched pinnies clutching dolls, adorable moppets in sailor suits with jam on their faces. Beautiful, well-tended children who somehow managed to make more noise than the late-night crowd at the Golden Spur Saloon in Carneiro, Kansas.

Dodging around moppets, Tess stumbled toward the first available flight of stairs and took to higher ground. Her father's golden rule: *When in doubt, run.* It didn't much matter where you were running to, just so long as you kept going. And going. Because while you were running, you couldn't think of where you'd come from or where you might land. Sometimes, it felt like she'd spent all her life like this, always in motion, going, going, going, because to be in motion meant never having to stop and think.

She'd hit the end of the line, as high as she could go. Above her, the great funnels belched out smoke and dark clouds blotted out the sky. Raindrops struck her face but Tess didn't care. She blundered to the rail and gripped it with both hands, feeling her stomach lurch in time with the movement of the ship. *I-won't-be-sick; I-won't-be-sick* . . . Her body hummed along with the ship's engines, every resource she had focused on the all-important task of not losing the soda crackers she'd choked down in lieu of breakfast.

She was on one of the promenades, she knew. The abandoned deck chairs told her as much. Ordinarily, there would be people here, strolling, chatting, talking, regarding the view. But the weather kept them away, indoors. She had the deck to herself, just the sea and the sky and the sound of the ship churning its way through the waters.

Or almost. Staccato footsteps passed behind her, paused, and circled back.

"Hullo," said the unmistakable voice of Robert Langford. "It's Cinderella."

Tess pressed her eyes shut. Not him. Not now. She didn't have the energy to match wits. "Shouldn't you be in first-class?" she rasped, not turning around.

"This *is* first-class," said Mr. Langford, with some amusement. "You just can't stay away, can you?"

Tess looked sharply at him, and wished she hadn't. The movement made her head swim. "Is it? I didn't—" When she'd made her detour around the children on the Shelter Deck, she must have gone up the wrong stair. They tried to keep second- and first-class apart, with separate rooms, separate walks, separate stairs, but trust her to have blundered into the one place she didn't want to be just now. "I'll just—"

Go, she was going to say, but her throat closed around the word, fighting the nausea that rose with the swell of the ship, so that it came out as something between a retch and a gag.

"It's like that, is it?" Mr. Langford was at her side in an instant. "You poor infant."

"I'm not an infant," Tess gasped, clinging to the rail with both hands. She didn't dare lift her head to look at him; if she did, she would disgrace herself for sure. "I'm twenty-four years old."

"As old as that?" Mr. Langford's voice was mocking, but it was a kindly mockery. A hand touched her shoulder. "Stay there. Don't move."

Tess wasn't sure she could. "Why? Are you planning to have me evicted?"

"I'm planning to get you a cup of tea," said Mr. Langford, and turned to hail a passing steward.

"No, don't—"

In the embarrassing interval that followed, Tess was vaguely aware of Mr. Langford steadying her, smoothing the damp strands of hair away from her face, murmuring encouragement. Tess's world narrowed to the immediate complaints of her body. Even the press of the rail against her chest and the warmth of Mr. Langford's hand on her shoulder seemed to come from somewhere very far away.

When at last there was nothing left in her, she fumbled for her handkerchief. A much finer one appeared in front of her. "Better now?"

Tess heard a moaning noise. She had the uncomfortable feeling it had come from her own throat.

"Glad to hear it," said Mr. Langford. "Ah, thank you, Patrick."

The world was beginning to come back into focus. From the corner of her eye, Tess could vaguely make out the same red-haired steward who had brought the flowers to Mrs. Hochstetter's cabin setting down a small table, followed by a tray. She would have admired his dexterity if humiliation hadn't overwhelmed just about every other sentiment.

"Here." A blue-and-white-patterned teacup appeared in front of her, like a conjurer's trick.

Tess jerked away. "Please, no. I couldn't."

"Never say never," said Mr. Langford. "*Excelsior.* Put your courage to the sticking point. And all that rot. Trust your uncle Robert. I've forgot more about hangovers than you've ever learned in all your long, twenty-four years."

"I'll be sick again," she warned.

"You won't." The cup jiggled insistently beneath her nose. "It's ginger. A sovereign remedy for *mal de mer*—or *mal* in general, really."

"Don't say I didn't warn you," croaked Tess. "Oh, for heaven's sake, I can hold it myself. You don't need to feed me like a baby."

"Don't I?" But Mr. Langford surrendered the cup into Tess's hand, where it shook so badly she could scarcely get it to her lips. She managed a small sip before the cup was whisked away. "Baby steps," he said. "Or baby sips, as it were."

Tess would have glared at him if she could have managed it. As it was, she contented herself with a deep breath, and found that the salt air didn't scrape against her throat the way it had a moment before.

"See?" said Mr. Langford. "Didn't I tell you?"

"A regular medical man, you are," retorted Tess. "Would you like to sell me some snake oil?"

"No," said Mr. Langford equably. "Just another sip of tea. A small sip." He watched as Tess complied.

He made the world's least likely governess, thought Tess irritably. "Happy?"

"Quite. One likes to see one's remedies succeed. Perhaps I'll patent it. Langford's Ginger Toddy." Dropping the patter, he said, with a rough sort of sympathy, "You're not accustomed to people looking after you, are you?"

Tess folded her arms across her chest, well enough now to feel the wind. It bit through her thin suit jacket. "What makes you say that?"

"I had a dog when I was young. A whippet. I . . . reclaimed him from some boys who had been training him to race. Starving him, really." He regarded Tess thoughtfully. "He showed the same charming lack of gratitude when I first tried to feed him. He'd been trained to mistrust good intentions."

Tess wasn't sure she liked being compared to a dog. She rubbed her hands up and down her arms to try to stave off the chills. "Forgive me for forgetting to tug my forelock. I'll just grovel a bit now, shall I? Do you need me to k-k-ow-tow, or will a simple th-thank you do?"

Mr. Langford's lips pressed together. "You're freezing. Don't you have a coat?"

"Downstairs. I hadn't exactly p-planned to come out for a constitutional."

Ignoring her sarcasm, Mr. Langford shrugged out of his coat and settled it over her shoulders like a cape. Tess could feel the warmth from his body sinking into her very bones.

Instinctively, she put her hands up to the collar, feeling wool that had obviously never seen the inside of one of Mr. Gimbel's bargain bins. "I can't take this."

"Calm yourself. It's not a gift, only a loan. I can't have you dying of hypothermia on my watch. I'll lose my membership in the Royal Order of Knights Errant and be forced to confess myself a hopeless cad. Consider it your contribution to my moral rehabilitation."

"Well, if you put it like that . . ." Maybe it was the cold, or the weakness of being sick, but Tess felt the fight draining out of her. Was it so hard to allow someone to be kind? Gruffly, she said, "Thank you."

"You're doing me a service, if you knew it." Mr. Langford looked out over the waves, his profile like something carved on the prow of a ship. "I hate the sea."

Tess looked at him in surprise, the wool of the coat collar tickling her chin. "You don't seem to be suffering."

"My brother drowned in a sea like this." The stark words rang like iron on metal. Mr. Langford breathed in deeply through his nose. "I don't know why I'm telling you this."

"I'm just that easy to confide in," said Tess. It wasn't entirely untrue. People tended to tell her things. Maybe because they saw in her what they wanted to see. "It must be my warm and sympathetic manner."

Mr. Langford snorted, momentarily diverted. "Ha. Shall we say that you have a certain astringent charm?" A wave crested around them, and Mr. Langford's lips went white.

"Do you need to sit down?" said Tess, her hand automatically going to his elbow to steady him.

"Do I look so feeble as that?" His eyes met hers, and there was a force that leapt between them, like the snap of the current. Mr. Langford broke his gaze first. "The waves—I've been sailing since. Get back on the horse, they say. In calm weather, when the sun is shining, I can pretend it doesn't matter, that I'm not chilled to my bones. But when the fog comes up and the sea gets rough . . ."

"How old were you?" Tess asked softly.

"Eight. And my father . . . My father . . ."

His fingers strayed unconsciously to his breast pocket. Tess could hear the crinkle of . . . something. Paper. A telegram.

"He must want you home," Tess ventured.

Her father had been like that after their mother died, not wanting to let either of his daughters out of his sight. Keeping them close, like a miser with only two coins. Not out of love, so much, but fear. All they had was each other, he'd told them, again and again. Each other, a gaudily painted wagon, and a store of bad ideas.

Mr. Langford gave a short, harsh laugh, and looked at her as though he'd just remembered her presence. "Hardly."

"You don't know that."

"Oh, but I do." There it was again, the unconscious move toward the pocket and whatever it contained. "The pater sent me a telegram telling me not to sail. It doesn't come much clearer than that. Don't look like that. I would feel the same way in his place. It was my fault that Jamie died."

Tess clutched his coat tighter around her. "How?"

"I'd pestered him to take me out with him. And then—I was the one who fell in. Jamie drowned trying to save me."

Tess tried to catch his eye. "You didn't mean it to happen. You weren't trying to hurt him."

"Does it matter? The result was the same. If I could go back—" The anguish in his voice cut to the bone. He shook his head, like a man coming awake. "Why am I telling you this?"

"Because I'm here?" She didn't tease herself that it was anything else. She might have been that whippet he'd been talking about: an object of charity. His coat hung on her shoulders, heavy and warm. Without giving herself time to think better of it, Tess blurted out, "I killed my mother. Not intentionally. I came down with scarlet fever and she took it from me. My father—he never reproached me with it. But I always knew that if he could trade us—well, I wasn't the one he'd keep."

Her throat burned with the words. No matter how many times she'd thought it, she'd never said it aloud, not to anyone. Not even to Ginny. But she owed Robert Langford, and this was the only coin she had with which to pay him.

Tess cleared her throat. "It's not easy, is it? Being the one who survived."

Mr. Langford lifted his teacup, his eyes never leaving hers. "Here's to the survivors. Unwanted though we may be." He paused, struck by a sudden thought. "Didn't you tell me you were going home to your mother?"

Damn and blast. That was what she got for letting down her guard. A cup of ginger tea and a warm coat and she'd nearly blown the game.

"Is there any more tea in that cup?" Tess demanded. As Mr. Langford handed it to her, she hastily cobbled together a lie. "I'm headed home to my stepmother. I wasn't—I wasn't really welcome in my father's new family. I was sent to America to live with an aunt in Kansas when I was five. It was easier for everyone that way."

That was the thing with lies: she could almost imagine it were true. She could picture the cottage she'd supposedly left, like something out of a picture book, all thatch and hanging kettles, and a woman with an apron tied over a cotton dress, holding a ladle.

"Then what brings you back?"

"It was time." Over his shoulder, she could see Ginny, waiting in the lee of one of the lifeboats. Ginny made a barely perceptible move of her chin. Tess knew what that meant. *Get a move on. Time's wasting.* Quickly, Tess said, "My father's dead. It was time to go back to the beginning again and start over."

"Can you?" Mr. Langford looked at her, his eyes as dark as the sea. "Or is that just a fairy tale we tell ourselves?"

"You don't know if you don't try, do you?" Ginny's foot was tapping impatiently against the deck, but Tess couldn't resist adding, "You're going back, aren't you?"

Something passed across Mr. Langford's face. When he spoke, his voice was a deliberate drawl, the flippant aristocrat at play, holding her at a distance. "Blighty needs all her sons these days, they say. Whatever my father may think."

"At least you still have a father." So much for confidences. Tess shrugged out of Mr. Langford's coat, thrusting it back to him with more speed than grace. "Thank you for the coat and the tea. I feel almost human again."

"Only almost?" There was real concern in his voice. And something like an apology.

Tess bit her lip. No explaining how she'd spent her life watching through windows, wondering what it must be, to be like everyone else. "If I don't, it's not your doing," she said. It was past time to go, but she stopped all the same, asking gruffly, "Will you be all right?"

Surprise and gratification chased across his face before the usual urbane mask descended. His hand covered hers for a brief moment. "Survivors, remember?"

And then he tipped his hat to her and was gone, with a speed that was almost like flight.

"Well," said Ginny.

Tess turned to find her sister standing behind her, arms folded across her chest. No matter how many times she saw her, Tess still couldn't quite get used to Ginny's latest incarnation, her fair hair dyed black and ruthlessly scraped back. It changed the entire nature of her face; it made her feel like a stranger. A very disapproving stranger.

Ginny looked darkly at the door through which Mr. Langford had departed. "Is that why you couldn't be bothered to meet me last night? Too busy sparking with the Mr. La Di Dah over there?"

"I wasn't sparking—with anyone. I was sick." Which you would know if you'd bothered to check, thought Tess mutinously, and then felt guilty for it. How many times had Ginny sat through the night with her childhood megrims? Hadn't been her father, certainly. It had been Ginny, always Ginny, with a cold cloth and a bottle of patent medicine.

Ginny was unconvinced. "What was all that, then?"

"Common kindness," said Tess tersely.

Ginny snorted. "Come on, now, Tennie," she said, and the use of her childhood nickname made Tess feel about five years old again, with a dirty apron and mismatched braids. "Don't you know better than that? There's nothing common about kindness."

Tess could hear Mr. Langford's voice in her ear. *He'd been trained to mistrust good intentions*. Was that what had happened to her? Had she become too hard, snapping in self-defense where there was no threat to be had? He hadn't had to be nice to her. He'd done it to no purpose.

"Maybe they're just bred to it, then, people like him." Tess fished out a phrase from a half-forgotten book. "Noblesse oblige."

"If you want to believe that, I've a bridge I can sell you. I just don't want to see you hurt, Tennie, not like that." Ginny clasped Tess's cold hands in her own, squeezing them tight. "His kind, they use up girls like us and toss 'em aside. You know that. Just because he has a handsome face—don't let yourself fall for it."

Tess shook her head. "He wasn't trying to romance me."

Ginny dropped her hands. "No, he's got Caroline Hochstetter for that." The words hit Tess like a blow. Just as Ginny had intended. Tough love for her own good. "But when has that ever stopped a man from having a bit on the side? Wham, bam, and a few coins if you're lucky."

Her words hung like coal dust in the air, acid, corrosive.

"Ginny—" Tess began, and broke off, not knowing what to say. She knew there were things Ginny had never told her, things she'd done to keep them afloat. To keep Tess safe and fed. But Ginny's closed face forbade sympathy. Instead, Tess said simply, "Don't worry, Ginny. I'll be careful. I promise. I was sick and he helped me. That was all."

Ginny put her face close to Tess's, frowning. "We can't trust anyone but each other. You know that."

"I know that." Mr. Langford's ginger tea burned at the back of her throat. Kindness. So much for kindness. Tess could feel the sickness rising again, and swallowed hard.

Ginny gripped her by the shoulders, looking at her with concern. "You all right, Tennie?"

"It's just"—what had Mr. Langford called it?—"*mal de mer*. I guess I'm not much of a sailor."

"Well, you'd better hope it subsides," said her sister, letting go and stepping back, all business again. "You have work to do tomorrow night."

"Tomorrow night," echoed Tess. "Tomorrow night?"

"Were you planning to wait until we disembark? This isn't a game, Tess. This is our future we're talking about."

No, it wasn't. It was Tess's past, and she couldn't seem to get clear of it. "All right," said Tess wearily. Without Mr. Langford's coat, she felt cold and exposed. "What do you want me to do?"

"You could at least pretend to be pleased." Ginny looked at her with pursed lips. "The manuscript is in the safe in the Hochstetter suite. Hochstetter had the safe put in specially—didn't trust the safe in the purser's office. Which should tell you something about just what this thing is worth."

Tess was supposed to be impressed, she knew, but she couldn't quite muster the energy. So she just nodded.

Ginny's lips tightened. "The Hochstetters will be at the captain's table at dinner. They'll both be there starting at six. The staff have their meal at six thirty. You have until seven thirty. Eight if you're lucky."

"That's not enough time to make a copy!"

"Then steal it and copy it at your leisure."

"In my cabin, which I share with three other people?"

"Do I have to do all the thinking around here? Just do it, Tess. Get it done somehow. And get it done tomorrow night." Ginny glanced over her shoulder, as if looking for eavesdroppers. "You don't know the people we're dealing with."

There was something in her voice that set all Tess's alarm bells ringing. "What people, Ginny?" It was a music manuscript, for heaven's sake. Admittedly, collectors could be cutthroat, but it hardly seemed something to engender such alarm. "What are you talking about?"

Ginny just shook her head. "Never you mind. Just do it. Tomorrow night."

CHAPTER 10

Sarah

Devon, England
May 2013

JUDGING BY THE state of the sun—falling, still falling, toward a reluctant May horizon—we had an hour or two to start work before night arrived. Or maybe John Langford planned to keep himself busy through the night, in order to stay his demons. He certainly walked like a man bent on business. I gamboled across the tender green turf like a puppy, trying to keep up with those long, determined strides, until he started and briefly turned his head.

"You should let me know when I'm walking too fast," he said reprovingly.

"You should *notice* when you're walking too fast," I said, "or else you're going to have to turn in your English Gentleman certification card."

"I apologize. I was counting on your shrill American voice to keep me in check."

He hadn't stopped, but he'd shortened his stride, and as I caught up and glanced at the side of his face, I saw he was grinning.

"That's why there were so many war babies, you know," I said.

"What?"

"Back in the Second World War. Cultural conditioning. The English girls expected the American GIs to act like gentlemen, basically, and the

GIs expected the English girls to slap them when they'd crossed the line. They were pretty much doomed to disappoint each other. Ergo, babies."

John made a thoughtful grunt.

"I take it you're not impressed with my historical insight?" I said.

"Not at all. I just think 'disappoint' is an interesting choice of terms, in the context of sex."

At the word "sex," delivered in John's masterful Oxbridge drawl, I stumbled, recovered for an instant, and then skidded spectacularly into the grass.

"Are you quite all right?" he asked, helping me back up.

I spat out a mouthful of turf and said I was just fine, thanks. "How far away is this folly of yours, anyway?"

"Not *my* folly. Robert's folly. It's just around the edge of those trees, up ahead. You'll see it in a moment. I say, are you sure you're not hurt? You seem to be limping."

"Totally okay. A few grass stains on my pants, no biggie."

John's cheeks turned pink. He looked away swiftly and cleared his throat. "*Trousers*, Sarah. When in England, always say *trousers*."

"Because?"

"Just trust me. Ah, here we are. Down that little slope. You see?"

I came to a stop and followed the direction of John's arm. "You mean there? On the island?"

"That's the one."

I didn't reply. I might have forgotten how to speak. Around the trees, down that gentle slope of spring green, nestled a small, tranquil lake; in the middle of the lake swam an island; in the middle of the island, surrounded by willows weeping and a couple of apple trees uncurling their new green leaves, sat an octagonal building like something the Romans might have left behind, made of crumbling red brick and pale stone. A swath of massive, purpling wisteria climbed up one side and over the crest of the dome, disappearing down the back. From behind us, the sun turned the stone a luminous rose-gold.

"Rather pretty in the dying light, isn't it?" John said, in the kind of vaguely ironic voice that probably disguised a deeper meaning, which I was too awestruck to deconstruct. "Although I expect all that lovely wisteria's done for the roof."

"I think it's beautiful."

"Of course it's beautiful," he said. "But what matters is what lies inside the thing. Wouldn't you say?"

He resumed his brisk pace, and I scrambled after. Though the air was turning cool, I hardly noticed; my blood was warm from exercise and anticipation. An elegant stone bridge came into view, linking the island to the shore, and as we approached it, I asked John when it was built.

"The folly? Oh, it's original," he said. "The old admiral had it built as an astronomical observatory—stars being essential to navigation back then—and also to keep watch on the Channel shipping. None of his descendants shared his obsession, however, so eventually they sold off the telescope and closed up the roof."

We reached the bridge, and I laid my hand on the round-topped pillar at its base. "But this is more recent, isn't it?"

"Why do you say that?"

"Um, the date? Carved into the stone? Nineteen nineteen?"

"Good Lord." He stopped so quickly, I had to sidestep the swoop of his shoulder. With one hand, he reached out to touch the numbers engraved in the stone balustrade. "You're right. I never noticed."

"Sometimes it takes a fresh pair of eyes."

"We used to play here all the time as kids." He shook his head. "I mean, of course I knew it was built later, after the war. Just not exactly when."

"So what happened to the first bridge?"

"There was no bridge. Just a boat, moored at the water's edge. To get to the island, you had to row. I reckon the admiral wanted to keep the lubbers away."

I looked at the date again. "So Robert must have had the bridge built, right? Because his father died in 1915. Right after the ship sank."

"Yes. Shot himself in his office in Whitehall when he heard the news. He never knew Robert survived it." John rubbed his chin. His voice turned quiet. "I used to wonder if that was a punishment, of sorts."

"For what?"

"Blaming Robert for his brother's death. Being such a miserable father."

I started forward again, up the slight curve of the bridge. I loved the tranquility, the tender silence. Our footsteps crunched softly on the gravel. Atop the dome, a horse-shaped weather vane stared east. The water itself was absolutely still, green-blue and depthless. Not as murky as I expected. I peered over the edge of the bridge and said, "So I guess Robert didn't want to have anything more to do with boats, after an experience like that."

"I don't suppose I blame him. Though it's a shame. Imagine the privacy. Once you rowed over, nobody could reach you without getting wet." He bent and picked up a pebble, which he tossed over the side and into the water, almost without breaking stride. A gentle splash floated back. "There used to be swans, my grandmother told me. Back in the old days. A pair of them."

"How beautiful. They mate for life, you know. Swans."

"Grandmama said they were nasty brutes. They'd score you for a crust of sandwich."

"So what happened to them?"

We reached the end of the bridge and stepped onto the island. John turned around to stare over the water and up the velvety lawn we'd just crossed—not to the Dower House on the left, but the pale, enormous building to the right at the crest of the rise, which I supposed must be Langford Hall itself, gilded by the aging sun. He crossed his arms and smiled grimly.

"We ate them during the war."

Though the grounds of the folly looked unkempt and overgrown, in the way of English gardens, I saw signs of cultivation. "I thought you said the place was abandoned," I said, pointing to the well-pruned limb of an apple tree.

"I didn't say it was abandoned. I just said my great-grandmother locked the place up. The gardeners come around. And Mrs. Finch gives the place a dusting every few months, as I said. Runs the taps, flushes the toilet. Makes sure the ceiling's not leaking and the bugs haven't taken over." John reached into his jacket pocket and produced a small bronze key. "Which means *this* should still work, God willing."

"So when you aristocrats say 'Nobody's been inside for years,' you don't count the hired help."

"Of course not. Where do you get these strange democratic ideas?" He eased the key into the lock, taking his time, and gave the mechanism a careful wiggle. The door was white and very plain, paint peeling at the edges, looking as if it had been cut into one redbrick side of the octagon as an afterthought.

"You look like a safecracker," I said. "Or a midwife."

"Locks are delicate, mysterious things, Miss Blake. Each one has its own quirks. Its own secrets. You've got to have patience. Slow and gentle. Feel your way in. Devote yourself wholly to the task at hand."

His face turned up as he said this, meeting mine halfway, one eyebrow slightly raised, and I felt the blood rush into the skin of my cheeks. I folded my arms and said, "And here I thought you gentlemen were no good with tools."

"Nonsense. We're deeply fond of instruments of all sorts. Wield them with skill and dash. After all, and as my father himself once told me, when I was but a wee lad, anything worth doing"—now the lock clicked, the knob turned under his hand—"is worth doing well. After you, Sarah." He stepped back.

"Well, just so you know, that particular metaphor—locks and ladyparts, I mean—is considered . . . is considered . . . hopelessly . . ." I came to a stop in the middle of the room and whispered, "Sexist."

"*Ladyparts*? What the devil? I was talking about keys, Miss Blake. Keys and locks. What an exceptionally dirty mind you've got. Are all American women so fixated on—"

"Wow. Wow. Oh my God. You weren't kidding."

John stepped past my elbow. "About what?"

"It really *is* untouched." I turned around slowly, trying to absorb every detail, except there were too many. Shelves and shelves, lining six of the octagon's walls, each one crammed with books at all angles, bent with books to its absolute maximum capacity. A big wooden desk strewn with stacks of paper. Papers stacked on the floor, papers stacked on more stacks, papers fallen from their stacks. Beneath the shelves, drawers overflowing with yet more papers. Objects crammed into the spaces where no book or paper would fit. I stepped to the desk and allowed my hand to hover over the green shade of a lamp without touching it. I whispered, "Like someone walked out one day, right in the middle of something, and never came back."

"As I understand, that's exactly what happened. Heart attack. Poor bloke, he was only in his sixties."

"His wife must have been devastated."

"Yes. She died not long after, as I said. Oh, look there. That's probably Himself." He pointed to a portrait hanging on the wall above the door: one of the two facets of the octagon not occupied by bookshelves. "Look at the rascal. Painted when he was still fairly young, I believe."

I stepped closer and craned my neck to study the picture. "Not bad."

"Yes, it's done with remarkable skill. My great-grandparents mingled with an arty set; I understood it was done by one of their friends." He squinted closer. "I can't make out the name. Can you?"

"I actually meant he's kind of hot. Look at those eyes. Like he's keeping a dirty secret from the artist. And all that gorgeous hair."

John cleared his throat. "I'm told I resemble him."

I turned away from Robert's handsome face to inspect the intent, strong-boned profile before me. The wave of hair falling on his temple. In the dusky indoor light, the gold had darkened to brown, and maybe the arc of that wave echoed the one on Robert's forehead. Maybe. But Robert's features were elegant, classically handsome, the proportions so clean and perfect. His eyes crinkled at a dashing angle, as if he was reaching through the ages to flirt with you, right there where you stood in the twenty-first century. Not at all like John's eyes, sober and steady.

"In your dreams," I said.

The room itself wasn't as big as I expected—maybe twenty feet in diameter, although the high, domed ceiling made it seem more spacious—and each octagon side contained a window, framed by bookshelves, except the wall with the door and the wall opposite, which presented an identical door.

"Symmetry," I said to John, as I reached for the knob of said door, expecting to find myself back in the great outdoors. Instead, the door opened to another, smaller octagon. "Oh, hey. Look at this. It's a bedroom."

"Ah, I thought so." John came in behind me and strolled to another door, smaller, on the right. He cracked it open and called back, over his shoulder, "And here's the famous bathroom. So it seems the stories are true, after all."

"How so?"

"According to family legend, he used to spend weeks on end here, when he was finishing up one of his books. My great-grandmother insisted on the lavatory being put in, at extraordinary expense, of course. The talk of the village. Being American, she made a great fuss about plumbing and hygiene. I expect Robert was too lovestruck to object." He pushed back the wave of hair from his forehead. "They would bring him food on a tray and leave it outside. Nobody dared to disturb him."

"Not even his wife? If they were madly in love, like you said."

"Well, I imagine she was allowed conjugal visits, from time to time."

At the same instant, we turned our heads to stare at the bed pushed against the wall, covered by a striped wool blanket. Some kind of sheepskin throw lay draped across one end. "You did say Mrs. Finch comes in to clean, right?" I said.

"Yes, of course," he said quickly. "A few times a year, at least."

An awkward silence settled over us. I turned away and stepped to the window, which looked east, toward the cliffs and the river. The horizon had turned molten, reflecting the sunset to the west. I could see it shimmering on the water, like a piece of gold foil laid atop the glassy surface. "I don't know where we're going to begin," I said. "There's so much. All those papers and books and mess. It's going to take weeks."

"Take as long as you need."

"I wish I could. But I'm supposed to fly back to New York in ten days. My mom . . ."

"Oh, right. Of course." He rubbed his chin again. "Well, you've got me to help. Although some might say I'm more of a millstone than an angel of mercy."

"You don't have to do that."

"But I insist. Haven't anything else to do, after all."

"Really? Don't you have—I don't know—work or something?"

He laughed. "Don't you remember? I'm unemployed, at the moment. Unemployed and unemployable. No work, no family. Hiding from the world at large. In short, I'm at your service."

"But you can't. I mean, I can't ask you to just be some kind of unpaid research assistant."

John stepped closer, not that he needed to. His size alone overwhelmed me, even from a few feet away, because of course he didn't step *too* close. That was not the English way. That was certainly not the Langford way. But I still found myself staring at the weave of his sweater instead of his face, until the clearing of his throat forced me upward. The dust motes flew between us. He spoke sternly. "You don't have a choice, Sarah. I'm breaking the rules just by letting you in at all. You surely don't think I'd allow you to ransack the Langford vault unsupervised, do you?"

"No. Of course not."

"Right, then." He checked his watch. "It is now nine o'clock, the sun is setting at last, and I, for one, am famished. Let's head back to the house for a spot of dinner, and we'll get started first thing in the morning."

Having spent most of my professional life—such as it was—studying the habits and traditions of the British Isles, I knew I shouldn't expect much when opening the larder of an English country house.

Still.

"When you said 'a spot of dinner,'" I said slowly, "did you actually mean 'a spot of HP sauce'?"

"Spoilt Americans. There's a perfectly good tin of beans, right there in front of you. And may I direct your attention to the Spam on the shelf above? Fry it up with a knob of butter and I'd call that a fine meal."

"You would," I said wearily. "No wonder you grew so tall. You will literally eat anything."

"Not true. I can't abide HP sauce."

"And I'm starting to wonder why you don't have any adult siblings."

But before I even finished the sentence, I knew the answer. I'd done my research, after all. The word "siblings" dropped like an anvil from my mouth, too late to take back. I started to apologize, but John answered first.

"Because Mum did a runner when I was an infant, and my father drank himself to death within a decade. So I had all the fruits of Mrs. Finch's kitchen to myself, lucky chap."

"I'm sorry. I knew that. I don't know what I was—"

"Don't bother yourself. My grandmother shielded me from most of it. I grew up imagining I had a charmed childhood, in fact." His long arm snaked around me for the Heinz baked beans. The lurid blue label seemed alarmingly faded to me. "I reckon there's toast somewhere, if we look hard enough," he said.

"Beans on toast. You know how to spoil a girl, Langford."

"If you were hoping for a glass of chardonnay down the gastropub, Blake, you've come to the wrong bloke."

"You're such a snob." I took the can and trudged to the Aga, and ten minutes later we sat at a large mahogany table in the dining room, washing down beans on toast with a stupidly priceless Bordeaux John brought up from the cellar. And maybe I was hungry, or maybe my taste buds were knocked flat by the sheer gorgeousness of the wine, but I kind of enjoyed it.

"It's a classic dish." John leaned back in his chair to squint at the dining room ceiling through the curve of his wineglass. The light bulbs in the wall sconces had failed to ignite when we flipped the switch, so John lit candles instead. Six of them, just enough to see dinner by, so I wasn't quite sure what details he aimed to discover on the dim plasterwork twelve feet above us. "You should try Mrs. Finch's recipe," he said. "She tops it with proper cheddar and Worcestershire sauce, if you please. Sort of a beany Welsh rarebit."

"Oh, a gourmet."

He didn't answer, so I returned my attention to the beans, while the clock ticked away on the mantel and the candles wavered bravely in the enormous silver candelabrum. (Purloined from Langford House in the dead of night, October of 1996, John told me as he lit the wicks from a box of old matches.) John's plate was already scraped clean, and the wine was half-gone. I swallowed another bite and finished the wine in my glass and tried to think of something to say, some comment on the glorious mess awaiting us tomorrow in the folly, but John rose suddenly from his seat and made to refill my wine. I put my hand over the glass. "No, please! I mean, it's amazing. But I've already had one hangover today."

He shrugged, filled his own glass, and sat back down. "I expect you think we're all mad."

"Actually, I was thinking about something else. I was thinking about when you were talking about the swans, and you said, 'We ate them during the war.'"

"Don't judge. The wartime allowance for meat was about nineteen ounces a week. Nineteen ounces. I daresay a brace of your McDonald's hamburgers contains more than that."

"I'm not judging. But you, John Langford, did not personally eat those swans. So you tell me I have an unnecessary allegiance to my Irish ancestors, but you're just the same. You're loyal to your family."

"Yes," he said.

"Just yes?"

"Yes, I am loyal to my family, Sarah. In fact, I've been sitting here wondering what the devil I'm doing, bringing in some woman I've only known a few hours straight into the beating heart of what remains of the Langfords, after the disastrous twentieth century. The inner sanctum, forbidden to pestering scholars and journalists from the moment old Great-Granddad shucked off his mortal coil. So perhaps I'm the mad one."

"For what it's worth, you can trust me. Honest."

"Well, in the inimitable words of Christine Keeler, you *would* say that, wouldn't you? Never mind. It's done. There's no turning back."

"Yes, there is. You could drive me back to London tomorrow morning. Let your sleeping dogs lie. Never find out what Robert Langford was really up to, the day the *Lusitania* went down."

"But that's the coward's way out, isn't it? Anyway, I didn't say I don't trust you." He finished his wine and stood. "Come along. I'll take you upstairs. Mrs. Finch should have your room ready by now."

"My room?"

"Well, *my* room, to be precise. I'm afraid the other options aren't especially habitable, on short notice."

"*Your* room?"

He tilted his chin upward and laughed. "My God, the look on your face! Relax, Sarah. I'm not going to be sleeping there myself."

"Oh." I swallowed back something that certainly, *certainly* could not have been disappointment. "Then where *are* you sleeping?"

John picked up his plate. Reached out to take my plate and stacked the knives and forks on top. "There's an old Russian saying your chap Reagan used to bandy about, back in the Cold War. 'Trust, but verify.'"

"Meaning?"

"Meaning that while *you* lay your head on my childhood pillow in the Dower House, Sarah, *I* shall be sleeping—trying to sleep, at any rate—in Robert Langford's folly." John reached for the wine bottle, worked the cork inside, and tucked it under his arm. "Surrounded, you might say, by all his secrets."

CHAPTER 11

Caroline

At Sea
Monday, May 3, 1915

WITH A FLOURISH, Jones held up the pale pink silk tulle and linen tape lace afternoon dress, her expression like one who'd just exposed a secret. "I pressed this last night, thinking you might like to wear it for your concert rehearsal. These sleeves are perfect for adding a little bit of drama while playing the piano."

Caroline had fallen in love with the long soft tulle sleeves with deep shaped buttoned cuffs and had ordered it at Bergdorf's without asking for the price. Her mother would have been proud. After being raised to be acutely aware of what everything cost while trying to pretend she wasn't, it was quite the accomplishment. The funny thing about it was that it wasn't the poverty that had bothered Caroline's mother so much as the fear the neighbors would find out how desperate the Telfairs really were. That it wasn't her mother's delicate constitution that held them back from traveling abroad or hosting lavish parties as they'd done while Caroline's father was still alive.

"It's perfect," Caroline said, barely glancing at the dress. She'd slept poorly, so distracted by the memory of kissing Robert Langford. Had she really kissed him? Or had he kissed her? Did it matter? She was a married woman. A married woman who loved her husband. What could she have been thinking?

"Are you feeling all right, ma'am?"

Caroline realized she'd pressed her fingers against her lips. She removed them with embarrassment. "Yes, perfectly fine. Thank you. What time am I supposed to meet Miss Schuyler for our concert rehearsal?"

"Right after breakfast, ma'am. In the first-class lounge. I took the liberty of asking Patrick to make sure the piano was tuned for you. I know what a perfect ear you have."

Caroline looked at Jones, as if seeing her for the first time, taking in the scraped-back dark hair, the somber features, and wondered what her story was. She was curious as to how Jones had come to be a lady's maid, and why she was so good at her job. And she wondered what it was that made Jones notice all the small things about Caroline's life, and then use the knowledge to make everything run more smoothly. It was a gift. She couldn't ask her, of course. Her mother had always warned her about being too close to "the help," as she'd called the two servants they'd been able to hold on to despite meager pay—most likely because they'd been elderly even when Caroline was a child and didn't have any other prospects.

"Thank you, Jones." She smiled brightly to show her appreciation, even though the guilt over the kissing incident continued to gnaw at her.

"Are you sure I can't bring you anything else for breakfast besides coffee, ma'am?"

Caroline shook her head. "I must be having a bout of seasickness because I really don't think I could face any food right now. I think I shall get dressed and make it up to the lounge before Miss Schuyler to test the piano. Exercise my fingers a bit. They'll need some warming up with all of this cold, damp weather."

She stood, prepared to slip her dressing gown from her shoulders, when there was a soft tap on the doorframe and a subtle throat-clearing.

"Darling," Caroline said with more force than she'd planned. She and Gilbert had had no time alone since she'd seen him after the infamous kiss, no time for him to rage at her, or accuse her, or any of the things he had every right to do or say. She eagerly scanned his face for any sign that he'd seen her with Robert. But he looked the same; same steady gaze and firm jaw. Same gentle eyes that stared back at her without recrimination.

She held back a sigh of relief. "Have you come to listen to me rehearse for Thursday's concert? I think I will need your help to survive spending an hour with Margery Schuyler." She hadn't realized until she spoke just how much she needed him to say yes, if only to give her the chance to lavish attention and affection on him. Not to assuage her guilt, she told herself. But to remind them both of how much she loved him.

He cleared his throat again. "I'm sorry, but I have business matters that need my attention. But I will be joining you for dinner this evening." He reached into a pocket and pulled out a handful of strung pearls. "I retrieved these from the purser's safe at Jones's instruction. She's suggested the sapphires for your dinner gown, which I will retrieve later."

He held out the pearls like a peace offering. She wanted to take them and hurl them against the wood wall paneling in her frustration. Instead, she held out her hand and allowed him to pool the pearls into her palm. "Thank you, Gilbert. Although I think it would be easier if you kept my jewels in the safe you brought from home and installed in the sitting room. Then you wouldn't have to run back and forth from the purser's office."

"My safe is filled with business documents I will be needing once we arrive in England. There's simply no room for anything else, I'm afraid."

"Fine," Caroline said, her voice sounding defeated even to her own ears. She forced a smile. "The pearls for now and the sapphires for later are perfect."

"Until later," he said with a stiff bow, most likely in deference to Jones's presence, then left, his footsteps swallowed by the thick carpet.

Caroline focused on the oozing sore in the corner of Margery's mouth to distract her from the horrendous sound of the older woman screeching out a high C. Although her voice could be diplomatically classified as a contralto, Margery was delusional enough to have selected Karol Szymanowski's "Songs of a Fairy-Tale Princess" for the Thursday evening concert, a vocal and piano arrangement that was clearly meant for someone with a first-soprano voice who could hit the high notes without startling mice in the walls. Or really, anyone who could sing at all. Caroline was quite sure she'd heard roosters crowing on early mornings back home in Georgia with more vocal abilities than Margery Schuyler.

Caroline lifted her fingers from the keyboard of the grand piano, conveniently situated in the middle of the lounge so it would be hard to avoid being seen, which, apparently, wasn't something Margery minded as she shrieked even louder when someone walked by. Caroline wondered if the tone-deaf woman had realized there was now a growing circumference of empty chairs surrounding them.

She reached for a stack of sheet music that had been placed helpfully on top of the piano by Patrick, their steward. She wasn't sure where he'd found the music, but it was clear that he knew something had to be done and was trying to be helpful. Perhaps he was afraid of a mass exodus over the side of the ship if Margery were left to continue her assault on not only poor Mr. Szymanowski's music, but on the human ear itself.

She pulled from the stack Schubert's *"Der Tod und das Mädchen."* Not one of his most inspired pieces, but a good starter song for a novice singer, and Caroline was already familiar with the piano music. "How about this one instead?" she suggested, holding it out for Margery.

Margery's lip quivered then turned down in a perfect frown. "Only if you believe you need something easier to play. I'm an artiste. And you are supposed to be accompanying *me*. I don't know why you can't play in the key in which I'm singing, or why you have to squeeze in so many notes so that it appears as if I'm coming in at the wrong time." She looked down her not inconsiderable nose and sniffed.

"Because that's the way the music is written," Caroline insisted, using great effort to unclench her teeth before speaking, even taking a brief moment to stare up at the exquisite carvings on the lounge's ceiling in an effort to calm herself. "I thought since we were performing together it would behoove us both to actually *read* the music. At the same time."

Margery frowned at the music, dabbing at her mouth sore with her handkerchief. "What about the Strauss waltz? As I'm sure I already told you, I'm quite the writer and I am very sure that I can create something magnificent to go with the waltz." She sniffed again. "Typical *German* not bothering with words for the music. As if lyrics are an afterthought."

"But it's a waltz—" Caroline began.

Margery cut her off. "Go fetch it now. I'll show you what I mean."

Caroline turned around on the bench to give the vile woman her full attention. "My husband has it under lock and key. I'm afraid it's simply not possible."

"Nonsense. Surely your husband isn't so busy that he can't acquiesce to a simple request from his wife?"

Caroline wasn't completely successful in keeping her annoyance and anger from her voice. "It's not that he's too busy, Miss Schuyler. It's that the manuscript is too valuable and will not be removed from the safe until we disembark."

"Well, that's just ridiculous. Let's go to the purser's office right now and demand to have it taken out."

"It's not in the purser's office. . . ." Caroline stopped, wondering why she was bothering to argue with this woman. She took a deep breath, then faced the keyboard again. "I am sorry, but it's just not possible. Shall we continue with another piece?" She looked up and forced a smile.

Margery didn't smile back. Instead, her eyes narrowed as she considered Caroline. "Exactly what I would expect from an upstart such as your husband. He might have all of that new money, but he doesn't fit in. Perhaps if he spent more time with you, some of your upbringing might rub off on him. But I hardly see the two of you together, as he always appears to have some urgent business to take him away. What in heaven's name could be more important than spending time with his young wife? It's no wonder you don't have children."

The older woman looked as if she actually expected an answer. Caroline picked up the stack of music and pretended to rifle through it, although her hands were shaking so badly, she was afraid she might rip the paper. "My husband has many business dealings, Miss Schuyler, and I'm afraid I'm not at liberty to discuss them with you. Shall we continue with our rehearsal?"

Margery pressed her lips together, making the sore bulge a bit at the corner of her mouth. "I'm finding it very difficult to work with you. If I could find another accompanist, I would, but it seems everyone else is already occupied so I'm stuck with you." She sucked in a breath. "I have a headache now and will retire to my cabin to lie down. May I suggest that you use this time to practice? Otherwise I'm afraid you will embarrass us both." With a quick tilt of her head, she turned and left, the swish of her outdated long skirts against the floral carpet loud now in the glaringly empty lounge.

Unable to keep it in one moment longer, Caroline let out a loud groan then slammed her hands against the keyboard in an admittedly childish fit of frustration. But people like Margery were amazingly good at bringing out childish emotions in normal people.

The sound of enthusiastic clapping brought her suddenly to her feet, nearly knocking over the heavy piano bench as she stood. She grabbed on to the brocade seat to keep it from toppling, looking around to spot her audience.

Robert Langford, who'd apparently been sprawled out of sight on a nearby high-backed sofa, stood. "That last bit was the best part of the entire performance. Will you be doing that again on Thursday?"

She started to laugh, but then remembered what his chest felt like pressed up against her. How his lips tasted. And then she wasn't smiling anymore. "You should have let me know you were here. It was quite rude of you to lie in wait like that."

He moved closer and she could smell the clean crisp scent of him. "And miss that lovely performance? Well, the piano was lovely anyway."

"Thank you."

Their eyes met and he wasn't smiling anymore either. "I could listen to you play all day. I suppose it takes me back to my childhood at Langford House, listening to my mother play. She was quite good, you see. Brilliant, even. Before she stopped playing, that is." He grinned, but the light faded in his eyes.

"She stopped?"

He nodded, his smile faltering. "The day James drowned. So I suppose that means that was my fault, too." His mouth lifted, as if that could erase his words. "She was beautiful. Like you."

A pregnant silence filled the space between them. She found her gaze resting on his lips, and wanting to take a step toward him as much as she wanted to run as far away as she could. "I love my husband," she said, wishing she didn't sound like she was trying to convince herself.

"I know," Robert said quietly.

"What happened yesterday . . ."

"Needed to happen," he finished for her.

"What do you mean?"

He shrugged. "You've had an infatuation with me for years. It had to come out at some point."

"Excuse me? You have some nerve. . . ."

He laughed. "That's better. You were getting far too serious. You kissed me, and we both enjoyed it. And if you want to leave it at that, we can. I just want you to know . . ." He took a step forward as if the room were crowded with people instead of completely empty, and he wanted just her to hear. "I've been in love with you from the moment I first saw you. I've tried to stop, but I can't. I just can't seem to accept that I will have to spend the rest of my life loving you from afar."

He hadn't touched her, but every inch of her skin was burning as if he had. And then she was smiling at a memory, even while she wanted to cry. "You held my hair back while I threw up in the Talmadges' rose garden," she said. "That was the first time we met."

"You had just turned sixteen and had too much champagne, as I recall. You were trying so hard to be grown up."

They were standing so close she could have kissed him. She was embarrassed by how much she *wanted* to kiss him. "That seems like a million years ago, doesn't it? I wonder what would have happened if you'd declared your love then? What our lives would be like now."

"Your mother wouldn't have sent you away to school in Pennsylvania, for starters."

"But then I wouldn't have met Gilbert."

There was a long silence. "No. You wouldn't have," he said, his voice barely a whisper.

"Caroline. There you are." Gilbert's voice boomed from the doorway into the smoking lounge. "It's almost time to dress for dinner."

She stepped back quickly, hoping Gilbert wouldn't notice. "Of course. I was just about to leave." She indicated Robert. "You remember Robert Langford, don't you, darling? He was at our bon voyage party."

The two men, nearly the same height, eyed each other speculatively and shook hands. "Yes. Of course. Your father is Sir Peregrine Langford, I believe."

"Guilty as charged. Do you know him?"

"Only by reputation. I understand he's at the forefront of trying to convince President Wilson to enter America into the war."

"You are as familiar with my father's position as I am, I'm afraid. My father and I don't discuss politics or anything else. We're estranged. However, I have read a lot recently about Hochstetter Iron & Steel being the leading supplier of shrapnel and barbwire to Great Britain. I suppose I should thank you for your efforts in fighting the Germans."

Gilbert coughed, clearing his throat as he indicated Caroline. "I'm afraid we are boring my wife. Please excuse us, we must get dressed for dinner now. Good evening."

Robert nodded. "I must be off myself." He turned to Caroline. "Thank you for allowing me to eavesdrop on your rehearsal. You'll be splendid." He said his goodbyes and exited the room, and it took all Caroline had not to stare after him.

"Shall we?" Gilbert said, offering her his arm.

"I wasn't bored," she said, not moving. "And is that true—what Robert said about you being a major supplier of shrapnel to the British?"

He looked uncomfortable. "It might be. Without the numbers in front of me, I can't be sure. But they're in dire need over there and it's a big market for the company. There, now you know. May we go back to our suite?"

"Yes, of course." She held on to his arm more tightly than warranted, hoping he'd think it was the tossing of the ship that made her wobbly on her feet, and not her encounter with Robert or learning from others what her husband kept from her.

As Gilbert led her through the lounge toward the lifts, a small group of children tailing two nannies ran in from the Saloon Promenade, all giggles and fresh air, eager for their tea. A little boy, not more than four years old wearing an adorable sailor outfit with matching hat, ran into Gilbert with such force that the air seemed to be knocked out of him.

"Now, now, little man," Gilbert said gently as he lifted the child into his strong arms. "What's the hurry?"

"Oh, Rupert—do say you're sorry," said the young nanny, her complexion a deep red from either the wind or embarrassment.

The boy smiled into Gilbert's face. "Nanny said I could have two ices if I was good." He held out a hand with two pudgy fingers.

"Well, then," said Gilbert, gently placing the boy on his feet again within easy reach of the nanny. "I'd say you've been very, very good. A bout of enthusiasm at the promise of ices should never be punished, I shouldn't think."

"No, sir," said the nanny as Rupert looked up at Gilbert with admiration, and something inside Caroline's chest pressed against her lungs, making it hard to draw breath.

Gilbert stared after them as the group made their way toward the stairs, then escorted Caroline back to their suite. "I have something to show you," she said when he opened the door to her bedroom.

Without waiting for his answer, she walked inside and when he followed her in, went behind him to close the door. And lock it. Seeing him with the child had reminded her of how much he wanted to be a father. How much she wanted to be the mother of his child. With everything else between them, this was the one true thing that had never changed and probably never would.

Gilbert raised a sandy brow as she approached him. "What are you doing, Caroline? It's still daylight."

"I know. And I'm still your wife. I've missed you in my bed." She began working the buttons on his waistcoat, then stood on her toes to kiss the underside of his jaw just where he liked it. "Love me," she said softly into his ear. "Right now." She pushed his jacket over his shoulders, relieved to feel no resistance. "Because I want you. And because I'd like to believe that you want me, too."

His fingers threaded through her hair, scattering pins, but he didn't seem or care to notice. He was like a man starved as he lifted her and carried her to the bed, neither of them waiting to get completely undressed.

His hands were tentative at first but Caroline, impatient and eager to erase the image of another man, showed him where she wanted him to touch her, how fast and how slowly, where to kiss and how hard and how soft. They forgot, for a short time, who they were and what had brought them there, and enjoyed themselves as if they were two new lovers.

Happy and satiated, Caroline fell asleep with Gilbert on the narrow bed, one bare leg thrown across his. And when she awoke alone to the sound of Jones calling her name and tapping on the door, she found a note written on *Lusitania* letterhead on the bedside table. She held it between her fingers for two long breaths, knowing what it would say without opening it. Gilbert had written her a note the morning after their wedding night, a night of excited anticipation and fulfilled passion. Which had only made the contents of the note more devastating. She opened the folded note, the stiff paper crisp and formal, and read the two simple words, followed with the lone initial *G. Forgive me.*

CHAPTER 12

Tess

At Sea
Monday, May 3, 1915

"PARDON ME," SAID Tess, as she dodged past a nanny and her charges on the Shelter Deck, just outside the upper level of the first-class dining room.

The children of the saloon passengers were being gently separated from their hoops and tops, extracted from their games, shuffled off to dinner and bed so their parents could come out to play. And by play, Tess meant dine and drink and play at cards and make a hash of amateur theatricals. It was, to recall a phrase from her childhood, none of her no-nevermind. It wasn't any of Tess's business what the swells did, just so long as it kept them from their cabins, visibly occupied elsewhere.

Really, thought Tess, it was terribly kind of the architect of the *Lusitania* to have included a rotunda over the first-class dining room. Not only did the balcony make an excellent vantage point, but the ornamental pillars provided cover, a place to keep an eye on the comings and goings. One coming in particular: Caroline Hochstetter. Once Mrs. Hochstetter was safely seated, Tess could hightail it to the Hochstetter cabin.

And then? Oh, nothing much. Just crack a safe, extract the contents, and get away before anyone saw her. Simple stuff.

It's the last time, Tess reminded herself, heading for a likely pillar.

There was one problem. Her pillar was already occupied, and by the look of him, the incumbent had been standing there for some time.

"Why doesn't it surprise me to see you here?" Mr. Langford lifted a silver flask in greeting. Tess caught a brief glimpse of a crest incised on one side before he tilted it back, drinking deeply.

"Because you just can't stay away from me?" Tess quipped, trying to decide what to do. He'd notice if she found another pillar. On the other hand, chatting with an acquaintance gave her an excuse for being up here.

On the whole, Tess rationalized to herself, Mr. Langford might be more of a blessing than a curse. Albeit a rather grumpy one.

"You seem to have recovered," said Mr. Langford. He did not sound particularly enthused. He waved the flask. "From your . . ."

"*Mal de mer*?" provided Tess with a grin, but Mr. Langford failed to smile back. Silly to feel hurt. It wasn't as if they were anything more than chance acquaintances. She nodded at his watch chain. "Do you have the time?"

"'I have wasted time and now time doth waste me.'" Mr. Langford took another swig from the silver flask before hoisting his watch from his waistcoat pocket. "It's half five."

Later than she had thought. "Ta," said Tess, as she had heard the English porters do. And then, "Are *you* all right? You look a little—"

"Beset? Besieged? Bewildered?"

"I asked if you were all right, not if you'd swallowed a dictionary," retorted Tess, but the ashen cast of Mr. Langford's elegant features took the bite out of her words. Moved by genuine concern, she took a step closer. "Is something wrong? Is it . . . your brother?"

"Jamie?" Mr. Langford raised a brow. He did it very nicely, one graceful arch, with no unsightly eye scrunching. He slouched back against the pillar. "It ought to be Jamie, oughtn't it? But no. Nothing that noble. Nothing that simple."

"I'm good at complicated," offered Tess. Mr. Langford gave her a look. Tess shrugged. "What? Call it payment for the use of your coat. It's a one-time offer."

"If you must know," Mr. Langford said testily, "I've been in love with the same woman for the better part of a decade, and she hasn't the slightest idea I'm alive."

Tess pressed her eyes shut. That was what she got for asking. "Oh, I'd say she knows you're alive, all right. If we're talking about the same woman."

"Oh, yes—as a dancing partner, maybe," said Mr. Langford bitterly. "As someone to play duets with while her bloody husband talks business. But that's all. I'm just a pair of legs and fingers."

"Legs and fingers?" Tess choked on a laugh and tried to turn it into a wheeze. "Sorry. Sorry. I shouldn't mock. Love's hell, right?"

Not that she'd know. The closest she'd come to romantic love was of the "if you don't move that hand, I'll shoot your fingers off" variety. She'd fancied herself in love once, sixteen and naïve, but her family had moved through town too quickly for her to do anything stupider than a bit of canoodling behind a cowshed. For which she was grateful. Really, she was.

Mr. Langford scowled at her. "Go right ahead, mock, mock, mock. You want something to mock? Your so-called accent. Where in Devon did you say you were from again? And did you emigrate via the moon?"

"I only went for the green cheese." Mr. Langford was not amused. But, then, this wasn't about her accent, was it? Tess let out a deep breath. "Fine. You caught me. I was faking the accent. Happy now?"

"Oh, blissfully," said Mr. Langford bitingly. "Why pretend?"

"Look, I was a kid when I came here. But I always knew it wasn't for keeps." Sometimes, the best lies weren't lies at all. "I thought—I thought people on the other side of the Pond might take me more seriously if I sounded like I belonged. Do you know what it is not to belong anywhere anymore?"

Mr. Langford's eyes burned through her. His clipped British accent very apparent, he said, "Do you need to ask me that?"

Her cheeks were too hot and her hands were too cold; Tess felt as though she had a fever, half-chills, half-flame, and all because of the strange, electric feeling of his eyes on her, seeing her, seeing through her. They had nothing in common; they were from worlds apart. So why did she feel like she was staring into the other half of her own soul?

"Oh, give me that," said Tess, and grabbed the flask from him before he had time to protest, tipping off the cap with an expert flick and emptying it gratefully over her mouth. It went down strong but smooth, the burn a welcome distraction. She wiped her mouth with the back of her hand, deliberately crude. "Lordy, that's good. You may have dubious taste in women, but you sure do know your whisky."

"Where," said Mr. Langford, ignoring the insult, "did you learn to drink like that?"

"Finishing school," said Tess, and took another swig, more for show than anything else. She didn't like getting drunk; she didn't like the loosening of her limbs, the dimming of her wits.

Mr. Langford gave her an incredulous look. "I'd like to see that school."

"I bet you would. My . . ." She'd almost said "father." Tess hid her confusion with a cough. "My aunt's husband made his own 'shine. Until the law caught up with him, that was." Ten dollars' worth of lovely copper coils reduced to rubbish. "You grow up being dosed with that, you can drink anything. But we're not meant to be talking about me. We're meant to be talking about you. Here you go, Romeo. Drink up."

"'He jests at scars that never felt a wound,'" said Mr. Langford darkly. He tipped back the flask and then looked owlishly at Tess over the silver cap. "You want to know what bothers me?"

"I expect I'm going to hear it," said Tess. She snagged the flask. "Shoot."

"I've loved her for years. Years."

Tess rolled her eyes at the elaborately painted ceiling. "Yes, you had mentioned that."

Mr. Langford glared at her. "Do you want to hear this or not? I've loved her ever since I met her at a ball just weeks after I arrived in the States. She wasn't meant to be there—she wasn't out yet—but her mother brought her all the same. And I found her casting up her accounts in the rosebushes."

"Last of the great romantics, you," muttered Tess, but for all she wanted to make fun, there was something about the story that hit her hard where it hurt. Because it was romantic, more romantic than all those fools who mooned over their perfect loves. You saw a woman at her most vulnerable and still wanted her? That was something different, indeed. "So what happened?"

"She married," said Mr. Langford bleakly. "A man a dozen years her senior. More. And I didn't have the sense or the will to stop it. I was traveling the country, satisfying my wanderlust. She was only sixteen when I met her. It never occurred to me—but it ought. I ought to have known. I ought to have at least sent her a bloody letter. But she was in school still! There was all the time in the world."

"You weren't the one who married," Tess pointed out.

"No, but . . ." Mr. Langford shook his head helplessly. He looked directly at Tess. "Do you know what I did today? I finally told her the truth. I told her that I've been in love with her since that night at the Talmadges' hideous party. I stripped myself to the bone."

"And?" Tess prompted, feeling a strange lump in her stomach.

Mr. Langford drew himself up to his full height. "She told me that she loves her bloody husband."

"Oh," said Tess, feeling both relieved and intensely sorry at the same time. Neither of which made the least bit of sense.

"Oh," agreed Mr. Langford. "She kissed me. *She* kissed *me*."

"I can see where that might give you ideas," hedged Tess, trying to suppress the urge to slap Caroline Hochstetter right across her pampered face.

"It did," said Mr. Langford shortly. "But I was wrong. It wasn't about me at all, it seems. I might have been anyone. I was just the teaser stallion. Warming her up for her proper mate."

"Ouch," said Tess, as mildly as she could. "No wonder you look like you want to kick out the rails of your pen. Should I give you some hot mash and tuck you up for the night?"

Mr. Langford scowled at her. "Why do I talk to you?"

"Because you can't talk to anyone else." And she was nobody, not even a whippet. Tess made up her mind. "You gave me some good advice yesterday. So I'm going to return the favor. Here. You might want to take a bit more of this," she added, shoving the flask back in his general direction.

"That's your advice? To drink? Forgive my skepticism, but I've already tried that. It doesn't work."

Fine words from a man who'd snatched up that flask faster than a frog on a June bug. "Now who's having trouble accepting a kindness? The drink isn't the advice. It's just a temporary panacea. Think of it more as . . . the anesthesia before the amputation."

"I'm not sure I like the sound of this," muttered Mr. Langford into the mouth of the flask. "Which part of me are you planning to sever?"

"The part of you that's wasted ten damn fool years on a woman who doesn't want you." Tess muscled up to him. He was considerably taller than she was; she had to crick back her neck to look him in the eye. Not like the elegant and willowy Caroline Hochstetter, who had only to tilt her head gently. Hmph. Tess enunciated slowly and clearly. "Any woman who uses you to get to another man isn't worth your time. She's not the one for you."

"Or she just hasn't realized it yet." The words seemed to come from deep in his chest, a raw, whisky-infused rumble that Tess felt as much as heard.

"Yet?" Tess poked him in the chest. Hard. "Didn't you say it's been ten years? How much longer are you planning to give her?"

"*And you should, if you please, refuse / Till the conversion of the Jews . . .* That's from a poem, you know. Marvell. 'To His Coy Mistress.' *Had we but world enough, and time . . .*" Mr. Langford regarded Tess with heavy-lidded eyes. "He was trying to persuade her to forget her virtue, of course."

He was trying to shock her, she knew, to get back at her for her unwanted advice. But she was no debutante to quail at the mention of what went on between a man and a woman.

Tess folded her arms across her chest. "Is that what you want from Mrs. Hochstetter? To get her into bed?"

"Damn your eyes," said Mr. Langford, but he said it without heat. He raised his eyes to the heavens. Or, rather, to the idealized imitation of the heavens painted in rococo splendor above their heads, mute gods and goddesses, shepherds whose pan pipes remained forever silent. "God, what did I do to deserve you? Have you been assigned as my own particular conscience? Or merely a goad? Yes, if you must know. And no . . . I want her, yes; who wouldn't?"

Who indeed? But Tess didn't say it aloud. She wasn't a woman here. She was a semi-detached conscience. Or perhaps a goad. She wasn't sure which was worse.

"But?" she prompted.

"I only want her body if it comes with the rest of her. Her heart, her soul, her conscious will." Mr. Langford laughed without humor. "That's a nice bit of ego, isn't it? Wanting to possess someone entirely, inside and out. But that's what it is: that's what I want, not a quick tumble in the sheets, but a love for the ages, the sort minstrels sing about centuries on. Troy lost, Camelot fallen, diplomacy upended, and kingdoms ruined."

"You talk like that and I'm confiscating your hooch," said Tess tartly. "No one is worth telling the world to go to hell. That's not love; that's arson."

"Love is to burn." He added, with deliberate provocation, "You might know that if you'd ever been in love."

Tess's teeth clamped so hard that her jaw hurt. "Did it never occur to you, perhaps, that you've loved her for so long that loving her has become a sort of habit for you?"

Mr. Langford looked at her with the appalled disgust usually reserved for the sort of people who picked their teeth in public. "What in the devil is that supposed to mean?"

In for a penny, in for a pound. "You want to talk about minstrels singing? Half the time, those knights were off on quests for things they didn't even want. Grails, wild boar, women, it didn't much matter, did it? The point was the chase." Like her father, always questing after something. "That's not to say Mrs. Hochstetter isn't a fine woman. She is. But have you thought about what you'd do with her if you got her? I mean, besides making kingdoms topple."

Mr. Langford's lips were pressed in a thin, white line. He stared at her with burning eyes, but made no response.

Couldn't argue with her, could he? Tess met him stare for stare. "Never mind, I'm sure you'd play lovely duets together. That would take up—what?—two or three hours in a day?"

Mr. Langford forced the words between his lips. "You know nothing about it."

"Don't I?" Tess shot back, and for a moment she wasn't sure if she was talking about him or about herself. "It's easy to love someone you can't have. There's no risk in it."

"Oh, isn't there?" Mr. Langford's jacket buttons scraped against hers, Savile Row against Woolworth.

Tess refused to back down. She blew out her chest like a pigeon. "What risk? That she'll divorce her husband and you might actually have to risk making your life around another person? Caring about another person? Trusting another person?" The words tore up from deep inside her, raw and painful. Tess bit down deeply on her lip, so hard she could taste blood. "Never mind. You asked my advice, and I'm giving it. Here it is. Forget her."

Something naked and vulnerable passed across his face. "How in the bloody hell am I meant to do that?"

Tess could practically taste the whisky on his breath. His fine-featured face was inches from hers, scored with torment. She didn't think; she just acted.

"You can start with this." Grasping his lapels, Tess pulled his face down to hers.

She'd meant to kiss and run. Just a brief smack on the lips, for effect's sake. But this wasn't a boy behind a cowshed. This was a man: a man with a fair amount of whisky in him, a man who'd already been kissed and left. His hands closed around her arms; his mouth slanted across hers, hot and hard, holding her to the promise of her kiss. Never mind that it had been meant as a false promise, she was caught now, caught fast, dizzy with the smell of whisky, tobacco, and expensive shaving soap. Dizzy with the smell of him.

Colors flared behind her closed eyes, like a Turner painting, all orange and red, purple and gold; she was drowning in it, drowning in color and light, and the only way to stay afloat was to pour it all back out on the canvas, kissing him back as good as she got, clinging to his shoulders with both hands, his buttons leaving dents in her chest, his hands burning through her back.

It was the dinner bell that brought them both to their senses, tolling loudly enough to make Tess's ears ring. Or maybe it was the kiss making her ears ring.

She stumbled back, feeling the painted wood of the railing hard against the small of her back.

"Steady on now," said Mr. Langford unsteadily, taking a half-step forward.

Tess held out a hand to ward him off. If he touched her again—well, it wouldn't be a good idea, that was all.

"Don't fret yourself," she said tartly, or as tartly as she could, with all her breath constricted somewhere below her corset. "I'm not flinging myself over the balcony. But don't you go getting any ideas now! That was just—just a thank-you for yesterday. Now we're quits."

Mr. Langford blinked at her. "You call that quits?"

It was gratifying, dangerously so, that he sounded as bemused as she felt. Now who was the teaser mare? Tess thought savagely. And she'd walked right into it herself. No point blaming Mr. Langford. This was all on her head. Not that she'd ever tell him so.

Below, Caroline Hochstetter, serene in pearls, entered the dining room on her husband's arm, Margery Schuyler close on their heels, her awkward gait serving only to emphasize Caroline Hochstetter's elegance, an elegance that went deeper than clothes and jewels, imbued in her bones, her carriage, the tilt of her head. She would never be caught slamming down 'shine, or flaunt her bosom to distract a mark. Tess tasted bile at the back of her throat, bile and whisky.

"Two women kissing you," Tess said mockingly. "Don't let it go to your head."

"Trust me," said Mr. Langford flatly. "My head has nothing to do with it."

And wasn't that the truth. It wasn't her head that was doing Tess's thinking either, a fact that spelled danger. "Did you book passage because you knew she was going to be here?"

Mr. Langford swiveled to face her, swaying slightly on his feet. "Are you mad? If I'd known she and her husband would be here I would never have—" He broke off, a dark lock of hair tumbling down over his brow, giving him a boyish, vulnerable look. "Whatever you think of me, I'm not such a glutton for punishment as that."

"Ten years, Mr. Langford," said Tess, and then, because she had work to do, even if she didn't seem capable of keeping her mind on it, she gave him a little push. Just a little one, hardly a touch. Because if she touched him again, she wasn't quite sure what might happen. Not for you, Tess, my girl, she reminded herself. "Don't you need to dress for dinner? Go make yourself presentable and make those debutantes swoon."

Because one of those girls, untried and unmarred, would be the one for him. Damn whisky, making her maudlin. Just like Pa.

Tess turned on her heel, the effect only slightly ruined by having to clutch at the railing for balance. Over her shoulder, she called, "Up and at 'em, Mr. Langford."

Behind her, his voice was very quiet, dangerously so. "Don't you think, after that, you should call me Robert?"

There was something in the way he said it that made her tingle straight down to her toes. It took all her willpower to keep going, flapping a hand in parting. "Don't flatter yourself . . . Robert. Now go and sober up!"

And she should do the same. Only it wasn't whisky messing with her head. It was Mr. Langford. Robert. His smile. His scowl. His accent, clipped and drawling by turns, teasing, exasperating, elusive, honest. He threw her more off balance than Pa's strongest moonshine, and, Tess reminded herself, was like to leave even more of a headache in the morning. Ginny might be driving her distracted at the moment, but her sister was right about one thing: Robert Langford wasn't for the likes of her.

Not even for Tessa Fairweather, newly minted Englishwoman.

Tess could have wept, but what was the point of weeping? She'd cried for her mother as a child, cried for her father's attention, but no amount of tears could bring either back. And no amount of tears would magically lift that manuscript from the Hochstetters' safe.

There was a ladies' lounge right off the dome. Tess ducked inside, just in case Mr. Langford had any inclination to follow her. Not that she thought he did, not really. In the mirror, her face was flushed, her hair escaping in dark blond wisps around her forehead. If Mrs. Hochstetter was an orchid, elegant and rare, she, thought Tess, was a common garden daisy. Or maybe a tiger lily, bold and blowsy.

Tess splashed some cool water against her face, letting the salt tang bring her to herself again.

No more whisky. And no more Mr. Langford. If she saw him in passing, she would hightail it the other way.

With that resolved, she set out for the Hochstetters' suite, conveniently located on the same deck as the dome. The passageways were, as Ginny had promised, deserted: everyone, master and servant alike, was at supper. Tess took the same path she'd taken last time, past the lifts, into the cul-de-sac, to the door that opened onto the Hochstetters' sitting room. She waited a moment, wraith-still beside the door, listening for noises within or without, half-expecting Robert to appear behind her, or that red-haired steward to pop up out of nowhere. But there was nothing, only the scrape of her own breathing, in and out, in and out.

Go in through the servant's entrance in the back, Ginny had said. *Mrs. Hoch-*

stetter's bedroom door will be left open. Tess wasn't quite sure she believed her, but, sure enough, when Tess put her gloved hand on the door handle, it opened. Just like that.

Maybe, when you owned the earth, you didn't bother to lock doors. Or maybe, thought Tess wryly, they thought that no one would be so foolish as to attempt to rob them when there was no place to run.

The room smelled faintly of perfume and something else, the smell that Tess equated with the house with all the nice ladies where they had briefly stayed when she was six. Very nice ladies. A dress that cost more than Tess's ticket had been left crumpled on the floor, the matching shoes kicked in opposite directions across the room. Someone had dragged the sheets back up on the bed, but not smoothed them. The ripples and dents told their own, unmistakable story.

If Robert could see this . . .

No. Tess averted her eyes and tiptoed through to the door that opened onto the sitting room. None of her no-nevermind. Besides, Robert already knew. Teaser stallion, indeed.

And what a tease. Tess's lips still burned from that kiss a moment ago. If he'd kissed Caroline Hochstetter like that . . .

Mind on your work, girl. The safe was exactly where Ginny had said, belatedly installed and barely hidden, relying on the large lock rather than secrecy to ward off thieves. But Tess was no stranger to locks. They didn't come easy to her, the way copying a page with her pen had, but she'd had years to learn their intricacies, to get to know the feel of a mechanism, the sound of the wards moving.

There was something soothing about the feel of the pick in her hand, the steady, calming work of fiddling a little this way, a little that, all her concentration on the infinitesimal sounds from within. The lock was an expensive one, but hardly unique. It took less than five minutes for it to fall open.

Twenty minutes left. Tess hastily opened the metal door. And there it was. The music manuscript in lonely splendor in the center of the safe. No jewels, no other papers, just the manuscript.

What was it that made this one manuscript so darn special?

Collectors, Ginny had said. Maybe if she were musical, she would understand better. As it was, Tess found all this security for a sheet of music rather baffling. *All right, time to get on with it.* She drew out the pages, assessing the job with an experienced eye. Usually, she'd be calculating matches: finding the right sort of paper, the right sort of ink to make an exact match. But that didn't matter for these collectors, Ginny had claimed. They just wanted the substance of it, copied precisely, down to the last jot and tittle. And they were willing to pay handsomely.

Ten pages, closely written with musical notes on long, lined staffs, cryptic words scribbled in the margins. Words and numbers. As Tess lifted the manuscript, a sheet fell out. It looked the same, all filled with notes, but there was something odd about it, something that looked wrong to Tess's trained eye, as though it had been written in another hand and inserted later. There was more marginalia here, more scribbled notes in German, more numbers—almost like an equation of some kind. Or a code.

Three Germans in the brig. Ginny's watchful eyes and tense shoulders.

You don't know the people we're dealing with, Ginny had said. Ginny, who spoke German still. Ginny, who had never explained, really, why a collector would be willing to pay such a sum for a mere copy.

Unless it wasn't the music they were after, but something else. A code. Plans.

CHAPTER 13

Sarah

Devon, England
May 2013

"PLAN," I SAID aloud, just at the instant I woke up. I needed a plan.

I opened my eyes to a painful cascade of white sunshine and Princess Leia in a metal bikini. For a moment I thought I'd been kidnapped by an Ewok. Then I saw that Leia wasn't moving—that she was, in fact, a poster fixed on a wall papered in navy blue stars—and I remembered where I was.

Not Ewoks. Langfords. John Langford.

I reached for my phone on the bedside table and stared in disbelief at the screen. A quarter to *nine*? I hadn't slept that late in years. My head fell back on the pillow. Several app alerts lurked invitingly below the slender numbers 8:46, but I couldn't summon the slightest interest in them. I felt heavy, drugged, slow, the way you do after a thoroughly deep sleep. *Plan*, I thought again, although this time I didn't actually say it. I needed a plan. If only I could bring myself to move.

Last night, when Mrs. Finch had led me upstairs to John's room, the hallways were dark and I was too exhausted to pay any attention to my surroundings. I'd allowed the flow of the housekeeper's chatter to carry me along—snatches of that monologue returned to me now, and none of it made any sense—until she'd closed the door at last. I'd rummaged in my carry-on, discovered my toothbrush and face cream, and stumbled across the hall to the bathroom, and all I noticed before crashing into John's freshly made bed was the R2-D2 clock lamp on the bedside table, and *that* only because I had to hunt for the off switch for a minute or two before finding it inside R2's shiny Cyclops eye. At the time, I figured the lamp was an ironic decorating touch. Or I was simply hallucinating.

Now, in the brilliant glow of a Devonshire morning, I realized Mrs. Finch had actually led me aboard an Imperial Star Destroyer.

A dozen *Star Wars* action figures were locked in combat atop the bookshelf opposite the bed. The *Millennium Falcon* dangled from the ceiling, pursued by an X-wing fighter. And was that a lightsaber resting in the lap of the giant stuffed Chewbacca in the corner, or was he just wishing me the top of the morning?

I turned my gaze down to the soft, worn sheets, which were chillingly festooned with Darth Vader masks, and flung myself upright.

Good Lord. No wonder his wife had left him.

I crawled out of bed and shook my hair. Opened my suitcase and dragged myself across the hall to shower behind plastic stormtrooper curtains. By the time I found my way downstairs to the kitchen, I half-expected to see a Tupperware cylinder of blue milk waiting for me inside the fridge. Instead, I encountered half a block of butter, a pitcher of curdled cream, and a head of iceberg lettuce, nicely browned.

I closed the door and turned to stare at the teakettle atop the Aga.

"I guess it's up to you, mate," I said.

"So I think we need a plan," I said to John as I handed him a mug of tea. The sunlight filtered in between the heavy curtains of Robert Langford's folly, obscuring the clutter, and the air smelled of dust and wood and human sleep. I pretended I didn't notice the foot and a half of bare chest curving above the edge of the white sheets, played it cool like I woke up every morning to the male form au naturel, but I don't think I would have convinced a keen observer. Luckily, John was wincing into his tea mug instead of looking at me.

"You call this tea?" he said.

"Gosh, you're welcome. The way you emptied that bottle of brandy last night, I would have thought you'd appreciate any form of liquid sustenance," I said. "And don't try to deny it. I saw the bottle in the kitchen trash."

"For your information, that bottle had about three ounces of brandy left inside to begin with. I was doing the poor thing a favor." He took another delicate sip of tea. Winced again. "Well, maybe six ounces. But it was excellent brandy."

I folded my arms and attempted a stern expression. "So what's with the *Star Wars* fixation?"

"I beg your pardon?"

"Your room. I can't believe your wife let you keep Chewbacca in the corner. With the lightsaber? That's just creepy."

"Christ. Mrs. F put you in *that* room?"

"Apparently, yes."

"I'm sorry. I told her . . ." He rubbed his hair. "I told her to put you in my room. I suppose she thought—well, she must have thought I meant my *old* room. From when I was a kid. Before I got married."

"Thank God for that. Princess Leia had me pretty worried, there. I'm not going to lie."

John set the mug on the worn Oriental rug and flopped back on the pillow. "I apologize. I guess she thought—well, the master suite—she probably thought you'd feel awkward, staying there. And everything else upstairs is closed up, filled with old furniture and moldy carpet. I'd hoped to make it a home again, one day, but Callie never—well, anyway. Sorry."

"Don't worry about it."

"Was it awful? I hope you managed to sleep, at least."

His eyes were closed. He'd made up a bed on the chaise longue in Robert's study, which was just wide enough to fit his shoulders, although his legs stuck out well past the end. A blanket of striped wool covered the southern end of him. The northern end, as I said, was bare, and I thought it was strange, out of character, that he didn't seem embarrassed. Was he a secret exhibitionist, perhaps? Or still drunk?

"I slept all right," I said. "Better than you, probably. That doesn't look very comfortable. Why didn't you use the daybed in the bedroom? Guarding the premises or something?"

"No, I wasn't guarding the premises. I just didn't want to sleep in there, that's all." He reached down and groped for the mug on the floor. "You're right. We do need a plan. But I think we should discuss said plan over some sort of breakfast, don't you think?"

"I looked for some eggs in the fridge, but you're all out."

"Eggs would be in the larder, Sarah."

"The larder? Are you kidding me? Don't you refrigerate your eggs?"

"Of course not. Do you?" He found the mug at last and set it on his chest. At the instant of contact, he startled upward, spilling tea over chest, sheet, and blanket. "My God! Where's my shirt?"

"Um, you're not wearing one? So I don't know where it is."

The mug went bang down to the floor. John snatched the sheets up to his neck.

"I've got a terrific idea, Sarah," he said to the ceiling.

"What's that?"

"Why don't you step outside for a moment, and I'll have a quick wash and get dressed. Then we'll head down the pub for a proper full English, hmm?"

"A full English? Is that like a full monty? Because between you and Chewbacca, I think I've already got that covered for one morning."

He grabbed the pillow from behind his head and threw it at me.

"Out," he said. "And take your damned lousy tea with you."

"Down the pub" turned out to be the Ship Inn, a ramshackle old pile about a mile along the lane from the Dower House. In typical English fashion, John insisted we walk, as if I didn't have enough appetite worked up already. The sun shone on our backs, but the air was brisk. By the time a waitress dropped a cup of coffee in front of me, I was ready to start nibbling the pink packets of sugar substitute.

John, on the other hand. He looked like he was ready to start nibbling the waitress's bosom, of which there was plenty to spare, exposed above the deep V of a snug white T-shirt bearing the faded image of a seventy-four-gun ship of the line. "Julie!" he exclaimed, face all aglow.

Julie set down his tea and flung her arms around his neck. "Johnnie-boy! I was waiting for you to recognize me."

John rose to return her embrace more thoroughly. You know, like the gentleman he was. She was much shorter than John—like, who wasn't?—and he had to bend his neck and most of his long torso to land the kiss where it belonged, on her cheek. They disentangled slowly, or maybe it was my imagination. "I didn't know you were working at the Ship," he said. "How are you?"

"I'm all right, I'm all right." She brushed back a few strands of hair, dark brunette streaked with startling violet. Her eyes were bright and round and faintly bruised underneath, like she'd had a rough night and needed comforting. "Davey took me on last summer when the hotel gave me the sack. How's yourself? Are you back at the house?"

"For a bit." He detached himself at last and settled back into his seat. Julie's bosom settled into the space next to his face. "It's good to see you. Can you spare us some breakfast?"

"I guess so." She glanced at me—not impressed, not impressed at all—and back again to John. "Full English for you?"

"Everything you've got. I'm famished."

"Bit of the worse for wear, are you?" She ruffled his hair. "I'll sort you out, never fear. Haven't I always?"

"You're an angel, Jules."

"Go on," she said, kissing the top of his head, and without sparing me another glance she swung away, headed for the kitchen. John smiled at her departing figure. The ties of her navy-striped service apron dangled across the pockets of her jeans, which fit her bottom like she'd painted them on just that morning. On the other hand, I couldn't blame her. If I had a rear like that, I'd want the world to take note.

"Old friend?" My voice came out a little high.

"Hmm? Oh, yes. Very old friend. We used to play together as children."

"I'll bet."

He raised his teacup and lifted an eyebrow. "Sarah, for God's sake. She's Mrs. Finch's *granddaughter.* We were practically raised together. She and Davey—he's the publican—she and Davey and I used to spend all summer running wild over the grounds."

"Let me guess. She was Leia? You and Davey were Luke and Han?"

"See here."

"Ha! I'm right, aren't I? The question is, were you Luke or were you Han? I mean, that's the key to everything, right there."

"The key to—" John began, but a short, beefy man walked up behind him and cut him off with a backslap that pitched him forward into his teacup. I could have warned him in advance, of course, but I chose not to.

"Johnnie-boy!" the man shouted. "What the bloody hell are you after, walking into my pub and fixing yourself on the shape of my sister's arse?"

"Davey bloody Finch. I'm committing suicide by breakfast, isn't it obvious?"

"Happy to oblige you, mate. Who's the bird?" Davey jerked his head in my direction.

I stuck out my hand. "My name is Sarah Blake, Mr. Finch, and I'm—"

"What, an American? Has it come to this, old bloke?"

There was something about the way he said that word. *American.* And my stomach was still empty, and my hair was still wet, and last night's wine hadn't done me any favors. I heard a faint cracking noise, the way a straw sounds when it strikes a camel's back.

"Okay, listen up," I said. "Here's the thing about Americans. Having sailed across the Atlantic to save your weak chins and skinny butts from the Germans, not once but *twice*, not to mention the Cold War, not to mention the Marshall Plan, we start to get a little salty when Limey Neanderthal idiots like you talk about us like we're not sitting right there."

Davey turned to John and gestured with the bar towel in his hand. "Oi. Is she for real, mate?"

I rose from my chair. "If you'll excuse me, I'm heading back to the house to fix myself a plate of scrambled salmonella."

"Davey," John said, in a low, slow voice. "Miss Blake is a writer and a friend of mine, and I believe you owe her an apology."

"An apology, is it?"

"An apology. Pronto."

"I have a Twitter account," I said, "and I'm not afraid to use it. Hashtag *asshole*. Hashtag *Ship Inn*."

Davey heaved a sigh. "Johnnie-boy, I hate to have to tell you this, mate, but you've let yourself in for it. Out of the fry pan—"

"Amusing," John said. "Now the apology."

Davey turned reluctantly to face me. "I apologize, Miss Blake. Bit of banter, that's all. Limey Neanderthal pig idiot that I am."

I sat back down. "I didn't say pig."

"You should have," said John.

"Just taking the mickey out," said Davey. "You know how it is. Breakfast is on me, all right?"'

"For Christ's sake, Davey, you weren't going to charge me for breakfast, were you?"

"Just don't ask for seconds, clear? The Ship ain't no soup kitchen for sacked toffs." Davey threw the kitchen towel over his shoulder and turned back in the direction of the long, oaken bar running the length of the opposite wall. "Oh, and Sarah? It's *arsehole*. With an *R*. I may be a pig, right enough, but I ain't no bloody donkey."

"Don't mind Davey," John said, slicing up his eggs in ruthless strokes. "He's just protective. They both are."

"Protective? You're six and a half feet of walking, talking white male privilege. You don't exactly need protection."

"Fair enough."

"Fair enough? That's it?"

"Fair enough, I don't need protecting. I'm a big boy and all that." He paused to shovel more food, swallow more tea. "Of course I'm damned lucky to have been born to all this. But privilege isn't easy, either. There's a massive responsibility to being a Langford."

"You're not actually bringing up the white man's burden, are you?"

"Don't twist words. I just mean that when you occupy a—whatever you call it, a privileged space, you have to find a way to deserve your good fortune. To make good. You've got a proper neck up on everybody else, true, but sometimes that only means you've got farther to fall. And in the end, you're only human. You make mistakes, like everybody else. Except *your* mistakes . . ."

I wanted to ask him about his mistakes. I wanted to stick a crowbar into that small opening and pry it wide, but instead I allowed John's voice to fade away into the dim, placid silence, the unmistakable pub atmosphere, stale beer and frying chips and something else. Centuries. Wooden beams cut from trees long dead. There were two other customers, both men, both forking breakfast with their right hands and swiping at their phones with the left. I felt my own phone vibrate in my coat pocket, slung behind me on the chair, and resisted the urge to check it.

I sopped up some egg yolk with the fried bread and said, "I've been thinking about how we're going to tackle that mess in there. The folly, I mean."

"Yes. That. I was snooping around a bit last night, before I turned in, and it seems it's a bigger job than I imagined. Robert was not a man of tidy, organized habits."

"Geniuses usually aren't."

"You think he's a genius, do you?"

"Of course! Those novels! I think he was better than Fleming, I really do. I mean, they've got great, twisty plots and all, but the real magic is between the lines. What he implies but doesn't say. His characters are so acute, you know? There's always some telling detail that makes you catch your breath. You know what I think?"

"What do you think, Sarah?" He was smiling at me.

"I think that for all the cynicism in those stories—and my God, it just drips from the page sometimes, not that you can blame him after what he went through—for all that, I think he's actually a romantic at heart. A romantic manqué. Lost in another age."

"Of course he was a romantic. He married his true love, didn't he?"

"Now *you're* sounding cynical."

"I'm not. I'm happy for him. He set his sights on the distant, beloved object and he won her. She loved him back. They had children and swans and no doubt bloody fantastic sex all their lives. Good on him."

"Ouch."

He swept up the last of his toast and finished his tea. "Are you done?"

"Almost."

"Then let's head off." He reached into his pocket and pulled out his wallet, and evidently he didn't mean what he said to Davey earlier about the free breakfast, because he took out a twenty-pound note and laid it on the table, anchoring it with a bottle of HP sauce.

Instead of plowing ahead, John restrained himself to a disciplined walk beside me, keeping his hands shoved in his pockets and his head bent pensively downward. The lane was unpaved, the grass still damp with dew. A few clouds had begun to gather in the sky, and the sun disappeared behind them, leaving the air even chillier than before.

When we came to the Dower House, we skirted around the side and headed down the slope to the folly. I spoke up at last.

"So why are you still so loyal to them? Your Langford ancestors, I mean."

"Because they're family, I guess. You have to forgive their faults. They're a part of you, aren't they? Their sins are your sins. Their blood is yours. It's the only inheritance that really matters."

"I know," I said. "That's what I'm scared of."

"Scared? Why?"

I fingered the edge of my phone in my pocket. There had been no messages from Riverside Haven this morning, no voice mails, and when I'd called to check on my mother last night, the nurse said she was taking a nap. Still, the edge of anxiety never really went away, like a small, dark bird living in my head. "My mom has Alzheimer's, like I said. Early onset. And as hard as it is, watching her fade away—forgetting stuff, sometimes forgetting me—there's this other shadow. I try not to think about it, but it's there."

"The same thing might happen to you, you mean."

"Yes." I squinted at the sky, trying to judge how much longer before the sun came out from behind the massive, rabbit-shaped cloud that obscured it. "I'm thirty years old. So if I'm like her, I have twenty, maybe thirty more years before it starts to hit. And it progresses faster in early onset. I mean, my mom was okay one year and almost helpless the next, and that's with the best care I could buy her. *Small Potatoes*, that's what bought her that private care and everything, a little more time, or at least I hope so, and now . . ."

"The sob story, eh?" He said it kindly.

"Yep. That's about it." I rubbed the corner of my eye with my thumb. "Anyway. I just feel like I need to know. I need to know what's hidden back there in the family closet. I need to know the truth, I need to know everything, before it's too late."

"What if you can't know everything? What if some secrets are hidden too deep? Or destroyed altogether?" He paused as we reached the bridge and laid his hand on the pillar, near the date carved into the stone. "What if you're better off not knowing?"

"You're always better off knowing. Anyway, I need to know. I just do. I need to know if my great-grandfather was a victim or a . . ."

"Or what?"

"I don't know. I guess that's what I'm here to find out."

John's hand dropped from the pillar and reached for mine. "Come along."

I was too surprised by the touch of his hand to reply. His grip was secure as he led me over the bridge, as if I were an oar and he was pulling me through the water. And it was warm. My own hands were freezing, for some reason, but John's fingers radiated heat. We came to a stop before the door and John fumbled for the key.

"Call me crazy, but I feel like you've got something to tell me," I said. "Did you find something last night?"

"Maybe."

The door opened. John stepped back to usher me through, and when I was safely inside he closed the door behind us and walked to Robert's large, Edwardian desk, positioned to catch the glow from the easternmost window. The sunrise, the morning light. He lifted an object from the corner and held it out to me.

"What's this? That's not Patrick's pouch, is it?"

"No. It's much like his, however. An oilskin pouch, the waterproof kind they kept at sea for important papers. But this one belonged to Robert Langford."

I took the pouch from him and opened the fastening. The sun came out suddenly, flooding the window and the room, illuminating the pattern of stains on the slippery brown leather.

John put his hands on his hips and watched me as I stuck my hand inside and drew out a small leather book. "I can't tell you whether your great-grandfather was an agent of some kind," he said quietly, "but it's entirely possible mine was."

"Why do you say that?"

"Look inside. I may not be a spy novelist, but I'm pretty sure that little volume in your hands is a codebook."

CHAPTER 14

Caroline

At Sea
Tuesday, May 4, 1915

CAROLINE FELT LIKE a traitor. She could barely look at the bed where just the day before she and Gilbert had made love. She convinced herself that it had been only her husband she'd thought of while he'd been touching her, only his skin she had felt beneath her fingers, only his voice she had heard whispering in her ear. Almost. Because as wonderful as it had been, she couldn't completely deny that there had been a third person in bed with them.

"Mrs. Hochstetter?"

Startled, she looked up at her maid, Caroline's dinner gown carefully folded over her arm. "Yes, Jones?"

"It's time to dress for dinner. I took the liberty of steaming your gown. I do believe that steward, Patrick, must have deliberately crushed all of your gowns while bringing the luggage to your stateroom. I suppose he's only used to handling potato sacks and can't tell the difference between straw and silk."

Caroline wanted to scold her, but found it difficult to look in Jones's eyes. When her maid had come to help her dress for dinner the previous evening, she'd found the bedroom in disarray, the bedsheets spilling onto the floor, Caroline's hastily discarded shoes and bits of clothing she'd removed before falling into bed with Gilbert splashed against the carpet like debris from a storm.

Jones, like any good lady's maid, hadn't said a word about it or even acknowledged the mess while she'd helped Caroline dress. The room had been set to rights by the time she'd returned from dinner, as if the romantic interlude had never happened. And it might as well not have, as Caroline hadn't seen her husband since, Gilbert having excused himself from dinner the previous evening and making himself absent for the entire day. Patrick had informed her that Gilbert sent his regrets, that pressing business matters required him to closet himself for most of the day with one of the stenographers on board. He would join her tonight for dinner.

Even the note Gilbert had written was conspicuously absent—most likely accidentally gathered and sent to the laundry with the sheets. Caroline was too embarrassed to ask Jones about it. And too humiliated to look for it and have to read the words again.

"Yes, of course. Six o'clock sharp for dinner—mustn't forget."

Jones frowned slightly at Caroline's tart tone. It couldn't be helped. Gilbert was so excruciatingly punctual, something she'd had to learn during their marriage. It simply hadn't been a priority in Savannah, as the pervasive heat and humidity were more a deterrent to rushing about than being a recipient of a disapproving frown from a hostess. Tardiness was accepted, and most likely encouraged, as nobody wanted to appear in a dining room or ballroom glowing with perspiration or—heaven forbid—smelling like a wet dog.

She stood from the dressing room table where she'd been rearranging her toiletries into straight lines as if she could force her thoughts to be as obedient. With a more neutral tone, she said, "What have you chosen for me this evening?"

Jones held up a cream silk-satin crepe evening dress. Caroline remembered trying the gown on the first time, and thinking of how Gilbert would love to see her in it. Elegant and demure, yet with more than a hint of skin from the low V in the back and the front, and sensuous from the feel of the fabric. It had a high-waisted bodice that emphasized her generous bust and tiny waist—small enough for Gilbert to encircle with his large hands, as he'd commented on their wedding day when he'd allowed himself to touch her for the first time. Gold and green beaded and sequined flower motifs matched the looped-up train, the draped ankle-length skirt wrapped over at the back allowing a generous view of her silk stockings and trim ankles.

"It's perfect," she said with a small smile that showed nothing of her immense satisfaction. Gilbert would not be able to ignore her in *this* dress. "And just earrings—this gown needs nothing more. I'm thinking the pearl and diamond drops that I wore last evening," she said, indicating the small velvet box on the dressing table.

"That's exactly what I thought, ma'am, which is why I didn't request Mr. Hochstetter retrieve anything else from the safe. I believe a simple long, flat bun at the back of your head would also showcase the earrings and the lovely neckline."

Caroline allowed herself to smile brightly. "You and I make a wonderful team, Jones. I must ask my husband about increasing your wages."

The maid bowed her head briefly, then placed the dress carefully on the bed before laying out two long cream kid gloves and a folding fan next to them. She excused herself for a moment then returned with a pair of gold brocade shoes, the pair adorned with two-buttoned instep straps, pointed toes, and Louis heels.

Yes, Caroline thought, imagining herself later, after dinner, wearing just her underpinnings, earrings, and those shoes. I will be irresistible. She smiled again, feeling empowered enough to believe that, of the three more nights aboard *Lusitania* she had with Gilbert, she would make each one count.

Gilbert stood as Caroline entered the parlor in their suite, placing a half-empty glass of spirits on a side table. "Good evening, Caroline," he said, clasping his hands behind him. He looked so regal and handsome in his white tie and tails, his shoulders so broad and robust that she felt the strong sense of security that she always associated with him. Her sister-in-law, Claire, had chided Caroline when she'd confessed these feelings, saying that was what a girl should say only about her father.

"Good evening, Gilbert," she said, giving a small twirl so he could admire her dress. "Do you like it?" she asked, trying not to be hurt that she had to prompt him. "I was hoping that tonight instead of leaving immediately after dinner perhaps we could stay for the dancing. They unbolt the tables beneath the dome to make room for a dance—isn't that splendid?"

His eyes held an odd glint as he regarded her steadily. "Your arms are bare. Won't you be cold?"

She kept the smile on her lips. "I'm fine—I have my gloves, after all. I was afraid a wrap would fall from my chair or get lost during the dancing, so I thought I'd leave it behind. It gets so warm in the dining room with all those people." Which wasn't exactly true. She remained cold from the moment she awoke until the moment she went to sleep, thankful for the hot water bottle Jones thought to put at the foot of her bed. But she'd wanted Gilbert to see her in the dress before anyone else, perhaps even be convinced to have a private dinner for two in their suite before retiring to her bedroom.

She was about to suggest it when they heard a soft rap. Gilbert opened the door to Patrick, who smiled warmly at her and tipped his cap before turning his attention to Gilbert and handing him a small envelope. "Telegram for you, sir. They are requesting a reply straightaway."

He opened it roughly and read the contents, a scowl on his face, before glancing back at Caroline. "I'm afraid this can't wait. It will only take a moment, so you may go ahead to the dining room and I'll meet you there. Perhaps find a larger group to sit with so you won't be alone until I'm able to join you."

Disappointment curdled in her stomach like sour milk. "What's this about?" she asked, unwilling to be kept in the dark yet again. Especially because she'd been kept awake the previous night with a niggling thought that wouldn't go away. "There are rumors that *Lusitania* is carrying munitions. Are they from Hochstetter Iron & Steel?"

His face darkened. "Don't bother yourself with these thoughts, Caroline. It is much more complicated than I have time to explain to you right now. And I really must go."

She swallowed her disappointment. "Of course. Don't be long."

He barely spared her another glance before quitting the room. Caroline followed him through the twisting corridor of their suite, sure he'd turn around and kiss her goodbye, or at least tell her he thought she was beautiful. Instead he walked out into the corridor without looking back. She recognized sympathy in Patrick's eyes, but glanced away because she was afraid she might actually cry.

"I'd be happy to escort you to the dining room, ma'am," he said, his soft voice and Irish accent soothing to her raw nerves.

"Thank you, Patrick, but I think I'll dine in tonight."

The sudden sound of whistling directed their attention to the corridor just as Robert Langford walked by, perfectly outfitted for dinner with his own white tie and tails. She recognized the song one moment before he spotted her beyond the doorway. It was a new song, she knew, something catchy and sweet. Something fun to dance to at parties.

"Caroline," he said with surprise. He drew back a step as an elderly couple walked past them, dressed for dinner. The man tipped his hat, the woman's face obscured by an extremely full fur stole so it was unclear if she'd seen anyone at all.

"Yes, that's it—the song you were just whistling. That's the name of the song, isn't it?"

He seemed to think a moment, as if he couldn't recall that he'd been whistling at all. His eyes registered surprise. "Close," he said. "It's 'Can't You Hear Me Calling Caroline?'"

"Good evening, Mr. Langford," Patrick said, stepping into the corridor. "I must see to Mrs. Hochstetter's dinner. It appears she's decided to dine in tonight."

"And miss the *salamoas a la crème* and the *pouding Talma*? Oh, the tragedy!" A look of exaggerated outrage crossed Robert's handsome features. "Please, ma'am. Allow me to escort you to the dining room so that I won't have to report you to the chef, who would surely weep into his *mousse de jambon* and ruin it for the other diners."

Despite herself, Caroline laughed. Taking his arm, she said, "Oh, Robert. What would I do without you?"

"Indeed," he said softly, escorting her down the corridor toward the lifts. As they departed, she caught a glance between Robert and Patrick that she couldn't decipher, but quickly forgot about it as Robert sang softly into her ear, *"I miss you in the morning . . . Caroline, Caroline . . ."*

She tapped him playfully on the arm with her fan. "You must stop, Robert. If somebody hears you, they might think you're pursuing me."

"Who says I'm not?"

She was spared from making a response as they entered the crowded lift taking diners down to the Saloon Deck and the main floor of the first-class dining room, nearly colliding with Prunella and Margery Schuyler. Too late to escape to the safety of the stairs, she smiled at the two women, being careful not to impale one of her eyes on the many ostrich feathers protruding from Margery's coiffure.

"How fortuitous that we run into you, Mrs. Hochstetter," Margery said down her long nose.

"Really? And why would that be?" Caroline asked.

"Mrs. Schuyler and I will be dining with the esteemed sculptress Ida Smythe-Smithson. We will be discussing art in its many forms, and how we can use art to amplify our minds and talents, no matter how small." She pressed her lips together as she regarded Caroline. "You must join us, of course. Perhaps it will help you in your quest to rise above your talents and perform at a new level this Thursday coming."

Only the warm pressure of Robert's hand on the small of her back prevented Caroline from either stomping on the woman's foot with her Louis heel or simply pushing her hard enough to make her topple. Instead, she said, "I'm afraid there won't be room. I've invited Robert Langford to join my husband and me for dinner."

"Perfect," Prunella said, standing behind her sister-in-law and nodding an ostrich-feather-festooned head in Caroline's direction. "We have a table for six reserved already so you all must join us." She closed her mouth, her edict having been issued and the jut of her jaw making it clear that there would be no disagreement.

"I'm not a little surprised that your husband has plans to join you, Mrs. Hochstetter, knowing how very busy he is." Margery sniffed slightly before dabbing her mouth sore with her handkerchief.

A voice from beside Caroline spared her from responding. "I would be delighted to join you," Robert interjected with a charming smile that fooled everyone but Caroline. She loved that she could read him like that. Loved that connection between them. It had always been there, ever since their first auspicious meeting.

"You look exceptionally beautiful tonight, Caroline," he whispered in her ear, his warm breath tingling the skin on her bare neck and back. "That dress. It does something to a man that might be called . . . indecent."

She kept her gaze forward so she could pretend she hadn't heard a word, but she was glad for the general noise of the crowd around her to drown out the sound of the blood soaring from her heart and racing through her body.

The lift gates opened and the diners spilled out, the stifling scent of different perfumes that had overwhelmed the small space suddenly dissipating and leaving behind only the lingering aroma of flowers. They moved en masse the short distance to the dining room, their collective voices echoing off the marble floors and then seeming to lower. Even on this third night of dining, it appeared the passengers could still be awestruck by the opulence of the two-story room.

More than one person glanced up. The ceiling of the first-class dining saloon was capped with a stained glass dome that sparkled with all the reflections from the candles and lighting fixtures below. Done in the style of Louis XVI, the gold-capped Corinthian columns and the intricate scrollwork surrounding oval paintings of cherubim adorning the dome were much more to Gilbert's taste than to her own, but even Caroline couldn't deny the beauty and elegance of the space. It made one want to sip one's consommé a little more slowly, to savor each bite of food, and to perhaps take the time to enjoy the conversation with fellow diners. Perhaps. Unless one's dinner companions were Mrs. and Miss Schuyler. In which case, there was always a never-ending supply of good wine.

"Here we are," Prunella announced, bustling her way through the crowd like a cannonball at Gettysburg. Feeling as if she were a duckling in Prunella's feather-festooned wake, Caroline followed obediently, glad to have Robert beside her. They approached a round table covered in white linen with crowns of starched serviettes protruding from each place setting as at all the other tables, except this one was conspicuously tucked into the farthest reaches of the room, as close to the silk-lined wall as possible. As Caroline accepted the chair Robert held out for her, she couldn't help but wonder if this seating had been arranged intentionally by the staff, having had two nights' experience with the dining Schuylers already.

"Hello," said a very proper English voice from across the table. "I'm Ida. Just Ida, as I do not believe in formalities. And you are?"

Caroline stared in the direction of the voice and saw immediately why she'd missed the woman at first. She was tiny, her shoulders barely reaching the table from her seated position, so that she was nearly hidden by the crystal vases filled with fresh flowers and the multitude of glasses meant for every kind of wine. Her gaze was focused on Caroline, unblinking, as she took a sip from her glass of champagne. At first glance, the woman didn't look much older than twelve. But when Caroline actually looked into the woman's face and saw the knowing eyes and lips set in a sensuous smirk, she realized the woman had to be in her thirties. She had flaming-orange hair—not a color Caroline had ever seen in nature—cut into a short bob, and wore not only bright red lipstick, but *rouge*. On her cheeks. Where everybody could see.

Before responding, Caroline glanced at Prunella, but the older woman didn't seem to notice that anything might be amiss. Turning back to Ida, she said, "I'm Mrs. Gilbert Hoch—" She stopped short at the look of disdain Ida gave her. "I'm Caroline. And this is my friend Robert."

"We've already met, haven't we, Robert?" Ida said, her words laced with innuendo.

"Indeed we have," he agreed, seating himself last. He didn't offer any explanation as to the circumstances of their meeting, but simply smiled back at Ida. A pang jolted Caroline that felt oddly like jealousy. Which was ridiculous, really. Robert wasn't hers and he was free to entangle himself with any woman. Except . . .

The woman's high-pitched voice interrupted her thoughts. "You must be Caroline the woefully lacking accompanist with the preoccupied husband," Ida said before taking a sip of champagne.

Caroline opened her mouth to defend herself but stopped when Ida winked. "I can't imagine anything more difficult," Ida continued, "than to accompany such a superior voice as Miss Schuyler's. Granted, I haven't yet heard her sing, but from what she's told me, she must rival Lucrezia Bori."

Margery closed her eyes and lowered her head for a moment in mock modesty, allowing Ida to smile fully at Caroline. Caroline was relaxing back into her seat when she felt a presence behind her and turned to see Gilbert.

His eyes were guarded as he bent toward her ear. "Hello, my dear," he said quietly before making his apologies for his tardiness and turning to greet the other diners at the table. His face registered momentary surprise when he spotted Robert on Caroline's other side.

"Mr. Langford," he said in greeting.

"Mr. Hochstetter," Robert replied. "I heard you were delayed and took the liberty of escorting your lovely wife to the dining room. I hope you are staying for the dancing afterward. Her gown really must be shown off."

Gilbert looked down at Caroline's dress as if seeing it for the first time. "I suppose it's one of your new ones?"

"Yes, it is. Don't you like it?" She wanted him to look at her the way Robert had. To see what Robert had seen.

"You look cold. Would you like me to fetch your wrap?"

She met Ida's assessing stare and felt a frigid smile form on her lips. "No. I'm absolutely fine. I'll let you know if I change my mind."

She was acutely aware of the two men by her sides as the meal progressed and they were served course after course that smelled delicious but that Caroline couldn't taste. It was impossible to keep track of how much wine she drank as another glass would be filled or refilled with each course. She was aware of Robert conversing with the three other women at the table, and she interjected her own comments occasionally so as not to appear uninformed or uninteresting. Gilbert remained mostly silent, studying his food with meticulous attention as he prepared each bite.

"Are you unwell, Caroline?" Gilbert glanced briefly at her mostly untouched plate.

She turned to her husband. "I'm fine. Really. It's just that we ate lunch at one o'clock, which hardly gives me enough time to build up an appetite for dinner." She put down her knife and placed her hand on his. "Please say you'll stay for the dancing. Please, Gilbert. For me."

He looked down at their hands. "You know I don't dance. I believe you once told me that I had two left feet." He smiled gently. "I wish I could—I would be proud for people to know that you were with me. You go ahead and stay and have fun. I might even watch for a little while."

"I'm sorry if I ever said that. But I'm a good enough dancer for both of us, Gilbert. Really. I won't allow us to make fools of ourselves."

He was already shaking his head. "My father was a coal miner who taught me the value of hard work. It wasn't our way to make spectacles of ourselves, or spend our time doing frivolous things. It's not my way. But I want you to do what makes you happy."

"Being with you makes me happy." She wanted to squeeze his hand, but he was already pulling away, as if afraid somebody might see her show of affection.

"Don't you agree, Mr. Hochstetter?" Margery was looking at them, a spot of *choron* sauce from the sea bass clinging to her mouth sore, which seemed to have grown even larger since the day before.

"I beg your pardon?" Gilbert asked.

"Ida was making the point that nude sculptures should be placed in every home so that we see the human body—especially the female form—as a thing of strength and beauty, and not something to be ashamed of."

Ida was nodding emphatically. "When God made Adam and Eve, they were nude, and perfect in his eyes. Why we choose to hide our bodies under clothing is really mystifying when you think about it." Her gaze traveled to Caroline. "Your wife, for instance, has the most remarkable figure. I would love to sculpt her in the nude—that bone structure is begging to be immortalized in marble. I wouldn't charge my usual rate because it would be such an honor, and because I think it would be a point of pride in what I'm sure is already an impressive art collection in your home."

Spots of color sprouted on Gilbert's cheeks. "I beg your pardon, ma'am. I believe you have just insulted both my wife and myself. I must ask you to apologize."

Margery frowned at Gilbert with disapproval. "Really, Mr. Hochstetter," Margery said, her voice cajoling. "Perhaps if you were an artiste like Ida and myself, then you might understand better what we're trying to say. Then you might comprehend the superiority of a Goethe or a Wagner, unconstrained by repressive Anglo-Saxon notions of morality . . ." She waved her hand, trying to conjure something from the air. "Or the genius of, perhaps, a *Strauss waltz* over the mediocre talents of Anglo-American composers." She paused, her gaze casually settling on Caroline for a moment before turning to Gilbert.

Gilbert slid his chair back. "I don't need to be an artiste to understand what you're suggesting and that is nothing short of obscene. To even consider my wife for such a show of vulgarity . . ."

"Mr. Hochstetter," Robert began. "Gilbert, if you will allow. Ida is a world-renowned sculptress. It is the highest compliment to your wife and to you to be considered as a muse for one of her fine works of art. Your wife is a very beautiful woman, sir. If she were mine, I'd want to show her to the world."

Speaking across Caroline as if she weren't there, Gilbert hissed, "But she's not yours, is she, Mr. Langford?" He stood, jerking the table enough that he knocked over a glass of eleven-year-old French wine, the red startling against the white tablecloth. "I've heard enough," Gilbert said with barely suppressed anger. "My wife and I will be leaving, and I would appreciate you not speaking to her again for the remainder of our time on this ship."

Caroline stared down at her half-eaten plate of food, blinking rapidly, what she wanted to do and say warring with what she would probably say and do.

"Caroline?" Gilbert said firmly, his hand on the back of her chair.

"Perhaps you should ask your wife if she's ready to leave," Ida suggested, not completely hiding her smirk.

Robert stood, too. "Gilbert, please sit down. I'm sure Miss Smythe-Smithson would be amenable to a different topic of conversation, and we all promise to behave civilly."

As if Robert hadn't spoken, Gilbert looked down at Caroline, who was still staring at her plate, the blue-and-white floral pattern of the china seeming to spin around the circumference. "Caroline? Are you coming?"

Slowly, she lifted her head and managed to raise her eyes to his, remembering what her mother had taught her about being a woman: *Appear to be weak and docile when it suits, but never forget that a soft and gentle outer appearance simply masks a spine of steel.*

"No, Gilbert. I'd like to finish eating, and then perhaps dance."

For a brief moment, she thought her husband might forcibly remove her from the table. Instead, he took two deep breaths, the second louder than the first. "As you wish. Please know that I will be extremely busy until we reach England, and I doubt you will see me until then. Good night."

He left without another word, walking quickly and almost knocking into a waiter bearing a silver tray of desserts. Heads turned as he walked past them toward the exit and then, one by one, as if on cue, they all turned to look at Caroline.

She felt as if she might be sick. From embarrassment and humiliation. From disappointment. "Excuse me." She stood quickly, her gloves falling from her lap, but she did not care enough to pick them up. "I'm not feeling very well. It was a pleasure meeting you, Ida." She nodded to the other ladies. "Good night."

She could feel Robert standing next to her but couldn't look at him as she bolted toward the exit adjacent to the one Gilbert had used. Despite her need to leave the room, she would not give anyone the satisfaction of believing that she was running after her husband.

Caroline ducked into the first corridor she came to and pressed her forehead against the nearest door, desperate for something cool to stave off a surge of what felt like fever. She wondered if it could be the wine, or the rich food. Anything, really, other than believing her husband had just effectively put her in her place in such a public manner, and then dismissed her for the rest of the voyage. As if she were a pet dog who needed scolding, and whose absence wouldn't be noticed overly much.

"Mrs. Hochstetter. You seem distraught. May I be of some assistance?"

At the sound of the steward's soft Irish accent behind her, Caroline lifted her head and blinked, the brass label on the door announcing she was at cabin D-61. She was about to accept his offer, having no idea how she was to manage putting one foot in front of the other without assistance, when another voice spoke.

"I'll take care of her, Patrick," Robert said, his words soft yet precise, as if he were as agitated as she was.

"Are you quite sure, sir?"

"Quite," Robert said, the gentle feel of his hand on her elbow doing much to calm her.

"Ma'am?" Patrick asked her, as if making sure this new arrangement was agreeable to her.

"I'll be fine with Mr. Langford. Thank you, Patrick."

The man bowed slightly then left, looking back at them once before disappearing around the corner.

Robert slid her hand into the crook of his elbow. "Come on. I'll take you back to your suite."

She shook her head, refusing to move. "No. I don't want to go there."

"Then let me fetch you a drink. Perhaps the lounge . . ."

"No," she said, thinking more and more clearly. "I don't want to go to the lounge."

"Then I'm afraid . . ." He stopped, his eyes searching hers.

"I want to be with you."

"But you are with me."

She didn't blink. "Alone."

"Alone?"

She nodded. Either emboldened by Ida's words or by Gilbert's secretiveness and rank dismissal, she finally understood what she wanted. *Who* she wanted. She found herself smiling at her own boldness and Robert's seeming reticence, and finding the role reversal almost amusing. "You don't have a bunkmate, do you?"

In response, he put his hand over hers on his arm, and led her to the lifts. Owing to most everyone else being at dinner, they had the lift to themselves, but stood on opposite sides without looking at each other just in case someone was waiting on the Promenade Deck level when the gates opened. With a steady pace they passed her suite then took a left in the second corridor.

Checking to make sure nobody was lurking in the hallway, Robert opened the door to allow her inside, then followed, shutting the door behind him. It was a small room with a single bed, but, as he'd pointed out before, he had a window looking onto the sea. A dim lamp sat on the bedside table.

He stood near enough to touch her, but didn't move. "Are you sure, Caroline? I don't want there to be any regrets. And I certainly don't want to be your teaser stallion."

"My what?"

"Never mind." He took a step closer, his breath warm on her face and smelling of wine.

"What about Ida?"

"Ida?" He seemed genuinely confused.

"She said you'd *met*." She emphasized the last word to make it clear she understood it could have a myriad of meanings.

"She has a whippet, which is how I met her. She was walking her dog in Regent's Park and mine—also a whippet—had just died. I couldn't resist."

"And that's all? You're not lovers?"

"Of course not," he said. "Why? Are you jealous?"

"Of course not. I just wanted to make sure that . . . this isn't something you do on a regular basis. I want to be special."

"Oh, Caroline," he breathed. "You have no idea how special you are to me." He closed the distance between them but still didn't touch her. "Are you sure you want this?" he asked again.

She brought her arms around his neck, threading her fingers through his hair, realizing that she'd been wanting to do that for a very long time. She pressed her lips against his, needing to show him that regret was the last thing on her mind.

"Well, then." He spun with her in his arms, pressing her against the door. "It's just the two of us here. No one else exists right now but the two of us. Here. In this room. What was before or what is to come doesn't matter."

"Even Ida?" she said against his neck, her words almost a gasp as he pulled her closer so there could be no doubt of his desire.

"No one." His fingers slid around to her back. "I do love this dress, but I'm afraid it must go." Expertly, he unfastened the small buttons down her back, while she pulled at the tie around his neck and then the fastenings on his waistcoat, all the while their lips and mouths explored each other, afraid to separate, as if any space between them would allow in thoughts that didn't belong in their here and now.

She was barely aware of their clothing being removed, or any sound from the engines or the corridor outside. She was only aware of him, of Robert, and the taste of him on her tongue, and the feel of his fingers on her bare skin in places she'd never been touched before.

He placed her on the bed and smoothed his long body over hers. She wore her stockings and garters still, but not the shoes. Her fantasy had to give way to practicality at some point. But it didn't matter. He didn't turn off the lamp and refused to let her cover herself with her hands.

"Don't," he said, raising her arms over her head to rest against the pillow. It was wanton, but she didn't care. This room was her new world where she could be someone else. Or perhaps this was the room where she could finally be *her*.

"You have no idea how long I've wanted to do this." He lowered his mouth to one breast and licked slowly. "Or this," he said, moving his mouth to the other breast.

"How long?" she gasped.

"Since the first words you ever said to me. In the Talmadges' rose garden."

She arched her back, needing to be closer to him. "What did I say?"

"You called me your knight in shining armor." He trailed hot, wet kisses up to her throat. "And then you said you'd love me forever. You kissed my cheek and then ran off to dance with someone else."

"Oh, Robert," she said, remembering now, remembering the girl she'd once been. "Why did you go away?"

"Shh," he whispered, pressing his lips against hers again. "Before or after doesn't exist. It's just you and me. Here. Now."

She lifted her hips to meet his, feeling the rocking rhythm of the great ship beneath them until her limbs crumbled like sand and the buttery light of dawn stained the walls.

CHAPTER 15

Tess

At Sea
Wednesday, May 5, 1915

TESS'S EYES AND mouth felt like they'd been scrubbed with sand. Even the pale dawn light was an affront, too bright by far.

But there was no use trying to sleep. When she had, all she saw in front of her was that roll of music, those odd diagrams on the last page. And Ginny's face, familiar and foreign at the same time.

Nellie, Mary Kate, and the woman whose name none of them had learned—Inga? Helga?—were snoring in their bunks when Tess crept out onto the deck. It was so early that not even the most ambitious English nannies were filling their lungs with freshness or forcing their charges to perform open-air calisthenics.

She found a chair on Shelter Deck. It wasn't hers, of course. She couldn't afford the fee. But it was too early in the morning for the owner to demand his rights. She was doing him a service, really, warming it, Tess told herself, and hunched her shoulders against the morning chill as she concentrated on sketching the stragglers who were beginning to appear on deck: a nurse rocking a fractious child; an elderly woman being wheeled in a Bath chair, so draped in rugs that she looked like a perambulating bolt of cloth. Out to sea, Tess could see the hazy outline of a ship. It wavered in the mist and was gone. There was nothing but Tess and open sea and open sky. And her sketchbook.

It was what Tess always did when she felt like she couldn't quite breathe. She put her emotions into pictures, letting her pencil do her thinking for her. Words might lie, vows might be false, but a picture was what it was, as long as one had the wit to see it.

She sketched the vague outline of the ship. One of the British naval escort the captain had promised them? It was too far away to tell. Tess knew about as much of naval ships as she did of spies and codes and secret plans. Which was to say, nothing at all. She added a jaunty British flag to the top, as if by drawing it she could make it more real, more solid, anchor it by them for protection.

Line by line, image by image, Tess could feel the tension in her shoulders release, the grip on her pencil relax. She wore the lead to nothing, sharpened it, and began again. Two girls appeared together with their nanny, playing. Sisters. Tess's imagination replaced their starched pinafores with calico, their hoop with a bag of marbles, or possibly three shells and a pebble. Tennessee and Virginia Schaff, rolling into town just in time to roll out of it again.

It had been shell games for the under-twelves when Tess was only six and Ginny sixteen. Shell games and marbles and trick cards. They'd moved on to more elaborate cons as Tess's skirts lengthened with her legs and she began to pile her hair on top of her head instead of plaiting it in braids. It was Ginny who'd come up with the idea of using Tess's skill with a brush to play a different kind of shell game, a grown-up shell game. A game in which, she swore, no one would get hurt.

But that page in the Hochstetters' safe. That was something else entirely. Numbers, codes, plans. They wouldn't get slapped on the wrist and sent to kick their heels in the British equivalent of the Tombs for a few months. What did people do to foreign agents? To spies? Tess didn't know, but she had the uneasy feeling it involved blindfolds and firing squads. Whatever they were paying, it wasn't worth it.

A piano. That was what she was drawing now, without even thinking of it. A piano with a woman seated on the bench. But it wasn't Caroline

Hochstetter she placed at the keys. The hair on the woman at the piano was fair, not dark, her hair curly, not straight; her figure was an hourglass, not a fashionable rail. Tess's fingers faltered on the pencil. She'd drawn herself at the piano, not in the elegant Hochstetter parlor, but in a simple front room, with antimacassars on the chairs and an oil lamp on the table. What she might have been, perhaps. What she still might be, if she and Ginny could only go straight.

Not that she'd ever play the piano like Caroline Hochstetter. Being tone deaf was something of a barrier.

But, all the same. If she could only convince Ginny to drop whatever this was, to come away with her. . . . This could be the two of them. This could be their front room, somewhere in Devon.

Tess's pencil, as always, was ahead of her mind. She was already sketching a second figure in the doorway. But it wasn't Ginny. It was the figure of a man, tall and lean, propped against the doorframe.

"Hullo, Cinderella." The man's face disappeared in a jagged line of lead as someone tweaked one of the curls that had escaped her haphazard chignon. "Taking the air?"

Tess breathed deeply, relaxed her death grip on her pencil, shamefully glad for the error that had eliminated the man's features in one fell stroke. "I might, if people around me didn't insist on breathing it."

"Now, now," said Robert Langford, leaning comfortably against the arm of the neighboring chair. "Didn't your nanny ever tell you it's important to share?"

"I didn't have a nanny." Just a sister. A sister who told her it was important to take, because if you didn't take first, someone else would and then you'd be left with nothing at all. Tess squinted up at Robert's blurred outline, lifting a hand to shield her eyes against the sunlight, which seemed to be coming as much from within him as without. "You're bright and cheerful this morning. What happened to the whisky and tears?"

"Who needs whisky when they can sup on the nectar of the gods?"

"You mean moonshine?" said Tess grumpily. All of this gratuitous cheer was distinctly grating when all she wanted to do was brood in peace.

Robert beamed beatifically upon her. "I mean love, you ignoramus. 'Drink to me but with thine eyes and I'll not ask for wine'—or whisky or 'shine. My inebriation is an exaltation of the soul."

"Oh, the soul, is it?" Tess applied her pencil to her sketch just a little too hard. The lead left grooves on the page. "Is it the soul that left those marks on your neck, then?"

Robert had the grace to look abashed, but only for a moment. He grinned at her. "Thanks for that. I'll raise my collar points and look like a Regency dandy, all chin in the air."

"And head in the clouds," retorted Tess, sticking her pencil behind her ear. No use wasting good lead. "What happened to all that highfalutin rubbish about wanting to possess heart and body together?"

"What makes you think I haven't?" Robert rested a hand on the back of her chair, making her skin tingle with the proximity. "Don't try to fright me out of my good humor. 'Sufficient unto the day' and all that. I appreciate your concern for me, but . . . 'The heart has reasons of which reason knows nothing.'"

"Ha. If you're fool enough to believe that . . . But you're right. It's none of my nevermind." Grudgingly, she added, "I hope you'll both be very happy."

"So do I." Robert's face lit up like a boy's, and Tess found herself wanting to give Caroline Hochstetter a swift kick in the shin. Just on general principles.

"Shouldn't you be off writing ballads to your ladylove?" inquired Tess disagreeably, retrieving her pencil.

"She's sleeping," said Robert, as though Caroline were the only woman who had slept in all of history. Probably garbed in white samite and wreathed in roses. He leaned a hand against the back of Tess's stolen deck chair. "What's that you're doing?"

"Sketching." Tess hastily flipped the page. Robert leaned over to squint at the picture, a quick sketch of two girls playing hopscotch while their governess hid a yawn behind her hand.

"You're quite good," he said.

"You don't need to sound so surprised."

"You're right, I needn't." Robert smiled down at her, golden in the sunlight. "You're a woman of many talents, Miss Fairweather. May I?"

There was nothing incriminating in this book, Tess had seen to that. This was for her own thoughts and fancies, nothing to do with a job. But she handed it over reluctantly all the same. This was her book, her private place. Letting someone else see it felt a bit like strolling the deck in public in her combinations.

Robert flipped past studies of the boat, the sea, Mary Kate with her mouth open in a monologue, Nellie pointedly writing letters, a group of second-class passengers clustered around the piano by the balcony. He laughed out loud at a picture of Captain Turner looking pained as Margery Schuyler tugged on one arm and Prunella Schuyler on the other. A seagull eyed Prunella's hat in a distinctly considering way.

When he caught his breath, Robert said, "Have you thought of setting up as a caricaturist? *Punch* has nothing on this."

"If anyone would hire me," said Tess, repossessing her sketchbook. Haltingly, she added, "I would have liked to be a proper artist. To paint my own compositions. But I never learned properly. My—my aunt couldn't afford lessons."

"You're self-taught? That's all the more impressive."

It wouldn't be, thought Tess, if he knew the means by which she had acquired her practice. Most students, she knew, copied Great Masters to study their technique. Few tried to pass them off as originals. Tess tucked her sketchbook protectively under her arm. "I have a knack, that's all."

Robert drummed his fingers on the back of her chair. "I know a few people on Fleet Street. It's one of the benefits of being a lowly journalist. If you would do me the honor of entrusting me with a sample sketch or two . . ."

Tess looked swiftly up at him. "You'd put in a word for me?"

She couldn't quite hide her surprise. *No one gives you something for free, Tess. Always look that gift horse in the mouth.* That's what Ginny would tell her.

"Why not?" With disarming charm, Robert said, "I'd be doing them a favor, not the other way around. Besides, I don't feel we're quite quits. I owe you for holding my hand through the Slough of Despond the other day."

Not just his hand. But that was all behind them now. And, as Ginny had pointed out to her so eloquently, there had never been much "them" to be behind. Just one impulsive kiss. It wasn't as though he had kissed her. She had kissed him. No matter how much he seemed to enjoy it at the time.

Not enough, apparently, to dim his ardor for Caroline Hochstetter.

Stop it, Tess told herself. A kiss was a kiss, but a job was a job. A proper job, not the sort that might land them behind bars. She could make a home for herself and Ginny, convince Ginny to drop this latest scheme. There was the money, yes, but also the prospect of being an artist, a proper one, paid for her work. Not that she hadn't been paid for her work before, but it would be nice to be able to own it, instead of skipping town with each effort.

"I told you," said Tess gruffly. "No thanks required."

Robert raised a brow at her. "No witty rejoinder? No attempt to put me in my place? I rather thought you were looking a bit wan, Miss Fairweather. Have you had breakfast?"

She hadn't even thought of breakfast. "I think I've missed my sitting."

"That's easily remedied. What ho! Patrick! There is a lady dying of famine in our midst."

In the warm glow of being called a lady—a lady!—it took Tess a moment to react. "No, don't. There's no need . . ."

"There's every need," said Robert gravely. "Don't you agree, Patrick? Cunard rather frowns on famine."

"We can't have that, sir," agreed the steward, appearing like a genie. "If I might, I would suggest an immediate repast alfresco."

"Just the thing, Patrick. I'll leave the details to you. Crumpets, kedgeree, what have you." A coin passed from Robert's hand to Patrick's, a substantial one from the look of it. Tess didn't know whether to feel cosseted or indebted. Or perhaps both. Neither, she decided, was good.

"Mr. Langford. *Robert.*" Tess yanked at his sleeve and Robert finally looked down at her, his eyes dancing with amusement.

"Did you have a special request I neglected to convey? Do you object to kedgeree?"

"We can't do this." Not just because Robert bore the marks of his night with another woman on his neck. Tess scrounged for another excuse, one that would save her pride. "He's a first-class steward."

"And I'm a first-class passenger," said Robert, "ministering to a damsel in distress. Hunger ought to count as distress, don't you agree?"

"I'll be more distressed if they boot me off the boat."

"It's hardly a hanging offense," mocked Robert. "Here now! Don't look like that. Patrick won't say a word. I've known him since my first trip out. He's as true blue as they come."

Tess thought about Ginny, about the stranger looking out at her from Ginny's face. They'd shared a bed for years. She'd thought she knew everything about her sister. But Ginny was lying to her, hiding something. Something big. Something dangerous. Something coded among the numbers and letters on the last page of a Strauss waltz.

"Do you really ever know that about anyone?" Tess knotted her hands together, feeling the bones hard beneath the skin. "You think you know someone—but what if they're not who you thought? How do you know?"

"That's a grim topic for a fine morning." For a moment, she thought he meant to change the subject, but he didn't. He mulled it over, before saying, quietly, "People like simple stories. Good and evil, hero and villain. We try to mold people into familiar roles, roles we can understand. The devoted mother, the heartless adulteress, the wastrel, the toady, the patriot—the traitor. But it's never that simple, is it?"

Tess shook her head mutely, not so much because she agreed, but because she hoped that he was right, that it wasn't that simple. Because if it was, then she definitely wasn't on the side of the angels.

Robert stared out over her shoulders at the whitecaps forming in their wake, lost in his own thoughts. "I used to believe in those sorts of stories, the sort where evil wore a curled moustache and a cloak and good carried a shining sword. I grew up on them." He looked down at Tess. "There's a gallery at Langford Hall with portraits of my ancestors. Most painted centuries after, out of pure imagination, but what's a bit of creative license in a good cause? Armor and ruffs and knee breeches. As a boy, all I wanted was to live up to them, heroes every one."

He didn't sound as though he found them so heroic now. "Were they?" demanded Tess.

"Ah, that's the question, isn't it? If there was a battle, we were in the thick of it—or so my father claimed. There was a Langford at Hastings, a Langford at Agincourt, a Langford at Bosworth—just don't ask which side. A Langford was hovering by the bedside, dutifully transcribing the words as John of Gaunt went on about this sceptered isle. A Langford stood beside Elizabeth I as she wittered on about her heart and stomach, and a Langford helped Charles I hoist his standard at Nottingham. We sailed from Holland with Charles II at the Restoration and whispered words of encouragement in William of Orange's ear. Am I boring you?"

Perhaps her eyes had glazed over, just a bit. "So what you're saying," translated Tess, "is that your family has been toadying to people wearing crowns since there were crowns to be worn."

Robert gave a brief bark of laughter. "That's one way of putting it. My father would prefer to say that we have an exemplary record of service. But . . ."

"But?"

"*Et in Arcadia ego.*"

Tess cocked her head. "Let's have that again, shall we? In English this time. American English, if you please."

"There's a serpent in every garden. Is that plain enough?"

"Biblical, even." Tess lounged back in the chair, doing her best Eve imitation. "What's your fatal apple, then?"

"It's all lies." The word hung stark in the air between them. "It was only after Jamie died that I began to dig into the family archives. The Langfords were no one until my great-great-grandfather had the good fortune to sink a French ship. The portraits in the gallery are all wishful thinking, the product of an artist's dream. Our grand history is a fraud. It's all a fraud. I'm a fraud."

There was something about the way he said it that made the hairs on the back of Tess's neck rise. Maybe because she knew more than a bit about being a fraud herself. "Surely you're not responsible for what your family did?"

"The sins of the fathers?" There was a grim set to Robert's mouth. "And why not? If we're willing to claim their credit, why not their blame?"

Her father, selling snake oil, skipping town. Ginny, embroiled in goodness knew what. The name on her passport, a lie. "But what if you use those lies to make something true? What if the myth turns into something real? Like—like your father and all those make-believe ancestors. They made you want to make something of yourself, didn't they?"

"And look how that turned out." His hand moved reflexively to his breast pocket. "*Christ*. What a farce."

"What do you mean?"

"Nothing. It's nothing." Jamming his hands into his pockets, he said rapidly, "My father is a big mucky-muck in government. 'Rule Britannia and pass the port.' He can't bear the thought that his one and only surviving son is doing nothing for the war effort. The last of the Langfords, nothing but a wastrel."

"Well, you're going back now, aren't you?" Tess pointed out. "I assume it's not just to follow Caroline Hochstetter."

"Yes. I'm going back . . . for my sins."

Tess looked up at him, cursing the sunshine that played havoc with her vision, wreathing Robert in rainbows. "And what might those sins be?"

"Nothing out of the ordinary. Ah, Patrick! You've done me proud, I see." Turning back to Tess, he said, in the old, bantering tone, "If you want a sin, here's one for you: gluttony. If one must fall, at least one can do so for more than a bite of apple."

More than a bite of apple, indeed. The tray the steward carried was weighted down with heavy dishes with silver domes. It was too much, in more ways than one. Her sister was right. Kindness only went so far.

"I see the partridge," said Tess dryly. "But where's the pear tree?"

Robert laughed, and she could hear the relief behind it, relief that she wasn't going to pursue . . . what? His sins? The sins of his fathers? "Eat up, Miss Fairweather. I won't be satisfied until the roses are back in your cheeks and the insults on your lips."

"If I eat all this," said Tess, trying to keep her tone light, "they're like to put an apple in my mouth and roast me for supper. You don't intend me to eat all this alone, do you?"

"If you insist, I might be prevailed upon to suffer one of those delightful cakes with maple syrup," said Robert. "And possibly a poached egg or two. Purely for chivalric purposes, of course. Yes, Patrick?"

The steward had paused, murmuring something in Robert's ear, pressing a piece of folded paper into his hand. Robert opened it, and the lines cleared from around his eyes. He looked like a greyhound waiting for the opening call to race—or like Tess's father with a new town in view. Focused. Intent.

"Thank you, Patrick." Casually, he tore the note in half, and in half again, letting the pieces flutter away into the sea. To Tess, he said, "I'm afraid I'll have to leave you to suffer those cakes alone."

Tess looked down at the array of elaborate dishes Patrick had laid out. The minced veal and stewed fruits had suddenly lost their savor.

"Let me guess," she said, trying to make a joke of it. "You're going to sup on the nectar of the gods."

"Or at least the crumbs from their table," said Robert, but she could tell that his mind was elsewhere, on the note Patrick had passed him. Absently, he said, "Do justice to Patrick's work for me."

Tess hoisted the syrup jug in salute. "How could I not?" she said lightly.

But she found, as Robert walked away, that her appetite had gone. She tried to return to her sketching, but her fingers felt clumsy. Stupid to care, she told herself. Stupid to care that he'd probably gone to his Caroline. A happy Robert was a useful Robert; if he'd remember to send her sketches along, that would be enough. Men might fail you, but a job, a proper job, that was something she could hold on to. She didn't need Robert Langford conjuring banquets; she just needed enough to feed herself and Ginny.

And if she kept telling herself that, she might even believe it.

A shadow fell across her page. "That," said a flat voice, "is my mistress's chair."

A woman in a black dress stood with arms folded, glaring down at her.

Ginny.

Tess stepped automatically into her role. "Is it? I didn't know. I'll go away now."

"You'll come with me," said the woman loudly, taking Tess roughly by the elbow and hauling her up. "Riffraff."

"Aww," Tess whined. "It was just a chair. No one was using it."

"We'll see what the stewards have to say about that."

Around them, there were a few raised eyebrows. A portly woman nodded in a satisfied way, pleased the proper order was being upheld. Ginny marched her sister into the stairwell, down a flight, around a corner, into a dark alcove. Tess wasn't quite sure where they were, but she could hear the sound of typing nearby. The ship's secretarial pool? The clacking made a good cover for their voices.

"Ginny," Tess said with relief. "I've been wanting to talk to you."

"It's not talk we need." Her sister snatched the sketchbook and shook it, then leafed rapidly through. Tess winced as a page tore. Ginny thrust the book back at her. "It's not here."

"This is my sketchbook," said Tess apologetically. "I was just sketching."

Ginny made an impatient gesture. "Well? Do you have it?"

Impulsively, Tess put a hand on her sister's arm. "What's going on,

Ginny? We've never worked like this before. Not being able to find you—not knowing when I'll find you—not knowing who we're working for—this isn't us, Ginny. This isn't what we do."

"Isn't it?" Tess couldn't quite get used to her sister's new appearance, the strange and the familiar all mixed together. But this was more than hair dye. There was someone Tess didn't know looking out at her from behind Ginny's eyes and it chilled her to the core. "What do you know about it? You just do the drawings. And you can't even be trusted to do that properly anymore."

Tess could feel her cheeks coloring. That Holbein miniature. "One mistake . . ."

"One mistake that nearly landed us both in jail," said Ginny sharply. "Do you know what I had to do to buy off that detective? Do you know what your freedom cost me?"

"Not just *my* freedom," said Tess softly, but her sister didn't seem to hear her.

"They're still looking for you, you know. Any word about where you are and you'll find yourself cooling your heels in the Tombs. If those fancy new papers of yours were to be proved false . . ."

"Are you saying you'd turn me in?" It was impossible even to think it. This was her sister, the sister who had stolen milk for Tess's supper and combed her tangled hair and made sure she had more than her share of the blanket in winter.

"I'm saying," said Ginny, "that you're treading a fine line. Darn it, Tennie. Did you do it or not?"

Tess stepped back, away from the dangerous look in her sister's eyes. "The buyers, Ginny . . . Who are they?"

Ginny stiffened, her eyes darting to one side, then the other. "They'll pay well. That's all you need to know. Where is it?"

Tess looked both ways before lifting her skirt and drawing a tight roll of papers out of the secret pocket. "Here."

Without a word, Ginny untied the string and flipped through. She went through once, then again, before looking up, her eyes wild. "There are only nine pages here. There were supposed to be ten. This is worthless, Tennie! Worthless!"

"It's a Strauss waltz," said Tess, in a small voice. "Surely that's worth what your client will pay."

Ginny brandished the papers, shaking them in Tess's face. "Where is the goddamn tenth page?"

Tess took a deep breath. "In Mr. Hochstetter's safe." The chagrin and anger on her sister's face confirmed all her worst fears. Softly, she asked, "What's on that last page, Ginny?"

Her sister turned her face away from her. "Why ask me? You've seen it yourself."

Numbers and symbols. Tess's chest felt tight, fighting for air, like the time she'd fallen in the mill pond fully clothed, her dress and petticoats dragging her down, water scraping the back of her throat. "Why does that last page matter so much, Ginny?"

"The music won't be complete without it, will it?" said Ginny belligerently. "You can't expect the client to pay for only part of a waltz."

"That didn't look like music."

"The composer's notes, then. What do you care? Paper is paper and ink is ink. Just *do the job*."

Tess fought the urge to step back from her sister's anger, to apologize, to scurry and do her bidding. Instead, she lifted her head. "Not unless you tell me what this is about."

"It's about getting paid," said Ginny brusquely. "You like to eat, don't you?"

The wrongness of it hit Tess like a hammer. It wasn't that Ginny had ever been particularly forthcoming. She'd never been one to share more than she had to. But she'd never been like this, angry and threatening. Afraid. "This isn't about the music, is it? I saw the writing on that page. I saw the diagrams. This is about the war. Those Germans in the brig—are they part of this?"

Tess knew she was right as she saw Ginny's lips settle into a hard line.

"Do you even know what those papers are about?"

"I know they're something important. I know they're something the German navy will pay well for. *Is* paying well for," Ginny corrected herself. Her voice dropped as she took a step toward Tess. "Which is why you had better swallow those scruples of yours and get on with the job."

"No," said Tess.

"I'm going to pretend you didn't say that."

"I can't do it, Ginny. It's one thing to—to switch a painting." Tess found she had trouble putting the words together. What had once seemed easy to justify was harder and harder. "But this? The German navy? I don't like the sound of it."

"It doesn't matter whether you like it or not," said Ginny sharply. "We've promised it to them."

"You've promised it to them." At the look on her sister's face, Tess bit down hard on her lip. "I didn't mean it that way. Come with me to England, Ginny. Forget all this. We'll start over together. We'll come up with new names, new identities. We've done it before. We can make a new future for ourselves."

"Nursing at the front? Serving rationed food in some miserable tea shop in a London slum? And that's if we're lucky."

"Mr. Langford thinks he can find me a job," Tess said eagerly. "He's a journalist. He knows people. He has a friend at *Punch*—"

"Langford." Ginny's voice dripped with scorn. "I should have known. That's what this is, isn't it, Tennie? That's why you've suddenly discovered a conscience. Is that what it is, Tennie? You planning to marry Mr. Langford and have loyal British babies?"

Tess winced. Her sister always had been able to read her like a book. Far better than she'd ever been able to read Ginny. "Mr. Langford is a friend. That's all." Except for the memory of the other night's kiss burning on her lips. Primly, Tess said, "He has nothing to do with this."

Ginny gave a harsh laugh. "Hasn't he? Gosh darn it, Tess! Forget about whatever he promised you. There are only three days left. Do what you have to do, but get me those papers. Or I can't answer for the consequences—Tennessee Schaff."

Something about the way her sister said her name made Tess's insides curl like a shriveled leaf. "Are you threatening me?"

"I'm warning you." Her sister made an abortive move toward her. "Listen to me, Tennie—you don't want to cross these people. Those Germans in the brig, they're not the only agents on board, not by a long shot. You don't know what they're capable of."

Wasn't that all the more reason to steer clear of them? Tess reached for her sister. "Ginny . . ."

But Ginny dodged away from her, slapping aside her hand. "Just do it. And one more thing."

"Yes?"

"That Langford. You think he follows you around for your witty repartee?" Tess felt her cheeks flushing at the sandpaper roughness of Ginny's words. "You think he's really nothing to do with this? I thought I'd raised you to have more sense than that."

Around them, the clatter of the typewriting machines went on, but Tess felt as though she were encased in ice, the whole world frozen. "What are you talking about?"

"I'm telling you. There's no such thing as a free meal," said Ginny. "Stay away from Robert Langford. Or he might just have you for breakfast."

CHAPTER 16

Sarah

Devon, England
May 2013, one week later

AMONG THE ASPECTS of John Langford that bemused me: nothing ever affected his appetite.

I scowled at the Meissen dessert plate perched on the corner of Robert's desk, which had, until recently, contained four slices of Mrs. Finch's iced lemon cake. A few crumbs remained. "Are you going to finish that?" I asked.

"No. No, go right ahead."

"I was being sarcastic. And you *were* going to finish it, weren't you?"

"I—of course not."

"You do realize I haven't scored a single bite?"

John looked up at last from the folder of papers before him. "Didn't you bring your own?"

"I thought you had me covered with your four thick slices."

"I am so sorry. I genuinely thought—"

"Never mind. You have a lot of engine to fuel."

He started to rise from his chair. "No, really. I'll go fetch more."

"Sit down. Please. It's almost dinnertime, anyway." I stretched and set aside the book in my own lap. "You'd have fit right in on that ship. The length of these menus. I mean, what even *is salamoas a la crème*?"

"Salamanders in cream sauce, perhaps?"

"It's listed among the desserts, along with *pouding Talma*."

"Oh, that one's easy. Sort of a spotted dick, except molded into the shape of Talma."

"Spotted *dick?*"

"Calm yourself. It's a pudding. Although not intended for dessert."

"Then who's Talma?"

"Haven't the foggiest."

I leaned back on my elbow and considered his benign face. "Have you ever considered work as a historian's research assistant, Langford? Because you're amazing at this."

"I do what I can, thanks."

"Well, like I said, you'd love shipboard life. Breakfast, lunch, dinner. It's like all they ever did was eat."

"And other things, according to the evidence." He winked at me and returned to the papers before him. He sat at Robert's desk, sifting through yet another of Robert's bulging brown folders, which might contain anything from correspondence with his publisher to receipts for his shirts to incomprehensible sketches on cocktail napkins, in no particular chronological order. We'd been sorting them out for a week now, and the rug was covered by stacks of Langford detritus, laid out in rows, organized first by subject matter and then by date. The largest pile was dryly labeled *Miscellaneous*, into which I had just chucked a Lord's cricket scorecard from 1932.

"What evidence?" I held up a program for a piano concert at Carnegie Hall, April of 1952. "That he liked music? He was a fan of the cricket? He got his book ideas in the middle of cocktail parties?"

"Well, we know he fell in love with my great-grandmother on board, so there's your evidence for amorous frolics, Sherlock." He squinted at the program. "Carnegie Hall, eh? That's a long way to travel for a piano concert."

"It was Mary Talmadge," I said. "One of the greats."

"Never heard of her."

"Philistine."

"If she'd rowed the eight at the Olympics, on the other hand . . ."

"She couldn't have. Women didn't start rowing in the Olympics until the 1970s."

He cocked his head at me. "Really? Where did you learn that?"

"Oh, I don't know." My cheeks went hot. "I must have heard it around somewhere."

"You're not doing research on the side, are you? Interest piqued just a little, perhaps?"

I tried to throw the Carnegie Hall program at him, but it caught the air and fluttered to the ground instead. "Everyone needs a break now and again. This is pretty tedious work. Plenty of material for a 'Robert Langford, spy novelist' biography, but it's like he's blocked out his entire life up until 1920. He never spoke about *Lusitania*, never wrote about it, not even in letters. You wouldn't even know he was on that ship unless you'd seen the passenger manifests and the newspaper accounts."

"And even the newspapers hardly mentioned him." John thumbed through a few papers. "I suppose, if he did commit treason, it's possible he destroyed all the evidence. Even likely."

"And left the codebook behind in an oilskin pouch? Why? As a souvenir?"

John made a grunt that might have meant anything. Agreement or frustration. He sat back in the chair and said, "Speaking of. Any more ideas on that code?"

"No. Every time I try to match the message on my great-grandfather's envelope with one of the ciphers in Robert's codebook, it doesn't make any sense. It's still just letters and numbers. Like a code layered on top of the code."

"Then maybe we're wrong. Maybe the codes don't match at all. Maybe Robert and Patrick were running different rackets. Working for different people, I mean."

"That would be one pretty big coincidence."

He shrugged his big shoulders. "Stranger things. Like I said before, I don't know much about spycraft—"

"Despite the fact that your ancestors seem to have been knee-deep in it."

"But I do know that the intelligence agencies weren't very well organized back then. There were rivalries and conflicts. They were stepping on each other's toes all the time, and sometimes on purpose. So—"

"So maybe they were actually rivals? Double-crossing each other?" I frowned. "But that doesn't make sense, either. They were obviously . . . well, not friends. But they seem to have worked together. I mean, the watch Robert gave Patrick? That was a nice watch."

"Maybe a case of keeping your enemies close? Don't forget, the Irish sided with the Germans in the Great War, if only to spit in the eye of the English. Not even Robert might have known for sure where Patrick's loyalties really lay." John ran a hand through his hair, which was in need of a good cut. The weather had turned gray, and he wore a dark green cashmere sweater that might conceivably have been handed down from Robert himself, judging by the variety of moth holes. Or maybe not, unless Robert was a very tall, very broad man. Which, according to the evidence, he wasn't. Maybe Mrs. Finch had forgotten to put the sweater away in a cedar closet. Maybe Mrs. Finch had forgotten there *was* a cedar closet. Still, it suited John. He had the kind of face that went well with worn, moth-eaten cashmere sweaters. The color brought out the green in his hazel eyes. He looked so much softer-edged, so much kinder than he had in that Costa Coffee shop eight days ago. I liked the familiar angle at which his shoulders slanted from his neck, the way his eyes widened when he sipped his tea. The look of happy concentration on his face right now, as he considered the complicated problem of Patrick and Robert. Our two ancestors, skulking about a ship together, exchanging messages, plotting to do—what?

"You know something?" I said. "I think you're enjoying yourself."

"Of course I'm enjoying myself. This is a thousand times more enjoyable than dodging photographers in the capital and waiting for the next half-truth to turn up in the *Daily Mail Online*."

"Even if you have to keep company with money-grubbing Americans?"

He grinned. "I've found they start to grow on one, after a while. Once you get accustomed to their strange habits and penchant for frankness."

I rose to my knees and gathered his gaze into mine. "Can I be frank right now, John?"

His smile faded slightly, replaced by an expression of wary interest. His hands curled around the knobs of the armrests. "Certainly, Sarah. Speak your mind. God knows I expect nothing less of you."

I leaned forward and caught the edge of the desk with my fingers. His eyelashes, I thought, were remarkably thick. I said, in a husky whisper, "I'm so hungry right now, I could eat a swan."

"Ah, that's the proper spirit." He rose from his seat and walked around the corner of the desk, holding out his hand to me. "Let's find ourselves some dinner, shall we? But there's one rule."

I took his hand and swung to my feet. "What's that?"

"We can't talk about my great-grandfather, or your great-grandfather, or any aspect of the history of the Langford and Houlihan families. For just one bloody hour, I want to talk about something else."

"What else is there?"

He kept hold of my hand. "I'm sure we can think of something," he said.

When was the last time I'd held a boy's hand? I couldn't remember. When you attend an all-girl Catholic high school, you graduate with a fine, well-rounded education in pretty much everything except holding hands with boys. Or anything else with boys, really. Then you go to college, and you're so damned shy around the male of the species, he might as well *be* another species. Eventually, around sophomore year, you find a boy as shy as you are, such that your shynesses cancel each other out—he might explain this to you as a math equation, to which you nod earnestly because you've maybe had a few beers and a boy is actually holding your hand for the first time in your life—and he's smart and kind of cute, and you're not in love but you're close enough, and at last you get to learn the great mystery of life. Then you graduate, and he goes to grad school on the West Coast, and you go to grad school on the East Coast, and anyway you're sick of him by then. It's only later that you realize nobody really holds hands anymore. That nobody holds these quaint, old-fashioned rituals quite as dear as you do.

Or is it just me?

Anyway. There was this other guy, a guy I met at grad school, working on my history PhD, before that fateful semester in Ireland. I'd gone to this mixer at somebody's stinkhole apartment on West End Avenue, and I'd felt somebody's gaze on my cheek, my neck, my hair, except every time I turned around, nobody looked back. But I did catch sight of this boy, sleek brown hair and sharp eyes, medium height, holding a beer in one hand and a cigarette in the other. I hated cigarettes, so I don't know why the boy kept claiming my attention. He just did. But I couldn't catch his eye, and even when I almost did, I chickened out at the last instant. Too intimate, too exposed, to catch a stranger's gaze. I got my coat and left. He caught up with me in the stairwell and apologized. *For what*, I asked. *For not introducing myself*, he said. *I'm Jared Holm. Journalism school, second year.* And he held out his hand.

Probably that wasn't the last time I held a boy's hand. Probably Jared and I held hands a few times, during the lazy course of those four or five months before Ireland, half-baked friends with some benefits, the kind of itch-scratching relationship that serves its purpose when there's nobody to entrance you. Maybe I'd even held hands with that Wall Street guy, although I don't think so. He wasn't the hand-holding type, at least not in the traditional sense. But certainly not since then. Once Mom got sick, I had no room in my life for anything else. No space in my emotions for everything that came along with putting your hand in his hand, palms touching, fingers touching, skin against vulnerable skin.

And I still didn't have that space, did I? I was still booked on that nonrefundable flight back to New York in three days. Mom was still sick. Her fate stuck to my mind and my thoughts like some kind of black substance, like wax, shutting out light, impossible to ignore, even under the welcome distraction—the temporary relief, the *lightening*—of England and my Langford research. To make matters worse, the hand in question belonged to a completely unsuitable, unattainable man, a man who'd just separated from his wife, in painful circumstances that he still refused to discuss in anything other than general terms. The last thing he needed was to jump straight into a new relationship. The last thing *I* needed was to be somebody's rebound fling.

So we'd stayed squarely in the friend zone, this past week. Of course we had. Every night, John walked me back to the Dower House, and though we sometimes shared a glass of wine or sherry or whatever was burning a hole in the Langford liquor cabinet, chatted and laughed together like friends do, he always signed off with a smile and a little salute and disappeared out the garden door.

Except once. Once he kissed my cheek, the night before last. I felt like a teenager, when you lie in bed and review the scene over and over in your head, and you can't stop smiling, and your nerves sort of heat and buzz like an electrical circuit, and you feel the kiss on your skin for hours afterward and don't want to wash it off, ever, even though it was just an ordinary, meaningless *mwaa* on the cheek like you give to people, even strangers at a dinner party, when you say goodbye.

Nothing more than that. A reflex, almost.

Still. His lips had touched my skin.

And now, two days later, here we stood. Here *he* stood, keeping my fingers hooked loosely in his, looking down from his six and a half feet to my five and a half feet, expecting me to speak. Some reply to *I'm sure we can think of something*, which, by itself, wasn't especially suggestive, at least compared to some of the lines we'd volleyed back and forth over the course of the past week. It was the way he said it. The lowering of his eyelashes. The wry little smile in the right-hand corner of his mouth. The way his hand kept mine, and the way mine didn't pull free.

Until the smile fell away, and the hand released me.

"I'm sorry," he said. "I didn't mean—"

"No! I mean—"

"We can talk about whatever you want. If you'd rather stick to Langford—"

"I don't—I mean, if you *want* to stick to Langford—"

"Only if you do."

"Are you asking me what I want?"

"Yes. Yes, I suppose I am." He stuck his hands behind his back and frowned at the top of my head, a few inches away from actual eye contact. "Tell me what you want, Sarah."

I took a deep breath, because this was important. This wasn't Jared Holm or the Wall Street guy. This was John. I couldn't screw it up.

"Okay. I want to—"

A rapid clicking noise interrupted me. We jumped and turned to the door, which we'd left open to allow the fragrant May air into the room, and where a sleek, winsome, mottled-brown whippet now galloped across the threshold.

"Walnut!"

John stepped forward and threw open his arms, just in time to receive a missile of canine ecstasy. In the next instant, they were rolling on the rug, John on his back while Walnut licked his face like it was coated in liver pâté. "Easy, boy! Easy!" John said, laughing. "Hold on. All right, all right. Enough. Get off, you bloody mongrel. I've got someone for you to meet. You're going to like her, I promise."

I knelt on the rug and held out my hand. "Even if I *am* a vulgar Irish American who refrigerates eggs."

Walnut lifted his head and turned a pair of melting brown eyes toward me.

"Her name is Sarah," John said, "and I'll bet you a tennis ball she likes dogs."

"Hello, Walnut." I let the dog sniff my fingers. He must have liked what he smelled, because he licked them, too, and though his tail was already wagging furiously it now seemed as if it might launch him into space. I laughed and rubbed his head, and he turned back to John, who sat up and grinned with such genuine, unchecked, unprecedented joy, I nearly cried. Nearly. Instead I blinked, looked down, and patted Walnut's backside as it shimmied back and forth, propelling that tail.

"You're a good boy, Walnut. You missed your daddy, didn't you?"

"Of *course* he did," said a tragic voice from the door.

I fell back on my bottom and craned my neck to take in the visitor. She wasn't hard to find. She stood just inside the doorway, six feet tall and about a hundred and three pounds, wearing a pair of indigo skinny jeans under a black lace top and quilted black Chanel flats on her long, slender feet. Her hair tumbled about her shoulders with the artless flaxen streaks of a six-year-old girl just back from a beach holiday. She took off a pair of aviator sunglasses and said, "I'm so sorry, John. I meant to bring him back sooner, but I just—I needed—you know what my therapist said—and all those fucking photographers! It was so awful."

John rose carefully to his feet. His smile faded. Beside him, Walnut whimpered. The tail slowed, stopped, and fell, as if it had run unexpectedly out of gas. Or petrol. Whatever whippets fueled up with here in the United Kingdom.

"Callie," he said. "I wasn't expecting you."

She glanced at me with red, swollen eyes. "*Obviously*. Can we talk for a minute? Or am I *interrupting* something?"

John looked at me. "Sarah?"

"No, of course not," I said brightly. "You're not interrupting anything. I'll just—I'll just go for a walk or something."

There was a small, brittle silence. Walnut, sitting next to John's feet, wagged his tail against the floor, as if to whisk away the tension. Callie blinked her eyes and put her sunglasses back on.

"I'm going back to the house," she said. "You know where to find me, John. Walnut? Come on, boy."

Walnut cast John an apologetic look and bounded after her. John turned to me with the same expression, only somewhat more human and heavy-hearted.

"I'll be right back," he said.

In John's absence, the folly took on an uncanny silence. He'd never left me alone there for more than a few minutes, and I couldn't get used to the stillness, the vacuum he left behind. Everywhere I looked, I saw a hole where he should have been. The desk. The sofa. The rug where he lay yesterday evening during a break, hands behind his head, staring at the ceiling as he told me about the Boat Race his last year at Cambridge. How the weather was so blustery there were actual whitecaps on the Thames. *So we're sitting there in our seats at Putney Bridge, waiting to launch, and I'm staring at the cox, first-rate chap, and his face is white as a ghost, and all I can think is, bloody hell, I reckon we've got a fifty-fifty chance of capsizing. . . .*

I turned my face away from that empty rug and stared at the piles of Langford flotsam instead. In addition to Miscellaneous, there were piles for Literary Correspondence, General Correspondence, Literary Research, Drafts and Manuscripts, Receipts, Catalogs, Financial Affairs, Photographs, and Press. None of it had anything to do with the *Lusitania*. None of it had much to do with Robert's life before and during the First World War at all, in fact. It was as if he'd emerged from the Irish Sea as a new man, without a past. It was like the dark side of the moon—you knew it was there, but you had no light to shine on it, no means of examining the surface.

Except the oilskin pouch. He'd kept that. Why?

I had half a drawerful of papers and notebooks to finish sorting. They lay there in a mess on the rug, next to the sofa where John slept, and they weren't going to sort themselves, were they? But I knew what they contained. Plenty of material for that "Robert Langford, spy novelist" biography somebody was going to write someday. What I wanted was something else. And maybe that thing, that clue did indeed lie hidden somewhere on the floor, like a tiny diamond waiting to be unearthed in a great, big mine. Maybe I should just get back to work and keep myself busy while John did whatever he did with his ex-wife in the house across the lawn. After all, I only had three more days. Three more days to figure out Robert Langford.

I couldn't stay away from my mother any longer, could not hide away from the imminent financial collapse back home. I had to finish sorting these papers.

Instead I went to the desk and opened the drawer on the lower right, where John kept Robert's codebook and Patrick's telegram envelope and the notebook we were using to work out the ciphered message. I sat down in the padded leather chair, which was still a little warm from John's body. In less than two minutes, everything had changed. The door was still open, and the wind came from the Channel, from the mouth of the river Dart, where John went rowing in the morning before I came down from the Dower House. I could smell the faint marine whiff of the sea, of the green things growing on the banks, and it made me think of John. Throughout this magical week, I'd meant to wake up early enough to watch him row. It hadn't happened. The boathouse stood down a path at the bottom of the cliff overlooking the river. It had a primitive shower, so John washed there before he came up, and the scent sort of imprinted itself on him, hung about him in a cloud as he whooshed into the kitchen, brilliant with exercise, and took over the buttering of the toast.

I picked up a pencil and opened the notebook.

There were twelve separate ciphers in the codebook, and we had no way of knowing which one had been used to transcribe the message on the envelope. No way of knowing who, in fact, had written it down in the first place, although my instincts screamed that it was Robert himself. In the first place, it was his telegram envelope. In the second place, I'd come to know Robert's handwriting intimately in the past seven days, and there was something about the brushstroke, something about the weight of the pen on the envelope's paper, that told me this was the same hand holding that pen.

I'd bought the notebook from a stationer in the village, and it contained fifty pages of graph paper. I'd transcribed the message in all twelve different ciphers, one to a page, and transcribed again to be sure I hadn't made a mistake. And none of them made any sense. I ran my pencil along the lines of the first page, examining the letters and numbers, trying to find some kind of pattern. The second page. The third.

It was the fourth transcription that interested me the most. There was something familiar about the arrangement of characters, like I'd seen it before somewhere. But not recently. A long time ago, high school or college, something I'd learned and forgotten. A mathematical formula, perhaps? Calculus? (Oh God, anything but calculus.)

But what? Why? What did it mean?

Across the room, my phone buzzed. I'd left it on the rug, next to the papers. I'd been ignoring it lately, other than to make sure there wasn't some urgent message from Riverside Haven—for some reason, hanging around with John, the *ping*s of the outside world were less interesting—but this time I jumped from the chair. Might be John, I thought. Might be an emergency. A whippet emergency. A crazy ex-wife kind of emergency.

I dove for the phone and read the alert. It was a text, all right, but not from John.

Hello there gorgeous. Livin in London now n heard ur here too. Lets meet up for drinks hmm? Jared xx

For a moment or two, I stared at the words on the screen. My God, I hadn't thought about Jared Holm in months, maybe years, and now—just minutes after remembering that encounter in a piss-scented Morningside Heights stairwell, his hand reaching for mine—he sends a text. An incoming communication from some strange, unsettling universe, that Twilight Zone in which a person's image flashes across your memory, just before the phone rings and it's him. And you can't help thinking, you can't help wondering—*why?*

My mother's voice intruded. My mother's brusque, pre-Alzheimer's voice in my head: *Oh, for God's sake, Sarah. It's just a coincidence.*

I sank on the sofa and replied—Sorry, I'm in the country now, headed back to NY in a couple of days, looks like we missed each other. Hope all's well ☺. Pressed *send*. Stared at the screen, at the *dot dot dot* of Jared replying, and then I looked back at the desk.

Why not?

A little gust of wind came through the door, fluttering the papers. I wound my way around the piles, back to the desk, and picked up the notebook. In my hand, the phone buzzed again—Jared's reply—but I tapped the internet browser instead and entered the first set of characters in the search field: *FE3C*

The search results came back an instant later, but not quite in the way I expected. At the top of the results page came the dry question: *Did you mean* Fe_3C *(iron carbide)?*

"Holy crap," I whispered. "That's it."

I burst through the garden door, panting, calling John's name, and crashed into Mrs. Finch. She was dressed in floral blue and an ecru apron that might once have been white, and her face wore an expression of extreme displeasure.

"I'm so sorry! Are you okay? Where's John?"

"No, Callie. I am not *okay*." She placed a withering emphasis on the last word.

"Um, it's Sarah. Not Callie."

She peered at me through her inch-thick spectacles. "You're not Callie."

"It's Sarah!" I said. "Where's John?"

"In the sitting room."

I flew down the hall, past the door to the dining room, around the doorway to the sitting room. I'd never actually gone inside. John and I stuck to the kitchen and dining room. Any lounging took place in the folly. So when I whipped open the door, I wasn't really thinking about what lay inside.

Silly me.

"John!" I said. "I figured out—"

John looked up from the corner of a cream-colored sofa next to the fireplace. On his lap curled his ex-wife, sobbing softly. Her hair spilled free to dangle in a shining, sun-streaked waterfall from the sofa's edge. Walnut lay at his feet, next to Callie's discarded shoes, looking anxious and miserable. He lifted his head at the same instant as John.

For an instant, our gazes met. The room faced north and the air was cool and dim, but I could still see the stricken expression on his face, the lines of worry on his forehead. He opened his mouth to say something.

Before he could speak, I turned away. Left the room and closed the door quietly behind me.

An hour later, John walked through the door of the folly and said my name. I looked up from my place on the rug, surrounded by paper, and thought how tall he looked from this angle. How big-boned, and how lean, and how his face had lost all its hard-won handsomeness and now looked exactly as it had in the Costa Coffee shop, grim and square and cold in the eyes.

"Hey," I said. "How'd it go?"

"I'm going to take her home now. I'll be back in a day or two."

"A day or two?"

"Do you mind?"

Did I *mind*? Did I mind if John Langford left with his beautiful ex-wife and went to her home—whatever that was, probably *their* old home, the one they once shared as newlyweds, having blond, skinny, long-limbed sex all over the furniture—and came back in a couple of days? Possibly even after I'd departed for New York?

I crossed my arms. "Of course not. She's your wife."

"Ex-wife."

"I understand. Seriously. Go ahead."

"No, Sarah. You don't understand. She's an addict, she—" He ran a hand through his hair. "Look, I can't say more. But I can't turn my back on her. We've known each other since we were babies."

"John, it really is okay. I'm just your research buddy, remember? Your annoying houseguest. You don't need my permission to go anywhere. With anyone. Do what you need to do. I'll be right here, sorting through all this precious Langford memorabilia without supervision, keeping myself busy. Don't mind me at all!"

He cracked a small, grateful smile. "All right, then. I won't."

"Really? You trust me? No more guarding the stacks?"

"I trust you, Sarah."

He turned to the door and stopped, and I stared at his profile, his too-large nose, his neck, his shoulders covered in worn green cashmere.

"Something wrong?" I asked innocently.

"Your flight back," he said. "When is it again?"

"Um, it's Sunday. Three days away."

He swore softly.

"But you don't need to worry. I'll make sure everything's locked up, and—"

"That's not what I'm worried about." He turned to face me. "Can't you extend your ticket or anything? Another week, perhaps?"

"No. I need to get back to my mother. It's killing me, not being there for her. And I need to figure out . . ."

"Figure out what?"

"Nothing," I said.

"The money side of things?" he asked gently.

"Like I said, I'll figure it out. You do what you need to do. And if this is goodbye—" This time I had to cut myself short; I actually choked on the word, like a teenager.

"Sarah." He turned his head to stare at the wall next to the window, and

I realized he was looking at Robert's portrait. He frowned at his great-grandfather for several seconds, not speaking or even moving, until at last he turned back to me.

"Yes?" I said.

"Don't mess with my Rubik's Cube while I'm gone," he said, and he walked out the door.

CHAPTER 17

Caroline

At Sea
Wednesday, May 5, 1915

CAROLINE FELT AS if she were playing a game—a game where the rules hadn't been completely explained and one in which she had no idea if there could be any winners. She burrowed a little deeper into her pillow, unwilling to open her eyes and face the daylight. And the truth of not only what she'd done, but the glaring reality that she couldn't replace her elation with justified guilt no matter how hard she tried. *You said you'd love me forever.* Maybe she'd spoken the truth all those years ago. Maybe she and Robert were meant to be together. If only she hadn't been sent up north to school. If only she hadn't met Gilbert. If only.

Her bedroom door opened and she feigned sleep, imagining it was her maid, and felt more than a twinge of embarrassment. She'd had no regret the night before in Robert's arms, nor when he'd had to get Patrick to go to Jones's room at dawn and ask the maid's help to safely deliver Caroline into her bedroom. Caroline had no experience with this sort of thing. How did one act when faced with a servant who knew your darkest secret? Pretend that nothing had happened? Or acknowledge it and ask for discretion? Despite her commitment at pretending to be asleep, her mouth formed itself into a smirk. Yes, she thought. A game, indeed.

"Mrs. Hochstetter?"

Caroline didn't move, hoping to postpone the inevitable as long as she possibly could. Maybe she could say she was ill and wouldn't have need of her maid's services for the duration of the voyage. But how could she? She'd made her proverbial bed, and now she must lie in it. If only this game came with a rulebook, she'd know how to proceed.

"Mrs. Hochstetter?" the woman said again, her voice more urgent. "Your husband would like to see you. I told him you were indisposed, but he's most insistent."

Caroline opened her eyes, then shut them again when she remembered Gilbert's departure from the dining room the previous evening. Her humiliation. And then she remembered that he'd told her that he would be too busy to see her until they'd reached England. Her eyes fluttered open, wondering if this might be a peace overture, and something that felt like the stirrings of guilt began to gnaw at her insides.

She sat up, taking stock of her body, of the sore places and the raw skin where the bristle of Robert's chin had left its mark. *No regrets*, Robert had said. And so she wouldn't. Except . . . Her gaze locked on her maid. "Did Mr. Hochstetter . . . ?"

"He checked in on you an hour ago, ma'am. When you were tucked into your bed sound asleep."

"So . . . ?"

"There was nothing amiss. Just your husband worrying a bit because you don't usually sleep so late. I told him you were overtired and to let you sleep. But he's asking after you so I thought I'd come wake you and help you dress. Won't do to have tongues wagging." Jones raised eyebrows that were oddly lighter than the hair on her head.

"What do you mean?" Caroline asked, as if she didn't already know the answer.

Jones placed a long-sleeved afternoon dress of crepe de chine on the opposite bed and slid open the curtains so that Caroline couldn't see her face as she spoke. "I'm just saying that at breakfast this morning, several of the servants mentioned that you and Mr. Hochstetter had a row last evening at dinner, and that another gentleman followed you out of the dining saloon.

It might be best if you and your husband are seen together, to still any tongues that feel too loose."

Heat burned Caroline's cheeks. It took two attempts to force the words from her throat to her lips. "Thank you, Jones. I will take your advice." She swung her legs to the side of the bed, realizing too late that her nightgown had ridden up high enough to expose skin rubbed pink on the insides of her pale thighs. When she looked up, she saw that Jones had seen it, too.

"I thought a dress with sleeves would be best. There's quite a bit of chill to the air as we head toward the Irish coast. I've drawn you a hot bath, too. It might help wake you up along with the coffee I've asked Patrick to bring for you."

"Thank you," Caroline managed without meeting the maid's eyes, still unsure of her role. If this were a game of chess, she had no idea if she were the queen or a mere pawn. The one thing she knew for certain was that the board was set precariously on the rocking waves of the Atlantic Ocean and she couldn't quite gain her footing.

She bathed and dressed in record time, glad that Jones's usual stoic silence had suddenly turned to an uncharacteristic chatter. If Caroline had to guess, she'd say that her maid seemed almost giddy. It was as if she'd been tested by her employer's indiscretion and on her own strength of will and superior abilities had navigated them both into safety.

As Jones placed the last pin in her mistress's coiffure, her eyes met Caroline's in the mirror. "You're a picture of loveliness, ma'am," she said. "Just make sure that you don't tilt your head too far to the right. There's a mark on your neck that your dress collar won't completely hide."

Caroline stood suddenly as heat rose from her chest and neck, and focused on straightening her silver brushes on the dressing table. "Thank you, Jones. That will be all."

"Yes, ma'am. Mr. Hochstetter is in the parlor." Jones inclined her head as Caroline walked past her to the door, acutely aware of where her collar brushed the skin on her neck.

Gilbert sat reading the *Cunard Daily Bulletin*, the liner's attempt at keeping *Lusitania*'s passengers mildly knowledgeable of a world at war, and the battles being waged on land and sea. Gilbert usually folded it and tucked it out of sight, thinking the contents too disturbing for her, but Caroline was adept at finding his hiding spaces and had been successful so far at reading it daily. Not that the news was painted with anything but the broadest strokes, giving readers a sanitized version of the war. It was like the entire world was conspiring with her husband to soften all possible edges of life. Except that Caroline, as her mother had once told her, knew that one could never appreciate the beauty of a rose without having once been stuck by its thorn.

She watched her husband for a moment as he read, unaware of her presence. His blond hair was combed back and perfect, showing a broad, smooth forehead that belonged on a boy and not a man closer to forty than thirty. She felt the old tenderness as she watched him, the same feeling she'd had when Claire had first introduced them and he'd been so awkward with her. He'd barely said a word and she'd assumed it was because he was shy, which, considering his size and stature, she'd found endearing. It wasn't until much later that he'd admitted he'd simply been smitten and afraid of embarrassing himself if he'd uttered a single word.

He looked up and their eyes met, and she had a flash of memory of the night before, of his anger and her humiliation, and any words she might have said died in her throat. She almost asked him why he was there since he'd all but promised that she wouldn't see him for the duration of the voyage. But she couldn't. Only those without sin should cast the first stone.

He stood and placed the paper on a side table. After clearing his throat, he said, "Patrick brought your gloves from the dining room and gave them to Jones. You must have dropped them last night."

She nodded tersely, swallowing back her disappointment. Assuming that's all he had to tell her, she began to back out of the room.

"Caroline."

She stopped and their gazes met again. "Yes?"

"Are you unwell?"

She started to answer then stopped as Gilbert's eyes flickered to her waist and then back up again. “Just tired,” she said quickly, finding her way to a chair and sinking into it before she collapsed. His implication was clear. *Dear God. What have I done?* It was too early to tell, of course, but there was always the possibility.

He was at her side in a moment. “You’re looking very pale. Let me get you a glass of water. . . .”

She waved him away, but couldn’t meet his eyes. “No, really. I’m just tired. I’ll feel better after I have a cup of coffee.” As if waiting for his cue, Patrick entered with a tray upon which sat a coffeepot and two cups. Glad for the interruption, she took her time pouring the coffee, lots of sugar and cream in hers, plain black for Gilbert. Her hands shook a little, but at least doing something kept her mind away from Robert and what they’d done together in his bed. *No regrets.*

Gilbert sat down in the chair next to hers and picked up his coffee cup. He seemed nervous, something she rarely saw. It put her on edge, causing her to take a quick sip of her coffee and burn her tongue. He cleared his throat awkwardly. “I received a telegram from Claire. She sends her love. She also cautions us to wear our life belts about the ship at all times. The Germans are apparently nondiscriminatory with their sinking of ships.”

Caroline was surprised he’d confided this much to her. “Are you worried?” She found herself holding her breath.

Without pausing, he shook his head decisively. “No. I feel quite confident that the Germans would not wish to sink *Lusitania*.”

There was something in his tone that broached no argument. It was infuriating yet comforting at the same time and she felt herself exhale. “How can you be so sure? I’ve heard the talk about munitions being on board. And how my husband might be responsible for having them on the ship, but he won’t tell me. Wouldn’t that make us a target? Unless, of course, you’re aware that there’s something else on this ship that might be more valuable to them, in which case they wouldn’t want to send us to our watery graves.” She wasn’t sure where the bitter hardness came from in her voice. Perhaps it was simply the manifestation of her guilt.

With a disarming smile that reminded her of the young man she'd fallen in love with, he said, "There are a lot of Americans on board. I doubt the Kaiser would want to shake that particular lion's cage."

But there was something in his smile, something that told her there was more, and she was just as sure that he would not tell her what it was.

He surprised her by standing and moving next to her chair. He took her cup and placed it on the low table, then reached down and took her hand. "I'm sorry you're so tired. Not the least because I know I'm to blame for your not sleeping well last night."

"How . . . ?" This time she did meet his eyes, expecting accusation but finding only contrition.

"I should never have spoken to you the way I did last night at dinner. I allowed business matters to sour my mood even before I sat down. And then that woman . . . that *artiste*." He said it with the same inflection one might use to say the word "Kaiser." "I won't take back my disagreement with her, but I should never have allowed myself to be goaded by her and then to take out my anger on you. I love you, Caroline. I would never wish you to feel as if you didn't matter to me. Will you ever forgive me?"

She kept her gaze on their clasped hands as betrayal, love, anger, and every emotion in between tangled in her head like seaweed. Softly, she said, "That's the thing, isn't it? You say you love me, and you buy me things to show this, but I can't say you've ever made me feel as if I mattered to you. There are things a woman needs. . . ." She let her voice trail away, aware of a stiffness in the fingers that laced hers.

He let his hand slide away from hers. "You know I don't like to talk about those things, Caroline. It's not my way." He knelt by her chair and took her hand again. "But I want to try. I want to be a better husband." He closed his eyes for a moment. "When this . . . business deal is finished, I'll be able to clear my head and focus on other things. Like you. Us." He gripped her hand more firmly, as if to show his conviction. "We'll go somewhere—somewhere far from this war. Like a distant island. Just you and me. Or maybe we'll do all the things you've always wanted to do back home in New York. I know how much you love going to museums and plays—we'll go to every single one, on opening night so we'll be the first. And we can take rides in Central Park just like you've always wanted but that I've made you go with your friends on because I was too busy. It will be different, Caroline. I promise. I just need to get through this one business matter."

She tried to suppress the stirrings of hope. "It all sounds like exactly what I've always wanted our marriage to be, Gil. What I've always prayed for. But they're just words. I need you to show me you love me. Show me that you respect me and my opinions. That what I think is important." She leaned closer. "Tell me about this business matter. I won't presume to be able to have the knowledge to solve anything, but sometimes just telling a sympathetic person can help. And perhaps I can reassure you that you're doing the right thing." She smiled. "It would be a true partnership. I don't think I was ever intended to be put on a pedestal and admired from afar. I want to share your life. Even the unpleasant parts, and what you might think are boring business dealings. I want to know everything about your life."

The light in his eyes dimmed. "You don't know what you're asking, Caroline. There are things I can't possibly share with you. Trust me, it's for your own good."

Anger flared in her chest as they stared at each other, each seemingly determined not to be the first to look away. Gilbert glanced down at their hands before abruptly letting go and standing.

"Please, Gil. Nothing will change if you can't tell me what it is that is so preoccupying you."

When he didn't say anything, Caroline stood, too. "Your silence tells me that I don't matter to you. That all of your plans for us mean nothing. Just some smoke and fog." She was on the verge of tears, yet she wasn't sure which part of the last twenty-four hours was tugging hardest on her heart.

She walked past him to leave, but he held out his hand to her. "Caroline, please. Don't."

She waited for him to say more, but when he didn't she kept walking until she'd reached her bedroom. Jones was still there, tidying it up and making the bed. Caroline had intended to have a good cry in the privacy of her room, but had to swallow back her tears. Jones already knew too much about her private life as it was.

"May I get anything for you, ma'am?"

Caroline managed a smile "Just my box of stationery, please. I think I will retire to the writing room and write a few letters." She hated writing letters, yet it was the first thing she could think of that would make this day seem normal. And because the reading and writing room was the sole domain of the fairer sex, it was also the one place where she'd be guaranteed not to run into Robert. She couldn't bear to face him now, especially not after her conversation with Gilbert.

"Yes, ma'am." The maid opened the door of the satinwood armoire and pulled out a small box from the top shelf.

"Thank you, Jones. I'll be back to dress for lunch." Caroline took the box then turned to leave.

"Mrs. Hochstetter?"

"Yes?"

"If there's anything you need, or anything you need to confide—anything at all—you can trust me. Discretion is one of the requirements of being a good lady's maid, and I'm one of the best."

Caroline regarded her coolly, wondering why she'd never noticed the woman's eyes before. How cold and appraising they seemed. Not the eyes of a lady's maid at all.

"I'll keep that in mind, Jones. Thank you."

It wasn't until much later, after she'd written letters to her mother and Claire that said everything about the ship and the voyage and nothing of what was in her heart, that Caroline remembered Gilbert's parting word. *Don't*. She spent the rest of the day wondering what it was he didn't want her to do.

CHAPTER 18

Tess

At Sea
Thursday, May 6, 1915

DON'T GET TOO close!"

Strong hands grabbed Tess from behind, dragging her out of the way of a rapidly unraveling coil of rope.

Dry-mouthed, Tess turned, finding herself chest to chest with a furious Englishman with a night's growth of beard on his chin. In that startled moment, she had to resist the urge to lift her hand to his chin, to feel the prickles against her palm. She had never seen Robert Langford anything but perfectly soigné, but here he was, looking as though he'd just tumbled out of bed, his hair rumpled, his chin shadowed, smelling of sleep in the gray, cold dawn.

He looked different. Dangerous. The sort of man who could fight dirty in a dark alley, who could level a man with a fist.

Stay away from Robert Langford.

Robert took her by the shoulders and shook. "What were you thinking? Do you want to be knocked overboard?"

Tess wiggled out of his grasp. "Not particularly, no. I just—" She had been staring, transfixed, as the ship's crew had heaved and hauled the lifeboats from their places on the Boat Deck, cursing and sweating, ropes tangling, boats bumping. "I'm not used to, well, ships."

"I gathered that much," said Robert dryly, and Tess belatedly remembered that he was. And why he was.

No wonder he had grabbed her like that. No wonder he looked so wild-eyed. He'd seen his brother swallowed by the sea and been able to do nothing to save him.

Unless that was a lie, the same way everything she had told him about herself was a lie.

Tess swallowed hard and turned pointedly back to the blunders of the crew, watching Robert out of the corner of her eye. "Are they supposed to be like this? The lifeboats, I mean."

"Do you mean, are they meant to be out like that? Yes. We're only a day from the Celtic Sea. I gather it's a standard precaution."

"If it is standard," said Tess, "you'd think they would be better at it."

Nothing about what was going on looked standard to her. Some of the men weren't sailors at all, but waiters from the second-class dining room, porters, and other staff, presumably pressed into service. On the Boat Deck, the ill-formed crew tried and failed to get the boats into position, the captain getting redder and redder in the face, and tighter and tighter in the lip, as the exercise progressed. The rising sun only illuminated the crew's clumsiness and the expressions on the faces of the gathered passengers. Nobody looked impressed.

Robert's lip curled. "It doesn't precisely fill you with confidence, does it?"

Something in his voice made Tess look up at him sharply. "Are we going to get off this ship?"

Robert shrugged. "One way or another."

His voice was grim. He might have been a different man entirely from the one who had burbled to her of love yesterday, who had conjured a feast from thin air. There was something rather disconcerting about the transition, that he could change his skin so entirely.

Tess frowned up at him. "That's a bit gloomy for a man who was—how did you put it?—drinking the nectar of the gods?"

Robert turned abruptly away. "The fountain has run dry. The tap appears to have been shut. The lady won't see me."

The term "lady" was debatable in Tess's opinion, but she decided to leave that one be. "Won't or can't?"

"Does it make a difference?" Robert paced rapidly toward the other end of the deck, Tess tagging along behind.

"I should think it would."

Robert stopped so suddenly that Tess nearly skidded into him. "*I* should think that if one really wanted something, one would make a way."

And what was it that he wanted, really? Caroline Hochstetter's love? Or the plans she carried in her safe?

"Isn't that a bit medieval of you? Setting tests for your ladylove's devotion? Also, I thought it was supposed to be the other way around. Aren't you meant to be proving yourself to her?"

"I would be if I could bloody well get near her," he snapped, and again Tess wondered what it was that he wanted to get near. The lady? Or her waltz? He didn't sound like a man in love. Not that she knew what a man in love sounded like, not really.

Tess backtracked a bit. "So I take it you haven't been able to infiltrate milady's chamber?"

Robert glanced down at her, his brows drawing together. "'Milady's chamber'? What sort of novels have you been reading?"

"It isn't a novel; it's a nursery rhyme. *Upstairs, downstairs and in*—oh, never mind."

"*There I met an old man who wouldn't say his prayers / I took him by the left leg and threw him down the stairs*. Are you suggesting I boot her husband down to C-deck?"

"I'm suggesting—oh, I'm not suggesting anything. I was simply trying to lighten the tone."

So much for subtle. How did one introduce the topic of espionage? *Pardon me, but are you trying to get into Mrs. Hochstetter's drawers or her* drawers?

No, she didn't think that would go over well. Tess could feel crazy laughter welling in her throat. She was just a good, honest thief. What did she know of spies and plots?

And if he was involved, who might he be working for? Not with Ginny, not if she wanted Tess away from him. For the British, then? Hochstetter was an American; whatever it was that the German navy wanted might be up for grabs to the highest bidder, with everyone trying to nab it first.

But Hochstetter was heading to London, which would seem to imply that he was working with the Brits. In that case, where did Langford come into it? There were other agents on board, Ginny had said. Other Germans. Were there rival groups at work?

Or was he just a man in love?

Trying to work it out made Tess's head ache. She needed coffee, a gallon of it.

Wandering back to the rail, Tess flapped a hand in the air. "What *do* you see in Caroline Hochstetter? Oh, I know she's pretty enough and she's accomplished, but why this sudden urge to go slay dragons for her?"

"It's not sudden," Robert said woodenly.

"Oh? You've been behaving like this for years, then? Let me put it this way. You've been in love with her for years, you say, but you've never done anything about it. Why here? Why now?"

Robert shifted uncomfortably. "I don't know. Maybe it's because we're here now. Isn't that reason enough?"

"That's one of the least gallant things I've ever heard. You want her because she's here?"

"That's not what I said. You make me sound like a—"

Tess folded her arms across her chest. "Like a what?"

Robert sketched a frustrated gesture. "Like an opportunist. No, that's not the word. A fraud. Someone only playing at love when it's at hand."

Tess looked at him sharply. "Well, you don't seem to have spent the past decade repining."

"Maybe it took me this long to realize that she might be more than just a distant dream. Maybe I—oh, I don't know." Robert glowered into the eastern sky, streaked with rose and gold. Slowly, haltingly, he said, "There's something about her. Something—like a rose furled under glass, just waiting for the glass to be broken so it can bloom properly. . . . What? I never claimed to be a poet."

"You're not doing too badly." Tess couldn't figure out if the words were stilted because they were wrung from his heart or because he was making them up as he went on. She cocked a hip. "Go on, convince me."

Robert looked away from her, out at the waves. "She's so well bred, so reserved, but there are times . . . There are times when you can feel the real Caroline, underneath it all, just waiting to be freed. The night before the ship sailed . . ." He took a deep breath, paused, and started again. "The night before the ship sailed, there was a party at her husband's house. Caroline and I found ourselves alone, in the music room, playing duets. She has a manuscript, an unpublished waltz by Strauss. . . . The way she looked as she played it, the magic of it—I can't describe what it was."

He didn't have to. Tess had seen it, seen them together, lost in the magic. Or so she had thought. But was it romance she had seen, or strategy? Curious that he had brought up that manuscript, that manuscript that was something more than music and something more deadly than magic.

That was the first time she had seen him, seeking Caroline Hochstetter out in her music room. Now that Tess thought about it, it was increasingly suspicious. First the music room, then lurking outside the Hochstetters' stateroom, then watching Caroline from the balcony—in fact, all the same places Tess had been, at the same time. Possibly for the same reason.

Craftily, Tess asked, "Will she be performing the Strauss piece in the talent show?"

Robert glanced down at her, his expression inscrutable. "No. It's kept under lock and key, I gather. Much the way her husband seems to be keeping Caroline."

"Wouldn't you if you were in his shoes? He's probably seen the way you look at her." Mustering her courage, Tess gave him her cockiest grin. "Come clean with me. She's the reason you're on this ship, isn't it?"

"What makes you think I'm not heading back to do my bit for old Blighty?"

Tess raised her eyebrows at him. "Do you really expect me to believe that?"

"No, I guess not. Not a wastrel like me." Robert's voice was clipped, at its most British. She had, Tess realized, offended him. "If you must know, I'm going home for family reasons."

And if she believed that one, she'd also buy a bridge. "I thought your family didn't want you home."

"*Et tu,* Miss Fairweather? Sometimes it doesn't matter whether you're wanted or not. There are some things that one must do, regardless." Abruptly, he asked, "If you knew that someone you cared about was involved in something unsavory, what would you do?"

Ginny. But no. He couldn't know about Ginny, could he?

Carefully, Tess said, "It would depend on the person, I suppose. And why he was doing it."

Robert's face gave nothing away. "Say the person was being blackmailed. For an indiscretion."

Robert Langford, for example? Ginny didn't share all the details of her exploits with Tess, but she knew her sister was no stranger to blackmail. The threat of the Tombs still hung over Tess's head.

Not that Ginny would follow through on it, her own sister, Tess hastily assured herself.

But Robert Langford? He would be fair game. Just another mark, just the sort of man of wealth and birth Ginny despised on principle. She would think it a virtue to wrench the silver spoon from his mouth.

His father was a mucky-muck in government, he had said. If Robert had been involved in an indiscretion, it might threaten the family position, the family Robert mocked but clearly cared about, more than he would admit. She had heard it in his voice when he spoke of the portraits of his ancestors. However much of a lie they might have been, they mattered to him all the same.

And Ginny would know how to take advantage of that.

It would certainly explain why she had warned Tess away. Sending Robert to get the manuscript from Caroline, that would be insurance, just in case Tess didn't come through. Tess hated the idea, but it rang painfully true. Ginny was a big believer in insurance.

And she didn't, after all these years, totally trust Tess. To Ginny, Tess was, and always would be, that girl with scabbed knees and scraggly blond braids, to be made use of in her fashion, but never a full partner.

Keeping her voice carefully neutral, Tess said, "By an indiscretion—I'm assuming you mean something of a personal nature?"

"Possibly."

"Couldn't you—I mean, that person—just tell the blackmailer to go hang?"

Robert's hands flexed at his sides. "What if there were larger stakes involved? What if it might bring down a man's name and career? What then?" He looked at Tess, and the bleak look in his eyes cut her to the bone. "What if the price were worse than the original sin?"

"I would run," she said, without hesitation. "Get out. Get away."

"There's no outrunning Nemesis. Say you can't run. What then?" Robert didn't wait for her to answer. He laced his fingers together, pushing them backward until the knuckles cracked. "There was a story my father read to me when I was a boy, back before . . . It was called 'The Lady or the Tiger.' Do you know it?"

"It sounds familiar." It sounded like a sideshow at a fair. "But . . . no."

"A condemned man is given the choice of two doors. Behind one lies a beautiful lady. Behind the other, a tiger. There are no markings on the doors, no signs. Pick the wrong one, and . . ."

There was a problem with this story. "What if the lady *is* the tiger?"

That was not the reaction he had been expecting. "In most parts of the world," said Robert testily, "a tiger is generally a tiger. Sharp teeth, stripes, all that sort of thing."

"What I mean is . . ." What did she mean? Tess took her tangled thoughts in hand. "All I'm saying is, sometimes trouble can come in all sorts of forms. Just because something looks charming doesn't mean it can't hurt you. And sometimes the rougher path might be safer in the end. The tiger might be safer than the lady."

"Have you considered hiring yourself out for summer fetes? You can don a turban and tell people to cross your palm with silver," said Robert crossly. "It would be just about as helpful."

"If you don't want advice," said Tess bluntly, "don't ask for it."

Robert took a deep breath, and Tess could see him donning his mask again, the urbane gentleman with the rueful smile. "I'm sorry. I'm in a beastly mood. I'd best take myself back to my cabin and see if a bit of cold saltwater won't improve my temper."

Gosh darn it. Whatever chance she'd had of getting Robert to confide in her, she'd gone and put her foot in it.

Impulsively, Tess put her hand on his sleeve, holding him before he could get away. "If you're in some sort of trouble, any sort at all—you do know you can talk to me, don't you? Whatever it is. I won't judge. And I won't snitch."

For a moment, she thought he might take her up on it.

But then a chain clanked somewhere and a sailor cursed. A rattle toppled to the deck and a baby wailed. And Robert Langford gently detached her hand from his arm.

Much to her surprise, he lifted her hand to his lips, in the Continental way. She could feel the press of his lips straight through the cotton of her gloves. "Whatever strange quirk of Fate threw you in my path . . . you've been a brick, Miss Fairweather. A bit rough on the ego, but a brick all the same."

Caroline Hochstetter got to be a flower yearning to be free; she was masonry. "Any time you need a building block, you know where to find me."

Robert squeezed her hand before releasing it. "When we get to Liverpool, I'll stand you dinner at the finest hotel in town."

"I'll hold you to that," said Tess. She could feel the touch of his lips like a brand. "Once we get to Liverpool."

Robert looked out at the lifeboats bobbing ominously over the slate-gray sea and his expression turned as dark as the waters. "If we ever get to Liverpool."

Two more days to Liverpool. If they ever got to Liverpool.

Tess returned to her cabin, splashed cold water on her face, ate breakfast with her bunkmates. But with every spoonful of porridge, her resolve only strengthened. They had two days left of the voyage. And she'd had enough of dancing to Ginny's tune. Whatever her sister had gotten into this time—whatever her sister had dragged Robert Langford into—it was time to nip it in the bud.

Tess resolutely pushed aside images of flowers blooming under glass. For all that he claimed not to be a poet, Robert's description of Caroline had stuck with her, haunted her. Of course, Tess told herself, just because he was being blackmailed didn't mean that he didn't also fancy himself in love. That might be the worst of it: to have to seduce the woman he thought he loved in order to betray her.

But what did Ginny have over him? What did he fear she might betray?

There was only one way to find out.

Tess set herself up at the end of a corridor, holding her sketchbook, pen, and a precariously balanced inkpot. It took half an hour for her prey to come into view. Old skills kicked in. Tess hurried down the corridor, head down, seemingly in a hurry, bumping into Ginny with just enough force to send her inkpot tumbling, sending red ink (she had deliberately chosen red) right down the front of Ginny's black frock.

"Oh, dear. I'm so sorry. You must let me try to make it right." Whipping out a handkerchief, Tess scrubbed vigorously at the front of Ginny's dress, while Ginny tried futilely to waft her away. Under her breath, Tess said, "I need to talk to you."

"Really." Ginny yanked her dress out of Tess's grasp. "There's no need."

"Oh, there's every need." Tess could be as stubborn as her sister when she wanted to be. She shooed Ginny in front of her, giving her a hard push on the small of the back. "I can't think how I came to be so clumsy! I couldn't possibly just leave you like that. There's a washroom just here. Let me at least see if I can't lighten the stain a bit. Before it sets. You know how impossible it is to get a stain out once it sets."

Tight-lipped, Ginny allowed herself to be herded. In the washroom, neither said a word as they checked for other occupants. It felt strange working together like this. Or maybe it was that it didn't feel strange working together like this. They'd done this a hundred times before. Only this time, they weren't on the same side.

Tess waited until they had finished their check before leaning her back against the door and saying, "What's going on, Ginny?"

Ginny plucked at the front of her frock. "What's going on is that I'm going to have to make an extra trip to the laundry."

Tess decided to start sideways. Twisting her hands in her skirt, she looked appealingly at her sister. "They were putting out the lifeboats this morning, Ginny. Everyone's talking about a German attack."

"You should know better than to listen to rumors." Taking in Tess's alarmed face, Ginny softened, just as Tess had hoped she would. Gruffly, she said, "You shouldn't fret yourself. No one is sinking this ship."

Tess made a helpless gesture. "How do you know that?"

"I just do," said Ginny shortly. If Tess knew how to manipulate Ginny, then Ginny also knew far too much about Tess. She'd already smelled a rat. Or possibly an Englishman. "Was that all? I don't know about you, but I have work to do."

Tess put out a hand to stop her. "What about that advertisement in the

Times? All the warnings? Are you telling me that was just so much . . . hot air?"

Ginny made an annoyed noise, resigned to another night of soothing Tess's nightmares. "Call it a smokescreen. Let's just say that there's something on this ship that's worth far more than the value of sinking it—as long as they can be sure of getting it. And I'm going to make sure they get it."

"This thing—what is it?"

"A formula. Something to do with a weapon," said Ginny vaguely. "Does it matter? What matters is that the Germans want it—and they're willing to pay handsomely for it."

The tenth page of the manuscript, the bit that didn't look like the rest of the music. Not messages to the Germans, then. A formula.

"It's a win-win," Ginny was saying. "We get the money. And we don't drown. *If* you're still with me on this."

It took a moment for her to make sense of Ginny's words. "But . . . I thought you said they wouldn't sink the ship. If they want this formula that badly . . ."

Ginny scowled at her. "Are you that naïve, Ten? Sure, the Germans want it—but they'll do what they have to do to keep the English from getting it. If they can't have it, no one can have it. So I plan to make darn sure that they have it."

Tess scrambled desperately for a solution. "There has to be another way. . . . We could copy out the manuscript, but do it wrong, switch up the details. Just think! It could be the best heist we ever pulled. You get the money for the manuscript, and then we go to the powers that be in London and tell them we diddled the other side. Why, we'll be set for life! They might even give you a medal."

"Sure, they will," scoffed Ginny, but Tess could see she'd caught her attention, that she was tempted.

"Why not?" said Tess recklessly. "I've already got British papers. You could, too. Wouldn't it be nice to be working with the authorities instead of against them for a change? Robert tells me his father's some sort of government mucky-muck . . ."

She realized her mistake in an instant, but it was too late.

Ginny's face closed as tight as the shutters on an abandoned saloon. "Oh, Robert, is it? Didn't I tell you to stay away from him?"

"You did, but . . . How is he involved in this, Ginny? What do you have on him?"

Ginny stiffened as though Tess had slapped her. "Oh, now I'm the enemy, am I? Protecting your precious Robert from your cruel sister?"

"No! Of course not." Even if it was true, just a little bit. Weakly, Tess said, "I just wanted to know, is he with us? Or against us?"

"Us?" Ginny folded her arms across her chest. She was broader than Tess had ever seen her, but it wasn't a pleasing plumpness. Her face looked sallow, unhealthy, not that of the girl who had slept under the stars, who could swim better and run faster than anyone Tess knew. "From the woman who told me she wanted out? You made it very clear that there is no 'us,' not as far as you're concerned."

"There's always an 'us,'" said Tess softly. No matter what Ginny had done, they were still sisters. They could see their way out of this together. She put her arms around her sister, felt her sister's shoulders stiffen beneath her touch. Tess pressed her cheek against her sister's, the sister who'd been the closest thing she'd ever had to a mother. "We're a team, that's what you always told me. You and me, Ginny. The two of us against the world. But you need to fill me in. I need to know who I can trust."

Ginny pulled away from her. "Me," she said fiercely, hurt and love and wounded pride all mixed together. "You can trust *me*."

"But you're not telling me anything! How can I trust you if you won't let me know what we're in for?"

"I'm trying to keep you safe!" Ginny's hands flexed over Tess's shoulders, stopped just short of shaking her. Her hands dropped to her sides as she said, in a low voice, "Believe me, Tennie, the less you know, the better."

As if she were still five, being bowled along in her big sister's wake. *Trust me, Tennie; listen to me, Tennie; follow my lead, Tennie.* No questions, no back talk.

"I'm not a child anymore, Ginny. You don't have to button my pinafores for me anymore. Trust *me*, Ginny. Let me help you. Help us."

Their shared past was there between them, a tangible thing, the sun shining hard on dirt roads, the smell of coffee over a charcoal burner, crushed wildflowers on the seat of a wagon, the hoot of a train whistle, Ginny's work-hardened hand holding Tess's soft little one.

There, in the washroom, Tess saw not the woman in the black dress, dark hair scraped back, but Ginny, with her light brown hair touched with summer sun, barefoot in calico, sweeping Tess up from the dirt and carrying her home, feeding her, caring for her. And she knew Ginny was seeing, not a woman in Gimbels' take on current fashion, but a little girl in a torn frock.

They would do this, they would get out of this scrape, make a new future together. And then . . .

"No," said Ginny, and the past crumpled around them, scattered like so much dust. "No. You wanted out? You're out." She took a step back and looked Tess up and down with the dispassionate chill of the collector assessing an inferior article. "I can't afford any mistakes, not this time."

Tess's throat felt like she'd been swallowing knives. "If it's that Holbein—"

"It's not just the Holbein," said Ginny crisply. "You want to be Tessa Fairweather? Be Tessa Fairweather. Don't look for me, don't talk to me. Go enjoy your *respectable* life as an *honest* citizen."

She made it sound like a slur.

Tess stared at her sister in alarm. "Ginny, I never meant—I never wanted you to think—I wanted us both out. I wasn't trying to turn my back—"

"Oh, no?"

She was hurt, that was all. People lashed out when they were hurt. "It's true, I took you for granted. I know you've always looked out for us both. Isn't it time for me to look out for us a bit?"

"And get us both killed?" Ginny stalked around Tess, grabbed the door handle. "Forget about it. You don't have to sully your lily-white hands. I'll find another way."

"Blackmail?" Tess grabbed Ginny by the arm. "Is that your backup plan? Blackmailing Robert Langford?"

Slowly, deliberately, Ginny extracted her arm from Tess's grip. "Don't try to contact me again. It's safer for both of us."

The door slammed shut behind her, right in Tess's face.

CHAPTER 19

Sarah

Devon, England
May 2013

I WOKE TO the sound of a slamming door, sometime in the middle of the night.

According to R2-D2, it was eight minutes after two o'clock in the morning, but who really trusts a droid? I lay motionless on the pillow, not quite certain whether the sound came from outside of my head or inside. Like when you're drifting off to sleep and start to fall down what feels like a solid, genuine flight of stairs, and you jolt back awake and realize it was just your imagination.

But I hadn't been drifting. I'd been deeply unconscious, dreaming about—what was it?—something to do with John and whippets and a cold, shingled beach—

Was that a voice?

Just a word or two, quickly hushed. A faint thump, felt rather than heard.

My heart thudded against my ribs. I stared into R2-D2's Cyclops eye, illuminated luridly by the reddish glow of the LED clock on his blue-and-white chest, and felt the blast of adrenaline shoot through my veins. John had texted me yesterday to say that he and Callie had arrived safely—*Where?* I thought—and he'd be back before I knew it. (Walnut misses you, he tacked on at the end, and I'd spent the rest of the evening wondering if by *Walnut*, he really meant *John*. Or whether a whippet was just a whippet.)

So if John wasn't messing around downstairs, looking for a middle-of-the-nightcap, who was?

Stay where you are, I told myself. Don't be that dumb chick in the movies. If it's burglars, they're not going to come hunting upstairs, to this room, unless they got a hot tip on a hoard of vintage *Star Wars* memorabilia to sell on eBay. They want the silver and the artwork, the priceless contents of a venerable English country house, unguarded and unoccupied (as far as anyone knew) except for a single, ancient housekeeper with the eyesight of a baby mole.

This is not your business, Sarah. Not your *house. Not* your *family silver.*

Anyway, John wouldn't want you to rush downstairs and get your head bashed in just to save his great-grandfather's Asprey christening cup.

Or would he?

Call 911, I thought. Just call 911. Or wait . . . it's something else here, right? Not 911. Nine-nine-nine. That's it. Call 999.

But what if the cops come and nobody's there? Or it's just Mrs. Finch fixing herself a cuppa in the kitchen because she can't sleep?

I lifted my head from the pillow and listened. The air was mute, but I felt a presence inside it, somewhere. A movement, the vibration of life, whatever you want to call it, like the strumming of a silent guitar. *A disturbance in the Force*, a voice intoned in my brain, and that was the last straw. I threw off the covers, grabbed my phone, crossed the floor on tiptoe, and cracked the door open.

"Mrs. Finch? Is that you?" I called down threadily.

A toilet flushed. Somebody called out a few words in a clipped, annoyed voice.

A *male* voice.

Damn, I thought. Damn. Damn. Damn.

I lifted the phone. As I tapped the first 9, a furious clatter broke out from the staircase, claws on wood, startling my frayed nerves. I dropped the phone, swore, bent down to grab it back, and as I half-rose and ducked back inside the room, a beast flew out of the darkness and commenced to lick my face from mouth to forehead with a long, wet tongue.

"Walnut!" I sputtered.

John met me halfway down the stairs. "I'm so sorry for waking you," he said, reaching for Walnut's collar. "Damn it, old boy, you were supposed to stay in the kitchen."

"It's okay. As long as you're not here to steal the silver and decapitate Mrs. Finch."

He laughed and straightened. He stood two stairs below me, so our faces lay on the same plane, hovering only a foot apart, and his exhilaration startled me. "Mrs. Finch could sleep through a ship sinking. Come on. Since you're already up, I've got someone for you to meet."

"Another whippet? I don't know if my face can take it."

"Not a whippet. Not a dog of any kind, actually. More like—"

A muffled, enormous voice boomed up from the hallway, sounding as if it belonged to Ian McKellen sending off a rival wizard. "John, my good man! I'm afraid you're out of loo roll down here!"

"—an uncle," John finished, with a rueful smile. "Uncle Rupert. Hold on just a tick."

"But who's—"

John turned and leapt nimbly back down the stairs and around the corner, Walnut at his heels. I blinked after them. The smell of outdoors hung strangely in the air. Outdoors and coffee and John and dog. Down the hall, a round golden glow spread across the air from the direction of the kitchen, matching the glow spreading across the interior of my chest, and I released my death grip on the banister and started down the stairs.

Whoever Uncle Rupert was, I had the feeling he'd want some tea.

The kitchen was now familiar to me, and I found the china and the tea and the spoons without thinking. Smelled the old-kitchen smell, whatever it was, spice and linoleum. Filled the kettle from the tap, lifted the lid on the hottest plate of the Aga, placed the kettle right in the middle. The warmth of the stove, I thought, was surely the reason my cheeks felt so hot.

When John swung back into the kitchen a moment later, he was bristling with energy, almost whistling with it.

"Everything all right in there?" I said, playing it casual.

"Oh, Uncle Rupert? Right as rain. Have you gone and put the kettle on, like an angel?"

"Straight down from heaven, if by heaven you mean a galaxy far, far away."

He came up next to me, and now his face was in its usual place, a foot above me, falling into earnestness. His hair was rumpled and tawny, and he hadn't shaved. He rubbed an absent hand against the stubble on his left cheek and set his other hand against the edge of the Aga. "Sarah—" he began.

"Sarah!"

We jumped and turned to the kitchen entrance, where a tall, stout, somewhat grizzled man stood inside a cloud of wild white hair, like Einstein. He wore a tweed jacket over a threadbare, pilling sweater-vest of burgundy wool, and though his lips smiled thinly, his puckered forehead didn't share their optimism.

"John's told me a great deal about you. Delighted to make your acquaintance." He started toward us and stuck out his hand.

John cleared his throat. "Sarah, this is Uncle Rupert. My father's brother. Uncle Rupert, Sarah Blake, my—"

He stopped short after "my" and started to blush.

"Visiting historian," I blurted, taking Rupert's hand. "So nice to meet you, even in the middle of the night."

"For which I apologize again," said John. "Rupert rang me up just as I was leaving, and I had the happy thought of swinging round to pick him up on my way out of London. I don't know why I didn't think of it before. My uncle, you see, happens to have dabbled in naval intelligence at one point in his checkered career."

"John exaggerates, of course. They merely consulted me on a purely mundane matter or two, from time to time." Rupert's left eyebrow made a funny little movement. He raised my hand to his lips and kissed the knuckles. "Enchanted. Speechless, indeed, and unutterably pleased to find John so—"

"In any case," John said, rather loudly, "as a military historian, Rupert has a bit of inside knowledge on the doings of our Langford ancestors, and while he's kept tactfully mum on the subject until now, I thought he might be persuaded to bring us up to the mark on—well, whatever he thinks might be useful. I've already explained the nature of what we're after in Robert Langford's study."

"*Lusitania*." Rupert nodded. He was still holding my hand between his, and he patted it now, as if comforting a child. "Poor old dear. I'm terribly sorry to hear about your great-grandfather."

"Um, thanks. I mean, I didn't exactly know him personally, so it's not what you'd call a fresh wound—"

"Still, he's your ancestor, Sarah. *May* I call you Sarah?"

"Of course—"

"This man is a part of you, my dear. His blood runneth in your veins, his heart beateth in your chest. His—"

The teakettle began the soft climb of its whistle, and I tore my hand from Rupert's sympathetic grip and spun in relief to the Aga, before he could see me smile.

"Uncle Rupert's always had the most tremendous regard for the past," John said.

"It's a living creature," Rupert said. "It keeps a mystical hold over me. I often imagine the old admiral doddering about the folly, adjusting his machine and peering out to sea, or Great-Grandfather Peregrine poring over his dispatches by the fire in the study. It's the modern age, you see, this brutal modern age with its ugliness and its hypocrisies and its false preening moral virtues—I beg your pardon—"

There was a faint choke, almost a sob, and I looked over my shoulder just in time to see Rupert turn away and slump toward the kitchen table. I glanced at John, lifting an eyebrow, and he returned me a small shake of his head and loped across the floor to the chair opposite Rupert's.

I turned back to the two elegant teacups before me—Limoges or something, no coarse coffee mugs around the Langford kitchen, not even the Dower House—and added leaves to the teapot, which was equally priceless, though not the same pattern as the cups. John had shown me how to make proper tea right after I'd asked him where to find the tea bags. *You don't drink tea from* tea bags, *do you?* he'd said in horror, the way you might say *You don't drink wine from* boxes, *do you?* He'd taken out the tin of tea and the mismatched elegant teapot and the silver strainer, explained how much tea and how long, and I followed his recipe now. While the tea steeped, I set the cups in front of John and Rupert. Rupert was staring at the table, counting the grains in the wood, and John was frowning at the top of Rupert's head. *Men*, I thought. John looked up when I set the cup and saucer next to his clasped hands. "You're not having any?"

"God, no. I need my beauty sleep."

He rose. "I'm sorry. Let me help."

We fell into step without words, John finding the cream and sugar—tasting the sugar first, just to be sure—and me bearing the teapot and strainer to the table, while Rupert hunched over his cup and drew his thumbs restlessly around the edge of the saucer. He looked up gratefully when I hovered the spout over the cup's delicate rim.

"Strong, I hope?"

"I think so."

He added cream and sugar, and John wandered over with a whisky bottle. "Yes, yes," Rupert said, brightening. "That's the stuff. My God. I didn't know we had any left."

John added a dollop and set the bottle next to Rupert's cup. "Just for special occasions."

"I've heard of Irish coffee," I said, finding the chair next to John's, "but Irish tea's a first for me."

"Call it Scotch tea, if you like," Rupert said. He lifted his cup and closed his eyes as he drank. "Or ambrosia, as *I* like."

John swung back into his own chair and poured his tea, adding cream and sugar but no whisky, which surprised me mildly. I wouldn't have said that he'd drunk a lot over the past week, but he hadn't exactly drunk a little, either. If I had a glass of sherry with him in the evening, he'd have two. When we split a bottle of wine at dinner, the split wasn't what you'd call fifty-fifty. Not by twenty-five or thirty. He was never drunk, but he seemed to know exactly where to lay down his glass on the *brink* of drunk without quite going over, and who was I to judge? He'd lost his wife. He'd lost his career. More vitally, perhaps, he'd lost what—back in that mystical past his uncle Rupert so worshipped—they used to call honor. The man had a right to drown his sorrows.

All the same, I was glad to see the bottle remain on Rupert's side of the table.

"So," I said brightly, weaving my fingers together, "how was the drive?"

"Marvelous," said John.

"Miserable," said Rupert. "Sheets of rain. And there was some awful show on the BBC, what was it, some American rubbish—I beg your pardon, Sarah."

"Eh, I've heard worse." I sent a friendly elbow into John's ribs.

"Rupert," said John, "tell Sarah what you told me in the car. A bit of a shock."

Rupert sputtered his tea and set the cup hastily back in the saucer. "What, about Nigel? I really don't think the poor child wants to hear my—"

"No, no. Not about Nigel. About Peregrine. Peregrine and his dispatches in the study?"

"Oh, yes. Naturally." Rupert wiped his chin with his handkerchief and reached for the Scotch. He poured about three ounces into his remaining tea, stirred it with a delicate spoon, and gazed thoughtfully at the damp stain on the ceiling. "Sir Peregrine Langford, our venerable ancestor, knighted for his services to a grateful nation, the chap who blew his brains out in grief when he heard his son was lost on *Lusitania*—"

"Yes, yes," John said, "she knows all that."

"—learned of this tragedy before the rest of the world, you see, because he was a director of Room 40."

"Room 40?" I asked.

"My dear child," he said tenderly, "the secret department within the Admiralty responsible for cryptoanalysis."

"Decoding things, in other words," said John.

"Oh," I said, and then, "Oh!"

"Yes. Of course, his involvement was all kept quite hush-hush, and I didn't learn of it myself until they had to give me clearance for one damned thing or another. Never told the rest of the family, because—well, at the time, it was secret. And while the facts have been largely declassified since—I discovered all this back in Cold War days, mind you, when they used to call me in for various panicky little briefings—I'm afraid I simply forgot." He shrugged and smiled one of those sad, vague, old-man smiles. "At any rate, it never came up around Christmas dinner."

"Well, now it's come up." John turned to me. "What do you think, Sarah?"

My head was spinning a little, whether from shock or glee or plain tiredness. I squinted across the table at Rupert's long, lined face. I'd taken out my contacts, of course, and I hadn't grabbed my glasses before leaving the bedroom, but even my nearsightedness couldn't account for the bleariness of his expression, the way someone seemed to have smudged his edges with a pencil eraser. Next to me, John crackled with a strange, tensile energy, just as if he hadn't actually been awake for twenty straight hours and driven all the way to London and back in the company of two different emotional vampires.

And I hadn't even told him about the coded message yet.

"I think it's too much for a coincidence," I said. "It's a breakthrough. How—I mean—what are the implications? Did he know his son was involved? Were they working together?"

Rupert shrugged his tweedy shoulders. "I've got no idea, I'm afraid. Never imagined until now that Robert might also have been involved in—well, in espionage, to put it plainly. Given the subject of his books, I suppose we ought to have wondered about it, but nobody in the family ever raised the least hint that he was an *actual* spy, not just a creator of imaginary ones. Least of all Robert himself."

"Well, Robert certainly hasn't left any hints about his father among his personal papers." I sat back in my chair and crossed my arms. "Nothing we've uncovered yet, anyway."

John drummed his fingers on the table. "What about Peregrine's papers? Have you ever had a look at those?"

"No," said Rupert. "It's not my field of study, really. I'm afraid I never got around to any kind of comprehensive analysis. In any case, as you well know, you've got to know what you're looking for in these types of papers, or else it tends to blow straight over your head."

"Where are they kept?" I asked.

"His private papers were sent to the archives at the Bodleian, I believe. He was an Oxford man. Isn't that right, John?"

"I believe so, yes."

"As to his official papers, I imagine they're gathering dust in the National Archives."

I uncrossed my arms again and leaned forward. "And how hard would it be for us to have a look?"

Rupert set his fingers around the edge of his saucer and peered into the empty cup, one eye shut, as if trying to read the leaves. For some reason, his hands transfixed me. They were large but slender, gracefully shaped, the kind of hands you might call aristocratic, except that the joints of his knuckles were pink and swollen. I wondered if he had arthritis, or whether it was just the long car journey, or something else. A tiny ceramic rattle made itself known in the silence, and I realized his fingers were trembling. He seemed to have forgotten my question, and I was about to prompt him when he looked up suddenly and said, "I imagine I could pull a string or two."

"Excellent." John rose from the table and picked up the teacups. "Shall we pop over there tomorrow morning, then?"

"Certainly, if you like," Rupert said. There was something shaky and brave about this sentence that made me peer into his eyes, profoundly tired, pink with exhaustion.

I reached across the table and touched Rupert's wrist, just below the sleeve of his white shirt. "In the meantime, though, how about getting some sleep?"

As it turned out, Uncle Rupert had a room of his own in the Dower House—one presumably not stuffed with relics from the Galactic Empire—and he didn't seem to care whether the sheets had been freshened or not. I watched him trudge up the stairs, followed by John, who'd insisted on carrying the small, old-fashioned valise that Rupert had brought along with him.

I returned to the kitchen and finished drying the teacups. Just as I slung the dish towel back on its hook, switched off the light, and headed for the doorway, John appeared around the corner, rubbing his hair with both hands, like he'd just discovered his own fatigue.

"You should go to bed, too," I said.

"Yes." He stopped just inside the doorway, a few feet away. The light from the hall slanted across the side of his face, which had lost its expression of boyish rapture and now looked grave.

"Everything all right with Rupert?" I asked. "He seemed upset."

"Rupert? Oh, he'll be all right. He's had another row with Nigel, that's all."

"Nigel?"

"His partner."

"Oh!" I hesitated. "Business partner, or *partner* partner?"

"Partner partner." He smiled. "Nigel's one of those chefs on the telly. A bit temperamental. Every month or two Rupert rings me up in tears and tells me it's over, but they always kiss and make up. I don't think Nigel could do without him; Rupert's the only chap in his entire entourage who won't take his guff."

"Good for him. Everyone needs someone like that. Someone you can . . ."

"Yes?"

My skin warmed. I was glad for the dimness, so he couldn't see me blushing. "Be comfortable with. Be honest."

"Funnily enough," John said, looking at me steadily, "I was thinking the same thing, driving Callie up to London this afternoon. Or yesterday afternoon, I suppose."

"How *is* Callie? I thought you said you were going to stay a couple of days."

He shifted his weight and leaned his shoulder against the doorframe. "Callie is just fine, Sarah. As fine as she'll ever be, anyway. I took her to her mother's house in Richmond. The old dear was a trifle taken aback, but as she's between lovers now herself, it dawned on me that this might prove an excellent opportunity for the two of them to lend mutual comfort. Or maybe that was just an excuse to follow my own, rather urgent inclination to jump straight back in the car and return home before you flew off back to New York."

"I doubt it," I said. "If you didn't think she was in good hands, you wouldn't have left her there."

"Possibly you're giving me too much credit." He smiled. "But they're quite alike, after all, except at least Lady Hammond's got her alcoholism all sorted. My hope is that . . ."

"She'll show Callie the way to sobriety?"

"Something like that." His gaze shifted a few inches, lengthened, so he seemed to be staring at the darkened kitchen landscape just past my left ear. His smile faded. "She's not a bad egg, Callie."

"Of course not. You wouldn't have fallen in love with her if she were."

"I don't know if I ever *fell* in love with her. I loved her, that's all. Knew her all my life. Was sort of dazzled by her, I suppose, when she transformed into this glamorous London It girl, surrounded by her *Tatler* crowd, and still had time for plain old John Langford. I thought I could save her from it all."

"I'm afraid it doesn't actually work that way."

"No, it doesn't. As I discovered. But she's got a good heart, underneath it all. She said something to me in the car, on the way to London."

"What's that?"

His eyes moved, returning to meet mine, and even though the light was dusky, even though his face had slipped into shadow, I could see every detail, every black eyelash. Without noticing, I'd stepped closer to him as he spoke, and I had to tilt my head up, while he tilted his head down at the exact complementary angle. "I'll tell you some other time, maybe," he said. "If she turns out to be right. And now I think I'd better step out of your way so you can go back to bed."

"Back to my berth in the Imperial Star Destroyer."

"I hope it's comfortable. You could always take the master bedroom, you know. Mrs. F could freshen it up in a jiffy. Well, perhaps not a jiffy, but—"

"Oh, I'm all right. It's grown on me. More comfortable than that sofa in the folly, I'll bet."

The corner of his mouth turned up a little. "Actually, that sofa is more comfortable than you'd think. Well cushioned. Wide, if a bit short."

"I guess I'll have to take your word for it." I forced a yawn I didn't feel. My nerves were buzzing, my heart smacking. I caught the drift of scent from his old green cashmere sweater, the faint warmth of his skin. "Good night, then."

"Good night." He reached out and touched my elbow. "Nice shirt, by the way."

"What, this?" I looked down. "Oh, gosh. I'm so sorry. That's yours, isn't it?"

"My jersey from the 2003 Boat Race, in fact. Where did you find it?"

"It was folded up with my laundry yesterday. I think Mrs. Finch must have slipped it in by accident. I was so tired last night, I just kind of grabbed it without thinking. You can have it—"

"Sarah," he said quietly, "don't worry about it. I don't mind. In fact . . ."

"Hmm?"

"I was happy to see you wearing it. When I saw you on the stairs."

"Oh." I swallowed. "Oh. Good, then. I mean, thanks. Thank you. So. We should really go to bed."

"Yes, we should."

"I mean, you should go to your bed, and I should go to my bed, and—"

John took hold of my other elbow and kissed me, brief and gentle, on the lips. "Do you mind?" he asked, raising his head a little.

"No," I whispered. "Do you?"

"Not the least bit." His hands moved, one to my waist and one to the side of my face, and he drew me closer and kissed me again. I had time to taste the tea on his breath, to feel the damp, delicious curve of his bottom lip and the scratch of his unshaven chin, before he lifted his mouth away and said, "Thank God. I've been wanting to kiss you all week."

"Really?"

"Yes. But I was afraid you'd think it was unethical and leave me."

We laughed nervously, looking downward into the thin, hot chasm of air between our two bodies. His fingers slid from my face to the back of my head. I said, "Probably it *is* unethical, though."

"Then I suppose we should stop."

I looked up. His face was so tender, it bruised me. "Yes. We really should stop."

We didn't move. Went on looking at each other in awe, in disbelief. His palm at my waist lay heavy, his fingers in my hair were as warm and light as sunbeams.

I lifted my own hands to rest on his collarbone, so that my fingertips just reached over the ridge to touch the hollow of his throat. The extreme softness of his sweater absorbed my skin. "For the record, though, you're not plain old John Langford. You're not plain or old. You're *John*."

"John," he said. "John and Sarah."

There was nothing I could say to that. No possible reply, except one.

I went up on my tiptoes, slipped my hands around the back of his neck, and kissed his lips, which parted just in time.

CHAPTER 20

Caroline

At Sea
Thursday, May 6, 1915

W*HAT TIME IS it?* Caroline sat straight up in bed at the clatter outside, metal and wood clanging together as if an angry cook had run amok with all of her utensils and pots. Except this was much louder, the objects being slammed against each other much bigger and heavier than mere pots and pans.

A gray, filmy light filtered through the edges of her curtains, telling her that it was predawn. She turned on the bedside lamp so she could see the small clock on the writing desk. Five forty-three. *Bang.* Not from the corridor, then. The noise was outside the ship, and a little above her. Something on A-deck.

Caroline sat up, blinking as if that might clear her head. Maybe it was one of the daily lifeboat drills, a subject of quite a lot of derision among many of the other passengers Caroline had met. Not about the drills exactly, but more about the fact that the passengers were not invited to attend.

Sliding on her wrapper, she padded across her room then down the short hall to Gilbert's bedroom. Perhaps he'd know what the noise and commotion was all about. If anything, he would be able to put her worries to rest. She placed her palm against his door and smiled bitterly to herself. The first person she'd sought to set things right was her husband. Her reliable and dependable Gilbert. The man she'd thought she loved. The man she'd betrayed.

She rapped on the door. "Gilbert? It's Caroline. May I come in?" In the past, she would have knocked briefly, then entered. But she felt as if she'd given up that right and now needed his permission.

When there was no answer, she knocked again. "Gilbert? Are you awake?" After waiting another long moment, Caroline hesitated only briefly before turning the door handle and pushing it open. His room was similar to hers, although slightly smaller and without access to the outer corridor. She'd been surprised when he'd selected it, assuming he'd want the space and the access. But he'd told her he wanted her to be more comfortable and given her the larger room. Caroline had hoped he'd really meant that he'd be sharing the room with her, but she'd realized the very first night that she didn't actually know her husband's intentions at all.

The curtains on one of his windows had been pulled open, allowing her to see the unmade bed, the indentation still on his pillow. "Gilbert?" she said to the empty room, not sure why. Maybe it was to finish their conversation from the previous morning, to ask him what it was he didn't want her to do.

The banging on the deck above continued unabated, yet she didn't care anymore. She sat down on the edge of the bed, smelling his scent, feeling his cold sheets. Missing him. She'd seen him only briefly the previous evening for a politely formal dinner with two other couples before he'd excused himself to attend to business. Not wanting to cause awkwardness, Caroline had also left the dining room and headed to her suite shortly afterward, desperate not to see Robert. Yet here she was, longing for both of them, feeling their absence as the tides must ache for the moon.

Do not rely on any man for your happiness, Caroline. You must find your own. Caroline sat up as if her mother were standing next to her, telling her daughter what she'd told her the day Caroline's father had died. Annelise

Telfair had loved her husband, and the security his position and money had offered her, but she had not stopped living just because he had.

Caroline stood. It wasn't the same thing, of course, but she could certainly appreciate the sentiment. Her mother hadn't raised her to wallow in misery. She simply must decide where her happiness lay, and chart her course accordingly.

With renewed purpose, she made her way back to her bedroom, planning to dress quickly and without her maid's assistance, have a quick and quiet breakfast in her suite, then wait in the first-class lounge until her appointment with Margery Schuyler for their final rehearsal before that evening's performance.

Yes, she loved her husband. But, as she'd realized in the darkest hours of the night as she tossed and turned in her lonely bed, she loved Robert Langford, too. Perhaps she needed to tell him how she felt, and then depending on his reaction, she'd know what to do next. She *had* to know what to do next.

She was so preoccupied with rehearsing what she'd say when she saw him that she almost missed the envelope that had been slid under her door from the outside hallway. Had it been there when she'd awakened? She wasn't sure. She'd been focused on the noise from the deck above, and could have easily overlooked it from where it lay on the blue carpet, shoved just past the edge of the door.

It had to be from Robert. Of course he'd been wondering why she was avoiding him. Maybe he wanted to meet with her, too. Eagerly, she stooped and picked it up, examining the envelope. It was cheap paper, thin and lightweight, not the heavy linen of her own stationery. She flipped it over, frowning at the *Mrs. Hochstetter* written in an unfamiliar hand. Not feminine or masculine, and definitely not tidy. It seemed as if someone had written the words using the opposite hand the writer was accustomed to using. As if the writer might be trying to disguise their identity.

Caroline ripped open the envelope, letting it fall to the ground as she unfolded the single sheet inside.

I know your secret. If you do not wish your husband to find out, you will deliver to me that which I ask. Wait for further instructions following this evening's concert. I will find you.

Caroline felt as if she'd been plunged into the icy Atlantic, suffocating and freezing, the suck of the waves pulling her under. *Who else knew?* She remembered what Jones had said, about there being gossip among the servants about Caroline's fight with Gilbert and then her fleeing the dining room followed by Robert. Had they been followed? Had Robert told someone? She dismissed the second thought almost as soon as it appeared. He would never have betrayed her. He loved her, she knew that. He'd said it often enough the night they'd spent together. And she knew his character. He wasn't capable of hurting her like that. *Then who?*

She remained standing, unwilling to give in to the urge to collapse on the bed and fall into a pathetic ball of fear and self-pity. That wasn't the daughter her mother had raised. She had no one else to blame for her predicament except for herself, and only she could extricate herself from it.

Closing her eyes, she forced herself to think. To consider the motives of the blackmailer. It only took a moment. Jewelry. It had to be that—she had nothing else of any value, at least that's what everyone except for a select few would assume. She'd been wearing various pieces since she boarded the ship, visible to anyone who glanced in her direction. She wondered which pieces her blackmailer would demand, and how she'd be able to get them from the safe in the purser's office.

Taking a deep breath, Caroline pressed her fisted hands against her chest as if she could slow the pounding of her heart. *Think.* She wasn't sure if the purser would grant her access to the jewelry, seeing how Gilbert was his only contact. But she could ask Gilbert to take out all of her jewelry from the safe and bring it to her room, claiming she wasn't sure what she wanted to wear that evening for the concert. It would make him happy to think she wanted to wear one of the gaudy pieces he'd bought for her. She swayed but didn't buckle, the burden of yet another betrayal almost too heavy to bear.

She finished dressing, then wrote two brief notes: one to Gilbert requesting her jewelry, and another to Robert asking him to meet her in the lounge, where she'd be alone for the next two hours. Then she shoved the blackmailer's envelope and note into the back of the desk drawer and gathered her piano music. She hurriedly left the room, intent on finding Patrick to give him the notes to be delivered, letting the door shut behind her with a decisive snap.

"I'm quite sure that's supposed to be an F sharp," Margery said down her long nose as she peered over Caroline's shoulder to examine the music on the piano stand.

"It is," agreed Caroline. "Which is why I'm wondering why you're singing an A flat. I could certainly play the piece in another key, which would make the A flat correct, but that would change all the other notes to the same key, which I'm afraid you might find too challenging."

Margery's rather large nostrils flared, at least making her mouth sore seem slightly smaller by comparison.

Caroline returned to the keyboard and began playing, not even caring that she and Margery were apparently performing in separate keys. She simply wanted this day to be over. After she'd delivered the notes, she'd waited in the lounge for two hours, her anxiety growing with each ticking of the giant clock over the green marble mantel. Despite assurances from Patrick that he would deliver her note to Robert straightaway, he had not appeared.

She needed to speak with him before the concert and her encounter with her blackmailer. Not to seek his advice, but to let him know that she was prepared to give in to the blackmailer's demands, whatever they might be, if only to protect Gilbert. Whatever happened between them, Caroline would not make her husband a public cuckold, an object of ridicule.

Only once had she ventured outside the lounge to see if she could spot

Robert, thinking maybe he'd misunderstood, but she had spotted only the lifeboats on the Boat Deck hanging on the outside of the great ship—apparently the commotion from that morning. It was sobering to see, a reminder of the necessity of last-minute emergency preparations. The Germans had not been keeping it a secret that their U-boats were lurking in the waters off Ireland, and despite the captain's assurances that *Lusitania* could outrun a U-boat, it was apparent that he was taking the possible threat seriously.

Caroline remembered what Gilbert had told her about the Germans not wishing to risk the ire of the American public over the potential loss of so many American lives. And how she'd thought there was more to his conviction than he was telling her. He was holding something back from her, she was sure of it. But she was no longer sure of his motives for keeping her uninformed, his actions since boarding the ship convincing her that his reticence wasn't all about protecting her delicate sensibilities. Watching the dangling lifeboats, suspended like a held breath, had erased any comfort his words had offered and filled Caroline with enough apprehension to force her back inside.

It had taken her a while to return to the Saloon Lounge as she was stopped several times by on-board acquaintances to sign their memento books. She felt odd not having one to offer in turn, but it had never occurred to her. She wondered how many of these people would remember her after only a year as they stared at her name and tried to put a face to it. But she signed several with a smile and then made her way back to the lounge, avoiding large droves of children led by stewardesses—apparently taking advantage of the fine weather—before finally arriving at the lounge to an annoyed Margery. She'd hurriedly sat on the piano bench and begun to play. Half an hour later, she was ready to toss either herself or Margery Schuyler over the ship's railing.

"Really, Mrs. Hochstetter, if you can't play the right notes then perhaps I should perform a cappella."

Caroline was tempted to agree. Her anxiousness over Robert and discovering the identity of her blackmailer had done nothing to keep her mind focused on the music and keyboard in front of her. Not that it mattered. The most gifted pianist in the world stood no chance of sounding better than snarling traffic when paired with Margery's screeching soprano and grating contralto voice.

Keeping her anger in check, Caroline said, "Perhaps we should try it one more time. I promise to try harder." She stifled a yawn behind her hand.

"Perhaps you'd play better if you got more sleep," Margery said, her eyes sharp.

"Excuse me?" Heat flooded Caroline's cheeks.

"You're yawning. I'm thinking lack of sleep isn't helping your somewhat pedestrian abilities on the piano."

Caroline stood abruptly and picked up her music from the piano stand. "I think I'm done for now. Please feel free to continue practicing without me. I'm retiring to my room to rest and I will see you at dinner." She bowed her head slightly. "Good day."

Despite Margery's sputtering protests, she hurried toward the lifts, halting suddenly at the strident notes of Prunella Schuyler's voice expounding on the virtues of her stepson, Phillip, at Harvard Law School. She watched as Prunella and her unfortunate victim disappeared into the lift, quickly lifting her skirts to head down one flight to the Promenade Deck and her suite.

Caroline had somehow managed to fall into a restless sleep, roused by Jones in time to dress for dinner. She watched her maid carefully, to see if she might give away any signs that she might know something of the blackmail note. But the woman was efficient as always, even expressing concern over the amount of jewelry that would be left behind in the cabin after Caroline and Gilbert went to dinner, promising to stay in the room to guard it until it could be returned to the safe. She'd even suggested storing it in Gilbert's safe in the stateroom, but Caroline had declined, telling her it would be taken care of and not to worry.

Gilbert escorted her to the dining room, his conversation stilted. "You look lovely," he said, indicating the thick collar of rubies and matching earrings she'd chosen, a set she detested.

"Thank you," she said, forcing a smile, trying to think of something else to say. But they were silent on the way to the dining saloon, as if both were aware of the gaping potholes into which any words might lead them.

They had joined the Schuylers for dinner, minus Miss Smythe-Smithson. It seemed no one was eager to repeat the earlier night's disaster. Caroline glanced at her dining companions, wondering if they'd noticed how she'd been unable to eat a bite of the quarters of lamb in mint sauce or the cauliflower au gratin she'd allowed a waiter to place on her plate. Her stomach felt as knotted as a ball of twine, her nerves filling any reserve space.

"Are you feeling all right?" Gilbert's words were solicitous and without recrimination, making Caroline feel even worse. "Are you quite sure you're not . . ."

He stopped as Caroline felt the blood drain from her face. Gilbert handed her a glass of wine. "It's possible, you know. Perhaps you should see the on-board doctor?"

She shook her head, horrified to think that the one thing she and Gilbert had always wanted was now the one thing she most dreaded. What if she were expecting a child? Could she ever tell Gilbert that it might not be his? She took another sip of her wine, her next thought making her even more ill. Because even if he suspected it wasn't, Gilbert would love the child as if it were his own.

"Are you nervous, then?" he asked. "About the concert. You haven't eaten a bite." He leaned closer. "You shouldn't be nervous, you know. You're quite brilliant on the piano. I don't think I've told you that enough. How proud I am of you."

He smiled his old smile, the smile of a handsome and eager young man. The smile she'd fallen in love with, and she found herself relaxing as she returned it. "Thank you, Gil. I'm not really nervous about the concert. It's just . . ." She looked up at that moment, forgetting what she was going to say. She'd spotted Robert across the room being seated at an empty table for two. It stunned her for a moment. She'd been looking for him for an entire day without success and then, when it was too late to speak with him, there he was.

Gilbert followed her gaze, settling on Robert for a long moment before returning his attention to Caroline. "Yes?" he prompted.

She brought her attention back to her husband, trying to remember what they'd been saying. "It's just . . . I don't think I've had enough time to practice."

He placed his hand atop hers. "You'll be fine. Even the most shrill voice couldn't hide the music you can coax from a piano."

"Thank you," she said, attempting to focus on the food and the conversation at the table, painfully aware of Robert watching them from across the room. She dared not look directly at him, aware that Gilbert's attention also seemed split between their table and Robert's. When the waiter brought the desserts and offered her a *bavarois au chocolat*, she quickly shook her head, feeling as if she might be sick.

As soon as dinner was finished, everyone headed up to the Saloon Deck and the lounge for the evening's entertainment. Caroline looked through the throng of passengers for Robert, but he'd left his table by the time Gilbert held out her chair. "I asked Patrick to bring your music to the saloon," Gilbert said into her ear.

"You always think of everything, don't you?" She'd meant it as a compliment, but somehow it didn't sound that way.

He met her eyes. "I do. Always." He put his hand over hers where it rested in the crook of his arm, then led her to the lifts and into the lounge. He settled them into two wing chairs near the piano, and asked a passing waiter to bring a Scotch for him and a sherry for Caroline. She didn't want it, but figured it could help settle her nerves. She and Margery weren't scheduled to perform until after a brief intermission, which meant she had to remain seated and not appear jittery through each performance. According to the program, the entertainment included a passenger dressed as Bonnie Prince Charlie in full Highland regalia singing six Scottish songs, various poetry recitations, singing, and solos on the euphonium and mandolin.

There seemed to be more enthusiasm than talent, and Caroline would have enjoyed the performances more if she hadn't been eyeing the group for a glimpse of Robert, or a potential blackmailer, assuming she'd be able to ascertain such a thing just by looking through a crowd. Gilbert seemed nervous, too, either because he was picking up on her own uneasiness, or because there was something else. Something else, indeed. Several times when she glanced at him, she saw him watching the entrance leading to the main staircase as if he were expecting to see someone.

Exuberant applause followed an elderly man's rendition of "Down by the Old Mill Stream," owing, Caroline suspected, to the copious drinks generously being served by the waitstaff. She looked down again at her program, relieved to see they were at the intermission. She counted how many more performances until the end of the concert, the last two items being the obligatory "God Save the King" followed by "My Country, 'Tis of Thee." Same tune, two vastly different sets of lyrics. At least another hour then. She wasn't sure she could stand it.

Caroline had planned to excuse herself at the intermission and pretend to head toward the ladies' room, intent on finding Robert. But before she could stand, Captain William Turner appeared in the center of the room, resplendent in his navy dress uniform, and asked for everyone's attention.

The room quieted, faces directed toward the man who'd done little to ingratiate himself with his passengers but who still garnered the attention and respect due a captain of such a vessel as *Lusitania*.

"Ladies and gentlemen, I just want to offer a brief statement to address a few concerns you might be having. As many of you are aware, we are entering a war zone, where it is acknowledged German U-boats may be lying in wait for enemy ships. I want you all to put your worries at rest, and reassure you that we are taking every precaution on board the ship and will also soon be securely in the embrace of a Royal Navy escort." He gave the audience a perfunctory smile. "Thank you for your attention. Enjoy the rest of the concert." He walked quickly from the room, as if eager to escape further questions.

Caroline stood, desperate now to find Robert, but felt someone pulling on her elbow. She turned to find Margery Schuyler, wearing the sort of expression one might find in a painting of a martyr being burned alive. "We are first following the intermission and should settle ourselves at the piano now so we are not rushed. You might wish to do a few finger exercises to make sure they're better able to hit the correct notes."

She started to protest, but Gilbert stood, too, and greeted Margery. "You are absolutely right, Miss Schuyler. I will leave my wife in your good hands while I step out for a moment. Not to worry, I won't want to miss a minute of your performance."

He bowed to them both and was already walking toward the exit before Caroline realized she was trapped. She sat down at the piano and adjusted the bench, spreading out the music that had been placed there earlier, and began to play.

Her playing was no better than it had been at practice, distracted as she was by the blackmailer's promise to meet her after the concert, her aborted need to speak with Robert, and Gilbert's continued absence from the room. Matters certainly weren't improved by the finger jabs on the back of Caroline's shoulders each time she missed a note.

She was near weeping with relief when they got to the end of the piece, but the surprisingly loud clapping and calls for "Encore! Encore!"—surely they were only being made in jest?—thwarted her request to excuse herself. Despite having made three steps away from the piano, she was pulled back and forced to sit while Margery flipped through several pieces of sheet music that she assumed would suffice for an encore.

From the corner of her eye, Caroline spotted Patrick, his face expressionless but walking with purpose, an unmistakable telegram clasped in one hand, approaching a man hidden in a corner. She hid a gasp as Robert stepped forward to take it. But she could not hide her surprise at seeing Gilbert appear at Robert's side and the two acknowledge each other before, as if in mutual accord, they left the room together.

She tried to stand, but Margery's strong hands on her shoulders pushed her back down. "Play," the older woman hissed. And, because Caroline knew there was nothing else she could do, she played. Perfectly, this time, her brain finally being allowed to escape to the place Caroline went to in her music, a place where she could ignore the realities of her world, even when it appeared that world was about to explode as so much dry timber at the mercy of a single match.

CHAPTER 21

Tess

At Sea
Thursday, May 6, 1915

THE GERMANS WOULDN'T really send the *Lusitania* up in flames, all to keep the English from getting that formula. Would they?

And Ginny wouldn't cut Tess out, not like that.

The night was chill and Tess's hands were even colder, but she made no move to go inside. She'd escaped from supper as quickly as she could and come up here, to the Saloon Deck, where the air might be no clearer, but at least she could think in peace.

Along the sides of the boat, the crew labored silently, tacking dark cloth over porthole windows. In a matter of hours, they would be making their way into the North Sea, into the territory where U-boats lurked beneath the surface, ready to strike. A group of first-class passengers was practicing getting into the new Boddy life vests, debating over the arrangement of the straps, punctuating the exercise with the odd raucous joke. The wine had been flowing freely at the first-class tables.

By the rail, couples stood arm in arm, making the most of their second-to-last night on shipboard, lavishing whispered "darlings" on each other, the lifeboats dangling conspicuously in front of them adding piquancy to their lovemaking. Friends giggled and shared secrets. From the grand saloon came intermittent bursts of music and applause.

Tess passed by it all, past the lovers, past the confidantes, past the lighted windows that one by one were being darkened. She had never, in all her born days, felt quite so alone.

There was a whist drive in the second-class lounge, but Tess had never learned to play cards for pleasure, only for profit. She couldn't see herself sitting there, making conversation with Mary Kate, pretending an interest in the cards.

We're all we've got. That's what Ginny had told her time and again. *You and me against the world, Tennie.*

But now it was Ginny against the world and Tess on the other side of it.

Was this how Ginny had felt when Tess had told her that she wanted out?

No. No, it wasn't like that. Ginny knew that Tess would rather they stay together—whether it was keeping a tearoom or painting pictures on shells or taking a course in nursing. It was only the cheating she wanted out of. Yes, she might have proclaimed her independence to Ginny, but it had been an independence predicated on Ginny being there all the same. She had assumed that Ginny would come with her, would be part of her new life in England. If not a large part, at least a "pop in from time to time and send a postcard" part.

But Ginny, if Ginny was telling the truth, had taken on a dangerous job without telling Tess. They didn't do dangerous. That had been part of the arrangement from the beginning. Just forgery. Just substitutions. Nothing to hurt, nothing with any repercussions.

Nothing like this.

Ginny was just angry, that was all. She was lashing out. People did that when they were hurt. The idea that her sister would repudiate her, would walk away like that—no. She got heated up, Ginny. She didn't take kindly to being crossed. But they were sisters. And whatever scheme Ginny was messed up in, surely it couldn't be so bad that they couldn't get out of it with a little ingenuity. Together.

But the thoughts felt as hollow as Tess's footsteps on the boards of the deck. The Atlantic stretched out in front of her, dark and cold, with no sign of a shore. She could lie to herself all she liked; for all intents and purposes, she was alone, unsure who or what to trust. And there was no denying that Ginny was scared, scared in a way Tess had never seen before.

Scared enough to close Tess out to save her?

Alone in the dark, Tess found herself gravitating to the lights of the first-class lounge, like a child in a threadbare coat pressing her nose against an expensive toy store window, yearning for a Paris doll when she couldn't afford bread. Some clever soul had placed windows all around so that the hoi polloi might feast themselves on the sight of their betters—carefully separated by glass, of course. The stained glass skylights set into the ceiling cast a warm light down on the polished mahogany of the walls, the green marble of the great fireplace. Everything seemed to glow: satin gowns, white silk scarves, jewels, carefully washed and coiffured hair. It was an embarrassment of richness, and, at the center of it, the grand piano, where a performance was just ending.

The room exploded into applause and cries of "Encore!"

Tess knew she shouldn't, but she couldn't help it. She moved closer to the glass, a shadow among shadows. And there, sure enough, was Caroline Hochstetter sitting at the piano bench, poised and self-contained, rubies at her ears and throat, her ivory silk gown managing to be both refined and alluring. The woman standing beside her acknowledged the plaudits with a series of elaborate bows that would put any opera house diva to shame, but not Caroline Hochstetter. She inclined her head a fraction, but otherwise made no sign, accepting the accolades as her due, unworthy even of comment.

Would the moon acknowledge the frantic movements of the tides? Some people, thought Tess, were so comfortable in their own sphere they didn't even need to try. They simply exerted magnetic power. And maybe it was that lack of trying that was the most attractive thing of all.

All very well if you were born with rubies.

Tess was about to turn away—what was the point of crying over the moon?—when she noticed a minor flutter at the side of the room. Gilbert Hochstetter had risen from his seat. And so had Robert. The two men moved quietly toward the exit, not looking at each other, not talking. Tess wondered, momentarily, madly, if they meant to duel for their lady's honor, like something out of a film at the cinema.

It was an absurd thought—pistols on the Saloon Deck? vengeance at ten paces, with the loser to take to a lifeboat?—but something about the tension between the two men made Tess follow them all the same. The shadows were her friend in this. The men's eyes must still be dazzled by the bright light of the saloon. But it wasn't just that. Tess doubted they would have been aware of her if she had been wearing clogs and playing a tuba.

At first, Tess thought they meant to go into the gentlemen's smoking room. And wouldn't that be just like men, to smoke cigars over their rivalry? But they didn't. Instead, they stopped a little short of the closed doors to the gentlemen's lounge, in the lee of one of the great funnels. Tess ducked back, her dark skirt and jacket blending with the shadows.

It was Hochstetter who spoke first. "We need to speak frankly."

Robert made an involuntary movement, something like a fencer's defensive stance.

Gilbert Hochstetter's lips twisted in a grim smile. "No, not about that. It's about the plans."

Robert blinked at him. "The . . . plans?"

Tess didn't miss the way his eyes darted first one way, then another, as though checking for eavesdroppers, instantly on alert. Alert because he knew.

The plans. Tess could picture the safe in the Hochstetter suite, the waltz that was more than just a waltz.

Oh Lord. They'd been rumbled. Somehow, Hochstetter had found out. Tess's mind raced, tumbling through a dozen dodges. A diversion, perhaps. She could stumble into Hochstetter as if by accident while Robert made a run for it. But where? Where could he run? This wasn't Topeka, where they could jump on board the next train out and thumb their nose at pursuers.

Hochstetter drew a cigar from his pocket, turning it around and around in his hand. He had large hands, square and capable. "There's no need to pretend. I was told from the first that you were my contact."

Contact. Tess froze. Contact? But Robert had said—

What had he said, really? Nothing definite. Just that his father was a big mucky-muck in government. That he was meant to be doing something for the war effort.

Oh Lordy.

"You were told," said Robert, with deceptive mildness, but Tess could hear the tension beneath it. "It would have been nice if someone had informed me. I've been searching this ruddy ship for days, trying to find the man and the documents I'm meant to guard."

It took Hochstetter a moment to reply. He stared down at the cigar, unseeing. "I was meant to approach you sooner. But—"

The cigar cracked in Hochstetter's hand. He looked down at it as though he had forgotten it was there.

Robert drew in a deep breath. "But."

"Be that as it may." Hochstetter tossed the broken pieces of cigar over the rail, the movement hiding his face. Straightening, he brushed tobacco crumbs from his hands, saying briskly, "That's beside the point. It was unconscionable of me to allow my feelings to get in the way."

"Understandable," said Robert. His face was in shadow, unreadable. "Not unconscionable."

"Don't pretend to sympathize." Hochstetter's voice cracked like a lash. With an effort, he forced something resembling a smile. "Or I may have to strike you. And then we'll be back where we began."

It wasn't quite a joke and they both knew it. Tess watched as Robert weighed Hochstetter's words and then said, slowly, "Right. Do you have them?"

"I do." There was an expectant silence. Hochstetter let Robert wait before adding, "In my head."

"But I'd thought—"

"There was a coded paper?" Tess could hear the amusement in Hochstetter's voice. He was a man, she suspected, used to having the upper hand, used to doing whatever he needed to do to maintain it.

"Yes."

"That's what we wanted them to think. A nice diversion in case someone was on the trail." He didn't need to point out that Robert had fallen for it, too. Waiting for that to sink in, Hochstetter added, "And a means to smoke out any traitors along the way."

"But the formula . . ."

"I have what they call an eidetic memory. I can reproduce anything I've seen."

"I see," said Robert. "Or rather, I don't. I can't very well put you in my pocket and haul you ashore."

"If all goes well, you won't need to. I'll make my way to the Admiralty on my own. But just in case . . . These preparations give a man pause." The smoking room windows had already been veiled in dark cloth. The two men contemplated that in silence for a moment, before Mr. Hochstetter said, "Do you have something to write on? The more innocuous, the better."

Robert fumbled in his waistcoat pocket, producing a torn envelope. "Is this innocuous enough?"

"It will do." Stepping closer, Mr. Hochstetter murmured something to Robert, pausing so that Robert might transcribe it. Whatever it was, it wasn't long. Strain though she might, Tess couldn't make out much at all, and what she could sounded like gibberish.

But it seemed to make sense to Robert, who paused with his pencil suspended over the envelope. "Is that all?"

"It's enough," said Mr. Hochstetter grimly. "It's enough to have the governments of two countries in a lather. You'll keep it safe?"

Robert clapped a hand over his pocket. "It won't leave my body."

"No?" There was an ironic note in Mr. Hochstetter's voice.

Even in the dim light, Tess could see the color deepen in Robert's cheeks. "I am sorry—for any complications I caused."

"But not for loving her?" Mr. Hochstetter gave a short, mirthless laugh. He reminded Tess of a lion she had seen once in a traveling show, caged, cornered, but still king of the jungle for all that, majestic in defeat. She knew how he felt; her own heart felt rough as sandpaper, every overheard word an agony. Idiot, she told herself. *Idiot.* Of course she'd believed the worst of Robert. She'd wanted to believe the worst of Robert. Because then it meant he didn't love Caroline Hochstetter. That he might, just might, love someone as flawed and twisted as Tess, two rogues together. "It would be easier if I could blame you for that. But, you see, I love her, too. More than she'll ever know."

Quietly, Robert said, "What makes you think I don't love her more?"

"You couldn't." Mr. Hochstetter took Robert's hand in a firm grasp and gave it a brisk shake. "Good night, Mr. Langford, and good luck. I trust we shall not have to meet again."

Robert inclined his head. "Sir."

Mr. Hochstetter departed without looking back, making for the first-class lounge and his wife, leaving Robert staring after him, tobacco crumbs at his feet, and the doom of nations in his pocket.

Tess should leave now, return to second-class, pretend to play whist. Only a day and a half more. *Lie low,* her father told her. *Not your business.* Never mind that her heart was breaking in two; that was her folly. She ought to have known he was never hers to lose. She could slink off into the night, pretend none of this ever was. No kiss. No promise of dinner at the finest hotel in Liverpool.

But she couldn't. The horrible reality of it hit her, sharp as the fingernails biting into her palm. She couldn't just walk away. Because Ginny was in trouble, in danger, and Robert was the closest to a solution she had. He was working for the British. He could protect them—protect Ginny.

No matter how much it cost Tess.

"Oi, there," said Tess, stepping out of the shadows, catching Robert's arm as he made to pass.

He yanked away fast, sending her staggering back. It took him only a moment to recognize her, letting out a brief exhalation of annoyance. "What in the devil are you doing here?"

Tess straightened her jacket, wishing her hands weren't shaking so. "I need to speak with you."

Robert ran his fingers through his hair. "I seem to be in high demand this evening. Can it wait?"

"No, it can't," said Tess, and placed all of her five feet four inches in front of him. She looked up into his eyes and said, as quickly as she could, "I know that you're a spy. I know that you have plans the Germans want. And I know who their agent on the ship is."

Robert stared down at her, his face like granite. After a moment, he said, "I didn't know they served absinthe on this ship. Have a cup of tea and sleep it off."

"And wake up to the same? There's nothing to sleep off. I know, Robert. I know all of it. I'll tell you everything, but only if you'll promise amnesty." Tess gripped his lapels, her knuckles white against the dark fabric of his coat. The words tore out of her, each one an aching wound. "I—the agent is my sister. Ginny. She's been working with someone on the ship. I think it might be those Germans in the hold."

She expected incredulity, anger, even. But this was something beyond anger. There was something in Robert's face Tess had never seen before and it chilled her to the bone. He made no move to detach her fingers. "Why are you telling me this?"

"Because she's in over her head. I'm afraid for her. I'm afraid for us." It was true. It just wasn't the whole truth. Held by that unflinching gaze, Tess blurted out, "She wanted me to steal the plans for her. I'm not really from Devon. But you knew that already, didn't you? My real name is Tennessee Schaff. Tess, for short."

"German?"

"No! My parents were—but that was long before I was born. I can sing you a bit of a German lullaby, if you like, but I can't tell you what the words mean. Just the sound of them when someone sings them."

"Or so you claim."

"I'm as German as—as your royal family! I've never been to Germany. I was born in Tennessee, but we didn't stay there long. We traveled a lot. Kansas, Nebraska, Wyoming . . . Wherever we could find a town with a saloon and a susceptible population." Now that she'd started, she couldn't seem to stop. The words kept tumbling out, like water through a broken dam. "We were swindlers, petty con men. My father brewed up patent remedies. My talent is forgery. I can do you a nice da Vinci, if you like."

"I'll remember that the next time I need to redecorate the family estate," drawled Robert, and the disdain in his voice hurt worse than any number of rebukes.

Tess flushed. "It was all fairly harmless stuff. Well, not harmless. But no one got hurt. Not even from Pa's potions. Just . . ."

"Conned? Fleeced? Gammoned?"

"All of those. I can't defend what I did—what I've done. But it was—well, it wasn't like this."

Robert cut right to the point. "You say your sister wanted you to copy the plans. What plans?"

"She didn't tell me." Somehow, they had stopped being Tess and Robert. This was an interrogation now, and she was in the witness stand. "Not then, at any event. She told me that a collector wanted the Strauss waltz and would take a good copy. I was supposed to copy it out and bring it back to her. Whoever it was she was working with, they thought there was something coded into the manuscript."

"And did you? Copy it?" Tess had never imagined that Robert's voice could be so clipped, or his eyes so cold.

"No!" This had gone all wrong somehow. "At least, not the bit that looked wrong. I told you. This isn't my sort of con. And I'm getting out. I'm going straight. That's why I'm here—to start all over. Ginny knew that. I didn't think this was anything different from usual. Just a copy for a collector. One last time, that was all."

She was floundering, helpless before that unwavering gaze. This must be how a fish felt on the hook. For the first time, Tess felt sorry for the fish. And she'd swum right at it herself.

Fool, she could hear Ginny say.

Ginny was right; she couldn't be trusted to look out for herself. She should have made him promise amnesty first. But she'd liked him, trusted him.

Loved him.

Robert took a step back, folded his arms across his chest. "So our chance encounters weren't so chance. Did you drop that shoe on purpose, Cinderella?"

"It wasn't you I was following—not at first. I was following Mrs. Hochstetter. I just needed to copy that waltz, that was all. But you were always there." Tess's voice was growing hoarse. She licked her dry lips, wishing she could find a way to make him understand. "I had no idea you were involved in any of this. Until—"

"Until?"

"You asked me what I would do if someone I loved was doing something I knew was wrong. I thought you meant Ginny. I thought you knew. Or"—she barreled on—"that you were talking about yourself."

Someone she loved.

There was a horrible silence as the full impact of her words exploded between them. Tess's hands curled into fists at her sides. She felt naked, exposed. But she wasn't going to take the words back.

Slowly, Robert said, "You believed I was working for the Germans."

Tess didn't know whether to be disappointed or relieved. Her throat dry, she said, "I believed Ginny might be blackmailing you into helping her. What was I supposed to think? You said it yourself! All of that about treason—and your father in the government—and not knowing the truth about you—and the lady or the tiger—what would you have thought?" Her voice cracked with stress and frustration.

"I don't know," Robert admitted, and the anger was gone from his voice. Instead he sounded tired, deathly tired. "Any more than I know what to make of you."

Tess wanted nothing more than to bury her face in his waistcoat and weep. But why? Because he loved another woman? Because she had just betrayed her only kin?

There was no going back, no showing weakness, so she straightened her shoulders, meeting his eyes defiantly. "That's the truth, all of it. I just want this to be over, that's all." She dug her teeth into her lower lip, trying to keep her voice level. "And I want my sister safe."

Robert's face softened. Or maybe it was only the uncertain light, lending the illusion of sympathy.

Not sympathy. Pity. Tess stiffened. "I'm not the only one with problems close to home. Didn't you hear Mr. Hochstetter? The only way someone would think the code was in the manuscript is if someone on your side betrayed you."

There was an expression on Robert's face that cut her to the core. He'd gone all bones and angles, the skull showing through the skin. When he spoke, his voice chilled her to the bone. "That detail had not escaped me."

Tess backed away. "Well, then. That's about the long and short of it. So I'll leave you to it, then, shall I?" She couldn't quite resist adding, "If you hurry, you might be able to hear Mrs. Hochstetter play."

"Oh, no, you don't." Robert snagged her arm. "This sister of yours. How do I find her?"

Tess stayed stubbornly where she was. "I'm not giving her up until I have some promises from you."

"You're not in a position to make demands, Miss Schaff."

"And you're not in a position to be particular!" Tess glared up at him. "You're missing the point. Didn't you hear me? You've one of your own to look for."

Robert appeared as though it were taking every ounce of self-control not to shake her. She could feel it in the flex of his fingers. But he was a gentleman, when all was said and done. At least she hoped so. "And who is most likely to be able to tell me who that person is? Where—do—I—find—your—sister?"

"What do you plan to do with her?"

"Hang her by her toes until she talks," said Robert acerbically. "Don't look like that, blast it. I'm fresh out of thumbscrews. I'll serve her tea and politely enjoin her to share her information."

She believed that just about as much as the other. "You might try looking for someone who looks like me."

"You're going to need to do better than that."

"I—Ginny is ten years older than I am." She could give him this much. And then she'd find Ginny and tell her the game was up. No harm done. They could disappear into the sunset together. Canada, Australia, somewhere people spoke English. Let Robert track down the malefactors, clear the way for their escape. Tess cleared her throat, trying to think of details that wouldn't be details at all. "She's a few inches taller. Everyone always said we had the same nose, though. And we have the same color eyes."

"Brilliant," said Robert, in a clipped voice. "I can go passenger to passenger inspecting noses."

Tess shrugged. "What did you expect? A distinctive birthmark? We're neither of us anything special, Ginny and I."

"What you are," gritted Robert, propelling her forward, "is a thorn in my side. Come along. You're coming with me."

Tess tugged back. "What do you mean I'm coming with you? I've told you everything I know. This isn't my racket. I'm only in this by the way."

"Or so you say." Robert kept moving, his longer stride forcing her to scramble to keep up. "Do you have any idea what you've been playing at? Do you know how ruthless these people can be?"

"Which is why you need to let me go!" She had to find Ginny, warn her. She tried to yank her arm away, but he had her fast. "Where are you taking me?"

He glanced briefly down at her. His face was in shadow; all she could see was the bright flash of his eyes. "To my cabin."

Tess stumbled, her legs tangling in surprise. "Well, now. That's rather forward of you, isn't it?"

"Call it prudent," said Robert tightly. "Did you really think I would just let you go after that?"

"Why not? There isn't anywhere I can go."

"Isn't there?" Robert's grip tightened, keeping her locked against his side like a lover. Or a prisoner. "Oh, no, Miss Schaff. I'm keeping you close—until I figure out what to do with you."

CHAPTER 22

Sarah

Five Miles West of Stonehenge
May 2013

AS THE GRAY English miles flew beneath the tires of the Range Rover, I couldn't quite shake a feeling of imprisonment. Maybe it was the drizzle, which had begun to drum the windows shortly after we crossed the river Dart and never let up, creating an atmosphere of damp, leather-scented enclosure; or maybe it was the fog of gloom that surrounded Rupert.

Or maybe—just speculating, here—maybe it was John's absence. When I'd tiptoed into the folly that morning at eight o'clock, I hadn't had the heart to wake him. He lay sprawled on his stomach on the sofa, one arm curled around the pillow and one arm dangling to the floor, and even though a crack of brilliant sunlight fell on the side of his face, his expression was so slack and relaxed, so utterly void, I could have mistaken him for a college kid sleeping off a hangover. I'd smiled and thought, Some hangover.

Oh, he'd been a gentleman, all right. I mean, what else could you expect from John Langford at two o'clock in the morning? Instead of deepening that last kiss, instead of swooping me into his arms and hauling me up the stairs like Rhett Butler—cue orchestra—he'd pulled away. He'd rubbed my cheek with his thumb, very gently, and said, *Good night, Sarah*. Said it in the kind of husky, intimate baritone that makes a girl's blood simmer in her sleepy veins, I confess, but "Good night" means "Good night" in any tone of voice.

And as I stared down at him on that sofa, at his long limbs boneless with exhaustion, I'd forgiven him. Walnut sat on the rug next to John's dangling arm, wagging his tail in quiet, protective welcome. I'd rubbed his ears and told him to take care of his master for me, and I'd gone to the desk and scribbled a note.

Dear John (hmm—always wanted to write a Dear John),

Played Trumpet Voluntary but you wouldn't wake up, so I'm headed to Kew with Rupert. Rest up and have a look at what I discovered on the code front (hint—it's right underneath this page).

Be back tonight.

S.

PS Took your car—Rupert said you wouldn't mind

PPS All right, his actual words were "better to ask forgiveness than permission"

I made no mention of kisses. Not even a casual *xo* before the *S*. I mean, what did you say to John Langford the morning after kissing him for the first time? Possibly the only time, given the fact that I had only two days left in the same country with him. I turned over several phrases in my head and didn't write any of them down, because if I wrote what I wanted to write—if I wrote what I actually *thought*, God forbid, what I actually *felt*—he would probably change all the locks. To wit:

PPPS I think I may be falling in love with you

Yes, perfect. Wonderful. Just what he needed to hear right now. Just what he needed in his life at this particular moment, a fantasizing American stalker.

I turned to Rupert, who was hunched over the wheel, his gray hair now tamed by some kind of old-fashioned pomade that made the car smell faintly of medicine. "This friend of yours at the National Archives," I said. "Does he know we're coming?"

"She. Yes. I rang her up this morning." He fiddled with the windshield wipers, making them speed up briefly to monsoon strength and back down again. "Used to work in the Admiralty, so she ought to know where to find old Peregrine's remains. She's pulling everything out for us right now. Terribly efficient, Priscilla, sort of a modern Miss Moneypenny. I knew him, you know."

"Peregrine?"

"Good heavens, no. Not that old, am I? I mean Robert. I must have been about seven or eight when he died. And Grandmama. Oh, she was a laugh. Always knew how to bring him out of his funks. They adored each other. She only lasted another year or so. Smashed her heart to bits when he went."

"John told me they fell in love on board the ship."

"Yes. I gathered it was some sort of scandal, actually. They never talked about it, for one thing, and a void of information—as you must know, being experienced at research—only ever means skullduggery. For another thing, nobody ever knew where she came from to begin with."

"Your grandmother, you mean? She was American, I thought."

"Yes, American, but from where? What family? Never heard a word about her childhood, about her past. As if she came into being on the ocean itself."

"Or maybe she just didn't want anyone to find her. Shipwrecks are convenient that way. You can escape your past. Your family, your marriage. You can start your life all over again, if you want to." I glanced down at my iPhone, thinking I'd felt a vibration. But the screen was black. Nothing. No message of any kind.

"Any word from John?" asked Rupert.

"Nope."

"Ah, I expect he's still asleep. Poor lad. Been through an awful ringer."

I looked out the window, where the hills rolled by, wet and silent. "Yes. It makes me mad, when I think about it. He doesn't deserve any of it."

"Oh, but it's never a question of what we *deserve*, Sarah. It's a question of what we can bear. And John, I'm afraid, happens to be one of those chaps who can bear a great deal. So he does. My God, he bore Callie all those years, until she broke him at last."

"He doesn't like to talk about it."

"No, of course not. He still protects her, it's absurd. Oh, she's not a bad sort, not at heart. But all the women in that family require a great deal of attention, a great and constant amount of fuss and admiration—"

"High-maintenance?"

"Is that the current term? Well, Callie needed it more than all of them. Instead of going to university, she went up to London and started modeling and—oh, what's the word—'hostessing,' I think they call it. A pleasant little word; I'm not entirely sure what it actually means. But you understand me. Then she discovered cocaine and that was it, I'm afraid. There was nothing he could do for her. He'd had a stint in the army after university, you know, and when he came back from Afghanistan, she simply latched on to him, the way the weak latch on to the strong. He was a bit of a hero, some sort of medal—"

"It wasn't some sort of medal," I said. "It was the MC."

"The MC, then." Rupert waved his hand. "Whatever it was, it was catnip to Callie. They were married straightaway—he's that sort of chap—and for a short while all was well. She helped him win his seat—she's got a knack for publicity, I'll say that—but once he settled into Parliament, devoted himself to politics, she got bored again. Took up her old friends, her old habits, except this time even worse than before."

"What about kids?" I said. "Didn't they want to start a family?"

"Oh, I expect John wants children. I don't know about Callie. One doesn't inquire. In any event, it's just as well they didn't. Something happened, I don't know what, and he moved out. Started proceedings, on the hush. The next thing you know, she's photographed with that Russian blackguard at One Hyde Park—"

"And throws John under the bus."

"More or less. It will all blow over, however. The inquiry's in a month or two, and once it's established that they were living apart, separate lives, divorce proceedings already begun, no reasonable conflict of interest, he'll be back in good graces."

"Do you really think so?"

Rupert nodded vigorously. "Haven't you been reading the papers? His constituents are outraged. He's a popular fellow, you know. Oh, he'll be back. He's a Langford, after all."

"Yes, he's a Langford." My phone vibrated, this time for certain, and my pulse jumped in response. I looked down.

Srry ur leavin so soon. I can come down to u. Need ur help on a littl project. Lunch tmrrw? JH

"John?" Rupert asked.

I sighed. "No. Just this old grad school friend of mine, wanting to meet up. He's visiting London right now."

"*He*, is it?"

"Oh, you know. He's probably just writing a book and wants me to help him find an agent or something."

"Ah, yes. *Small Potatoes*. Nifty title, that. John told me something about it last night. I'm terribly impressed. An authoress in our midst."

"Thanks. But nobody says 'authoress' anymore, just so you know. It's the kind of word that can get you banned from Twitter."

"Ha! I rather fancy I'd find that an honor, being banned from twittering, or whatever they call it. Unless you're actually offended, in which case I beg your pardon. An old has-been like me finds it hard to keep up with the niceties."

"Don't worry, I'm a New Yorker. If you want to offend me, you'll have to bring your A game."

"Oh," he said, a little blank. "Yes, of course. In any case, well done. I look forward to reading your work."

I laughed. "Are you sure about that? I'm trying to prove that your grandfather's a traitor, after all."

"'Trying' being the operative word. Well, time will tell. Time and old Sir Peregrine's papers, I hope. Poor chap. Bad enough he should kill himself because he thought his only remaining son had drowned. If he killed himself because he thought his only remaining son had betrayed his country—"

"Wait, is *that* what you think?" I exclaimed.

"I think it makes a great deal more sense than the former explanation. The one we've always been told. You must understand, Sir Peregrine was a Victorian. Family honor far more important than mere personal feeling. Nor was he particularly enamored of Robert to begin with. You've heard about the older brother, I'm sure."

"The one who drowned. And Peregrine blamed Robert."

"Yes. So I always thought it strange he'd go mad with grief like that, without even waiting to find out whether Robert had actually survived."

"Maybe he got a false report?"

"Maybe. Or perhaps he received a report of another kind entirely." Rupert turned briefly to me and winked, just as my phone buzzed again. "What? Aren't you going to look?"

"Eh."

"My dear girl, can't you see he's besotted? He spent four hours driving through a proper rainstorm last night, just in order to get back to Devonshire."

"For your sake."

"*My* sake?" Rupert laughed out loud, a beautifully hearty British laugh. "Believe me, Sarah, the heartsick uncle was merely a convenient excuse. A fact I realized by the time we crossed the M25, when he nearly missed the junction because he was going on about your cleverness in discovering the existence of some poor chap's Irish bastard in 1871."

"*That* was not clever. It was just that no one had ever looked before."

But I glanced down anyway. The screen had gone black again, but when I pressed the home button the message alert lit before me.

The penalty for auto theft is damned severe. Don't expect mercy.

I tapped a reply.

Just remember what happened to Jabba.

"Everything all right?" asked Rupert.

I leaned my head back against the seat and closed my eyes. "Oh, you know," I said. "The usual."

I'd first visited the National Archives several years ago, while I was researching *Small Potatoes*, and I felt the same sense of crushing disappointment now as I did then. For some reason, I still harbored an irrational expectation that the home of the Domesday Book would present a more dignified face to the world than the cheap architectural squalor of a postwar office block.

Rupert must have felt my sigh. Felt it, and understood its reason. He glanced up from under the dripping edge of the umbrella and said, "Rather uninspired, isn't it?"

"If by 'uninspired' you mean 'ugly,' then yes."

"It's not the outside of the building that matters, remember."

"Yeah, well, *as* I remember, the inside's pretty ugly, too. And that watercooler in the cafeteria is possessed by demons."

"Then I suppose it's fortunate we'll be working inside the comparative luxury of Priscilla's private office." Rupert jumped nimbly over a puddle.

"Priscilla," I said. "Tell me about this Priscilla."

Priscilla, it turned out, was waiting for us in the lobby: a large, handsome woman with sharp eyes and a mane of glossy supermodel hair the color of hazelnuts, wearing a leopard-print ponte dress I recognized from a recent Boden catalog. "Rupert!" she exclaimed, throwing her arms around his shoulders and kissing both cheeks. "You bloody bounder! You haven't been to see me in ages."

"And you've only gotten younger, my dear. How's that delicious crumpet of yours? The young, strapping fellow, what's his name?"

"Married, it turns out. How's Nigel?"

"He's well."

She narrowed her eyes. "You haven't rowed again, have you?"

"Oh, darling. It's a frightfully long story. We'll have a nice boozy dinner soon, I promise, just like old times, but in the meantime poor Sarah here—"

"Oh! I'm so sorry. Sarah . . . Blake, isn't it? The potato book? Adored it, by the way." She held out a long-fingered hand. "Priscilla Smythe-Bowman. I'll sign you in."

She turned away and clattered to the visitors' log atop a pair of nude patent leather heels at least four inches high. I leaned in to Rupert. "You're the gay best friend, aren't you? A walking cliché."

"Can I help it if the young ladies seek me out in droves? I happen to be a good listener, Sarah, and an excellent judge of shoes. If more men were like me, the divorce lawyers would go straight out of business."

Priscilla turned and waved us to the security gates. Up we went in the anodyne elevator, painted that particular color of industrial white that makes you feel empty inside. The air smelled of old carpet and cheap supermarket coffee. Rupert and Priscilla were chattering again about people I didn't know and love affairs gone wrong, and as I stared at the floor numbers above me, ascending with painful turpitude, something clicked softly in the back of my head, like a thumb trying to ignite a butane lighter. Something about fathers and sons and spies. Secret papers.

I turned to Rupert and interrupted. "Which book was it? The one where the spy discovers his father's also a secret agent?"

"What, what? A book?"

"Robert's book. I can't remember the title. One of his later ones."

The bell dinged, the doors jolted open.

"Haven't the foggiest," said Rupert, as we stepped into a rat maze of gray cubicles. "I'm afraid I never read them."

From Rupert's hasty description outside the National Archives building, I hadn't quite understood what position Priscilla actually held there. I still didn't, but whatever it was, she had somehow managed to acquire a private office with a partial view of the Thames from its dirty window, and a cluttered, maximalist décor that suggested she'd occupied it for some time. "I pulled the Langford papers for the years 1913 to 1915," she said, directing us to the lacquered coffee table before the sofa. "It's all been declassified, so take your time. Want me to send Tanya for coffee? I've got my own Keurig. Status has its privileges."

"Yes, please!" I shouted, while Rupert shuddered and refused.

Priscilla disappeared out the door, and I settled myself on the sofa and reached for the file box.

"What about it, though?" Rupert sank into the cushion next to me. "Robert's book?"

"Oh, it's probably nothing. Overanalyzing. You know how it is with books. We spend semesters pondering the meaning of the blue paint on the character's bedroom wall, and sometimes it's just blue paint, you know?"

"But sometimes not."

"Anyway, I'd have to go back and look it up. I pretty much chain-read them when I started the project, so it's kind of blurry. I can't even remember which book I'm thinking of."

"John will know. He's read them all. You should type him."

"You mean text him?"

"Don't be cheeky."

I pulled out my phone and sent a quick message.

Just arrived TNA. Which book of Robert's had the father and son spy plot?

Next to me, Rupert lifted a stack of old brown portfolios from the file box marked *1914*. "Why don't you start with 1915?" he said. "We'll finish sooner."

"There's no hurry."

"My dear Sarah," he said, opening the first portfolio, "I have the distinct impression that if I fail to return both John's car and his *resident historian* before nightfall, I shall never more be welcome on his doorstep. Which gives us"—he checked his watch—"approximately four hours to work."

Three and a half hours later, I leaned my elbows on the edge of the coffee table and frowned at the white cardboard face of the file box. "Rupert," I said. "Rupert!"

There was a startled snort from the body lying next to me on the sofa, followed by a comfortable snore. Rupert's head lay on the sofa arm, cradled by a tweedy elbow, and his hair fell in neat, shiny pieces over his forehead.

"Something wrong?" asked Priscilla, who was just crossing the threshold. She bore a fresh cup of coffee, an iPhone, and an expression of deep concentration, like she'd just come out of a meeting.

"Are you sure these are all the files?" I tapped the edge of the file box. "All the Langford files from 1915?"

She looked up from her phone and set the coffee cup on the corner of her desk. "All we've got. Untouched, too. Nobody's signed them out since they were first moved here from the Admiralty offices."

"And when was that?"

"I can't remember. A long time ago. Why? Is something missing?"

I picked up the last brown portfolio. It crackled under my fingers, releasing the familiar smell of old paper. "You might say that. The archive basically stops short in the middle of April."

"You mean April of 1915? No papers at all?"

"Yes. There's nothing at all here that accounts for the month before the *Lusitania* went down. Which is, as far as we're concerned, the most important part."

"Let me see that." Priscilla reached for the portfolio and slid the papers out. She thumbed through them carefully, scanned each typewritten page with the sharp, experienced gaze of someone who scanned pages for a living. Next to me, Rupert stirred and lifted his head.

"Something wrong?" he asked.

Priscilla reached the last page and looked up. Met my gaze and raised one eyebrow. "Uh oh," she said.

"Uh oh, what?" asked Rupert.

My phone buzzed. I picked it up and read the message, John's reply.

That would be Night Train to Berlin, 1948.

"Uh oh, someone's been up to no good," I said. Three dots appeared on the message screen, pulsing softly.

"What do you mean?" Rupert said.

Priscilla handed him the papers. "Seems we have a gap in the documents for the weeks preceding Langford's death."

"Good God."

He shuffled through the stack while I stared at my screen, counting the beats of those dots. *Night Train to Berlin*. Of course. Father and son. Both of them working for British intelligence during the thirties, except different departments, neither one knowing what the other was doing, until—until what?

A train crash. Sabotage. The son—the son was on the train, seducing a married woman whose husband had vital information—

"You're right," said Rupert, in an astonished voice. "My God. It's all missing. Just ends right here with this damned memorandum on April seventeenth. Are you quite sure they haven't been misfiled elsewhere?"

"I looked through every portfolio," I said. "Three times."

"Then who the devil's removed them? The Admiralty?"

"No way of knowing, I'm afraid," said Priscilla. "As I said, according to our records, you're the first researcher to have a crack at these. Of course, that doesn't mean nobody *has* had a crack at them. Just that nobody's done it officially."

"Which could be anyone," I said. "Anyone wanting to blot this out, for whatever reason."

Priscilla folded her arms. "What about his personal papers?"

"At the Bodleian," said Robert.

"Well, I suppose you might want to have a look there, if you can. They might have been mixed up, if he brought his work home with him. Which he wasn't *supposed* to do, of course, but in practice . . ." She shrugged her shoulders.

"Except he did the deed in his office," said Rupert. "He'd spent the night there. Shot himself sometime in the late afternoon of May the seventh. His secretary discovered him at his desk at ten past five, still bleeding."

The phone buzzed again.

Brilliant cipher translation, Bond. Still trying to make sense of it. Chemical reaction obvs but haven't been able to discover what. Carbon, iron. Metal of some kind?

I bent down, reached into my laptop bag, and pulled out my notebook. "I don't suppose you happen to have a chemistry background, do you, Priscilla?"

"Not much, I'm afraid," she said. "But I happen to know a chap who does."

I called John as soon as we were clear of the M25. The drizzle had diminished into a fine mist, and the motorway was a sea of red brake lights.

"Hello, Sarah," he said. "How's my car?"

"Your car's lovely, and so are you for letting us take it."

"I didn't exactly have a choice, did I?"

"I know, I know. I'm sorry. Filled with remorse. Rupert's sorry, too. Right, Rupert?"

"Sorry!" Rupert called out.

"Just listen, though. That chemical formula, whatever-it-is? It's the recipe, basically, for a metal, a new kind of alloy made with molybdenum that would have been stronger and more wear-resistant than any other steel alloy at the time."

"Fascinating," John said, in a strange, subdued voice. Sort of a weary voice, not at all like he sounded last night. "I was actually about to ring you up myself."

"Is something wrong? You sound upset."

"Not upset, exactly."

"Are you angry about the car? I really am—okay, now I feel terrible. But you were sleeping so soundly, I just couldn't bear to wake you, and we really needed to make this trip. I'll make it up to you, I promise."

"It's not the damned car, Sarah. It's the telegram."

I glanced at Rupert, who hunched back over the wheel in his familiar position, intent on the road. The lines on his forehead were deep and old, and his hair had begun to frizz from its retro prison of pomade.

"Which telegram?" I said.

"The one *inside* the envelope, Sarah. We were so bloody obsessed with the code written on the envelope, we overlooked the obvious. The telegram inside it." He paused, and his voice dropped almost to a whisper. "The one Robert never opened."

CHAPTER 23

Caroline

At Sea
Thursday, May 6, 1915

A TELEGRAM? CAROLINE HAD no recollection of any of the notes she had just played on the piano, her mind completely focused on the scene she'd witnessed—Robert receiving a telegram and then leaving the room with Gilbert. She lifted her hands from the keyboard, the notes quickly evaporating over the gathered audience. Now that it was over all she could think about was finding Robert and Gilbert, but before she could gracefully exit the piano bench, she was distracted by an awful noise. It was as if the heavens above had opened and all the cherubim and seraphim painted on the ceiling above were applauding as loudly as they could, the sound nearly deafening as more and more people shouted, "Encore! Encore!"

Margery bowed so low for a moment Caroline thought the King of England must have entered the room, and then she decided Margery must pretend to be an opera diva quite a bit in the privacy of her own room. She was really that good at it—the bowing, not the singing.

When Margery once more leaned over Caroline's shoulder to find yet another encore piece, Caroline saw her chance to escape and quickly slid from the piano bench, the ivory silk of her gown facilitating the movement.

"Mrs. Hochstetter, they're asking for another encore. . . ."

Although Margery's insistence on keeping her at the piano did make Caroline question the other woman's motives. Was she truly that much of a sadist? Caroline ignored the grating voice while making her way as quickly as she could out of the room, her progress halted by the many people who wanted to stop her and compliment her on the performance. She smiled and smiled, her cheeks beginning to hurt, wondering if she'd ever make it to the exit.

She made it to the place where she'd last seen Robert and Gilbert, the exit to the hallway leading into the saloon smoking room. She looked back into the lounge, intent on finding Patrick in the hopes of sending him into the smoking room to search for her husband. And her lover. *What could they be saying to each other?* Robert was an English gentleman, which meant he most likely hunted and knew how to shoot. Wouldn't he? She was quite sure that Gilbert had never held a gun in his life.

She spotted Margery coming toward her, her thin lips pressed together and her face a mottled red. Caroline considered her possible escape routes, quite certain that Margery would have no compunction at running after her to discuss her disappointment in Caroline's performance and her willful disobedience regarding another encore.

Realizing she had no alternative, Caroline made an about-face and entered the gentlemen's smoking room, rather certain that Margery wouldn't follow here in there. Thankfully, due to the concert, it was mostly empty. Several men looked at her with surprise, and one elderly gentleman, his white moustache oiled to a frightening point, regarded her as one might regard a rat in one's soup bowl.

Ignoring the stares and doing her best to pretend that she had no idea that she wasn't supposed to be there, Caroline quickly walked the width of the room examining every spot where two men could go to have a discussion. A private one, she hoped.

She made it to the hallway by the smoking room bar without spotting them, then continued into the Verandah Café, which was completely deserted. No sign of Robert or Gilbert. She grasped the back of a chair, suddenly unsteady on her feet and unsure if it was the roiling sea beneath her or the uncertainties in her life that threatened her equilibrium.

Unwilling to go back through the smoking room and desperate for fresh air, she headed to the Saloon Promenade, eagerly searching for the two men, ducking into shadows just in case Margery was as determined to find Caroline.

In the pitch dark it took Caroline a moment to realize that all the windows had been covered with black cloths to block the light and hopefully disguise the large ship on the open ocean from unwanted attention. A chill ran through her that had nothing to do with the evening air. Her mother would have said it was just someone walking over her grave. And for a brief moment, while staring out at the inky black of the ocean, she believed it to be true.

Being very careful not to trip in the darkness, she made her way around the promenade, finally ending up at the spot where she'd started. She pressed her fingers against her mouth, afraid she might lose what little food she'd managed to eat, the worry and fear over what Robert and Gilbert were saying to each other making her physically ill.

Knowing any decision was better than none, she headed down the promenade, bypassing the lounge, where she could hear someone playing a ragtime piece on the piano. She recognized it as the "Maple Leaf Rag"—a song forbidden by her mother, which of course made it irresistible to Caroline—and she wondered if the audience had become so drunk they weren't protesting the scandalous music. Not that Caroline had ever understood why everyone considered it so scandalous.

She made her way to the main staircase and, after making sure she didn't see Margery or anyone else she recognized, headed toward her suite. She paused for a moment in front of it, then continued walking. She'd already decided that she'd try and find Robert first.

She turned a corner and stopped in front of room B-38. It was the right one, of course. She'd been in it only that once, but it wasn't a visit she'd likely ever forget. Gently, she tapped on the door. "Robert? Are you in there? It's me. Caroline."

She thought she heard movement inside, but when the door didn't open, she knocked again. Keeping her voice as quiet as she could, she said, "Please, Robert. Open the door. I need to speak with you."

Again, the slight sound of something—someone—moving inside the cabin. What if he were hurt? What if Gilbert had done something to him?

"I'm coming in," she said, hearing the panic in her voice. She turned the knob, and found it locked.

"May I be of assistance, Mrs. Hochstetter?"

Caroline jerked back at the soft lilting voice of Patrick Houlihan, relieved to see an open expression without prejudice or accusation. Something she was sure he'd perfected after years of being a steward and for which she was extremely grateful. He knew her shameful secret, but would maintain a false ignorance as long as she did. He always seemed to be showing up right when she needed him, and she was too happy to see him at that moment to question it.

"Yes, thank you. I'm afraid I've . . . lost a sheet of piano music I would like to perform for the concert tonight."

It was a terribly constructed lie that a small child could see through. Yet there wasn't even a twinkle in Patrick's eyes.

"And you believe it might be found in Mr. Langford's room."

She nodded vigorously, as if to add veracity to her statement. "And if it's not, I think I'll wait for him here so I can ask him himself when he returns." Whatever was behind the door, she didn't want Patrick to see before she could weigh the situation herself.

"Of course," he said, pulling out a key ring upon which she assumed was a skeleton key for the cabins on B-deck. "In that case, I will be happy to assist. The show must go on, mustn't it?"

"Yes," she agreed. "The show must go on."

Patrick unlocked the door, but she reached for the handle before he could turn it. "I'll take it from here. I don't wish to take up any more of your time. Thank you, Patrick."

He smiled and this time she was quite sure his Irish eyes were twinkling. "If I see Mr. Langford, I shall be sure to let him know that you're in his room looking for your lost music." With a brief nod of his head, he left. She felt the color rise in her cheeks as she watched him walk away, waiting until he'd disappeared around a corner before turning the knob.

Before she could open the door it was flung open, the knob snatched out of her hand. She looked up, expecting to see Robert, and instead found herself staring into the face of a girl with tousled dark blond hair who looked as surprised to see Caroline as Caroline was to see her. The girl was pretty, she supposed, if one liked that sort of fresh-scrubbed look of a milkmaid, her brown eyes snapping with anger.

"Pardon me," Caroline said, her manners reacting before the rest of her could. As if she should be apologizing to this *person* in Robert's cabin. A *girl*. Actually, a *woman*, Caroline realized with some surprise. A woman around the same age as herself. They took each other's measure, and Caroline had the odd impression that they'd met before, although she couldn't place exactly where. Looking at the woman's rosy cheeks and bright open stare, not to mention the rough material of her cheap clothing, it was apparent they didn't run in the same social circles. Still . . .

"You're Caroline Hochstetter," the woman said, her voice distinctly American.

It wasn't the manner in which Caroline was accustomed to being addressed. "I'm afraid I'm at a disadvantage," she said, copying Margery Schuyler's grating haughtiness, and groaned internally at the accuracy of the imitation.

"I'm Tess . . . er . . . Fairweather."

"Are you the maid?" She hadn't meant for it to be insulting, but she couldn't imagine why this woman was in Robert's cabin.

"Do I look like a maid? Never mind." Tess flushed, her eyes bright with anger. "Don't answer that. I presume you're looking for Robert."

Robert? He was on a first-name basis with this person? Caroline stared at the young woman for a long moment, then glanced behind her into the cabin. "Is Mr. Langford here?" As much as she wanted to see Robert, she didn't want Tess's answer to be yes.

"No, he's not here," Tess said, trying to get past Caroline, her tone of voice one that would have made Margery proud.

Caroline blocked her exit. "Then why, pray tell, are you in his cabin?"

The woman drew back, and Caroline braced herself for what Tess would say. But whatever it was she was preparing herself to hear, it wasn't what flew from Tess's mouth.

"Robert and I are not lovers, if that's what you're thinking. As to why I'm in his cabin, ask your husband."

The words caught Caroline off-guard so that she barely noticed the woman moving past her and into the passageway. She didn't even jerk away when Tess placed a hand on her arm. "Be careful who you trust."

Their eyes met briefly before Tess dropped her hand and began walking away. A thousand questions swirled in Caroline's head, none of them coherent or logical, and none of them moving past her tongue. "Wait!" she called after her.

Tess turned.

"Do you mean Robert? I'm afraid I don't understand."

Tess seemed to consider Caroline's words a moment before replying. "Be kind to him." The woman turned back around and continued walking.

Caroline paced the small cabin while she waited for Robert to return, surprised her footsteps hadn't left a threadbare mark in the rug. She'd decided waiting in his cabin while Patrick searched for him would increase her chances of speaking with him before she had to face Gilbert.

She sat down on a chair, then stood to pace again, then sat down on the bed momentarily before jerking herself back to a stand. It wouldn't do to have Robert walk into his cabin and find her sitting on his bed. She began pacing again. The time spent waiting forced her to think, to examine the two paths her life could take once she disembarked. A life with Gilbert, perhaps changed from what she knew if he'd been serious about his plans for their future lives together. Or a life with Robert. Even if she would have to endure the social condemnation of a divorce, she couldn't deny the rush of exhilaration, of sheer *joy* she felt at the mere thought of a life with him. Or the heat that pushed the blood through her veins at the image of waking up next to Robert Langford every morning for the rest of her life.

She loved Gilbert. She knew this with the same certainty that she knew the sun would rise in the east the following morning. Yet she also loved Robert with the same conviction. Could a heart be split in half, each part loving a completely different person? And if that were true, how could she choose without the other half shriveling like a rose left too long on the vine? It might as well be a choice of the sun or the moon, except she understood that her days would be dark and her nights empty without both.

The door opened and suddenly Robert was there, staring at her with the same surprise Tess had just an hour before. Caroline faced him but didn't move, knowing she needed answers first, and if she touched him, just once, she would be lost and the answers would no longer matter.

"Who is Tess Fairweather?" Caroline asked, proud that she'd kept her voice steady.

He closed the door behind him, glancing around the cabin. "Where is she?"

His concern over Tess's absence sent a sharp stab of what felt a lot like jealousy poking Caroline in the ribs. "She left, that's all I know. She wouldn't answer my questions, instead telling me that I should ask my husband." Caroline heard her voice rise, like a woman on the threshold of hysteria. She took in a deep breath. "I saw you. With Gilbert. And I would like . . . I demand to know what is going on."

He made a move toward her, but she stepped back, her legs against the edge of the bed. Robert dropped his hands to his sides. "Tess was here in my cabin as my prisoner—nothing else. I need to question her about her sister, another passenger on board this ship. Her sister is a German spy."

For the second time that day, Caroline struggled to find the words needed to voice a question, almost as if everybody were suddenly speaking a foreign language she couldn't translate. "But why are you . . . ?" She stopped, looked up at him imploringly.

"I work for British naval intelligence. I was on a mission, which is now complete. Tess and her sister are merely distractions."

"A mission?" She thought for a moment, remembering Patrick with the telegram, giving it to Robert, and then him leaving the lounge with Gilbert. "But I saw you with my husband, and I knew you were with him for a long while because I went to look for you, as I imagined the worst. Is he involved in your . . . mission?"

"I'm not at liberty to tell you. But it's all over now." He started to lift an arm toward her, but dropped it quickly.

"Not at liberty . . ." She closed her eyes, swallowing her anger at yet again being left in the dark about what was really going on. Her anger focused on Gilbert, for not trusting her with the truth. She was his *wife*. "Was it all about business, then? Or was there something more?"

His eyes darkened, studying her closely as he spoke, and for a moment she thought he wouldn't tell her what it was that haunted his face. "There was more. He told me . . ." A pained expression crossed his face. "He told me . . ." When Robert moved toward her, she didn't put a hand out to stop him, allowing his fingers to land lightly on her shoulders.

"What did he tell you?" Caroline kept her gaze down, away from those searching eyes, focusing instead on the mother-of-pearl stud in the middle of his stiff white shirt.

With a gentle finger, Robert lifted her chin so that their eyes met. "He told me that he loved you more than I ever could. But I know that couldn't be true." He bent his head to kiss her but stopped, his lips hovering over hers, and she felt herself relax. The blackmailer, whoever he or she was, had nothing to hold over her anymore. At another time and place, she might have found it odd that relief was the only emotion she felt at knowing Gilbert was aware of her infidelity.

Robert continued, "I want you, Caroline. Not just here, and now. Forever." He closed his eyes and pressed his forehead against hers, his warm breath caressing her cheeks. "I can't promise you the luxuries to which you've become accustomed, but I can promise you that we won't starve. And that I will love you with everything I have until the day I die." He took a deep breath. "But I can't keep doing this if I don't believe you feel the same way. It's wrong, if you don't. Wrong for all of us."

She knew he meant Gilbert, too, and was grateful he hadn't said the name out loud. "But I can't let you go," she whispered. She closed her eyes, too, afraid of what she might see in his. Afraid she might see him pulling away.

"Then you need to choose," he said quietly, keeping his lips separated from hers still, killing her by degree.

She licked her lips, then opened her eyes. "Give me one more day. Please. I'll let you know before we leave this ship. I just need one more day."

"All right," he said, moving closer. With a voice barely louder than a whisper, he said, "But until then, what should we do?"

Caroline didn't hesitate. "This." She placed her hands behind his head and drew him toward her, his lips finally against hers, his strong, solid body fitting into hers as if they'd been made that way. She fell backward onto the bed with him, as if it were the most natural thing in the world, with no remorse or regret or any of those things she should be feeling but couldn't while she was in Robert's arms.

They took their time disrobing, exploring each other's bodies as if it were the first time. Or the last. Robert made love to her tenderly, each touch, each kiss like a branding. *You are mine*, they seemed to say. She allowed herself to forget who she was or where she was, giving in instead to the slow, steady rhythm of their lovemaking, yet all the time aware of the brittle space around her heart that threatened to shatter if she made herself remember.

Afterward, they fell asleep in each other's arms, their legs entangled so that it was difficult to tell where he ended and she began. It was there, when she awakened in the small hours of the night, that she remembered. Remembered the one word she'd said as she'd hovered between the twilight world of sleep and wakefulness, pressed against the body of her lover. *Gilbert*.

Caroline jerked fully awake, praying it had been a dream. She listened to Robert's steady breathing, assuring her he was still asleep. After quickly disentangling herself, she slipped from the bed and dressed as well as she could in the dark. She crept from the room, offering up a silent prayer that no one else would be up and about at this hour. And that Jones would have thought to leave the door to Caroline's bedroom unlocked so that she could enter it from the hallway, and almost wept with relief when she discovered that it was.

The small lamp by the bed was on, allowing Caroline to see her turned-down bedclothes and her nightgown placed carefully on the bottom of the bed. She closed the door quietly behind her and had just turned toward her washbasin when a voice called to her from a darkened corner of the room.

"Mrs. Hochstetter."

Caroline jerked toward the sound of the voice, her hand pressed against her heart. "Jones. You startled me."

"I'm sorry, ma'am. I've been waiting for you."

"Is everything all right? Is Gilbert . . . ?"

"He's not in his rooms. But that Irish steward, Patrick, stopped by an hour ago with a message from your husband. There is a well-known collector on board, a Mr. Charles Lauriet, and Mr. Hochstetter wants to show him the manuscript. Patrick was made to understand that you'd know which one he was referring to."

"Can't this wait until morning? It's quite late."

"I'm afraid there's some urgency, and it's already been an hour. Patrick said that he'd tell Mr. Hochstetter that he saw you with the Schuylers on the Saloon Promenade, to explain your absence. But he made it clear that Mr. Hochstetter needed the manuscript as soon as possible."

Caroline wrinkled her brow, too tired to attempt to make sense of any of it. "Yes. Of course. Thank you." She was more embarrassed than thankful at the knowledge that two more people were being duplicitous because of her. And even if Gilbert knew the truth of where she'd been, she found herself grateful that at least in this regard they could both pretend.

She went into the parlor of their suite and knelt in front of the small safe. She knew the combination—it was the same combination as the one at their house in New York. Gilbert, for all of his intelligence, said he wasn't capable of remembering more than one combination.

With the dim light of a table lamp, Caroline turned the numbers left and right, waiting for the quiet *click* before spinning the knob and opening the door. As Gilbert had told her, the safe was crammed with folders stuffed with papers, yet on top, unprotected and quite in the open, was the unpublished Strauss waltz.

She gingerly picked it up, then handed it to Jones, almost reluctant to let it pass from her hands. "Please be careful with this. It's quite valuable and very rare."

Jones inclined her head. "I will treat it as if it were mine."

"I can get myself ready for bed," Caroline said. "Please, go find Patrick and make sure Mr. Hochstetter gets that as soon as possible."

"Yes, ma'am. Good night."

"Good night, Jones."

She watched as the maid headed toward the main door of their suite, then waited until she heard the door close behind her. Caroline stood in the quiet, listening to the dull throb and hum of the distant engines, going over the events of the evening, wondering what mission Gilbert and Robert might be involved in together, realizing all the things she didn't understand, including what was in her own heart.

Slowly, she walked to her bedroom and got dressed for bed, then lay awake for a long time waiting to hear Gilbert return. She tossed and turned, words like vultures picking at her brain as she remembered what Robert had told her. *He told me that he loves you more than I ever could.*

She turned to her other side, desperate to find a way to escape her thoughts. When she finally fell asleep, she dreamed she was running through fog so thick she couldn't see her hand in front of her, nor had she any knowledge as to from what or to whom she was running.

CHAPTER 24

Tess

At Sea
Friday, May 7, 1915

TESS DIDN'T RUN. She walked. Quickly.

Down the corridor, up a flight of stairs, down another corridor, not going anywhere in particular, just away. Away before Robert could find her. On deck, the fog was thick enough to lose herself, but the cold drove her back inside, searching for a place to hide. She knew she couldn't hide for long, not even on a ship the size of the *Lusitania*. She needed a respite, that was all. Time to think. Time to plan.

While Robert was otherwise occupied with Caroline Hochstetter.

Tess pushed aside the image of Caroline Hochstetter, all rubies and disdain. Tess should be grateful to her, for giving Tess a breather. She could make this right somehow, she knew she could. But only if she wasn't locked up tight in Robert Langford's cabin.

Whatever Robert might think, Ginny wasn't the problem. Well, maybe she was, but she was Tess's problem, not Robert's. The real danger wasn't Ginny; it was whoever Ginny was working for, whoever it was who was making Ginny glance over her shoulder and start at shadows.

A day and a half still until Liverpool, Tess reminded herself. And, more important, Ginny didn't have the manuscript yet. These people Ginny was working with, they wouldn't do anything until they had their prize in their hands. Ginny should be safe . . . for now.

It was late, late enough that the saloons had gone quiet, the concert over, the whist drive done. Tess found an abandoned deck chair and plopped down in it, trying to make her brain slow down and concentrate, to work out the problem as if it were one of her drawings, line by line, each unremarkable on its own, but adding up to a coherent picture. The Germans in the brig might have been part of it in the beginning—who knew how many agents were planted on the ship?—but, in retrospect, they couldn't be Ginny's contact. Not with Ginny jumping like a cat on a train track every time someone came up to her.

Tess gnawed on one knuckle, ignoring the chill that crept through her clothes, straight down to her bones. It had to be someone who wasn't stuck behind bars, someone who had the run of the ship, with access to passengers and, more important, the Marconi machine.

"Miss Fairweather?"

Once she'd got her breathing under control, Tess recognized the Irish voice. "Patrick," she said. "I didn't see you there."

It felt strange to be calling him by his first name, as Robert did, as if she were a lady and he her servant, but she realized she didn't know his last name. He was always just Patrick.

Patrick, who was always there.

Patrick, who could go anywhere he liked.

Patrick, who had access to everything. Who had Robert's trust.

In the fog, his face seemed distorted, uncanny. Sinister. Slowly, Tess said, "You're working late tonight."

"There's always a lot to do in the last days," said the steward. Was it Tess's imagination, or was there a double meaning to that? "You shouldn't be out here, miss. You'll catch your death."

"We don't catch death, death catches us. Wouldn't you say, Patrick?"

"I wouldn't know, miss." A sudden grin lighted his tired face. "Although my missus has made me promise that if there's some time before the next voyage, I'll learn how to swim. She doesn't want the sea catching me. I've told her the ship's safe as houses, but . . ."

Tess wrapped her arms about her chest. "Houses burn. And ships sink. What do you think, Patrick? Everyone's talking about U-boats. Are we safe?"

"I think, miss," said Patrick carefully, "that right now you're in more danger from the night air than the Germans. Shall I escort you back to your cabin?"

There was nothing in his face to give any clue to his emotions, or his intentions. Three days ago, Tess might have assumed it was a kindness, but not now. *Be careful who you trust*, she had told Caroline Hochstetter.

Flippantly, she said, "Don't you have other duties? You shouldn't be wasting your time on lowly second-class passengers."

"Every passenger is my duty, miss."

That, Tess knew, wasn't the least bit true. *Did Robert send you after me?* she wanted to ask. *Are you working with Robert or against him?*

True blue, Robert had called Patrick, but what did he know about him, really? Just that Patrick remembered how he took his tea and could be trusted to pass on a package. Robert might be that trusting, but Tess knew better. Who better than a steward to have access to information others didn't? He could go anywhere, talk to anyone on the boat, and no one would think anything of it.

He could steam open telegrams, with no one the wiser.

Or she could just be going slowly mad, spinning conspiracies out of the mist.

"All right," Tess said, rising jerkily from the chair. "It's your shoe leather. I'm on E-deck."

"I know, miss."

Tess narrowed her eyes at him through the fog. "Do you know everything about everyone?"

Patrick paused for a moment, and then said, "Mr. Langford has been a good friend to me, miss. I'm happy to be of service to his friends."

Which said absolutely nothing.

Tess's nails dug into her palms as the steward led the way to the second-class stairs. At least, she thought, with gallows humor, they seemed to be going in the right direction. He hadn't dumped her over the rail. Not that he would. If he were working with Robert, Robert would need her alive to identify Ginny. And if he were working with the gang driving Ginny . . . Well, then. They would want her as a goad.

It was some slight reassurance to know that, for the moment at least, she was probably more use alive than dead.

Or Patrick might be exactly what he seemed: a steward who had been well tipped by Robert Langford over successive voyages, trying to see one of Robert's acquaintances right.

"How long have you worked for Cunard?" asked Tess craftily.

"Going on five years now," said Patrick. "It's steady work and it pays well, although being away from the family is hard. My wife is expecting our sixth."

"Goodness," said Tess. "I mean—congratulations. You must miss them."

The steward's Adam's apple bobbed up and down. "I do. If I had the money—but what's that they say? If wishes were horses, beggars would ride. Here's your berth, miss."

E-22. He had led her unerringly to her door. Despite the fact that a first-class steward had no business knowing the location of second-class passengers. Unless he had a reason to know. Robert might have had him discover the location of her cabin after she'd gone missing. Or Patrick might have known all along.

Patrick held open the door for her. "Good night, miss. If you need anything, I'll make sure someone is near the door."

"How very kind," said Tess weakly.

Patrick bowed his head. "Just doing my job, miss. Good night."

"Good night. I hope you get to see your family soon," said Tess, and shut the door behind her, wondering if this was how a mouse in a cage felt.

From the bunk on the left, Mary Kate's head popped up around the curtain screening the bed. She wore curlers with her nightdress. "A first-class steward taking care of you! You must have grand friends."

Unbuttoning her boots, Tess looked up at Mary Kate. "How do you know he's a first-class steward?"

The curtain dropped back into place. Mary Kate's voice, slightly muffled, emerged from behind the fabric. "I told you my Liam knew one of the stewards, didn't I?"

"*Would* you be quiet?" Nellie's voice rose sharply from the bottom bunk. "Some of us would like to sleep. The foghorn is bad enough without you chattering on."

"Sorry!" caroled Mary Kate.

Silently, Tess unbuttoned her jacket in the dark, but she didn't undress. Just in case. Still in her skirt and waist, she climbed up to her bunk and swung in, pulling the covers up over her head to blot out the sounds of the foghorn and Mary Kate's apologies.

She would only rest for a minute. . . . Just for a minute . . .

Through the thickness of the pillow, the horn sounded again and again, a mournful sound, like a dirge for the dead.

When Tess woke, the cabin was empty.

According to the clock on the mantel, it was nearly one; she'd slept half the day away, and it felt like longer, like she was one of those princesses in a tale who awakens to find the whole kingdom buried beneath briars.

A cautious foray outside revealed that Patrick's words had been an empty threat. Or an empty promise, depending on how one looked at it. There was no one stationed outside the door. No one she could see, at any rate.

Ducking back into the room, Tess washed and dressed as quickly as she could, determined to grab Ginny while the others were at lunch. She could guess and speculate all she liked, but it was about as much use as trying to paint a landscape in a blindfold. There was only one person who knew what was going on: Ginny.

Don't find me, Ginny had said. *I'll find you*. But it was too late for that. They needed to have it out now, before the boat docked in Liverpool.

If the boat docked in Liverpool.

Tess ran up the stairs, slipping out onto the deck. The world outside seemed to have been born new while she slept. Golden sunlight poured down on the decks. Children ran about, savoring their last day of freedom, playing jump rope and hopscotch. Behind them, like a shadow, Tess felt as though she could still see the fog of the night before, the cloth stretched tight over the windows to block the light. In her imagination, she could hear the foghorn echoing, marking the minutes, blasting a warning.

The phantom sound lent urgency to her steps as she hurried past the Regal Suite occupied by the Hochstetters to the room reserved for their maid.

The corridors were quiet; the first-class passengers were all at lunch. Most of them, at any rate. Tess came to an abrupt stop as Margery Schuyler's strident tones emerged from the door of Ginny's cabin.

"Well? Do you have it?"

Cautiously, Tess peeked around the edge of the door. Electric light blared off blindingly white woodwork, revealing a small but well-appointed room. A chunk of soap clung to the corner of the washstand, one of the few signs of habitation. In the middle of the room stood Margery Schuyler, resplendent in a Liberty silk dress in a pattern that clashed with her complexion.

Sitting on the bed, in a dark frock, her hair scraped back, Ginny folded her arms across her chest. "Not yet."

Margery paced the width of the cabin, her draperies fluttering around her. "We're only a day out! I thought you said this forger of yours was reliable."

Tess felt as though she'd been hit in the head. Forger? She'd assumed Caroline Hochstetter had loaned her maid out to Margery for the pressing of a dress. But . . . Margery Schuyler? Forger?

Maybe Ginny was setting up another job on the sly. An art heist. But then, wouldn't she have told Tess? They were done, that was what Ginny had said.

"He is." The male pronoun stung like salt. Maybe that was what Ginny meant when she'd said she didn't need Tess anymore. She'd replaced her. "Some jobs take longer than others."

Margery glowered at Ginny as though she were a waiter who had delivered the wrong soup. "Well, we don't have that kind of time. I thought I made that quite clear when I hired you."

"You can't rush good work," said Ginny. "This is the forger who copied Mr. Frick's Jan van Eyck *Virgin and Child*. I can't tell you where the original is—but let's just say Mr. Frick has no idea he has a copy. My man is that good."

My man. Tess could remember painting that, the feel of the brush, the smell of the paint, the celestial blue sky through dark arches as the Virgin and child, flanked by saints, accepted the homage of a kneeling worshipper in white.

Ginny hadn't replaced her. She was protecting her.

Which meant—Ginny hadn't told any of the others who Tess was. If Patrick had been guarding her last night, it had been on behalf of Robert Langford, not Ginny's mysterious colleagues. No wonder Ginny had been so adamant that Tess stay out of the way, away from her. She wasn't keeping her in the dark; she was shielding her. As she had done, as best she could, from the time they were little.

"We don't need good work," said Margery in exasperation, "we just need the waltz!"

"I told you," said Ginny. "You can have the waltz, all nine pages of it. But if you want the tenth . . ."

"This is extortion."

"You want it, you pay for it." Pausing, Ginny looked up at Margery Schuyler with an expression Tess couldn't read. "What is this thing, anyway?"

Margery raised her sagging chin, lifting her draperies like wings. Liberty on the Battlements, if Liberty had a slightly supercilious air and a conspicuous cold sore. "Why should I tell you? Let's just say that it's a device capable of deciding this conflict once and for all. Think of it. All these military entanglements that are sapping the artistic energy of the German people ended! In one blow. The world under German rule, finally, finally, freed from their bourgeois shackles, appreciating the higher things, appreciating *art* . . ." Shaking herself out of it, she said crossly, "So I would very much appreciate if you would stop wasting our time. Bad enough that our man in the War Office is starting to get cold feet . . . I mean . . . Never mind. You don't need to know any of that. You just need to get me that tenth page."

"And how do I know you'll keep your end of the bargain?"

Margery drew herself up. "Would you doubt the word of a Schuyler?"

Under the circumstances, Tess would have said yes.

Ginny eyed the other woman speculatively. "You can tell your people I'll have the tenth page for them when we disembark. Not before."

"They won't like that. How do I know you'll keep *your* end of the bargain?"

Ginny smiled, baring her teeth. "Would you doubt the word of a German patriot?"

It was pure bluff. Tess could tell even if Margery couldn't. "All right, then. But the moment we disembark. Or I won't be responsible for the consequences."

And Tess had just enough time to duck behind the door before Margery swept out in a flurry of conflicting patterns.

"I'm sure you won't," Ginny muttered. "Crazy bat."

Peering around, Tess saw Ginny dive beneath the bed, emerging with her old leather portmanteau. Philadelphia, Delaware, New York. Tess had seen that same portmanteau on so many beds in so many cities, hauled down so many platforms, tossed onto so many trains. Moving with controlled haste, Ginny flung the contents of the dresser into the bag. Combinations, two skirts, two waists, a set of battered brushes. Two wigs: one blond, one brown.

Ginny flung open the wardrobe, ignoring the three identical black dresses. Another skin sloughed off, another costume discarded. From behind them, she grabbed a sheaf of papers tightly furled in a roll, tied with string. Hiking her skirt, she stuffed them inside her garter.

The Strauss waltz.

Ginny paused to take a quick look around the room. Muttering something to herself, she yanked open a drawer and grabbed a pristine life belt. Hooking her portmanteau over her arm, she strode from the room, kicking the door shut behind her, before hurrying down the hall to the Regal Suite. She didn't bother going through the parlor. She went straight to the door on the side that led to Caroline Hochstetter's bedroom.

Recovering from her paralysis, Tess hurried in her wake. From the Hochstetter suite came the sound of doors opening and closing, clothing rustling.

Tess didn't bother to knock. She pushed open the door, catching her sister by surprise. Ginny froze, Caroline Hochstetter's fox stole dangling from one hand. The rubies at her ears and neck glimmered like blood. Her portmanteau lay on Caroline's bed, a bit of beading betraying the evening dress stuffed inside.

"Dammit, Tess!" hissed Ginny. "You aren't meant to be here."

Tess stood, one hand on the doorknob. "What are you doing?"

"Taking my wages." Ginny's face twisted into a simper, her voice taking on an exaggerated drawl. "*Oh, Jones, what a treasure you are. Oh, Jones, I don't know what I would do without you. . . . Yes, ma'am; no, ma'am; tell me if I can go, ma'am.* Scraping and bowing to her highness, hiding her little affairs. It makes me sick." Ginny's hand went to the rubies at her throat. "I've earned every penny of this."

That was Ginny, truth and lies mixed all together. That wasn't why she was running and they both knew it. "But—there's still a day before we land. They'll search the ship for you!"

A satisfied smile spread across Ginny's face. She tapped a finger against a folded piece of paper. "Oh, I don't think so. Not once Mr. Hochstetter reads *this*. Mrs. High and Mighty will be too busy explaining herself to worry about a few lost jewels. And neither of them will want me to go public."

Tess could have shaken her sister. "I wasn't talking about the Hochstetters, Ginny! I thought you had bigger plans than a few jewels."

"Oh, I've got those, too. I said I'd manage it without you, didn't I?" A wary expression crossed Ginny's face. "Is that what this is? Now that I've got it all in hand, you want in?"

"No! I mean, yes." Gentling her voice, Tess stepped forward, saying, "You can steal all the jewels you like. I'll help you! Forget that waltz. We can take the jewels and disappear together—just walk off the boat. I'll help you. I'll do whatever you say. Let's just get away."

Ginny regarded her suspiciously. The light winked off the cold, glass eyes of the foxes on the stole, giving them an equally skeptical air. "I thought you wanted out."

"I do. I want both of us out. But—I'm scared for you, Ginny. What happens when you give these people that tenth page? Do you really think they're going to give you a pat on the back and send you off to the Motherland?"

"They call it the Fatherland." But Ginny's face relaxed into something between exasperation and affection. "Do you think I'm that naïve, Tennie? I've made plans. They won't get the better of me. Not now that you're out of it."

The echo of the past swept over Tess like the rumble of a departing train. But these weren't shopkeepers' daughters or arrogant Argentines they were conning. Not this time. "But what if they *are* better? This is their game." Desperately, Tess tried to think of anything that might move her sister. "Think about what Pa would say. He *left* Germany to avoid serving in their wars."

Ginny made a snorting sound. Turning away, she began rummaging on Mrs. Hochstetter's dressing table. "Is that what he told you?"

Tess took a step forward, trying to see her sister's face in the mirror, trying to catch her eye. "Don't hurt anyone, that was what we always agreed. Nothing to hurt."

"Oh, for the love of—" Ginny slammed a scent bottle down hard enough to make it crack. "What about the people who starved because Pa fleeced them? Or do you want to talk about the people who were dumb enough to drink his elixir?"

Tess bit hard on her lip. "There was nothing in it to harm."

"Oh, because drinking turpentine is so good for babies." At the look of alarm on Tess's face, Ginny gave a short, sharp laugh. "Don't look like that, Tess. It wouldn't kill anyone. Not unless they knocked back a barrel of it. It was mostly vinegar and red pepper, anyway."

"Pa said it gave them hope." And he'd believed it, too. He'd believed in the power of hope. He'd believed if he'd only hoped enough, believed enough, Tess's mother would have lived. That was why he'd mixed his potions, striving, always, for the remedy he'd lacked. Yes, it had been a con, but there had been a truth of sorts to it. "He was trying to help."

"He was trying to help himself—to their wallets." Ginny gave her head a quick shake. With a decisive gesture, she swept a pile of coins into her pocket. "Why are we even discussing this? Pa is dead, and wherever he is, I'm pretty sure he's not sitting on a cloud playing a harp."

"Ginny—"

"We're finished here." Relenting slightly, Ginny paused, and touched Tess's check with one finger. "Once I'm settled, I'll send for you, Tennie."

"If you're settled." Tess swallowed hard; her throat felt like it was full of pins. "I can't let you do this. They'll kill you. Once you hand over that manuscript, you're signing your own death warrant."

"They'll kill me if I don't." Seeing Tess's alarm, Ginny said, "Don't you worry about me. Now that I don't have you to worry about, there's nothing they can do to harm me. I'll play their game, but I'll play it my way."

"You mean Margery Schuyler's way?"

Ginny froze. "What do you know about that?"

"I heard everything."

There was a shiver in the ship, as though the sea itself were standing still.

Ginny cursed beneath her breath. "She's a lunatic, you know. I can handle her. It's the people she's working for that matter."

"And if you can't handle them?" Tess grabbed one of her sister's hands. "Please, Ginny, at least consider going to the Brits—if anyone can protect you—"

"Protect me? Tennie, you have no idea. They can't even protect themselves. This is Robert Langford's doing, isn't it? You ask him, Tennie. Ask him just who wants that code—and why. No. Don't do that." Taking her by the shoulders, Ginny gave her a quick shake. "You stay away from all of this. Do you hear me? Go paint your seashells and lie low. And *don't trust anyone*. Goodbye, little sister."

Letting her go, Ginny strode to the door, rubies glowing darkly against her black traveling suit, a suit Tess had never seen before. A wig and some makeup and there would be a different woman walking out of the cabin.

Tess jackrabbited after her, trying to get between Ginny and the door. "Ginny, wait."

"There's no time," said Ginny. And then, gruffly, "I do love you, you know."

Love you. Love you.

The words seemed to go on and on and on as a dull thud reverberated through the air. The floor rose and tipped Tess to the side. She could feel a pain in her head, and then the world went black.

CHAPTER 25

Sarah

Devon, England
May 2013

BY THE TIME we turned off the road to the Langford drive, the world had gone black. I hadn't quite gotten used to that, the way the countryside darkened to pitch at night. In a city like New York, you never could escape the light.

"Lamps are out," Rupert said, as he pulled up the Range Rover before the Dower House and switched off the engine. "He must be down in the folly."

I unbuckled my seat belt and opened the door. "Then let's go straight there."

Rupert made some noise of protest, but I pretended not to hear him. I stared down the infinity of black space that was the lawn, trying to make out which distant twinkle came from the folly and which from the houses on the opposite bank of the river, while he puffed around the front of the car and said something feeble about tea.

"John's got an electric kettle for emergencies," I said.

Rupert sighed. "All right, then, my beauty. Since you're so eager for the reunion. Just allow me to fetch a torch from the boot, hmm?"

Of course John kept a flashlight in the back of the Range Rover, along with a full emergency kit. The beam jogged along ahead of us, illuminating the imperfections in the damp, green-smelling lawn before we could stumble over them, and the sight was so familiar from all my nighttime crossings with John, I would have forgotten that Rupert walked beside me, if he hadn't taken my arm.

Because John had never taken my arm, not even at two o'clock in the morning, when we were both stumbling with fatigue. We'd hardly dared to touch each other, until last night.

"Dear girl," Rupert said breathlessly, "far be it from me . . . to stand in the way . . . of true love . . . and that sort of thing . . ."

"*Love?*"

". . . but do you think . . . it might be possible . . . to downshift . . . your manic pace . . . just a trifle?"

"Oh!" I staggered to a stop, and in the slight glow from the flashlight, I could see that Rupert's face was flushed and somewhat strained. "I'm so sorry!"

"Not at all, not at all. Good for the ticker, no doubt. You're dragging me along admirably. It's just that my ancient legs can't quite move fast enough."

"You're not *that* ancient. Anyway," I added, a little defiant, "it's not John I'm eager to see. It's the telegram."

"Oh, of course. The *telegram*." He drew in a deep, long breath. "All right, then. Carry on. Let's go find that *telegram*."

I pressed my lips together. We continued forward at a more sedate pace, and though my muscles ached to go fast, to absolutely sprint toward the illuminated windows poised below us—yes, definitely the folly, I recognized it now—I matched my stride to Rupert's stride, bent my will to his. In the distance, I could just make out the glow of Torquay, and I thought of what John had told me that first evening, describing the nearby geography. How new and unsettling everything had seemed, and yet how I'd felt as if I were on the brink of something important. Something like this, like the sight of the tall, rectangular windows growing and resolving before me, golden with the promise of John's presence.

"It's all rather beautiful, isn't it?" Rupert said quietly. "Easy to forget how beautiful it all is. Almost magical."

"No wonder Robert liked to write here," I replied. No wonder John liked to sleep here.

The bridge appeared at the end of the flashlight's beam, and we climbed the gentle rise. As we crested the arc, I saw that the door was just ajar, and I dropped Rupert's arm and skipped down the remainder of the bridge to solid ground. To the door left ajar for me.

John sat at the desk, cast in flickering blue by the light of his iPad screen. His brow furrowed into an expression of haggard concentration, and his thick, square chin rested on his hands, which were knit together and propped up by his elbows. He wore a different sweater, I saw. Red faded to a rusty pink. I switched off the flashlight.

"Hello, there," I said.

He jerked his head, and maybe I stood in some kind of shadow, because he didn't seem to recognize me. His eyebrows flattened, and his hands gripped the edge of the desk, like he was about to launch himself into outer space. So I stepped forward, into the pool of lamplight, and his whole face simply lifted into a smile that warmed my chest, that made my heart fall and fall. Made me forget, for just an instant, all about the tantalizing revelation waiting for me somewhere in this room.

"Well, hello," he said. "I was just—"

"John, my boy!" Rupert roared over my shoulder. "Have you got any tea in there? I'm beside myself with thirst. This resident historian of yours refused to let me stop even for petrol, let alone human sustenance."

John rose from the desk. "I'm glad she didn't. You're bloody well late enough as it is. I've been watching one of the old Langford movies just to stay awake."

"Oh, which one?" I asked.

"*Night Train to Berlin*." He moved to the electric kettle that perched on the edge of one of the cabinets and peered inside. "I was hoping to find some sort of clue to our little mystery."

"And the telegram?" I asked.

He nodded to the desk. "Right over there."

I snatched it up, and even though I already knew what it said, even though I'd already turned those words over and over in my head, echoing John's deep, measured voice, I read them aloud anyway.

MISSION COMPROMISED STOP EXPECT IMMINENT
COUNTERMEASURE STOP TAKE ALL NECESSARY ACTION
PERSONAL SAFETY

I looked up. John had left for the sink in the bathroom; Rupert stood in the middle of the room, arms folded, staring at the paper in my hand, while the sound of rushing water floated from the doorway. "So they were working together, weren't they? Robert and his father. Something to do with this chemical reaction, the one that gives the Allies a major advantage in manufacturing materials."

"So it seems," said Rupert. "It's just odd, though, isn't it? The wording of the telegram. Obscure, as if he didn't want the Marconi operator to smoke out his meaning."

"Exactly," John said, returning to the room with the kettle. He set it back down and plugged it into the nearby socket. "If this mission was compromised—if the Germans had caught wind, and Sir Peregrine knew it, knew they meant to sink the ship—shouldn't he have wired the captain himself?"

"Very strange," said Rupert. He took the telegram from me and pursed his mouth as he stared at it.

I sank into the armchair and watched the back of John's neck as he readied the pot and the teacups. The lamplight made his skin glow. I pressed my thumbs together and said, "But I think you know the answer to that question, don't you? You know why Peregrine didn't try to stop the ship itself from sinking."

"I don't know for certain," John said slowly, measuring the tea into the pot, "because there's no proof, is there?"

Rupert looked up. "You think Robert was a traitor? That his father found out and was trying to protect him?"

"No," John said. He fixed the lid back on the tin of tea leaves and turned around, propping himself on the edge of the cabinet. His eyes were sober, his mouth drawn. "I think it's the opposite."

In the shock that followed, I don't remember who spoke first. Who broke the stunned silence that turned the air to glass. Maybe the kettle started whistling, and John turned to pour the water into the pot, and that was when I jumped from the chair and said, "Peregrine? Sir Peregrine was the traitor?"

Or maybe that was Rupert. Rupert who found his voice first.

Either way, John didn't turn. He just went through the motions of making tea, applying all his concentration to this ritual while he spoke to us patiently.

"I could be wrong, of course. It was the telegram that made me suspicious, for all the reasons I just mentioned. I mean, if it were me, if I'd just decoded some sort of message in Room 40 that led me to believe *Lusitania* was in danger, I'd bloody well wire that captain the instant he came within range of the Crookhaven Marconi station. I'd want to save my son, I'd want to save all those people on board, and moreover, I'd want to save that precious chemical reaction, wouldn't I?"

"Unless the point was to allow the tragedy to take place," I said. "The old theory that Britain needed American outrage. Needed America to enter the war."

He shook his head. "I've never bought that one. Anyway, that wasn't Peregrine's angle, was it? He was clearly working on some sort of espionage mission, and so was Robert, and something went wrong. Something so catastrophic that somebody purged all mention of it from the official records, as you discovered today. And that's when I thought about what you said, Sarah."

"About what?"

He nodded toward the desk and the iPad propped atop. "*Night Train to Berlin*. Here you are, Uncle Rupert. No milk, I'm afraid, but there's sugar in the bowl."

"The book?" I exclaimed. "It's in the book?"

"I couldn't find any copies lying about here, and I couldn't find it on Kindle. But the film's available online. A classic. Carroll Goring directed it, his first big hit."

I hurried around the corner of the desk and pulled the iPad closer. John had paused the movie, but I could see he was about three-quarters through. The blurred, monochrome face of some half-familiar actor filled the screen, as he walked down the narrow corridor of a Pullman coach. "Tristan Beaufort," I said. "He's got the—what was it, the formula for some kind of explosive, right? But the Germans have sabotaged the train, because they don't want him to reach Paris and hand it over to his English contact there. . . ." I looked up. "Oh my God. It was his father. Tristan's father was working in British intelligence."

John was nodding. He hadn't taken any tea himself, and his arms were folded across his rusty-pink chest. "And was being blackmailed," he said. "Blackmailed by the Germans. Told them where the information exchange was taking place, so they could snitch the formula for themselves and then sabotage the train to cover their tracks, so to speak. Let the British think it was just lost."

"Christ," Rupert whispered.

"Only he didn't realize that his own son was the British agent on board the train." I sat in the chair and stared at the wild, blurred eyes of the actor. "He found out and tried to send a message, but it was too late. Beaufort discovers the plot and diverts the train at the last second, saves the day, but his father—"

"—has already killed himself. Not out of grief for his son, but because he knows his treachery is about to be unmasked."

Rupert sat in the armchair, white-faced, holding the tea with both hands. "It was right there, all along. Hiding in plain sight." He looked at me. "Well, you've certainly got your story, young lady."

"Not quite. I mean, this isn't proof. It's all just educated speculation. And I'd never publish anything this—well, incendiary, without more evidence to back it up."

"Why not? You've got the telegram. You've got a decent working theory. And now that you know what you're looking for—"

"But it would destroy his reputation." I turned to John. "I can't just accuse your ancestor of treachery."

John's eyes met mine, steady and earnest, and as I returned his gaze, it seemed to me that I understood at last why he looked so haggard. Why his voice over the phone had sounded so strained. "Sarah, it's history," he said. "It's what you do. The truth is far more important than the Langford family reputation. Besides, this is exactly what you need, isn't it? It's exactly what you've been looking for. Your book. Your big comeback."

I opened my mouth and found I had nothing to say. Both men watched me, waiting for me to speak, waiting for me to take this gift that John was handing to me. He's right, I thought. This was exactly what I was looking for. The big scandal, the big cover-up. And it all fit together so beautifully. A shocking narrative from the past finds its echo in the present Langford family scandal. For John, the timing couldn't be any worse.

And yet, there he stood, a few yards away. Arms folded, face haggard, presenting this terrible, miraculous gift to me. He could have ripped up that telegram, he could have kept its contents forever hidden. But he hadn't. He hadn't even hesitated.

I rose from the chair. "John," I began.

"Rupert!"

I don't know who jumped highest. I spun toward the door and ended up folded over the chair arm. John jerked around and caught himself on the edge of the cabinet.

And Rupert? He gasped and leapt from his chair, spilling his tea on the rug before he set cup and saucer on the corner of the desk. His hands shook as he turned to face the large, handsome, black-haired man who filled the doorway.

"Nigel!" he exclaimed, in a choked voice.

"Well, there's a happy ending, anyway," I said, watching the flashlight bob through the window glass, over the crest of the bridge to disappear on the other side. I turned to John and smiled. "How long should I wait before I sneak after them?"

"I don't know. Might be a little awkward, you know." John lifted his hand and rubbed the corner of his mouth with one finger, possibly to hide the beginnings of a smile. "They seem to have a great deal to talk over."

"So I noticed." I made a show of glancing around the room. "So what should we do in the meantime? Watch the rest of the movie, maybe?"

"You could sleep here," he said, and added hastily, in the same sentence, "on the sofa, I mean. I could take the daybed in the other room."

"I don't have a toothbrush."

"I might have an extra. For emergencies."

"Emergencies?"

"You never know."

He looked sincere, almost angelic. The dim lamplight softened the edges of his face. The color of that sweater was not his best—or maybe he was just pallid from fatigue and shock—but the surge of longing overtook me anyway, filling my chest, making my fingers tingle and ache.

"A toothbrush emergency," I said. "This happens to you often?"

"Not often. Hardly at all, come to think of it. Possibly it was just wishful thinking, on my part. A small flicker of human hope."

His voice lost its teasing edge, and my mouth went dry. I felt the intensity of his mood, the quiet Langford charisma radiating from his skin. I couldn't stand the intent shape of his eyes, so I turned away and pretended to inspect the sofa in question. Tried to think of something clever to say, something to keep up the banter, and I just couldn't. No banter left inside me. No desire for wit and fun. Instead I found myself opening my mouth and talking about my father. How he was an expert on sofas.

"A couch potato, was he? Er, no pun intended."

I turned my head and lifted an eyebrow.

"You know, potatoes," he said. "Like your book. Sorry, never mind. It's late and my brain isn't quite—"

"He slept on them a lot. Sofas. He was an alcoholic. I'd wake up early and come into the living room—I was only four when they split up—and he'd be snoring on the couch, reeking of booze. That smell still kills me."

I'd turned back toward the sofa, Robert's sofa, because I couldn't look at John while I said a thing like that. The air stirred as he stepped toward me and stood by my side, staring at the furniture with me.

"I'm sorry," he said, like he meant it. Like he understood the true meaning of the word, akin to *sorrow*.

"Eh, it was a long time ago. I'm over it. Sort of."

"I don't think you ever really get over a thing like that, do you? He was your father."

"They're supposed to be heroes, when you're small. Time enough when you're grown up to realize they're just human. Just people, muddling through life like you are, making mistakes. But when you're little, your dad should be Superman."

"Well, my father wasn't Superman, least of all to me," John said. "But at least I had a splendid family history to lean on. Or did."

"Now I'm going to blow that up for you, too."

"Oh, I'll be all right. As you said. I'm an adult. I don't require heroism from my ancestors anymore. In fact, I've found it's rather more interesting when they're not heroic, don't you think?"

I didn't answer. Maybe the lack of sleep was catching up with me, I don't know. Maybe my nerves were failing, after all that excitement. The air was cool, because the door had been left open so long, and it smelled of the outdoors, the damp grass and the muddy, wet scent of the river nearby.

John touched my shoulder.

I said, "He called us once, when I was a teenager, and Mom was at work. He'd cleaned himself up, he said. He still loved us, still loved my mother. Wanted to know if I could go to Mom for him and ask for another chance."

"What did you say?"

"I said I would. And I hung up and I didn't tell her a word about it. I never told her. I don't know whether it was because I hated him for what he'd done, or because I didn't want to share my mother with him, or because I didn't want to put her through all that hell again. Whether I was selfish or whether I was protecting her. And a few months later he drove his car into a parkway overpass. When they tested his blood, he had an alcohol level of point two five."

"It seems you made the right choice, then."

I stepped to the sofa and sat down on the edge of it, folding my hands around my knees and staring down at my interlocked fingers. "But what if he went out and got drunk that night because of me? Because I didn't tell Mom? And what if I *had* told her, and everything had turned out all right? I would have had a father and Mom would've had her true love back, and he'd still be alive—"

"Oh, Sarah." John sat down next to me and drew me against his chest. "Trust me, there was no happy ending there. *Trust* me. You absolutely cannot redeem another human being. You just can't. Only God can do that, I suppose, God or whatever it is you believe in. The only person whose behavior—whose *goodness*—you can control is yourself. You just get up every day and do the best you can."

I snuffled against his sweater.

"I mean, I'm not saying you shouldn't reach out and help others. Listen and love and support and whatever you can. But you can't expect to save them. You can't hold yourself responsible for their choices."

I turned my head to face the desk. My arms had come to rest lightly across his stomach; his arm held me securely around the shoulders. I said, "Is that what happened with Callie? You realized you couldn't save her?"

He laughed. "No, I realized that much earlier. But I'm sort of old-fashioned about the better-or-worse business, and I'd known about the drugs and all that before the wedding, so I wasn't going to call quits because of that. It was the sex camp that did it for our marriage."

I drew back, and his arms loosened to let me go. "*Sex* camp?"

"I can't remember what they called it officially. Something about a physical therapy retreat for couples. Callie said we hadn't been connecting in bed the way we used to, and that was why our marriage was falling apart, not the fact that she tended to stumble home high at six in the morning with one shoe missing. So I agreed to go, because—well, what did I have to lose, after all? I mean, it was sex camp."

"But what was it like?"

"Very New Age-y. In the beginning, you weren't allowed to touch each other. They had all these classes and seminars. Saucy stuff. I learned a great deal about the female orgasm, it must be said. And then—I believe it was the third night, just before we were given permission for what they called 'mindful touching'—I went looking for my wife after dinner and found her bonking the instructor in the bondage room, so I went straight home and filed for divorce."

My hand flew to my mouth.

"Are you *laughing* at me, Blake? Laughing at my misery?"

"Of—of course not. It sounds—how terrible—I mean, the bondage room—were they actually—"

"You *are* laughing. I can see your shoulders shaking."

"I am *not*—"

"What a hard woman you are." He reached out his long, rusty-pink arms and gathered me up. "Hard, cruel. Do you have any idea how shattering it is to see your wife mindfully touching another man?"

"Well, you know, I've never had a wife."

"*And* you're satirical."

"Also, I've never been to sex camp."

"Hmm. Never been inside a bondage room either, I expect?"

"Nope. I did read that book, though. Almost all the way through."

"Child's play," John said, and he bent his head and kissed me.

For an instant, when I opened my eyes, I expected to see the red LED lights glowing across R2-D2's perfectly round chest, telling me it was time to rise and shine.

But the air around me was dark and musky, and a heavy arm lay across my middle, and a massive chest moved in a deep, steady rhythm against my back. And something else. I was happy. A fog of contentment inhabited my body, breathing silently through each pore.

John.

His name streaked across my mind, and it all rushed back: long, intimate kisses, clothing parted, John carrying me to the daybed in the other room. I remembered a feeling of wonder, mixed in with all the physical ecstasy of sex, and how I saw that wonder reflected in John's own expression. *Oh my God,* I'd whispered, linking my hands around the back of his neck, and I don't remember what he said in reply to that. Just that it got even better from there, and when culmination finally arrived, it was like nothing and nobody I'd ever known, like a spiritual relief, followed by the kind of silence that means all the things you cannot say out loud. Then sleep.

And now? I couldn't say how long I'd slept. Not long, surely, because the world outside the windows was as black as pitch, and I was still too tired to move. My brain, however, was awake. Awake and jumping. Alive with the thrill of falling in love—falling in love with *John*, oh God, John Langford, this warm, sturdy man sleeping beside me, his whole body now known to me—and alive also with another thought, another nagging question, hovering beneath all that bliss.

Let it go, Blake. Close your eyes and go back to sleep. Concentrate on this precious arm against your ribs, on the thump of his heart at your back. His legs tangled comfortably around yours. Concentrate on all of this before it's gone. Before you fly back to New York and real life.

But my eyes wouldn't close. I picked out the shapes in the room, the faint outline of the doorway to the study. Robert Langford's study, where he wrote all his books, where his secrets lived and breathed. Small secrets and large ones, the mother lode of all secrets, which he might or might not have told the world, except the world didn't notice. *My father is a traitor. My father stood back and allowed the deaths of a shipful of innocent people, men and women and children, just to save his own reputation. My father nearly caused my own death.*

How did you forgive a man for that? How did you keep that secret, all those years? What did it mean? Was Robert the one who had purged Sir Peregrine's files? Why? Why not just let the bastard swing from the gallows of public opinion?

Or had we jumped to the wrong conclusion, after all?

Something was missing. Well, a lot of things were missing, but as I lay there, counting the beats of John's heart, savoring the warmth of his breath in my hair, it seemed to me that we were missing something essential. The key to it all, the puzzle piece that made all the others fit together.

Carefully I lifted John's arm and slipped out from the shelter of his body. He made a noise of discontent, but he didn't wake. The air was cold on my naked skin, so I gathered the first thing under my hand—the sheepskin throw—and wrapped it around my shoulders. The softness of it surprised me. I tiptoed from the room, shut the connecting door, and switched on the lamp on the desk.

John's iPad still sat in place, paused in the middle of *Night Train to Berlin*. The screen was dark, and I didn't know the passcode. I sat down in the chair anyway, bringing my feet up to rest on the edge of the seat, wrapping my arms around my knees. I couldn't recall the details of the book, but I did remember that it had been one of my favorites, as I sped through the Langford oeuvre. Everything had fit together so elegantly. And the characters. Rendered so vividly, so lifelike, I'd felt, as I read, that I knew them personally. That they actually existed, in some alternate book universe. Tristan Beaufort, of course, but also the secondary characters. The father, the passengers on the train. There had been a romance, right? He'd seduced a married woman. And there was some connection to the whole espionage plot, some reason he seduced her, or maybe he found out the connection afterward? I couldn't remember, and yet it felt important, somehow. Urgent. Maybe even the reason I'd woken up.

I unfolded my legs, one by one, constrained by a certain stiffness in my nooks and crannies. Sex with John Langford, it turned out, involved all the major muscle groups and most of the smaller ones, plus a few I hadn't even known existed until now. I bent down to the stack of notes and items of interest that I kept in a file box near the desk, and I sifted through the contents with more curiosity than energy. I should go back to bed. Nothing useful could possibly come of this. In the morning, my head would be clearer, my body renewed. I could search with purpose. Still my fingers kept flipping, looking for the right folder, my notes on Robert's books, until they came to rest not on a notebook, but something else. Something smaller. Thick, sleek paper.

I lifted it away from the stack.

The program from the 1952 Carnegie Hall concert. The pianist. Mary Talmadge.

I sat back in the chair and thumbed idly through the pages. The old advertisements, the concert notes, the thanks to benefactors. *The proceeds of this concert will benefit the Talmadge Musical Conservatory in Savannah, Georgia*. Of course. I'd heard of the conservatory, one of the most prestigious in the country. Founded by some legendary philanthropist and his wife, who were obviously related to Mary Talmadge in some way.

But of what interest to Robert? Why would he have kept this particular program, from a concert in New York? Was he that obsessed with music?

I peered at Mary Talmadge's photograph. She was beautiful, even and perhaps especially against the tailored black-and-white setting, looking off to some point in the distance, her long, elegant pianist's fingers displayed prominently against her cheek.

Maybe that was it. Her beauty. Robert was a bit of a connoisseur, wasn't he?

Except there was something familiar about her, wasn't there? I couldn't say what. The eyes, the expression that conveyed an age far greater than her smooth skin suggested. I'd seen her photograph before, of course—she was a legendary figure in the mid-century music scene—but it wasn't that. It was something more intimate.

I tossed the program on the desk, and as I did so, a small, ecru rectangle of notepaper slipped free from the last page. I caught it just before it fluttered to the floor.

Albert Hall next. Will you be there? XO

The handwriting was distinctly feminine.

"Sarah?"

I looked up. John stood in the doorway to the bedroom, blinking sleepily, wearing nothing at all. A warm glow spread across my skin. "Right here," I said, and I set down the program and rose from the chair.

"Thank God. Thought you'd bolted already."

I turned off the lamp, walked across the room, and wrapped my arms around his waist. "The thing about Americans?" I said, just before kissing him. "We're not as stupid as you think we are."

Only later, as I nestled in John's arms and drifted inevitably to sleep, did my scattered mind recall that nagging detail about *Night Train to Berlin*.

"The husband!" I exclaimed.

"What husband?" John mumbled. "Not yours, I hope."

"No. The one in *Night Train to Berlin*. It wasn't Beaufort who knew the plans, remember? It was the husband. The husband of the woman he seduced on the train."

John answered with a snore.

CHAPTER 26

Caroline

At Sea
Friday, May 7, 1915

A LOUD SNORE erupted from behind Caroline where she sat with Gilbert in the dining saloon, staring at the dish of ice cream Gilbert had ordered for her, but for which she had no appetite.

Caroline turned slightly and recognized the old man with the extravagant moustache from the smoking room the previous evening. He sat alone, his head drooping perilously close to his plate of *pouding souffle Tyrolienne*, sound asleep.

"In some countries, I'm sure falling asleep after a meal is meant as the highest of compliments." Gilbert's voice held the trace of a smile.

She turned to him with surprise. It had been so long since she'd seen him this relaxed, or make an attempt at light humor. His face brightened with a broad smile, showing the crease in his cheek she'd fallen in love with, reminding her of how they'd once been when he was courting her, and how full he'd made her young heart. She couldn't help but smile back, then immediately felt it falter. She stared down at her melting ice cream, wondering if she ate it very fast, if it would freeze her mind so she wouldn't have to think about the looming decision she had to make in less than a day. A decision she was no closer to reaching than she'd been the previous night as she crept from Robert's bed.

Caroline pushed the bowl away in disgust, remembering, too, the shared ice cream with Robert at another garden party, and how he'd told her to press her tongue against the roof of her mouth to stop the sensation of ice imprisoning her brain when she ate it too fast.

"I'm sorry, darling," Gilbert said. "I thought you liked ice cream."

"I do." She attempted a smile, but it felt more like a grimace. "I just have no appetite."

His eyes searched hers, and Caroline knew what he was hoping to find. Yet she couldn't look away. If he chose to believe that she could be expecting a child, and it was a thought that made him happy, then she wouldn't take that away from him. She couldn't. She'd already taken so much.

She glanced around the dining room at the other first-class passengers enjoying lunch, surprised to see everyone eating vigorously as if it might be their last meal for days instead of just a few hours. "I'm surprised anyone has an appetite," she said, attempting to continue the light tone. "It's as if we do nothing but eat on board, with our daily schedules centered around what time the next meal will be served. I'll be amazed if I can fit into all of my clothes once we disembark in Liverpool tomorrow."

"You could be as large as an iceberg and I'd still think you are the most beautiful woman in the world."

Caroline laughed, the genuineness of it surprising her. "Are you allowed to use that word while aboard an ocean liner, Gil? There must be some law."

"There might be, but no one will ever try to stop me from telling my wife how beautiful she is. Or how her laugh can brighten my sourest moods, and how her music lights the world. Or how very much I love her."

Caroline almost asked him then about what he'd said to Robert. And what Gilbert knew about Robert's mission. Even why he'd needed the Strauss manuscript the night before. The words were so close to the tip of her tongue that she could almost taste the sourness of them, the way they would snatch away this perfect moment. A moment she'd been trying to find since they'd embarked in New York. And if she spoke Robert's name out loud, it would remind her of where she'd been in the early hours of the morning, and whose lips had last touched hers. *He told me that he loved you more than I ever could.* Gilbert had said that to Robert. Gilbert—the man she'd married and sworn to love and cherish. The same man sitting next to her now with searching blue eyes and a warm smile, declaring his love and waiting for her to speak. There'd be plenty of time later, she decided, when it was just the two of them again. Time to talk, to confess. To plan.

"I love you, too, Gilbert. More than I can ever say." She swallowed, searching for the gumption her mother had told her she had, then opened her mouth to say more. But Gilbert spoke first, almost as if he knew what she'd been about to confess.

"I owe you an apology, Caroline." He took both of her hands in his, uncaring that there were people around them who might see.

"For what?" she finally managed.

"For not allowing you into my life—into all aspects of it. You have a keen mind, it's one of the many things I love about you. I thought I was protecting you from the harsh realities of life, of war. I wanted to believe that if I kept you ignorant of what was really going on, that when I returned home I'd return to a wholesome innocence. But that wasn't exactly fair to you, was it? Yet even when you asked to be let in, I still denied you with perhaps more than my share of masculine pride."

Caroline sat still, afraid to move in case he realized what he was saying and to whom.

Gilbert looked down at their hands. "I invented something. Something important. Something that could determine the outcome of this war. It's a new steel alloy that will make soldiers' helmets stronger, and stronger helmets will save lives. I knew the British have been looking for such an alloy, and I thought I might be able to help. I was good at chemistry in school and I started playing around with some of the compounds." He lowered his head. "I kept thinking about those young men in the trenches, how each of them is someone's father, or husband. Or son. My company makes weapons that kill. And here was my chance to save lives."

"And you invented this alloy?" Caroline said, her heart swelling with pride.

"Yes. By accident, actually. I didn't really know what I'd done at first. But there you have it."

She thought for a moment as pieces began to take shape and fit together. "That's why we're on *Lusitania*," she said. "To bring the formula to the British." She met his eyes. "That was the mission you and Robert are involved in. He was sent to protect you, to keep the formula safe."

"Yes," Gilbert said, looking up briefly at the mention of Robert's name. "I have the formula memorized, but I gave it to Robert just to be safe."

"So the Strauss waltz . . ."

"Was just a distraction. In case there were others on board who knew about the formula. We wanted them to believe the secret was in the manuscript." He grinned. "I even added an extra page with a lot of cryptic nonsense written on it just to throw them off if it was indeed stolen."

Caroline sat up straighter. "So why did you want the manuscript to show to Mr. Lauriet last night?"

Gilbert looked genuinely confused. "I have no idea what you're talking about."

"Last night Jones came to me and said you needed the manuscript and so I gave it to her."

Gilbert rubbed his chin. "Good Lord, Jones?" He made to stand, then returned to his seat. "I'll let Langford know. No good rushing off right now—there's really no place she can hide and we'll make sure to telegraph ahead to let the proper authorities know to arrest her when we arrive in Liverpool."

It was Caroline's turn to look down at their clasped hands. "I've been so stupid. And not just in hiring Jones without due diligence, but for not trusting you. I've been so angry, and yet I should have known that you were only doing this because you love me and wanted to protect me. To keep me safe. And I—"

"Don't say it, Caroline. If you were about to say something about

Robert, don't. Let this be about you and me from here on out. Let us start our new lives now—now that all of this is behind us."

He reached into his pocket and pulled out a linen handkerchief embroidered with his monogram. She purchased them by the dozen at B. Altman on Fifth Avenue and Thirty-Fourth Street because he lost them as quickly as she could buy them. "Here," he said gently.

She took it, surprised to find her eyes moist.

"Would you like to stroll the promenade? A walk in fresh air always helps with digestion and it's a glorious day outside. We're approaching Ireland and are close enough to see the coast." Gilbert placed his hand on the table palm-up, his eyes an open invitation.

"I'd like that," she said, putting her hand in his, enjoying the sensation of security and protection as his fingers closed over hers.

"We can talk about our future together and all the plans to be made. I'll even learn to ride a horse so I can ride with you in Central Park. You've been asking me since we were married and I think it's time."

"Yes." She squeezed his hand, her heart burning with love and shame and uncertainty. "I'd like that," she managed to say. "Very much. And I promise to be patient with you each and every time you fall out of the saddle."

He laughed, the deep, chest-rumbling laugh she loved and had heard so little over the last year. Gilbert's gaze drifted behind her and he quickly sobered. Caroline turned to see Patrick approaching, another telegram in his hand.

"Madam," he said, acknowledging Caroline before turning to Gilbert. "I'm sorry to disturb you, sir, but you have a telegram and they are awaiting your reply."

Gilbert opened the telegram and read it quickly. He glanced at Caroline, his eyes uncertain. "It's the New York office. I'm afraid it's rather urgent."

"I understand," she said, because she did. "But promise me you'll come find me on the Promenade Deck so we can enjoy a stroll together?"

"I promise." Gilbert took her hand and kissed it. "I'll escort you to the lifts."

Caroline shook her head. "I'm going to stay here for a few minutes and try and eat my ice cream. Patrick can escort me."

"Good," he said, as he pulled back his chair. "I'll see you shortly."

Gilbert excused himself and left. Caroline picked up her spoon but replaced it on the table as soon as Gilbert disappeared through the doorway. She reached for the paper luncheon menu and pulled a gold fountain pen, a gift from Gilbert, from her purse. She didn't stop to think about her words, only that she needed to write them. When she was done, she folded the rectangular menu into quarters and handed it to Patrick.

"Please make sure that Mr. Langford gets this as soon as possible."

He took the folded paper, his eyes blank. "Yes, madam."

"Thank you. And I can find my way to the lifts on my own. I just need you to hurry and find Mr. Langford."

For a brief moment it seemed as if Patrick were waiting to say something, to ask her if she was sure. As if he knew what she'd written, and what she'd decided. But Caroline didn't acknowledge it, realizing it must have been a trick of the light pouring in from the skylight above that made her think the steward was more than what he seemed. She turned back to her ice cream in dismissal and even managed a small bite while waiting for him to leave before she stood and left the dining saloon.

Passengers swarmed the promenade like bees around a hive in summer, taking advantage of the warmer air and bright sunshine. The flat smoothness of the ocean reflected the brilliant blue sky like a looking glass, giving the illusion of endless heaven. Children played jump rope and ran away from nannies and stewardesses who tried to appear stern as they attempted to corral them. But everyone seemed to be smiling, owing no doubt to the good weather and the fact that the long ocean voyage was nearing its end.

Caroline breathed in the fresh air, feeling as if there was more room inside her now that she'd made her decision. She tried not to think about it, having always been taught that once a decision was made the past was the past and there was nowhere else to go but forward. She had to believe she'd made the right choice. Moving backward was no longer an option. For the first time in a very long while, she felt happy, as if the world held only possibilities.

Even the sight of Prunella and Margery couldn't dim her mood or her smile as she approached the railing. She inclined her head in greeting, carefully avoiding the flapping feathers on Margery's wide-brimmed hat that from a distance appeared to be a large bird roosting on her head. At least it created enough shadow to hide the unfortunate mouth sore that still hadn't disappeared.

"Good afternoon, Mrs. Schuyler. Miss Schuyler. What a beautiful day, isn't it?"

Margery sniffed. "It would be, I suppose, if my rheumatism wasn't acting up. And if all of these . . . children weren't running wild. Isn't there some sort of holding pen for them? One would think a ship such as the *Lusitania* would have thought to have one."

Caroline's attention was focused behind the older woman where Gilbert had just appeared on the promenade, unaware as yet of her presence nearby. She started to lift her hand in a wave, but stopped as she noticed the man only an arm's length away, equally as oblivious to the other man's presence. *Robert.* He was talking to the steward, Patrick, their expressions serious. She wondered if it had anything to do with the note she'd scribbled on the menu.

Her decision came rushing back to her in a tidal wave of emotion, carrying with it the weight of loss and longing like so much debris. But not doubt. She'd made the right decision, she knew that now. She needed to talk with Robert, but she couldn't here. Not in front of all these people. Not while Gilbert watched.

She quickly turned back to Margery, but stopped at the odd sight of an object in the near distance protruding from the glass surface of the ocean. Her two companions followed her gaze and for once they both seemed to be without words.

Margery eventually found her voice. "I daresay, that looks like a periscope." Her expression was more outrage than surprise. "Nobody told me that this was going to happen."

She was still speaking when Caroline saw the insidious rippling of the water near where the periscope's eye peered unblinkingly at the large ship, a white foamy snake slithering directly at them.

Prunella sniffed. "That had better not be a torpedo. My husband will be most put out . . ."

Caroline had ceased to listen. To Prunella, or the laughing children, or the screaming gulls overhead. An eerie sense of calm enveloped her, everything moving in slow motion, the sound cushioned as if packed in cotton to be examined later. She turned once more to where she'd seen Gilbert, desperately needing to find him. To assure herself that he was there, that he was safe. That he was hers and they were going to disembark in Liverpool and live the lives they'd promised each other. She took one step in the direction of where she'd seen him and then the world exploded.

The entire ship trembled in shock, its tremendous speed suddenly halted by an invisible fist. Caroline was knocked to the ground along with most of those who'd just a moment before been standing with her on the Promenade Deck. Another blast sounded from beneath her as a geyser of black water splashed up and over the deck.

She looked around to where she'd just seen Gilbert. Gilbert wasn't there, but she spotted Robert and Patrick, both clutching the doorway, Patrick's hat missing. Robert took something that looked like an oilskin pouch from an inside jacket pocket, and handed it to the steward right before the ship buckled again and Caroline was thrown several feet toward the railing. When she looked up, they were gone.

Sound came back to her with a vociferous roar, the gentle noises of just a minute before replaced now with shrieking and wailing and crying children. She grimaced in pain as she tried to use her hands to right herself, realizing she must have hurt her wrist bracing herself when she fell. The great ship listed to one side, her skirts and shoes damp as water raced across the sloping deck to return to the unforgiving ocean.

"Gilbert!" she called, her word mingled with the shouts of despair from her fellow passengers. She began to rise and was pushed down again by a group of people running across the deck, shouting about life belts.

"Hurry," someone cried nearby as Caroline finally managed to stand. "She's sinking fast!"

A lifeboat, filled surely beyond capacity, was slowly lowered over the side of the ship from the Boat Deck above. Then, just as it came abreast the Promenade Deck, there was a loud cry as one of the ropes slackened and then caught, tipping the boat to an alarming angle. The two crewmen aboard the lifeboat tried valiantly to right it, but their efforts were in vain as the boat continued its terrifying dip until all the occupants, some without life belts, were thrown into the frigid sea.

Caroline might have uttered a cry of distress, but the sound was buried under the cacophony of panicking passengers and of steel bolts and wooden timbers popping and splintering like wounded animals. The deck was utter chaos and she knew there was nothing she could do for those hapless souls who'd gone overboard. She searched desperately for some sight of Gilbert, trying to determine what to do next, what Gilbert would do. People around her scrambled into their life belts, and she watched as a husband helped his pregnant wife fasten the straps of her life belt, remembering that her own vest was in her cabin.

Yes. Surely that's where Gilbert would have gone—to their staterooms to retrieve their life belts. He was always so logical and practical, and for the first time Caroline felt grateful. If he'd seen her on the promenade, he'd be with her now. Failing that, he would have done the next logical thing. She refused to consider any other option.

As carefully as she could she struggled against the tide of people pouring out onto the promenade and headed into the darkened interior of the ship. Whatever the torpedo had struck had taken out the electrical system of the great ship, throwing them all into darkness. At least she was on the same floor as their stateroom, and it was near enough that she could find it in the dark. Straight in toward the lifts, turn left, past two parlor suites and then the funnel hatch on the right and their stateroom would be on the left.

She heard a woman wailing in the darkness, calling out a man's name. Caroline paused, unable to ignore the abject distress in the woman's voice, and called out for the woman to come toward her, that they would at least be together. But the hysterical woman was unreachable, unwilling or unable to respond to Caroline's offer of help. With grim determination, Caroline turned down the corridor, remembering her mother once telling her that if she ever needed saving, she shouldn't rely on anyone else to do it for her.

Her fingers slid along the papered walls for balance as she made her slow progress in the darkness, brief pulses of light teasing her from open doors and the exit to the Promenade Deck behind her. She pushed down rising panic as the ship shifted and moaned all around her like a giant beast slowly awakening and preparing to swallow everyone on board. It listed more and more to the side, making it difficult to walk, creating an acute awareness of the passage of time as the *Lusitania* slowly sank bit by bit into the great abyss of the Celtic Sea.

Caroline nearly cried out with relief when she reached their stateroom and threw open the main door, the rooms awash in sunlight streaming carelessly through the windows as if unaware of the tragedy occurring directly beneath its rays.

"Gilbert!" she shouted, opening up the door to his bedroom, followed by the dining room and parlor, finding them all empty. "Gilbert!" she shouted again, her voice rising, realizing she hadn't thought of what she'd do if he wasn't here. And wondered if she'd miscalculated and if he was at that moment looking for her on the promenade, where she'd said she would be waiting for him.

She heard a voice from her bedroom and felt almost weak with relief. "Gilbert!" she called and rushed to the door and threw it open. It took her a moment to register what she was seeing. "Jones?" she said, as if she needed to make sure that the woman wearing Caroline's fox fur stole and ruby earrings, and splashing water on a prone Tess Fairweather, could actually be the same Jones who'd been her dutiful maid up until that morning. The same woman to whom she'd given the Strauss manuscript. The same woman whose name was to be telegraphed ahead so she could be arrested as a spy when she disembarked.

The woman looked up at her, her frantic expression quickly turning to abject hatred, then returned to her attempts to revive an unconscious Tess. "Tennie, wake up! C'mon, sis, you've got to wake up now."

Sis? Caroline wondered if Robert knew. Walking toward the two women, she addressed her former maid, "I know who you are, and so does my husband. And you're not going to get away with it."

Jones continued to ignore her, and instead issued sharp slaps to her sister's cheeks, creating bright spots of red on the pale skin. Tess's words came back to Caroline. *Be careful who you trust.*

Caroline frantically glanced around the room, taking in the pile of clothes and jewelry stacked on her bed, the canvas life belt lying next to it, and then back to the figure on the floor who'd just begun to moan and to move her head from side to side. "Ginny . . ."

Caroline kneeled next to Jones—Ginny?—and spoke firmly. "I don't care what's going on here—right now we need to leave. The ship is sinking and we don't have a lot of time." She positioned herself behind Tess's shoulders. "You get her legs," she said to Ginny, her anger at the betrayal and subterfuge making it difficult to meet her eyes. "We can carry her out to the deck."

Tess was struggling to sit up. "I'm fine. I can walk." She stuck out her hands toward her sister, her movements erratic and uncoordinated like a small child's. "Ginny. Please. Stay with me. We can do this together."

But Ginny was already standing, furtively glancing around the room. "Since you can walk on your own, little sister, it's time I say goodbye. For now." She paused. "But I'll find you." With something that sounded almost like softness, she bent down and whispered into Tess's ear, "I promise."

With a sneer directed at Caroline, Ginny grabbed the pile of clothing and jewelry on the bed and began backing out of the room. "And good riddance to you, *ma'am*," she said, emphasizing the one word.

Before Caroline could react, Ginny bolted out of the door, dropping a strand of pearls in her haste. She paused just a second then dashed out into the corridor.

The ship shuddered and groaned as Tess's eyes went wide. "What's happening?"

"We've been hit by a torpedo," Caroline said. "We need to get out of here quickly." She reached for the girl's shoulders to help her stand, but Tess pulled away.

"Where's Ginny? I need to go with her."

"She's gone. It's up to us to get out of here." Caroline glanced over at the bed. "She forgot her life belt." She stood, stumbling against the dresser as the ship trembled again. She grabbed the jacket and tossed it to Tess. "Here—put this on."

Without waiting to see if Tess followed her instructions, Caroline bent down to look under her bed where she'd stored her life belt at Claire's telegrammed request, "just to be sure." She'd hug her sister-in-law when she next saw her. Just the thought of a future plan gave her the courage to slip on the jacket and fasten it.

Tess struggled with the fasteners and Caroline hurried over to help. Tess tried to push her away, but it was clear she was still groggy and unable to coordinate her movements. "Let me help you. My husband showed me how to fasten these new Boddy life belts correctly. If we don't do it right we might end up facedown in the water." When she'd finished, Caroline grabbed Tess's arm and dragged her out into the darkened corridor, taking a moment to pause and get her bearings despite the panic that tugged at her hem.

"Where are we going?" Tess asked, her voice stronger now.

"Hopefully out to a lifeboat." Caroline moved forward into the corridor.

Tess tugged her back. "But what if there aren't any left?"

Caroline resumed her forward movement, pulling Tess with her. "Then I hope you can swim."

CHAPTER 27

Tess

At Sea
Friday, May 7, 1915

I CAN SWIM," Tess retorted breathlessly, trying to break free of Caroline Hochstetter's arm. "Can you?"

"Stop quibbling and run." Tess hadn't imagined that Caroline had such resolution in her. She'd always pictured her drooping romantically like a Tennyson heroine. But that was steel in Caroline's arm and her voice. "Unless you want me to leave you here?"

"You don't need to sound so hopeful," muttered Tess, but she upped her pace to match Caroline's longer stride.

The other woman moved like a cat through the dark corridors, taking the steps two at a time, never missing her footing. Tess's head felt fuzzy as she stumbled along behind her. Maybe this was all the fault of that blow to her head. Maybe she was lying on the floor, imagining being tugged along in Caroline Hochstetter's perfume-infused wake.

A torpedo, Caroline had said. A torpedo.

But Ginny had said . . . Ginny had been so sure . . .

Around them, the ship shifted and rumbled.

Tess yanked at Caroline's arm, pulling her back. "Are you sure? A *torpedo*?"

She could feel Caroline check for a moment, then keep going. "I'd hardly joke about it, would I?"

She didn't know. She didn't know anything. Trying desperately to keep up, Tess said, "I need to find my sister."

And Robert. She needed to find Robert and tell him about Margery Schuyler. Robert and Ginny, Ginny and Robert.

Caroline didn't bother to look back. "Then stop talking and move."

"Ma'am, yes, ma'am," Tess gasped, but she was grateful for the other woman's supporting arm.

She couldn't tell whether the shifting of the ground beneath her was the ship listing or the blow to her head. She could see her father standing in front of a patient, two fingers up. *How many fingers?* But she couldn't see anything in the dark stairwell, not her fingers, not anyone else's. There were other people on the stairs, she knew that from the thrum of footsteps, the swish of fabric against her side. But she could see them only as shadows. Like ghosts.

This couldn't be happening. None of this was happening. It had all been like a child's game, threatening letters in the papers, saber rattling and bluster. Tess knew—she'd known—that in France and Belgium men were fighting and dying, that in the Atlantic Ocean ships were going down beneath the waves, but it was like watching a game of soldiers played on a dusty wood floor, paper ships being sailed in a creek. Not real, not back in New York, where the lights glowed above Broadway and the El hissed and hummed on its tracks.

They burst through the door to the deck, the sunlight blinding after the lightless interior. *Just a drill*, Tess expected someone to say. *Everyone back to their cabins.*

But everything had changed. The tubs of flowers next to the Verandah Café had tumbled sideways, spilling flowers and dirt that were being trampled into the ground by terrified passengers darting this way and that, the rusty blacks and browns of the third-class passengers mingling with the bright frocks and lush furs of the parlor set, everyone made one, everyone brought to the same level by the fear that distorted their faces, twisted their limbs.

"You weren't joking," said Tess dumbly, but Caroline's attention was elsewhere.

"Gilbert!" Caroline released Tess, sprinting to her husband, who caught her in one arm, pressing his lips against her forehead, his eyes closed as if in prayer. The expression on his face—Tess had no words for it. He was like a man finding his chance of heaven.

Over them, Tess could see Robert freeze for a moment, watching them. Then he seemed to shake himself awake, going back to corralling women and children into one of the lifeboats.

"This way! Women and children first!" she could hear Robert's crisp voice rising above the crowd, taking command as though he had been born to it.

She watched him stoop to help a child with a life vest, and realized, suddenly, the unfamiliar weight of the vest on her own shoulders. Not her life vest. Ginny's. Ginny's life vest.

The straps were too tight across her chest. The pain in her head receded as panic flared through her, rendering her vision more acute, all her senses on high alert. Sweat, perfume, coal dust, smoke. The pink of a child's coat; the high-pitched sound of a baby's wail.

Ginny. Tess began fighting her way through the crowd, searching for a dark head, a stolen fur. She had to find Ginny. Ginny, who had no life vest.

A woman grabbed at Tess's arm. In her other hand, she held a small boy by the wrist, tugging him along behind her. "My baby—have you seen my baby? I gave her to a man in a plaid vest, but I can't find them."

"I—no, sorry." The haunted expression on the woman's face cut through to Tess's bones. "What does he look like? The baby?"

"She. She's a girl. I wrapped her in a yellow blanket. . . ." The woman surged forward again, pulling at someone else. "My baby. Have you seen my baby?"

A Scotsman put out a hand to steady her. "Don't worry yourself. The captain says the ship will not be sinking this day."

But the woman shook him off. The little boy stumbled, but his mother pressed forward, dragging him behind her.

Tess could hear her words, echoing behind her. "My baby—have you seen my baby?"

All around her, parents were searching for children, reunited families clutching each other. Those lucky enough to have life vests were shrugging into them as best they could. A portly man attempted to stick his neck through what Tess was pretty sure was an armhole. A woman struggled to tape hers over what looked like four layers of clothes and a heavy fur-lined coat. People, people, everywhere, but not one of them was Ginny. Or a baby in a yellow blanket, or a man in a plaid vest.

Have you seen my mother . . .

My husband . . .

My baby . . .

No, Tess said, and again *no*, hating herself more with each denial, trying to tamp down the rising fear as the boat listed to the side, the water beginning to creep across the deck, damping her shoes. She'd gone nearly full circle, but there was no sign of Ginny, no sign of her sister.

No! They hadn't come so far only to be separated now. Tess would find her, she would. And then—she'd deal with that when they got to *then*.

Tess pushed past the Hochstetters, who were having a low-voiced argument about lifeboats.

"I won't take a woman's place. Or, God help me, a child's."

"Then I won't go either."

"But, Caroline. What if . . ." Gilbert Hochstetter touched a finger to his wife's cheek with painful tenderness, his gaze dropping to his wife's elegantly cinched waist.

Caroline pressed his hand against her cheek, looking at him with such naked emotion that Tess had to turn away. "Then we'll all be together."

Robert strode over, his cut-glass tones slicing through their argument. "Both of you, in. This is no time to be noble, Hochstetter."

"I'd say this is precisely the time to be noble," said Gilbert Hochstetter quietly, but he made no move to step away from his wife. "Women and children first. You know it as well as I."

Robert pointedly avoided looking at Caroline's hand on Hochstetter's cheek. Brusquely, he said, "You have other obligations."

Gilbert Hochstetter pressed his wife's palm briefly to his lips and then lowered her hand in a courtly gesture of relinquishment. "Which I have discharged."

"Not until someone gets to London." The two men exchanged a long look.

"If you would be so kind as to look after her for me—" Hochstetter began, as his wife said furiously, "I'm not a jewel box to be carried to shore!"

But Robert cut them both off, his words like stones, immovable. "I'm dispensable. You're not."

"Robert—" The voice was Caroline's, the name ripped out of her.

Robert nodded curtly, his eyes not meeting Caroline's. "Both of you, in the boat."

And, behind them, Tess caught sight of a familiar profile. The hair was all wrong and the coat was too big for her, but blood called to blood; she felt her sister's presence like a tug on her bones.

Tess darted out around the Hochstetters, standing on her tiptoes, trying to keep sight of her sister. "Ginny!" she screamed. "Ginny!"

But her voice was lost in the din, in the cries of children and shouts of sailors and the caw of the gulls overhead.

Her sister lifted her hand, precious stones glinting on her fingers, a carnival of colors: red, green, blue. A king's ransom of jewels reduced to fairground baubles. Blowing a kiss, Ginny called out, "See you on the other side, Tennie!"

On shore. She meant *on shore*. But fear gripped Tess, sent a superstitious shiver down her spine.

"I'm not going without you!" Tess shouted, but Ginny was already turning away, the hem of her coat sweeping the deck, the crush of humanity closing around her, hiding her from Tess's view. "Dammit, Gin!"

Someone grabbed her by the back of her jacket.

"What are you doing?" demanded Robert furiously, hauling her up like a fish on a line, floundering and flailing. "Get into the boat!"

Tess paused for a moment, clutching his wrist. "Robert, I need to tell you—Ginny's contact. It's Margery Schuyler."

Robert manhandled her toward the lifeboat. "Right now, I don't care if her contact was the Archbishop of Canterbury. Are you going to climb in or am I going to carry you?"

"I only stayed to tell you." Tess yanked away, hearing a seam rip. What did it matter? The fish on the bottom of the sea wouldn't care. "My sister—"

"Won't thank you for drowning. Don't just stand there! Move!" Robert's voice was ragged, nothing like his usual calm self. His hands were shaking, and so was his voice, and Tess remembered, as from a long time ago, Robert, a different Robert, telling her about another boat, a boat that went out and never came back. He was afraid, she realized, deathly afraid, and it came out in a roar. "By all that's holy, Tess, get in the bloody boat!"

"I can't leave her. I thought you would understand. You, of all people! Your brother—" Tess's voice broke.

Robert stopped, staring down at her, an arrested expression on his face. "You really love her."

Tess resisted the urge to stamp on his foot as hard as possible. Love Ginny? Of course she loved her.

"Did you love Jamie? She's my sister. She's my *sister.* She's all I have in the world."

"Not all." Robert's hands squeezed her shoulders, and, for a moment, Tess felt a rush of warmth. But then he turned her around, pushing her toward the boat. "Don't be a fool, Tess. Get in the boat. Get in before it goes."

Tess plucked helplessly at the fastenings of her vest. "I have to—this is her life vest. Her life vest, not mine. I have to get it to her."

Robert's hands settled over hers, stilling them. "She'll find one."

"Or she won't." How many people were there on the boat? And most of them looking frantically for life vests. Were there enough on the boat for everyone? Tess hadn't thought to ask.

The boat shuddered, sending people stumbling into each other across the deck.

"You won't help her by dying." Robert propelled Tess toward the lifeboat.

"Dying." Tess looked at Robert with wide eyes as he boosted her up into the boat.

"What do you think we're talking about? A stroll in Hyde Park? This ship is sinking. I'm not letting you go down with it."

"Then you're coming, too." Tess's hand closed around his wrist, keeping him from turning away.

Robert made a harsh sound that might have been a laugh or a sob. "I already let one boy die. Maybe this is expiation. Maybe this is my turn."

"You were a boy yourself," Tess shot back at him. "Please. You said it yourself. You can't help them by dying. Please, Robert. Please."

"Get in, Langford." It was Gilbert Hochstetter's voice, and it had all the command of a man who was used to the world jumping when he spoke. Caroline sat frozen beside him, her arm threaded through his, pressed tight against his side, and Tess wondered what she thought of her husband summoning her lover. Or had it all ceased to matter now? Here, between the devil and the deep blue sea. "You'll be needed if something goes wrong."

"Wrong?" Next to the Hochstetters, a woman clutched her child so tightly that the toddler made a noise of protest, wriggling for freedom.

"Nothing is going to go wrong," Hochstetter said quickly. "Cunard employs the most skilled seamen in the world. They're trained for this. They could launch these boats in their sleep."

Even as he spoke, there was a cry from down the stern. Suspended above the deck in their flimsy craft, they watched as a rope went flying free, sending a fully loaded lifeboat tipping over, women and children toppling down, down, down, into the water below. It happened so quickly that there was barely time for the passengers to scream before they hit the waves, their voices muffled by the water.

And then—the horror of it would haunt Tess's nightmares, she knew—the hands. The hands reaching up, futilely waving for help.

Someone on deck started flinging down lifesavers. They looked painfully small, little specks against the vast sea.

On the water, a child's doll floated, facedown, buttoned boots and lace-trimmed petticoats sodden with water.

Not a doll. A child.

Bile rose in Tess's throat. Instinctively, she leaned over, reaching down, but she was caught, useless, in the cradle of rope that held their lifeboat suspended above the deck.

"Oh God, oh God, oh God." The woman with the child rocked back and forth, hugging her toddler to her. The little boy had begun to whimper.

Next to them, another woman's lips moved in a silent prayer, her fingers on the beads of her rosary.

"Why aren't we moving?" a woman in a fur coat demanded, her voice high with fear. "Why aren't they doing anything?"

The lifeboat was held by a pin. Although a sailor stood by with an ax, ready to free the boat, he made no move to do so.

"Yes!" echoed Tess, feeling the feverish color rise in her cheeks. "We have room! If you set us down, we could save them. . . ."

Robert's hand squeezed painfully tight on her upper arm, cutting off her words, and, without knowing why, Tess buried her face in his arm.

"Shhh," he said as though she were a child, and Tess wanted to know if this was what it had been like last time, if this was how it had felt as he watched his brother's head disappear beneath the waves.

She jerked away, putting all her fear into anger. "Don't shush me! We might *do* something."

"I'll second that." A portly man in a heavy overcoat and one of the expensive new life vests strode up to the sailor with the ax. "Why are you just standing there? Lower the boat."

"Captain's orders," said the sailor, holding his ax a little tighter. "No launching until he gives the say-so."

"To hell with the captain. Do you have eyes, man? Can't you see the ship is sinking?" The man drew a revolver from beneath his coat. He held it trained on the sailor, his hand steady. "Lower the damned boat. Don't think I won't use this. When I shoot, I shoot to kill."

A ragged cheer rose from the boat.

"Yes, sir. If you say so, sir." The sailor raised his ax and slammed it down on the pin.

Tess's head spun with the boat as it lurched the wrong way, not toward the sea but straight into the onlookers on the deck. The boat battered through them like bowling pins. Cries of fear and pain and the thud of breaking bones and shattering wood echoed through Tess's ears as she was flung sideways into Robert, her life belt cutting painfully into her ribs.

"Steady on," murmured Robert, his breath warm against her hair as he held her tight against his chest. Too tight.

Tess wriggled free, trying to sit up. One shin was going to have a powerful bruise, but Robert's chest had borne the brunt of her weight; she'd banged her already sore head on his breastbone. "What's that in your pocket?" she asked huskily. "A flask or a brick?"

But the words died on her lips as she looked up at Robert's frozen face.

"Oh Lord," muttered Tess.

It looked like a scene from a hellfire preacher's most dismal imaginings. People crawling, keening, cradling broken limbs. Blood trickling down people's faces, bones sticking out of skin.

"The Lord hasn't anything to do with this," said Robert grimly. "This is sheer, human stupidity."

"We didn't—" Tess couldn't make herself voice the words.

"Straight into the crowd," said Robert. His voice was hard, but she could feel him shaking next to her, holding her as though it was as much for his comfort as hers.

The man with the revolver was crawling from beneath the boat, dragging one leg behind him, his face a red mask of blood. He paused beside what looked like a crumpled pile of clothes, lifting something. A hand. A limp hand.

Not clothes. A woman. And there was another beside her, her neatly coiffed gray hair mussed, her modest skirts up over her knees. But she wouldn't care. Not anymore. Her sightless eyes stared up at the gulls circling above, cold and glassy.

Dead. They were dead. A moment ago, those two women had been standing there, talking, alive. And now they were dead.

The child in the water, the women by the wall. Only a day ago—an hour ago—there had been children in starched pinafores skipping rope, women in flowered hats promenading the deck, with no greater concern than which cake to choose for dessert. And now . . .

Damp crept down her cheeks. Tess lifted a hand to dash the moisture away, but it wouldn't seem to go. It just kept seeping down, dripping onto her lips, as salty as the sea.

"Hochstetter." Robert set her aside, his voice clipped, urgent. "Are you all right?"

"I'm fine," Mr. Hochstetter said.

Tess blinked. He wasn't fine. His lips were white, and the smile he gave his wife looked like a skull's grin, all stretched bone.

Buck up, Tess told herself. No time for vapors. Even if her head ached and her cheeks were wet with tears she couldn't remember shedding.

Ripping the scarf from around her neck, Tess thrust the cloth at Caroline. "Here. You need that set. Wrap it round as tightly as you can. It should be splinted, but—I think we'll be needing those oars." When Caroline just stared at her, she added defensively, "My father was a pharmacist. I know a broken arm when I see one."

"Thank you," said Caroline. She made no move to reach for the scarf. Her eyes were wide, dazed.

Tess dangled it impatiently. "Oh for the love of—it's not poisoned. Just take it. Or I'll do it, if you can't."

"I'm fine," said Mr. Hochstetter again, even less convincingly than last time. He was cradling his left arm, trying to look nonchalant and failing.

A spark awoke in Caroline's eyes. "I can do it, thank you." But before she could take the scarf, the boat rocked on its ropes. Two sailors were straining, pushing the boat out with the help of half a dozen bystanders, all enthusiasm and no skill.

"There she goes!" shouted someone, in half-exultation, half-terror.

A wavering voice began to sing, *"Eternal Father, strong to save / Whose arm hath bound the restless wave . . ."*

Another voice joined in, and another, *"Who bidd'st the mighty ocean deep / Its own appointed limits keep . . ."*

The boat was over the rail now, hanging out over the sea. This must be what it was to be a bird, coasting high above the waves, weightless on the wind. The voices rose around her, and Tess felt a strange elation grip her with the swell of the music, the motion of the ropes. Everything would be all right; how could it not be? They would sail away for a year and a day, or at least for as long as it took to get to the coast, and Ginny would be there, and this would all be a distant memory, an adventure to be told to one's grandchildren.

The sun shone above from a clear blue sky and Robert's voice joined the chorus in a well-trained tenor. *"O hear us when we cry to Thee / For those in peril on the—"*

The boat lurched. The song faltered. They were toppling, tumbling, falling, the final word of the hymn lost as they plummeted down into the sea.

CHAPTER 28

Sarah

Devon, England
May 2013

A SENSATION OF falling overcame me. I startled awake, gasping and terrified. The air pressed against my skin, so gray and damp and chilled that for a murky instant, I lost my place in the universe.

Then a hand touched my bare hip. "Sarah! What's wrong?" asked a sleepy voice.

I closed my eyes and sank back into the pillow. "Nothing. Goose walked over my grave, I guess."

"Mmm. Can't have that."

John's arm draped across my belly. He pulled me gently back against his chest and nuzzled the nape of my neck, and now I knew exactly where I was, exactly where I existed in the universe.

I was home.

But I didn't fall back asleep. The echoes of that terror continued to pulse down my limbs, striking each nerve, and though John's arms anchored me securely to earth, I still felt the faint, unsettling vertigo that had awoken me.

I stared at the outline of the window, hidden by old, dark curtains, and I whispered, "Awake or asleep?"

"Awake. Unless I'm dreaming."

"Nope. Not dreaming. Unless we're dreaming together."

"So we really *are* in bed with each other? Naked? Made love twice last night?"

"Affirmative."

He exhaled into my hair. "Thank God."

I turned in his arms, so we lay on our sides, face-to-face. The dear, soft expression on his face made my eyes sting, and I smiled in order not to cry. "Not bad for rebound sex," I said.

A serious expression sank across John's face. He picked up a piece of hair that lay across my cheekbone and brushed it back over my temple. And another piece. Apparently I was somewhat disheveled. "Sarah," he said slowly. "Last night was a lot of things, but it wasn't rebound sex."

"No?"

"Not for me, anyway. What do you think?"

"Um, well." I stared at the tip of his nose. "I mean, obviously, it was . . . very special."

"Very special, hmm?"

"Very."

He made a small, gentle laugh. "All right. I'll be the brave one. I know you Americans expect vast outpourings of sticky emotion—"

"Ewww."

"So I'll try to accommodate you as best I can, in my humble, restrained English way." He picked up another piece of hair, but instead of brushing it back, he kissed it. "Let me explain something. If I'd wanted to ease my sorrows by indulging in rebound sex with somebody, I would've done it by now. As it happens, however, I'm not that kind of bloke. I did recklessly snog one of the Parliamentary aides at the Christmas do last year, I'll admit, but as we were both quite drunk on the cheap prosecco, I managed to get my baser instincts back under control before any mistakes were made."

I glanced at the spot on my wrist where my watch would lie, if I had a watch. "Still waiting for the outpouring of emotion, here."

"Be patient. I'm not exactly an expert at this, am I?"

"I don't know. Are you?"

"No. I'm not. But neither am I going to allow you to leave this bed—to fly away from all this thinking—because it's too important—"

"John—"

"All right. Here it is, in plain language. Sarah Blake, the truth is, I've suspected for some time that I, John Langford—that it's possible—actually quite likely—almost certain, that I am, in fact—"

"John—"

"—falling in love with you."

I opened my mouth, but I had no breath to speak.

"All right?" he said.

I whispered, "All right."

"And?"

I cleared my throat and said huskily, "And I think it's possible—actually quite likely—that I feel pretty much the same."

His face was so close in that narrow, inconvenient bed. His heavy bones lay carefully around mine, so that I seemed to be tucked into every nook and cranny of him. I thought I felt his skin everywhere, the vapor of his breath, his enormous warmth, the weight of the words we'd just spoken, and the intimacy was so intense, I couldn't stand it. I started to shift away, but John gathered me up swiftly and rolled me onto my back. "Good," he said. "That's settled, then."

His eyelids were swollen with sleep, his skin creased. I laid my palms along his warm, thick cheekbones, and as I met his gaze at last, I felt it again: the sensation of falling.

"Sarah? What's wrong?"

"It's real, isn't it? This is real."

"Yes. Quite real. We are lovers, Sarah. No going back."

"Oh my God," I said. "The complications."

"Don't think about them. We'll sort everything out when the time comes. Right now, it's very simple, isn't it? You and me." He lifted my left hand away from his cheek and kissed the fingertips. "Just stop worrying and bloody enjoy it."

"*Stop worrying.*" I looked away, up over the top of his head to the octagonal ceiling.

"It's not impossible, you know. You can lay aside your neuroses for a minute or two."

The paint on the woodwork was starting to peel. I stared at a faint, irregular tea stain and said, "John, in less than thirty-six hours I'll be on an airplane to New York."

"I told you, we'll sort it out. Do you think I'm simply going to wave goodbye and resume my old life? We've got a great deal of research left to do, Blake. A great deal. Months and months."

"But I don't have months and months. I have a mother, John, a mother who needs round-the-clock care, very expensive care, and I'm all she's got. And last night was terrific—more than terrific—I meant what I said—but—I mean, I can't ask you to turn your life upside down over some American girl you met ten days ago, who comes with more baggage than the Orient Express."

"Shh." John brushed his thumbs under my leaky eyes. "Sarah, please. Trust me, all right? We've all got baggage, loads of it. It doesn't matter. We'll find a place to unpack it all somewhere, God knows. *This* is what really matters. This is real. This is—worth overturning one's life for. I knew the moment I sat across from you in that damned grotty basement bar in Shepherd's Bush—"

"Knew what? That I couldn't hold my liquor to save my life?"

"I knew I could trust you. I knew you were that sort of person, despite your money-grubbing American ways and your pathetic inability to hold your drink. You're *true*, Sarah, and God knows that means everything to me."

Falling, I thought. Falling in love. This is what it feels like. As if the world's gone quiet and tender around you, and there's no bottom, nothing to hold you. Just his eyes searching yours, and his words hanging like stars.

"And that's why you brought me here?" I said. "To Devonshire? Because you knew you could trust me with the family history?"

"Oh God, no. I brought you here to seduce you."

I made a noise of outrage and tried to wriggle out from beneath him, but he caught my wrists and started to press kisses along the line of my jaw and the quivering side of my neck.

"I thought to myself, Langford, you're a sorry prospect on your own, I'm afraid, gaunt and oversized and frankly, no David Beckham in the looks department—can't cast a smoldering glance to save your life—"

"John, stop—that tickles—"

"—to say nothing of all the disgrace and notoriety. But then I thought, there's no aphrodisiac like a massive ancestral pile, is there? I mean, look what it did for Darcy."

"Pemberley had nothing to do with it! She loved him because of what he did for Lydia."

"Bollocks. It was the house, full stop. And his Byronic good looks. And while Langford Hall is no Pemberley, and it's technically owned by the National Trust, you've got to agree it does come with a damned fine folly." He stopped kissing me and drew back an inch or two, and his face turned serious. "Which, if I'm not mistaken, has brought happiness and good fortune to at least one lucky couple before."

By the time we rose and found our clothes, it was past eleven o'clock. We walked hand in hand across the damp grass to the house, where I showered and dressed while John made coffee. He gave me a kiss as he handed me the cup, and for a moment we stood there in the middle of the kitchen, smiling idiotically at each other and at the new, unexpected intimacy of being allowed to kiss over a cup of coffee.

"My turn in the shower, I suppose," John said.

"I guess I could have invited you into mine."

"Not with all the stormtroopers staring at us through the curtains, thank you very much. We'll go away somewhere for our first shower together." He kissed me again, more deeply. "Hmm. Possibly tonight."

"What about my flight?" I asked, a little breathless. "And our research? I feel like we're on the brink of—of finding out everything, and if we can just make that happen, I can head back home and feel like I've got the ground paved under me."

John started for the stairs. "Then I suggest you head back down and get the morning's work going, lazybones, if you're hoping to spend the night in five-star luxury."

I sent the oven mitt flying just in time to catch him in the small of his back.

Still, I obeyed his instructions. Not for the sake of obeying him, mind you, but because the vague, unsettling sensation had returned to me as he disappeared around the corner of the landing, and my mind flew back to last night's preoccupations. *Night Train to Berlin*, and the concert program, and Sir Peregrine's guilt.

The program still lay in the middle of the desk, where I'd left it. I picked it up, and for some reason, as I did, my face turned in the direction of the portrait of Robert Langford that hung on the wall. I'd spent the past ten days underneath that image, examining that face, and I knew it the way I knew my own reflection. Handsome, nattily dressed in a dark suit and tie, a little devilish, one eyebrow raised in perpetual mystery.

"I wish you could speak," I said. "I wish you could just tell me what you meant."

Robert stared back at me with his tilted, enigmatic smile.

"But thank you. Whatever you did, whatever happened on that ship, it ended in John. So thank you for John. Thank you so much for him."

I looked back down at the program in my hand, at Mary Talmadge.

The Talmadge Conservatory, I thought. Founded by her, or her family? I wasn't sure.

I picked up my phone, which sat on the edge of the desk, untouched since last night, and prepared to Google "Talmadge Conservatory."

But the text alert on the screen before me stopped my fingers.

"Oh, damn," I said, and I bolted from the room.

I met John on the lawn, about halfway to the Dower House. "What's the matter?" he asked. "Miss me already?"

"No. I mean, yes! I just completely forgot I'd agreed to meet this old grad school friend of mine for lunch at the pub. I'm so sorry. He's been texting me and I couldn't ignore him any longer."

He raised one eyebrow. "Friend?"

"Friend. Totally. I mean, barely even a friend. Haven't heard from him in years. But you know the code. You go to school together, you have to answer the call." I went up on my toes and kissed his cheek. "I'll be quick, I swear. Don't worry."

"I'm not worried."

"Because you look a little worried."

"Sarah, I trust you. It's not that. I was just going to ask you about tonight."

"What about tonight?"

"What we were talking about in the kitchen. I was thinking about this place on the coast, not far away, lovely spot, renovated, got a spa and a decent restaurant and—"

"Wait. Whoa. I thought you were kidding."

"Kidding?" He looked blank. "Of course I wasn't kidding."

"John, you don't need to whisk me away on some luxury getaway—I mean, I've still got to pack and get organized—"

"Well," he said, squinting toward the river, pushing his hand through his hair, "truth be told, I actually chose it because there's this facility nearby, and I thought—well, we might just take a quick look—"

"Facility?"

He looked back at me. His hair was still damp, his face was still pink from shaving, and he smelled of soap and clean laundry. The sun, perched high overhead, cast his features in deep relief. His voice, however, was gentle. "For your mother. You know, in case the book takes longer than you thought, or something like that. I—well, I know you miss her, and these publishing contracts can take the devil's own time—"

"Oh, John—"

"And before you ask, don't worry about the money. We'll figure all that out. The important thing is that you're able to focus on your work, to say nothing of focusing on sleeping with me—Sarah, what is it?"

I threw my arms around his neck and buried my face in his shoulder. "I don't know what to say."

"So I should book a room for tonight?"

"Yes. *Yes!* I'm sorry, I'm—I'm speechless—How long have you been planning this?"

"Not that long. Maybe a few days."

"I don't—How can I ever—"

"Don't say it. Don't say 'repay.' Nasty word, 'repay.' What you've given me already is beyond price. So not one word."

I pulled back, kissed him, flung my arms back around him, pulled back again. Tried to gather my thoughts back together. Parted my lips to speak.

John laid his finger over my mouth. "Not one word, Blake."

I laughed for pure joy. "Stop, all right? Just stop, or I'll yank you into the grass and show you *repay.*"

"I've no objection to that."

"But I *can't!*" I kissed his hand and pulled away. "I've got to hop, or Jared's going to think I've stood him up and he'll never stop bugging me.

Just—while I'm gone, have another look at that concert program, okay? I left it on the desk. And the movie. There's something there, but I don't know what. We'll talk when I get back."

"*Talk*, hmm?"

"Or whatever you want."

"Unless, of course, you decide to run off with this persistent bloke of yours down the pub . . ."

I laughed and started away. "Trust me. I'm sticking with the bloke who's spent a week at sex camp, learning the nuances of the female orgasm."

"Remember, there's more where that came from!" he called after me.

I fluttered my fingers and bounded up the slope. John's Range Rover sat by itself in the driveway, and it occurred to me that I hadn't given any thought to Rupert and Nigel since last night. Presumably they'd driven off together, into the sunset. Or the sunrise, more likely.

I smiled and trotted down the lane in the direction of the Ship Inn. Happy endings all around, then.

The May sun was warm, and by the time I burst through the ancient doorway—twenty minutes late—I was sweating through my blouse. The fug of stale beer and fried food enveloped me. For a second or two, I stood blinking, as my eyes adjusted from the sunshine to the dim, cramped pub lighting. The dark hum of conversation ebbed away, and I felt the weight of a dozen disapproving male gazes on my breathless figure.

"He's over there," said a voice near my shoulder.

I turned. "Davey! Nice to see you, too."

I knew Davey wasn't exactly well disposed toward me, but his expression of disgust surprised me. He shrugged those stocky, tight-clad shoulders and jerked his head in the direction of the pub's most obscure corner. "Been waiting this half hour. Must have something important to natter about, mustn't you?"

"Which is none of your goddamn business," I muttered, turning away. In a stroke, my good spirits dissolved, replaced by the same uneasy sensation that had woken me this morning. Maybe it was something I ate, I thought, and then I remembered I hadn't eaten anything, hadn't stopped for so much as a crumb of food on our way from London last night.

So maybe that was it. Fasting. Nigh unto starvation.

I reached the corner and drew in a deep breath. Jared hadn't seen me yet; he was hunched over his phone, wearing a gray sweatshirt and a navy baseball cap. Funny, I could hardly even remember what he looked like. Just his dark hair and those sharp eyes, dark blue. Medium height, still sort of skinny, the way he'd been at Columbia. A runner's build. He'd done the marathon one autumn, hadn't he?

"Jared! So good to see you!"

He jumped out of his seat and turned to me, smiling. "Sarah! Wow! There you are. Look at you, you look amazing. Sit down, sit down. Can I order you a beer or something?"

The words came rapid-fire, in between the clumsy movements of clasped hands and a two-cheek kiss. I caught a blur of familiar large ears, and a memory flashed past—Jared arguing with some friend about freedom of the press in colonial America or something.

"Oh, gosh. No thanks. Maybe some coffee?"

"Late night?"

The heat rose in my cheeks. "Sort of. I've been doing some research out here, and we found a really good lead, which always happens right before bedtime, right?" I laughed feebly. "So I'm starving and undercaffeinated. Watch out."

"Sure, sure." He twisted his body to wave in Davey's direction. "I gotta say, the waiter is kind of flinty. Even for a Brit."

"Davey. He's the publican, actually. The owner. He sort of hates me."

"Hates you? Why?"

"Because—" I bit back the sentence and frowned at Davey's approaching figure, which reminded me of an afternoon thunderstorm cresting the horizon. "Oh, I don't know. Hates all Americans, probably. You know the type."

"Do I ever." He raised his voice. "She'll have some coffee, right? Americano?"

"Americano, sure."

"And I'll have another beer. Sarah, you ready for lunch?"

"Just a burger, I guess. With chips. Lots of chips."

Jared turned back to Davey. "Make it two."

Davey scowled even more deeply and snatched the menus from the table. He departed without a word, storming back to the kitchen, dish towel flung over his shoulder.

"Jesus Christ," Jared said. "What did you do to him? Steal his dog?"

"I have absolutely no idea." I picked up the water glass, which contained no ice but plenty of liquid, thank God. After that jog in the sunshine, I was parched. "So. Here we are in England, huh? Long way from grad school. How's it going? What are you up to?"

Jared laughed. "Isn't that the wrong question? It's not what *I'm* up to, Sarah. It's what *you're* up to."

"Me?" I swallowed, choked, coughed. Reached for the paper napkin. "I'm just researching a book."

"Um, at the country house of a member of Parliament who just sort of *happens* to be at the center of the year's biggest political scandal. How the hell did you meet? Are you, like, *together*?"

"Of course not!" I squeaked, using the choking thing to disguise my wanton lack of veracity. "I just—well, he very kindly agreed to let me into the family archives for this book I'm doing about the *Lusitania*. His great-grandfather was on the ship, and so was mine—"

"The family archives? Is that what they're calling it these days?" Jared waggled his eyebrows. "Come on, Sarah. 'Fess up."

"There's nothing to 'fess. Jeez."

Jared threw up his hands. "Fine! Have it your way. Nothing going on in the family archives. So what's he like?"

"I don't know. English."

"Oh, come on. You can do better than that. Why did he even let you in the gates? I mean, please. The *Lusitania*?"

"It's true. That's exactly what it was. I tracked him down at a Costa Coffee in Oxford Circus and—" I stopped. "Wait a minute. How did you know I was even here with him?"

"What, seriously? You haven't heard? Sarah, sweetheart, your photo was in all the damn papers!"

"What?"

"*Oh*, yeah. Meeting him in some shitty bar in Shepherd's Bush. I mean, I didn't see your name in there. You're just the 'Mystery Brunette,' as far as anyone else knows." He wagged his finger. "But *I* recognized you, gorgeous."

"Well, aren't you the clever one."

"Hey, chill out. I didn't tell anyone."

"Thanks. I appreciate that."

He leaned forward over his empty pint glass. "So tell me more. Tell me the dirt. What's going on with that wife of his and the Russian dude?"

By now, I sat rigid in my chair, arms crossed. I'd finished my water, but a sour, sticky taste was invading my mouth, and I wanted desperately to wash it out. To wash myself off. Why the hell had I ever answered Jared's text? Allowed even one curious friend—all right, friend with benefits, but that was way back in the way-back—to invade the private, magical world I'd inhabited these past ten days? *Go to hell*, I should have texted back, instead of thinking I owed him anything, owed him a face-to-face send-off, a professional favor of any kind. I was an idiot.

"Come on, Sarah. We're old friends." Jared grinned and flipped his hand back and forth between the two of us, illustrating the close nature of our bond. "Give me the scoop. I promise I'll make it worth your while."

"Sure, I'll give you the scoop," I said. "I'll give you the scoop when—"

I was going to say *hell freezes over*, but a coffee cup crashed into the table before me, sloshing wildly, followed by a pint glass of pale amber ale that promptly discharged half its head of foam over the rim.

"Oops, sorry," said a female voice, not sorry at all, and I looked up into the violet-streaked hair and narrowed gaze of that bonny, buxom lass, Davey's sister.

"Jesus Christ," Jared said. "What the hell?"

I pushed my napkin over the spill. "It's all right. Just an accident. Thanks—um, thanks, Julie." Her name returned to me just in time.

"Any time," she snapped, and walked away, wiping her hands on her teensy apron.

"Awesome pub," Jared said. "Can't wait to write my Yelp review."

"Just drink your beer," I muttered. I picked up the mug—she hadn't left any cream, and I didn't want sugar—and sipped cautiously. Tasted like regular coffee. But then the best poisons were undetectable, weren't they? I swallowed and went on, trying to steer the conversation, "So tell me about you! What have you been up to these days?"

"Oh, you know. Making a living."

"Doing what?"

"Writing, actually."

"Writing! That's great. Let me know if I can do anything for you. I know a few agents who owe me favors."

Jared drew off a long drink of ale and set his glass down. "I'd hate to use up your credit."

"Hey, what are friends for? I had to blurb some pretty awful books to win those brownie points, so you might as well put them to good use." I glanced to the bar, where Davey and Julie seemed to be locked in some kind of heated discussion. Davey stood behind the counter, hands braced on the edge, while Julie leaned on her elbows and spoke near his ear.

"I'll keep that in mind," he said.

I sipped more coffee and said, "So what do you write? Working on the Great American Novel? The next *Gatsby*?"

"Nope. Nonfiction."

"Oh, that's great. What subject?"

Over at the bar, Davey shot a keen glance in my direction and pulled his cell phone out of his back pocket.

"Ah, good question. It's sort of the nexus between celebrity culture and politics and social media."

"So, contemporary stuff."

"Pretty much. Not your wheelhouse, I know, but I think you might be able to help me out. You know, lend a little insight based on your recent experiences. Damn, where's my burger? I could eat an elephant right now."

He picked up his glass again. His cheeks were beginning to flush, and as I watched him drink, as he swiveled to check on the possible arrival of his lunch, I remembered how little I'd liked Jared Holm by the time I left for Ireland. How brief and boring the sex was, how even more brief and boring the conversation afterward. He was the one you saw at all the Thursday night mixers, drink in hand, conversing with everybody and nobody because he was forever glancing over your shoulder at another prospect while he talked to you.

I shouldn't have answered that damn text, I thought again. I should have remembered him better. I should have remembered how relieved I felt escaping for Ireland, because I wouldn't have to see him again, and I hadn't even had to endure the awkwardness of an official breakup scene. But now that bill had come due. We were still friends, technically. He could still text me and ask for help with his writing, like you do when your old friends reach high places.

"Here we go," Jared said. "Finally."

Julie stalked up, balancing two plates of burgers and chips at either end of the tall wooden ship that sailed across her bosom. I flinched under the scorn of her expression, or maybe I was just afraid she'd dump it on my lap.

But she didn't. She set each plate down, grabbed a bottle of ketchup from a nearby table and slammed it down between us. "I hear you Yanks like this stuff," she said. "So have at it."

"Thanks, *mate*," Jared said—heavy on the sarcasm, in case you hadn't guessed—as he reached for the bottle. "Anyway. As I was saying. I appreciate your helping me out with this little project. You're the best mole ever. Sent from heaven to deliver me the goods."

Julie, who was just turning to stomp away, made a noise like she was trying to rip the head from a Barbie doll.

"Julie, wait!" I called.

She froze and swiveled her head. The look on her face suggested she was currently employing her Jedi powers to impale me against the wall, without success.

"Um, maybe I'll have a glass of wine, after all," I said. "Red."

Looking back, of course, that was the wrong thing to say. I shouldn't have stayed and had a glass of wine with my burger. I shouldn't even have had the burger, though I could have eaten twelve of them by that point, I was so hungry.

I should've just risen from that table, told Jared he could stuff it, and walked away.

And I think maybe it was just a lingering case of impostor syndrome. I'd gotten lucky with *Small Potatoes*, no doubt about it. Yes, it was a good book—a really good book—but there were plenty of great books published that summer, plenty of authors putting out outstanding, original work, and I was the one who broke out. I was the lucky one. At the time, I told myself it was pure, raw talent, but I knew deep down that luck had played a role—good timing, an eye-catching jacket, the right reviewers—and so I felt a duty to stay in my chair and finish this conversation. The same duty that had impelled me to answer Jared's text in the first place, the same duty that had urged me to the Ship Inn for burgers and chips this afternoon, as if by engaging in grubby shoptalk with a struggling, aspiring writer of no known ability, I could win back the elusive karma that had made *Small Potatoes* a success.

By the time John arrived, pink-faced and thunderous, I was on my third glass of wine, which Julie had delivered promptly after the second. She and Davey had backed away to the bar, where they probably filled up a large bowl with popcorn and passed it between them. I don't know. I didn't see anything but John, didn't have any room in my head for any other observation.

I remember the way he paused in the doorway, blinking as I had done, breathless as I had been, searching for me. I think Davey pointed him toward the table I shared with Jared, but maybe it was Julie. Maybe it was both of them together. Luke and Leia, I thought. I realized now that John was Han Solo. Of course he was, despite his privileged bloodlines. Gruff on the outside, tender on the inside. Mistrustful of others. Capable of great devotion, once you gained that trust, and loyal to the core.

Anyway. Not that it mattered. He spotted me, and the misery on his face equaled the misery I felt inside. He inhaled deeply, gathering himself, and strode across the room. He wore his green cashmere sweater over a white T-shirt, and in his hand he carried a piece of paper and a book.

"John!" I said, and then the stupidest thing I could possibly have said, even more stupid than asking for wine with my burger. "What are you doing here?"

He took his cue, of course.

"I might ask what *you're* doing here, having lunch with a *Daily Mail* reporter, but I'd be wasting my breath, wouldn't I, as the answer is more than obvious. Mr. Holm, I hope you've gotten your story by now?"

"Actually—" Jared began, apparently not quite understanding that the question was rhetorical.

But John had already turned back to me. He tossed the book and the paper on the table. "Here you go. If that even matters anymore. I'm assuming it was all just a cover story, but you never know. Two birds with one stone, as they say."

I stared down at the book—a copy of *An Affair in Paris*, Robert Langford's third book—and the paper, which seemed to be the Talmadge concert program. The two items had fallen in such a way that the photographs—Mary and Robert—lay next to each other, in the same studied, monochrome pose.

"I don't understand," I said hoarsely.

"You're a bright girl, Sarah. I think you can figure it out, if you inspect it carefully enough."

He turned and walked away.

Jared whistled softly and picked up the book. I was too stunned to stop him. Too stunned to run after John. I just looked blankly at my wineglass and thought, *It's half-empty.*

"Wow," Jared said, holding up the book and the concert program, side by side. "That's kind of a weird resemblance, wouldn't you say?"

And I was falling again, except this time it was real.

CHAPTER 29

Caroline

At Sea
Friday, May 7, 1915

SHE WAS FALLING; twisting, turning, weightless. There'd been the sound of a hymn being sung, then an abrupt snap followed by screaming and crying and shouting and the sensation of being held suspended in space and time. For a fleeting moment Caroline wondered if this is what death felt like, to be neither here nor there, all senses held in check while the earth stops its rotation so a person could merely step off.

But the screaming was real, coming from the mother with the young boy in the lifeboat beside her. She turned her head to watch them tumble over the side, as they disappeared into the same dark gray water rushing up toward her. The last thing she was aware of was the sound of their lifeboat scraping against the steel and rivets of the side of the ship and of Gilbert beside her, squeezing her hand and telling Caroline that he loved her.

And then she was alone, submerged in the cold water, with bodies and debris piled on top of her. The water numbed and consoled, terrifying her. Muffled sounds penetrated the water, adding to her dreamlike state. She thought of Gilbert, of the promise of their future lives, and she began to kick furiously toward the milky light of the sun on the ocean's surface.

Something dragged at her ankle, fighting against her kicking and her life belt's attempts to rise to the surface, slowly pulling her deeper. Reaching her fingers down to her ankle, she felt a rope, thick and strong, wrapped around her foot, the other end of the rope disappearing into the murky water, attached to an unseen object and making its slow way to the ocean's floor, intent on dragging Caroline with it.

She began kicking again in earnest, seeing how close she was to the surface, desperate to reach it, to suck in a lungful of air just long enough to give her the energy she needed to free her leg. But she couldn't. It seemed the harder she kicked the more entangled she became. *No!* she screamed into the abyss. *Not now!* Not when she'd finally figured out everything. Not when she and Gilbert had everything to live for.

With renewed energy she kicked furiously, but to no avail. Spots began to form around the periphery of her vision, either from the cold or her lack of air. She was dying, and all she could feel was regret. She closed her eyes and thought of Gilbert, wanting her last moments to be filled with him and not fear.

Something nudged her shoulder and her eyes flickered open. Tess had unfastened her life belt and was thrusting it at Caroline. Her frozen hands missed it twice and Tess was forced to knot the ties to Caroline's vest. She could feel Tess's hands on her foot, the tightness of the rope lessening on her ankle. Caroline wanted to tell her not to bother, that her lungs were on fire and she was already dead.

But then her leg was free and Tess was pushing her up toward the surface and they were breaking free to a world of light and sound and air. She coughed and sputtered, turning her face away from the agitated water, trying to escape the constant splashing and screaming, the incessant reminder of how helpless they all were, each of them dependent on what little resources of strength they possessed, and on the kindness of strangers.

"Swim!" Something tugged on her jacket and she realized it was Tess pulling her away from the sinking ship, managing to free her own jacket.

"But Gilbert . . ." She searched the bobbing waves for her husband, remembering his broken arm. "He's hurt—I must find him!" She began swimming back toward the ship but found her arm nearly yanked from its socket.

"No—you can't. The ship's sinking and it will suck everything under when it happens. We have to get away. And then we'll look for Gilbert and Robert. And Ginny."

A look of mutual terror and uncertainty passed between them, along with an informal covenant to believe the impossible, to hope when all hope seemed lost. Without a nearby lifeboat to head toward, they both turned to the open sea and began to swim away from the ship as fast as they could.

When it was clear neither one had the energy for one more stroke, they stopped to fill their lungs, instinctively turning around to watch the death throes of the Queen of the Seas. The Boat Deck was raised at an alarming angle like an angry fist above the waters of the Irish Channel as a giant wave began to wash along the starboard side, swallowing the deck and remaining passengers, a carnivorous sea monster with an insatiable appetite.

Caroline forced herself to watch, wanting to somehow pay her respects to her fellow passengers during their last moments, for them to perhaps find comfort knowing they wouldn't die alone.

The ship rolled to its starboard side and Caroline imagined the giant wave forcing itself through the writing room and library, the grand entrance, the lounge and music room, stunning works of beauty and art that were being extinguished as quickly as a candle flame in a hurricane wind. Any people remaining futilely rushed up to the stern as if that might save them and then one by one the great funnels began to go under, and this time Caroline did turn away, unable to watch the final desecration.

A great roar went up, either the cries of passengers or the sound of the water claiming its prize, but it was awesome in its terror, and Caroline pressed her hands over her ears.

She and Tess bobbed alongside each other for a long moment, as if they were both waiting for the ship to reappear, as if it had all been some terrible mistake. Instead the water returned to its glassy aloofness, a criminal hiding its deeds under a false mask.

Small waves eddied out from the spot where the *Lusitania* had disappeared, pushing debris and bodies toward them. So many bodies, of adults and children alike. Fate had arbitrarily chosen her victims, sparing no one due to age or status, education or bank account. Too many of the victims wore incorrectly fastened life belts, their hapless wearers floating facedown in the water. The lifeboats that had somehow managed to be launched, some filled to capacity and others mostly empty, rose and dipped on the water in the near distance while a flotilla of debris carrying disheveled and white-faced survivors floated between them like lily pads.

A piano bench, most likely the one Caroline had sat on many times, moved past them, the unmistakable waterlogged figures of Prunella and Margery Schuyler listlessly clinging to it. Prunella shifted her body, trying to raise herself higher on the bench, jostling it enough to dislodge Margery's feeble grip. Caroline watched for a moment longer, screaming out a warning to let Prunella know that her sister-in-law had slipped off, but Prunella didn't seem to hear. Apparently unaware of what she'd done, Prunella didn't see Margery's lone bejeweled hand, the precious stones catching the sun's afternoon rays, slowly slipping beneath the surface of the water, unheeded by her companion. Prunella looked around, bewildered as to her sister-in-law's absence, searching for her erstwhile companion.

Her strident voice carried across the water toward them. "Margery? Margery? Are you hiding from me? You can't swim away from me. It's simply rude!" Her shrill tones faded over the waves, as the bench floated farther and farther away from Caroline and Tess.

"Gilbert!" Caroline shouted, her voice evaporating over the water. She glanced over at a pale-faced Tess, her lip bleeding where she had it clenched between her teeth. It was the face of worry, and Caroline imagined she most likely looked much the same.

"Are you all right, Tess?"

She paused only for a second before jerkily nodding her head.

"Thank you," Caroline said. "For saving my life."

Tess looked away. "I was just returning the favor. Besides, I didn't do it for you."

Caroline understood, knew what it was like to love Robert Langford.

Knew what a woman would do to have his heart. She could feel no animosity toward Tess. Only pity.

"All right, then. Let's go swim to one of the lifeboats. We'll figure out what to do next once we're out of the water."

"But what if—"

"Don't say it." Caroline sounded much harsher than she'd intended. "Let's swim, and we'll worry about the rest later," she said in lieu of an apology, already kicking her legs to propel herself forward. Her skirts and shoes made it more difficult, as did the life vest, but she needed them for any extra warmth they could offer. The life vest kept her buoyed when her arms grew tired and she allowed herself to rest for just a moment. She tried not to think of Gilbert without a vest, trying to keep afloat, his broken arm hindering his attempts to swim.

She pushed even harder, eager to reach the nearest lifeboat, which appeared to be getting farther and farther away. True to her word, Tess was a strong swimmer, keeping up with Caroline, her face set with determination. There was something admirable and oddly likable about the young woman, something that made Caroline think that if their circumstances had been different, they might have been friends.

Tess shouted, startling Caroline into taking a deep gulp of seawater. Coughing, she turned to look at her companion and spotted Tess heading away from her, paddling and kicking furiously toward an overturned lifeboat on to which two people clung. As she watched, one of them—a man—slowly let go and slipped beneath the waves without a sign of struggle or lament. The man next to him reached out, but his companion had disappeared.

"Robert!" Tess shouted, slowing down long enough to wave her arm before continuing on her trek to the lifeboat.

Robert. Caroline kicked harder, propelling herself in the direction of the boat, hoping against hope that Gilbert was with him. All she had left was hope.

Tess reached them first, but Robert's gaze was focused on Caroline, his eyes and face light and dark like the half-moon as he watched her, as if waiting for a sign from her as to which way he should go.

Caroline's fingers touched the overturned boat, slipping off twice before she found purchase. She felt Tess next to her, doing the same. "Have you seen Gilbert?"

Robert turned away, but not before she saw the darkness in his face eclipse the light. He moved and she saw a man behind him that he'd been clinging to with one hand, holding them both up as he clung to the boat with the other.

She tried to call her husband's name, but couldn't force the word around the lump in her throat. His head was thrown back, leaning on Robert's shoulder to keep it out of the water, a scarlet rivulet of blood dripping from his ear.

"Is he . . . ?" Caroline managed as she moved toward her husband. Neither man wore a life belt, and she was consumed with guilt, knowing that instead of going to the cabin to get his, Gilbert had remained up on deck looking for her.

"He's alive." Robert's voice was brusque, as if he were talking to a stranger.

Robert's hand on the side of the boat was pale white, his grip slowly slipping, lowering him and Gilbert into the water, forcing Caroline to wonder how long they'd been clinging to the boat. How long Gilbert had been bleeding. And how long Robert had kept her husband from going under. "I've got him," she said to Robert as she placed her free arm around Gilbert's shoulder and kissed his temple, moving him slightly so that she and her life belt bore his weight. "I'm here, darling. I'm here."

Robert forced words from tight lips. "Have you got him? I just need a moment."

Caroline nodded and Robert pulled back, using his freed arm to help Tess up onto the side of the boat where she could hold on.

Gilbert's eyes opened, those beautiful blue eyes Caroline had fallen in love with the first time she'd seen him, the ones that darkened in passion and turned up at the edges when he laughed. A stab of loss and regret stole her breath as he looked at her, and she wanted to cry, to mourn all the wasted days. Regret, too, over what she'd done and the sure knowledge that this was her just punishment for her sins.

Gilbert licked his lips. "I just . . . wanted . . . to see you . . . one . . . more . . . time." He smiled at her, and his eyes closed as his muscles relaxed under her hand.

"Don't say that, Gil. Please don't. There will be plenty enough time . . ."

She didn't finish her sentence. A large wave erupted from somewhere in the depths beneath and pushed at them, carrying with it a twirling mass of floating debris and wrenching Gilbert from her hold.

"Gilbert!" Caroline screamed. She held on to the boat with one hand as her frozen fingers from the other slipped and skidded over the straps of her life belt, desperate to be free of it.

Robert had already let go of the boat, the fear and fatigue she felt mirrored in his eyes. "Don't, Caroline. Stay here. I'll bring him back to you. I promise." With one last look at her, his gaze as frigid and hollow as the winter sky, Robert dove under the surface and disappeared, the wave continuing to push them farther and farther from the spot from which she'd last seen Gilbert.

"Robert! Gilbert!" She called their names over and over as the debris and the waves separated them until she was no longer sure of where to look for them. Full panic took over as she continued to scrabble with her fasteners, her pianist's fingers suddenly clumsy and thick, until a hand clamped itself over hers, stilling her movement. "Don't be foolish," Tess said, her eyes filled with tears and desperation. "Robert promised he'd bring back your husband, didn't he? Don't make him go after you, too."

Caroline struggled just for a moment before she realized the futility of her efforts. She placed her forehead against the cool, slick side of the overturned boat, and pressed her lips together so she wouldn't cry. Crying was for children, her mother had always told her, and for those foolish enough to cry for the moon and other things they could never have.

She wouldn't cry, but all the fight and hope were gone from her. "So what do we do now?"

Tess squared her shoulders. "We hang on. We wait. And if you think God will listen to you, then pray. I'm afraid He's all but given up on me by now."

Caroline regarded Tess for a long moment, wishing she could believe in mercy enough to convince Tess that it existed. She found a tighter grip on the boat and let the cork-filled pockets of her life belt buoy her up, preparing herself to wait for someone to find them and pluck them out of the sea.

They both managed to hoist themselves most of the way out of the water and onto the raised bottom of the overturned craft, their clothes drying by degrees, the sun warm on their backs. Caroline lost track of time as they drifted without speaking, the Irish coast seeming to get farther and farther away. The sun moved across the sky as it did every day, making a mockery of the tragedy that had just unfolded. To some, perhaps, it was just another day, but to Caroline it was a day she was afraid she'd lost everything. She found herself praying the familiar prayers of her childhood, hoping that the God of her youth was as forgiving as she'd been told, and that somehow, miraculously, Gilbert and Robert had managed to survive. She held on to that hope, knowing that as soon as she stopped hoping she'd have no reason not to let herself slip soundlessly into the waiting water.

She became aware of Tess on the other side of the boat. Caroline glanced over at her companion, seeing Tess's tear-stained cheeks and her fair skin beginning to redden in the sun. She should be wearing a hat, or her face would be covered in freckles. Caroline caught herself before she said something. Hats and freckles didn't matter anymore. Perhaps they never had.

"Are you thinking about your sister?" Caroline asked gently.

Tess hesitated a moment and nodded, then rubbed her nose with her sleeve. "She's all I've got left in the world. I couldn't stand to lose her, too. She's everything to me."

Caroline didn't care that the woman Tess was referring to had betrayed both of them, had stolen from her and was probably a German spy. The heart never seemed to recognize the imperfections in others, nor was one given the chance to choose one's family.

"I'm sure she made it to a lifeboat. She's young, and strong—even if she had to swim, she could have made it."

Tess regarded her quietly, as if they were both thinking of Ginny weighed down by the fur wrap and the jewels, unwilling to part with them even if it meant her survival.

"And Robert?" Tess asked. "Do you think he was able to save both himself and your husband?"

Caroline nodded without thinking. "He promised. And I choose to believe him."

Tess looked away. "I suppose out here there are worse things than hoping."

They were silent again for a long while until a rhythmic thudding carried on the waves toward them. They both raised their heads, looking out over the open water. "It's a boat!" Tess shouted. "Come on—wave and shout. Let them know we're here!"

It was a fishing trawler, its deck already crowded with people wearing life belts and covered with blankets, two crewmen waving back to show they'd been spotted. Caroline tried to smile, but her worry over Gilbert and the memory of what had happened to so many people stopped her. She would be relieved to be off the lifeboat, but even she knew the journey wasn't yet over.

She and Tess were helped aboard by crew members with thick Irish brogues who settled them on the deck with two chunks of dark brown bread and a blanket to share. Tess was shivering uncontrollably and Caroline moved closer to her, placing her arm around her shoulder to warm and comfort her. It helped Caroline forget about her own plight for a few moments, at least until Tess pushed her away to stand unsteadily.

"I need to look for Ginny. She might be here, or maybe someone saw her."

She was right, of course. If Tess chose to believe in miracles, then she could, too. They walked together, arm in arm not so much for companionship but to keep themselves upright. The shock from the day's events and what they'd seen had caught up to them, but neither one of them was willing to wait. They moved among the clusters of survivors, all but the youngest ones dazed and bewildered over what had happened to them. Most everyone was searching for a loved one—a husband, a son, a daughter. A mother. It was the same lament, a badge of belonging to a club no one wished to be part of.

Tess and Caroline answered each one before asking about Ginny, and Gilbert, and Robert, receiving the same sad shake of the head they had just given. They'd almost made a full circle of the deck when they reached a crew member trying to hold a man's head and help him drink from a tin cup.

The man's head was covered in dried blood, obliterating the color of his hair. But there was something about the jawline, the shape of the nose. Caroline held her breath for a moment before rushing toward the man.

"Gil—it's me. It's Caroline."

His eyes flickered in recognition as she kneeled in front of him and gently lifted his head into her lap. "How badly is he hurt?" she asked the crewman.

The man shook his head. "Not sure, ma'am. Captain thought a wee bit of whisky could help."

"Is he alone?" Tess asked. "Was there another man rescued with him?"

He shook his head sadly, then gave the cup to Caroline before taking his leave. She looked down at her husband and a black cloud seemed to settle around her heart. His face was too pale, his breathing short and erratic.

A stout man with kind brown eyes whom she remembered from the first-class dining room leaned over to her. "We're headed to shore now. There'll be doctors waiting, I'm sure."

"Thank you," she said. She slipped her hand into her husband's, feeling the icy chill of his skin. "Gilbert? Can you hear me?"

He gave her hand a weak squeeze, and she almost cried then from relief, from gratitude, and the unspoken joy of answered prayers. Tess approached with a blanket and placed it on Gilbert, then stepped back, pressing herself against the railing as if to make the boat go faster.

Caroline bent her head over her husband's, blocking the glaring sun from his face. "My darling," she whispered. "Let me be the strong one now. I need you to keep breathing, do you understand? That's all I want you to do. And to think of us back in New York, sharing our lives, and loving each other until we're old and gray."

She leaned closer to his ear. "I know it's too early to know for sure, but I have a feeling. A woman's intuition, I think you would call it." A tear fell on his face, and she was ashamed to see it came from her eyes. She picked up a corner of the blanket and used it to wipe up the tear and the dried blood from his cheeks. "Imagine that, Gil. Our own child to love. And for his aunt Claire to spoil." She tried to laugh but the sound died halfway from her mouth.

Caroline straightened, continuing to wipe at her husband's face to keep her mind busy from all the frightening thoughts she was managing to keep at bay. "Just keep breathing, Gil. Think about how much I love you, and all we both have to live for, and I promise I'll do the rest." She leaned down to kiss his forehead. "We've got everything to live for."

The boat's engine continued to chug and hum as it made its way to the coast of Ireland, the sea birds screaming overhead as they searched for food. And underneath it all came the ragged breaths of the woman leaning against the rail, searching for her lost sister and for the man who could never be hers. Caroline squeezed Gil's hand and closed her eyes, her heart growing heavier as she thought of all that had been lost. Tess continued her vigil, her sad, lonely figure pressed against the railing as she looked toward shore, reminding Caroline of a child crying for the moon.

CHAPTER 30

Tess

Queenstown, Ireland
Friday, May 7, 1915

THE MOON HAD risen by the time the fishing trawler chugged into Queenstown.

Gas torches flared along the docks, turning the mist brassy. Soldiers formed a human honor guard, holding the crowd at bay, making a pathway for the survivors. As they stumbled off the boat, the crowd broke into a cheer. The sudden noise made Tess start and pull closer to Caroline. In the dark, their hands fumbled together, holding on to each other as they followed behind the stretcher on which Gilbert Hochstetter lay, wrapped in blankets.

People were crowding forward, trying to push through the guards, shouting questions, crowing encouragement. Flashbulbs popped, the scent of sulfur lending a demonic twist to the red light.

There had been flashbulbs that night at the Hochstetters' party. It seemed a lifetime ago, instead of just seven days.

Rescue workers hurried toward them as they made their way to the end of the cordon, offering shelter, lodging. An official-looking personage came up to the stretcher. "Is he . . . ?"

"Alive," said Caroline sharply.

She let go of Tess's hand, taking command of the situation, every inch the polished society wife, despite her salt-stained dress and disordered hair.

Through a fog, Tess could hear Caroline saying, "Gilbert Hochstetter of Hochstetter Iron & Steel. Yes, *that* Hochstetter . . . badly hurt . . . a doctor, as quickly as possible."

Caroline's words worked their magic. Or maybe it was the fierce look in her eye.

"This way," said one of the men, and directed the sailors holding Gilbert Hochstetter's stretcher toward a rough infirmary that spilled out onto the street, stretchers lying on the floor, doctors and nurses moving from patient to patient. Caroline followed, but Tess hung behind, scanning the crowd, looking for Ginny.

The more able of the survivors were milling about, searching for family and friends. They seemed so many on the crowded docks, but how many had been on the boat? Row upon row of bodies covered in blankets, waiting to be delivered to wherever bodies went, gave silent testimony to the others, those who hadn't been so lucky.

Cries of joy and the keening of the bereaved rang in Tess's ears. Through it, she heard someone calling her name.

He appeared through the brassy fog like something out of myth, wrapped in a tunic like a Roman warrior, his hair turned bronze in the torchlight, his legs bare beneath his skirt.

"Robert?" Tess's legs felt like lead; she was half-afraid to move for fear that the vision would disappear.

"Tess." As he drew closer, she could see that his face was scraped and bruised, one eye half-swollen shut. It contrasted oddly with the garment that wrapped him about, which wasn't a Roman tunic, but something else entirely.

"You're wearing a bathrobe," said Tess stupidly.

"A pink one." Robert tried to smile, and almost managed it. "I wasn't in a position to be particular. Most of my clothing is now food for fish."

And he might have been, too, so easily. Tess's throat closed, as she remembered the sights they had seen from the deck of the fishing boat, men and women floating in the water like so much rubbish.

"How did you—"

"Survive? The sea doesn't want me, it seems. This is the second time it's spat me back." Before Tess could say anything, Robert said briefly, "I was picked up by a rescue boat. Is Caroline with you?"

There were so many things she ought to say, but Tess couldn't quite get her tongue or mind around any of them. She felt numb, numb straight through. Instead, she jerked a finger behind her. "She's over there. With her husband."

"He made it, then." Together, they moved toward the infirmary.

"In a manner of speaking." Tess dug her teeth into her lower lip, tasting blood from an old cut. There was no point in hiding the truth. "Not for long."

"How do you know?"

"My father was a pharmacist once." Tess looked up at Robert, too tired to lie to him. "I know what it means when someone looks like that."

"With all due respect to your father's medical prowess—"

Every bit of Tess's body ached. She spoke more sharply than she'd intended. "It's not medical training, it's common sense. There's a death look. Once you've seen it, you know it." She nodded toward Caroline, on her knees beside the stretcher. "She knows it, too. Don't think she doesn't."

They slowed as they approached, listening to Caroline speak to her husband in a low, sing-song voice, her Southern accent more pronounced than Tess had ever heard it. There was something musical about it, like listening to a lullaby.

"—and then we'll go to New Orleans," Caroline was saying. "Have you ever had a beignet? They're almost impossible to eat neatly. But they're worth the mess."

Tess shoved Robert in his fuzzy pink side. "You should go to her."

Robert stood rock still, feet planted like a gladiator's. "That's the last thing I should do. Christ, Tess, what am I meant to do? Taunt her husband as he goes to the grave?"

"She needs you."

Robert's eyes never left Caroline. He stared at her like he was seeing her for the first time. Or maybe for the last. "It's not me she needs."

Amid the bustle of the doctors, the slow, soft voice went on. "After New Orleans, I'll take you to Savannah. You've never seen the house where I grew up. It's not the house where I was born. That burned down long ago. There was a party, you see, and someone was careless about the lanterns. . . . The whole thing went up like a Roman candle, that's what my nurse told me. She said it was the best fireworks display the county had ever seen."

Gilbert Hochstetter's lips moved. Caroline leaned closer to listen, and although the night was cool, Tess could see the beads of sweat on her brow.

"Yes, an expensive one," Caroline agreed. "My daddy never did find the money to build it back up again. . . ."

Her voice faltered as she glanced up, catching sight of Robert. For a moment, her face lit like that Roman candle she'd just been talking about, the blood rushing to her cheeks, a glow in her eyes. And just as quickly, it disappeared again, her face reduced to bones and angles, gray and orange in the fog and torchlight.

Caroline whispered something to her husband. Gilbert Hochstetter's eyes were half-closed, but Tess saw him make a weak attempt to squeeze his wife's hand. Leaning over, Caroline pressed a kiss to his brow, and then, slowly, painfully, rose to her feet.

Next to her, Tess could feel Robert tense. "Caroline," said Robert. "I'm so sor—"

"Don't say it." Caroline's eyes glittered fiercely, bright with unshed tears. Formally, she said, "Thank you for saving him."

"I did what I could." Robert's voice was ragged with regret, the pain so raw that Tess could feel the ache down to her bones. "You know that, don't you? If there had been any way . . ."

Caroline put her chin up. Even without her rubies, she looked like a queen, the sort one didn't dare to defy. "You got him out of there. And I'm going to get him back to New York and make him well."

Robert bowed his head. "Naturally."

They were both lying, thought Tess, her chest and head aching. Why did they have to lie like that? Couldn't they see they needed each other?

"Mrs. Hochstetter . . ." she began.

"Caroline," the other woman corrected her. "After all this, I think you could say we've progressed to first names."

Caroline held out a hand to her. Tentatively, Tess took it. The other woman's grip, she realized, was stronger than she would have supposed. Caroline was stronger than she would have supposed.

"Thank you for saving *me*," said Caroline. And then, to Tess's great surprise, she wrapped her arms around her in an embrace. Her breath tickling Tess's ear, she murmured, "Be kind to him."

Before Tess could respond, Caroline released Tess, straightening and saying briskly, "I'd best see my husband to our lodgings. Warm broth and hot tea will do him a world of good."

There was nothing that would do Gilbert Hochstetter any good now. They all knew that. But no one would say it.

Robert bowed over Caroline's hand, in a courtly style that hadn't been seen for many years. "If I can be of service in any way . . ."

"You already have. Good night, Mr. Langford." Caroline withdrew her hand. Her voice softening, she added, "Good night, Tess."

Robert ought to have looked absurd in his pink bathrobe, but he didn't. There was something in his face that made Tess drive her nails into her palms, the sort of grief that toppled towers and made kingdoms fall.

But all he said was, "Goodbye, Mrs. Hochstetter."

Tess wanted to shake both of them, to shove them toward each other. In all this misery, shouldn't someone take what comfort they could? They had each other. Or they could have each other. To throw that away, now of all times . . .

She couldn't bear it. Tess pulled away, saying indistinctly, "I should go—I have to find Ginny."

Robert put out a hand, stopping her. "Tess. It's nearly midnight."

Tess gave a laugh that was just a little hysterical. "Where else do I have to go?"

"Several places," said Robert, with exasperated affection. It was as if scolding her made the tension lift from the corners of his eyes, helped stop the grieving. "Don't be a fool. Let these kind people find you lodging. Sleep a little. There'll be time enough in the morning."

"But what if—" The words faltered on Tess's tongue. What if Ginny was wounded, hurting? What if, like Gilbert Hochstetter, she had only hours left? Tess couldn't make herself voice it. She could barely make herself think it. "I need to look for her."

"In the morning." Robert's hands closed over her arms, supporting her, restraining her. "I'll help you."

He had looked for Ginny before, or meant to. Tess glared up at him, holding on to anger because anger was better than tears. "Because you want to bring her to justice?"

"What's justice now? No. Because she's your sister. And I know what it is to lose—" Robert broke off, but not fast enough.

"You think she's dead," said Tess accusingly. "That's it, isn't it?"

No life vest, weighted down with furs and jewels . . .

Robert rubbed a hand over his eyes. "I don't think anything. I'm too tired to think. And so are you. Stay here. I'll be right back."

Stay? What did he think she was, his lapdog? Tess tried to cultivate indignation. Anything was better than grief and fear.

Out of the corner of her eye, she could see Caroline Hochstetter giving directions to the stretcher bearers. Caroline caught her arm as Tess walked past. "Do you need anything? A place to stay? . . . Money?"

"Just my sister," said Tess, trying to make a joke of it and failing miserably. Gruffly, she added, "Thank you."

"No," said Caroline. "Thank you. And remember what I said. He'll need someone."

With a nod of farewell, she was off, before Tess could decide whether to be touched or insulted.

Not that she had time for either. The infirmary was crowded with people, some suffering little more than broken bones, others with that gray look on their faces. Tess picked her way through, searching for Ginny, not sure whether she was looking for a dark head or a fair one. The sea might have washed the dye off.

"Have you seen—"

But no one had.

A hand closed over Tess's shoulder, making her jump like a cat. "Didn't I tell you to stay?"

"I'm not your whippet."

Robert chose to ignore that. He gestured to a well-upholstered woman standing behind him. "This is Mrs. O'Malley, the apothecary's wife. She'll put you up in their spare room and find you something else to wear."

Tess lifted her chin in her best imitation of Caroline Hochstetter's queenly ways. "And what's wrong with what I have on? This is best Gimbels."

"Mr. Gimbel never advised saltwater immersion," said Robert dryly. "Go on. Mrs. O'Malley will take care of you."

Not for nothing, Tess was sure. She had no money. And no means of acquiring any. Everything she owned in the world had gone down with the ship. "Robert—I can't accept this."

"If I can accept a pink bathrobe . . ." As he looked down into her face, Robert abandoned any attempt at levity. "In a time like this, you take what kindness you can."

Be kind to him, said Caroline Hochstetter. *He'll need someone*.

But it was hard to give in so easily. "I have no way to repay—"

"Tess," said Robert. "If you fight me on this, I will personally toss you back in the Atlantic."

"If you put it that way . . ." Turning to the older woman, Tess said, feeling like a schoolgirl, "Thank you, Mrs. O'Malley."

The older woman clucked her tongue. "After what you've been through! There's no need to be after thanking me. Come along, hen."

"I meant what I said," said Robert. "About helping you search."

"There's no need . . ."

"I'll call for you at nine," said Robert, and strode away before Tess had time to protest.

Tess left Mrs. O'Malley's at eight, wearing a dress that must have belonged to her landlady's mother. It smelled strongly of camphor, but by the time a few hours had passed, Tess had reason to be grateful for the medicinal tang. It covered other, less pleasant odors.

Robert caught her at noon, just as the church bells were ringing the hour. The town hall had been turned into a makeshift morgue, body after body laid out on the floor. Survivors and family members moved quietly among the corpses, lifting sheets, searching for loved ones. Stoop and stand, stoop and stand. The faces began to blur. Men, women, children. A mother cradling her child. But no Ginny. Not yet.

Tess set down the last sheet as gently as she could, straightening with difficulty. All of her ached, still. She had woken covered with bruises. But it was the despair, the cold despair that permeated the room that crippled her movements, slowed her wits. She swayed as she rose to her feet and felt a strong hand on her arm, steadying her.

"Tess," said Robert. "What are you doing here?"

"What do you think?" Tess cleared her throat, but her voice still came out hoarse. "I've tried all the hotels. And the train station."

The station had been packed with survivors attempting to book passage away, away anywhere. Tess had hunted for her sister, searching for either a dark head or a fair one. But there had been no sign of Ginny at the booking office, at the station, by the quay.

Robert gave her elbow a squeeze. Tess made no protest as he led her away, out of the town hall. "They're still bringing in survivors."

Tess squinted up at him in the sunlight. "I was down at the wharves,

Robert. I know what they're bringing in." Bodies, in increasing stages of decomposition.

The bodies of first-class passengers were being separated out and embalmed, to be sent to their families back in the States for proper burial. Tess had seen Margery Schuyler laid out among the others, being readied for the long journey home to New York. Margery, who had played some part in bringing this upon them. And for what? A dream of a better world? A taste of power?

Tess felt that she ought to take a certain satisfaction in Margery's demise, but she couldn't. Not while Ginny was still missing.

Robert matched his pace to hers, as though they were any couple out for a stroll. Out for a stroll in a town thronged with death. "You might have missed her. For all you know, your sister is currently on a train to London. Or halfway to Germany."

"She wouldn't have left without me."

"Wouldn't she?" Robert looked down at her, and it was Tess's eyes that fell first.

"I don't know," she admitted. *See you on the other side*, Ginny had said. "I don't think so, but . . . I don't know."

Together, they strolled away from the quay, from the disturbing sight of the sea, up one of the narrow, hilly streets.

"There have been stories," said Robert conversationally, "of survivors being washed ashore far from the site of a wreck. When the Armada smashed on these shores back in the reign of Good Queen Bess, there was many a small town that found a ragged Spaniard in its midst. It's why so many Irish have dark hair and eyes. Black Irish, they call them."

Tess wrinkled her nose at him. "It sounds like a tall tale to me. You don't really believe that, do you?"

"Stranger things have happened." They paused in the shadow of the cathedral. The tower was still covered in scaffolding, the building under construction, but no one was at work today. Everyone who could be spared was down at the docks. Robert looked down at Tess, all the mockery gone from his face. "When Jamie died—I refused to believe it. I pictured him clinging to a spar, like something out of *The Tempest*, blown to a strange shore, fighting to make his way home. I thought . . . I thought if only I waited long enough, he would come home again. I fought like the devil when they tried to ship me back off to school in the fall. Our housekeeper says I was like a wild thing, kicking and clawing."

Tess rested her head fleetingly against his arm, aching for the boy who had been. "Did it work?"

"No." Looking away, he said abruptly, "I had some news from home today."

His expression was as stony as the façade of the cathedral. "Not good news."

Robert gave a humorless laugh. "It depends on who you ask." His lips pressed tightly together. Tess waited, tamping down the urge to pepper him with questions. "My father is dead."

Tess didn't know what to say. The spring sunlight seemed a mockery. Death, so much death. "Robert . . . I'm so sorry."

"So am I," said Robert flatly. "He killed himself. When he got news of the ship going down."

"Gosh all fishhooks," said Tess, reverting to the idiom of her youth. She felt her cheeks heat. "I mean—goodness."

"I think you had it with the first one," said Robert, his hands locked behind his back, standing as rigid as the carved saints on the side of the cathedral.

"He must have thought he'd lost both his sons to the sea," said Tess softly. She could picture her father, in his more maudlin moods, gathering her and Ginny in his arms, telling them he couldn't bear to lose them, too. Usually right before he dosed them with one of his experimental nostrums, his attempts at immortality. But for love, always for love. Love and fear of loss. "To know that he'd lost you . . ."

Robert made a snorting sound. In another person, Tess might have suspected a sob. "Lost me? That's not why he did it. It wasn't losing me that killed him. It was—"

"What?"

Robert looked down at her, his eyes bleak, the skin around his lips white. "There's no harm in telling you now, is there? He's gone."

"Tell me what?"

"That you weren't the only one with a traitor in the family." As if he couldn't bear to be near himself, Robert began pacing, his booted feet kicking up dust from the construction site.

"But I thought—" Tess hurried after him, coughing in the dust.

"That he was the very epitome of John Bull with a roar louder than the British Lion? For he *is* an Englishman, and all that. Oh, yes, all of it. But . . ." Robert lifted his hands to his temples. He looked at Tess and said flatly, "My father loved another man. I don't know how you Yanks deal with such things, but at home, here . . . It could have ruined him. And when he had to choose between his name and his country . . ."

"He was being blackmailed?"

"I don't know for sure. I may never know. But—why in the bloody hell else would my father be so eager to keep me off that ship? Those telegrams he sent—he knew something, something he wasn't supposed to know."

Tess stared at him with dawning horror. "My sister said—"

"Yes?" Robert whipped around.

"I can't remember exactly. But something about your father. Something about your not even being able to help yourself."

Robert gave a short, bitter laugh. "True enough. I couldn't help myself. I couldn't help him. Bloody hell, Tess. If he'd only *told* me . . ."

Without thinking, Tess went to him, wrapping her arms around his waist, resting her head against his chest. "It wasn't your fault," she said fiercely. "You couldn't help him if he wouldn't let you."

"Because I wasn't there. I ran away, Tess. I ran away, years and years ago. I wasn't there. . . . And now, all these people. All these people dead . . ." He was trembling in her arms and Tess could feel a suspicious moisture on her bare head. "What if I'd stayed, Tess? What if I could have stopped this?"

"*No,*" said Tess, pulling back. She stared into his eyes, forcing him to look at her. "Do you think anyone could stop this? You don't *know* that your father was involved. And even if he was . . . It's not on you, Robert. None of it. I refuse to let you blame yourself."

"Christ, Tess," said Robert, choking. "Has anyone ever told you that you can be bloody terrifying? All you need is a chariot and to paint your face blue and you could conquer kingdoms."

"Don't change the subject," said Tess, poking him in the chest. "You are not to drink yourself to death out of guilt. I forbid it."

"*You* forbid it?" Robert raised an eyebrow at her, then shrugged. "My flask sank."

"That's one good thing to come of this," Tess muttered.

"Good thing?" said Robert. He held out an arm to Tess and they began walking again, side by side, their shadows joined on the path. "I thought you liked my whisky."

"I like you more," said Tess. She hadn't meant to say it. But since she had . . . In for a penny, in for a pound. She looked up at him, cursing the lack of a hat to shade her face and hide her expression. "Promise me, Robert. Promise me you won't kill yourself over this. If not for me—for her."

She saw his Adam's apple bob up and down. After a long moment, he said, "Gilbert Hochstetter didn't make it. He died last night."

"Well, then," said Tess. "Have you spoken to her?"

"No. The clerk at her hotel told me." Robert kept his eyes on the street, looking straight ahead. "She's taking him home to New York to be buried."

Tess followed suit, not looking at him, but painfully aware of his every movement, every nuance. "When?"

"Monday. An afternoon train, and then a ship from Liverpool the next day."

"Have you thought of booking—" Tess began, but Robert cut her off.

"Aren't we meant to be looking for your sister? I suggest we try the hotels again. You might have missed one."

Saturday bled into Sunday and still the bodies piled onto stretchers. Tess knew because she viewed every one, going from morgue to morgue with Robert at her side, inspecting the new arrivals, as though they were a macabre sort of catch of the day. There were stories, stories that lifted the spirits, of survivors washing up on far shores, startling fishermen at their work. Some of them were even true. But for every story of survival, there were a hundred more bodies beneath blankets, some so battered as to be barely recognizable.

But none was Ginny. At least, none was recognizably Ginny.

She couldn't stay here forever. And she couldn't keep leaning on Robert. He had his own affairs to attend to. The telegrams had kept coming; there was a funeral to plan for his father.

And Caroline Hochstetter was due to leave on Monday.

Alone in her room at Mrs. O'Malley's on Sunday night—the room Robert had paid for—Tess borrowed two pieces of notepaper.

Meet me at the quay. R.

Meet me at the quay. C.

Not exactly inventive, but the best Tess could muster under short notice. She wasn't worried about the handwriting. It was time, after all, that her talent as a forger be put to some good use. Expiation, that was what it was. And, maybe, in a childish way, a bargain with God, just as she used to try to bargain with Him when she was young, offering to give up her stolen marbles in exchange for her mother back. It hadn't worked then, but old impulses died hard.

Robert for Ginny.

There was an eerie hush over the town on Monday morning as Tess dispatched her messages. Today was the day when the bodies from the ship were to be buried. Not the first-class passengers; they were to be embalmed and sent home, wherever home might be. But the others. The ones like her. And Ginny.

Throughout the town, the shutters were closed. No smoke rose from the roofs of the factories. There was only the sound of the army band playing something mournful and vaguely familiar.

Robert would know what it was, thought Tess, as she joined the mass of mourners at the back of the procession. Robert and Caroline. She wondered if they were together, right now. They could play their duets together, fall in love again. That was what she wanted for him, wasn't it? She tried to make herself be glad for them, but the slow, heavy footsteps of the mourners reverberated through her; the grim thrum of death and grief encompassed her.

Stranger things, Robert had said. Tess tried to picture Ginny, unleashed on some small Irish town, the dye washed from her hair, her fingers still adorned with jewels. She might have lost her memory. She might have woken thinking herself born from the sea, like a mermaid.

A Roman Catholic priest and Anglican minister were pronouncing words that Tess didn't hear; incense blurred the air from the altar boys standing by the side of the mass grave. Any moment now, Ginny would appear, walking out of the crowd, eighteen again, with her hair in braids around her head, grabbing Tess by the arm and pulling her, half-running, toward the train station. Tess could almost see her through the mist, an old carpetbag over her arm, saying, *C'mon, Tennie! Hurry!* as they fled yet another town with the law on their heels.

Running and running, running all the way across the Atlantic.

Drums rumbled all around as the soldiers beat a tattoo. Incense like mist and drums like thunder, but Ginny wasn't there, striding in out of the storm.

"Abide with me; fast falls the eventide / The darkness deepens; Lord with me abide . . ."

As the hymn began to swell around her and the sailors lowered the unmarked coffins into the grave, the sobs began to tear out of Tess's chest, great, gulping, ugly sobs. It didn't matter; no one could hear her. She was just one among many, lost in the singing and the sobbing. She cried for the sister she remembered, the one who had held her in her arms and sung German songs to her. For the sister who had taught her to steal marbles and cheat at cards. For the sister who had held her up and pushed her down and loved her as best she could.

For the sister who might be in an unmarked grave or at the bottom of the sea or lost on a far seashore decked in stolen jewels, but who would never, ever come to Tess again.

Was this how their father had felt, why he had tried and tried to come up with some magical elixir to bring their mother to life again? Why he had run and run as though by running he might catch up with all he had left behind?

A multigun salute shuddered over the gravesite. Tess could feel the reverberation straight through to her core, as if she were disintegrating, crumbling into dust.

"Tess." Robert wrapped an arm around her, moving her away, away from the other mourners and the guns and the dust.

"Go away," said Tess, but he didn't, he wouldn't. He just held her and held her as she cried all over his brand-new jacket.

A long, long time later, when the guns had stopped and the other mourners had gone, and the sobs had run out, leaving her feeling limp and tired, Tess said, "It's over, isn't it? It's really over. She's gone. Like your brother."

Tess felt Robert's chin press briefly against the top of her head. "I could say something soppy, about their still being here as long as we remember them. It might even be true."

"Or I might have to hit you." Platitudes weren't the only problem. Wiping snot on the back of her hand, Tess pushed ineffectually against him. "You aren't supposed to be here. You should be with—"

"I was. And now I'm here. With you."

"But—"

"Tess. Stop. Let me take you back to town." He led her like an invalid, supporting her steps back down the long road from the cemetery into Queenstown.

Tess shook free. "But what about Car—"

"When she said goodbye, she meant it." In a gentler voice, Robert said, "And she was right. We couldn't. Not now."

"Why not now?" It was absurd, Tess knew, to fight for her rival, but wasn't that the point? They'd never been rivals. It had always been Caroline. And someone deserved to be happy out of this. One selfless act, one truly good act to make up for all the wrong she'd done. "There's no more husband to contend with. You don't have to worry about divorce or scandal. . . ."

"I don't want to share my bed with a ghost," said Robert bluntly.

Tess looked up at him in shock.

Robert looked faintly sheepish, but didn't back down. "You were the one who told me not to mince words with you. You saw how she looked at him at the end. If he were alive . . . If he were alive, I could compete with him fairly. But now? I haven't a chance." A wry expression crossed his face. "If I'm being honest, I'm not sure I would have won, even then. For whatever reason, she loved the bas—She loved him."

"For what it's worth, I think she loved you. In her way."

"In her way?" Robert smiled crookedly at her. "That's my Tess. No false consolation."

"I didn't mean—oh, never mind. Will you go home now?"

"I suppose I shall have to. There are affairs to be put in order—secrets to be hidden for another generation."

I'll miss you, Tess wanted to say, but couldn't. With an effort, she mustered a smile. "Well, you made it home in the end. You just had a bit of a dunking along the way."

Robert didn't return the smile. Pausing by the side of the road, he said, "Come with me."

"Back to town?"

"To Devon." He raised a brow. "It is your ancestral home, after all."

He was teasing her, and, somehow, that hurt worse than all the revelations and loss. She could bear him serious; she couldn't bear him flirting with her, not when this might be the last time she saw him. "You know I was lying about that."

"I know. You told me." Putting a finger beneath her chin, he tilted her face toward his and said softly, "Has anyone ever told you that you're a very honest liar, Tess Schaff?"

Too honest to pretend she didn't care. "And if I came with you?" she said, knowing everything she felt was in her eyes, and hating herself for it. "What then? Will you find me a place in the scullery, scrubbing pots?"

"No, Cinderella," said Robert, with exasperated affection. "As my wife."

"This isn't a fairy tale." Or if it was, it was one of the darker, more gruesome ones. "You can't turn a goose girl into a princess."

"Is this your way of saying you don't want me?"

"What do you think?" said Tess, and rose on her toes and kissed him.

He tasted of dust and breakfast kippers, but she didn't care. It was Robert, kissing her back, kissing her with a desperation borne of grief and loneliness and goodness only knew what else. His lips were on her lips, her cheek, her throat, kissing away her tears, making her forget herself, until someone shouted from the road and they fell apart in embarrassment and confusion.

Robert shoved his hands in his pockets and took a step back. "My original offer still stands if you prefer," he said raggedly. "I can introduce you to my friends at the papers, get you set up as a satirist. My house in Devon is a quiet place—but there's a great deal to paint. And money to hire you teachers."

Tess didn't know whether to kiss him again or hit him. "You don't have to bribe me with oil paints."

Robert looked at her with naked eyes, not the man about town anymore, but just Robert, the man whose father never wanted him, whose lover turned him down for a ghost. "I've precious little else to offer."

You have yourself, Tess wanted to say, but she knew he wouldn't believe her. Not now. Not with the sting of rejection still on him. Instead, she said, "Why me, Robert? Why now? If it's because you're trying to help me—I've told you before, I don't need rescuing."

"No. But I begin to think I do. Need rescuing, that is." He swallowed hard, saying with difficulty, "When I'm with you . . . the shadows on the wall don't seem so monstrous. You argue my demons into trumpery things, nursery goblins. I—I'm not sure I can fight them on my own."

She could tell how much the admission cost him.

Before she could say anything, he went on, quickly, "You know the worst of me—the worst of my family—and you haven't run screaming. What do you say? Will you save me from myself?" He cast her a sidelong glance. "If it's not you, it will be the whisky."

"That's blackmail," said Tess, stalling.

"I mean it, Tess. Not the bit about the whisky, but the rest of it. Would it be so terrible to marry me?"

Quite the contrary. And that was what made it so hard. "I've always wondered what it would be like to be a lady," said Tess huskily.

Robert bent his head, murmuring, "Don't become too much of a lady. I rather like you as you are."

They weren't exactly words of love, but . . . Tess shivered as he did something very interesting and rather naughty to her ear. He might not love her, but he needed her. That was enough. It could be enough.

Breathlessly, she said, "A diamond in the rough, that's me."

"Nothing so dull as a diamond," said Robert. "I see you more as a ruby."

Tess could picture Caroline Hochstetter's rubies around Ginny's neck, wrapping her around, dragging her down. Rubies glinting in Caroline's ears as she played the piano in the grand saloon that now hosted concerts only for the dead.

"Not rubies," said Tess hastily. "I've never liked rubies."

"Good thing I haven't any, then," said Robert, setting his hands on her shoulders and looking benevolently down at her. "I can stand you some rather nice pearls that belonged to my mother. And I believe there's a rather dusty tiara locked away in a vault. I might once have offered you a slightly dyspeptic whippet, but he perished of old age not long before I left for New York."

"So long as you don't mistake a wife for a whippet," said Tess.

"Don't be silly. *That's* a whippet." He pointed to a dog that was watching them from the side of the road, a skinny creature that seemed to be all legs and a very small head. "Hullo, there. Who do you belong to, then?"

The whippet ignored Robert and went straight to Tess, butting the top of his head against her hand.

"He likes you," said Robert.

"He likes what I had for breakfast," retorted Tess, but there was something rather sweet about the way the dog was licking her fingers. "He looks hungry. And I don't see a collar. Do you think someone abandoned him?"

"Another survivor," said Robert. "Shall we find a meal for him?"

"If you feed him," said Tess, "you might never get rid of him."

"We have a tradition of whippets at Langford House."

"I never had a dog before. We never stayed in one place long enough." Tentatively, Tess ran a hand over the dog's back, marveling at the feel of the muscles beneath the skin, the way he arched closer to her touch. "He's the color of walnuts."

"Walnut," said Robert. "It's a good name for a whippet."

The dog sat back on his haunches and gave a short bark of approval.

Tess looked from the dog to Robert. She'd never had a dog before, or a real home. There was something solid-sounding about Langford House. And about Walnut.

"Walnut the Whippet," Tess said, and smiled up at Robert over the whippet's tail, dog and man blurring together in the sunlight and a sudden mist of tears. "Shall we bring him home with us?"

EPILOGUE

Sarah

Cobh, Ireland
May 2015

On the slim, shingled beach below the cliffs, about a mile to the east, a man is walking a dog. At least, I assume it's a man; at this distance, and in this weather, it's hard to tell. The dog is athletic and boisterous, probably still young, and though the wind blows in angry, wet gusts, he frolics heedlessly among the rocks, while his master marches in his peaked woolen cap and Wellington boots. The sight of them together, man and dog, makes my ribs ache.

I turn my head back to the sea, shrouded in gray. To my right, the Old Head of Kinsale stretches its neck bravely into the squall, and it seems to me, as I stand on that cliff, looking out past the shelter of the harbor and across the Irish Sea, that it's looking for something.

But of course that's just my imagination. My imagination, shaped by what a therapist would probably call projection. Because we're all looking for something, aren't we? Every last one of us looking in vain, looking with futile, unassailable hope for something we've lost.

Walking back into town, I'm struck by how little Cobh—formerly known as Queenstown—has changed in the hundred years since Caroline Hochstetter and Robert Langford came ashore here, along with the other 765 survivors of the *Lusitania*'s last voyage, including the unknown woman who eventually became Robert's wife. At every corner, my breath sticks in my throat at some familiar landmark, some identical sign or building from a long-ago photograph, brought back to colorful, three-dimensional life. All the trials and storms of the twentieth century have left little trace on these streets and houses. Perhaps they were just too sturdily built, here on the edge of the Irish Sea, where storms and shipwrecks occur at regular intervals, are endured and then consigned to memory.

It shakes me, though. Like now, as I climb the twisting streets and look up to find myself outside the Imperial Hotel, where Caroline Hochstetter spent her last night before returning with her husband's body to New York. An uncanny sensation overtakes me, a collapse of time and space, and I might almost be standing next to her. Might almost hear the sound of clopping hooves and wheels rattling over cobblestones, smell the coal smoke and the manure amid the tang of the sea air, bear the weight of incalculable sorrow on my shoulders. Underneath my feet, the cobbles seem to have absorbed the memory of that terrible day and preserved it somehow, cold and hard and unbreakable.

And something else happens, in those moments, inside this architectural landscape that brings England back to my mind. England, which I haven't seen in two years, not since I packed my suitcase under R2-D2's impassive LED gaze and called an Uber to take me to the station in Totnes, and then traveled by train to Heathrow.

I think of John. John Langford, whom I also haven't seen in two years.

Three hours later, as I stand at the front of a packed lecture hall in the middle of Cobh—the old Cunard offices, now converted to a *Lusitania*

museum—delivering animated sentences into the ears of a fascinated crowd, nobody would imagine me capable of standing in melancholy on a rain-dashed cliff overlooking the sea, or before the façade of an antique hotel. I consider my lectures like performances, in which I assume the role of Enthusiastic Professor, bounding about the stage like an intoxicated deer, in order to communicate my passion for the subject with such conviction that you—the reading public—are practically compelled to buy the book afterward. Inscribed with a flourish, of course. A signed book should be a work of art, I think.

As always, I accompany my talk with illustrations, transmitted from an elegant silver MacBook Air to the screen behind me. A portrait of Caroline Hochstetter Talmadge illuminates said screen just now, and the audience gasps at her beauty. They always do. It's a particularly flattering likeness, of course, painted two years after she married her first husband, but there's no such thing as an unflattering picture of Caroline. (Believe me, I've seen them all.) In another age, she might have been a model. She has that kind of beauty, the kind that photographs perfectly from any angle. You might almost hate her for it, except that she didn't seem to care much about that beauty. She never exploited it. She devoted her life not to personal vanity but to music.

"I know, right?" I say, after a brief pause, in order to allow Caroline's image to properly sink in. "She's absolutely gorgeous. She's a young bride in this one, but she's still got a certain dignity about her. You can see why people—and men in particular—found her so fascinating. According to contemporary accounts, she had a long list of male admirers, but there's no hint she admired any of them back. She remained devoted to Hamilton Talmadge throughout their marriage, as she was to Gilbert Hochstetter before him. With one exception."

I flash to the next slide.

"*This* fellow. Handsome devil, isn't he? They made a good pair, side by side. And if he looks a little familiar, it's probably because you like to read old spy novels. Anybody know who this is?" I scan the crowd, but I'm presenting from a small stage, and the lighting makes it difficult to distinguish any faces. "Anybody? It's Robert Langford."

Sighs of revelation crisscross the auditorium. I smile and wait for the whispers to die down. Pick up my water glass at the edge of the podium and take a small sip.

"Scion of a prominent English family and, of course, writer of—in my humble opinion, anyway—some of the best espionage fiction in the universe. If you haven't read any of his books, I highly recommend them. *Night Train to Berlin* is a doozy. Spies and lovers, fathers hiding unspeakable secrets. You've probably seen the film, directed by the legendary Carroll Goring."

I pause again and turn my head to take in Robert's image. The resemblance to John sends a shock along my nerves, as it always does. Funny, I never noticed it back in England, when Robert's portrait stared down at me daily from the wall of the folly, and Robert's photograph stared up from the jackets of his books, and John himself was constantly nearby for comparison. Only afterward did the sight of Robert cause my breath to stop in my lungs. Only afterward did I notice how the shape of the eyes, the slant of the eyebrows, the curve of the mouth, were exactly John's.

By then, of course, I had nothing with which to compare them, except my memory.

I turn back to the crowd and smile.

"Of course, we don't know exactly what went on between these two aboard the *Lusitania* in the days before her sinking. We have only a letter from one Prunella Schuyler, posted right here in Cobh—what was then Queenstown—on the ninth of May 1915 to her stepson in New York, in which she assures him of her safety and makes a reference to Hochstetter's death, in such a way that suggests both his widow and Robert Langford will be pleased at this convenient turn of events. Now, *that*, my friends, is what we in the business call hearsay, and it proves exactly nothing. *This*, on the other hand . . ."

I flash to the next slide, a photograph of Mary Talmadge, and the image, arriving directly after that of Robert Langford, causes another wave of gasps to seethe about the room.

"Mary Talmadge," I say. "Caroline's only child. Born in Savannah, Georgia, on the tenth of February 1916, nine months almost to the day after the *Lusitania* went down. As we know, a year later Caroline remarried her childhood friend Hamilton Talmadge, who shared her Southern background and her love of music, and gave her all the love and security she needed after the trauma she'd endured. Not a passionate marriage, you might say, but a stable and happy one, based on mutual interests and genuine friendship. He adopted her daughter and was, to little Mary, the father she'd never known. And when Mary first showed signs of her prodigious musical talent, Caroline—with Hamilton's support—founded the renowned musical conservatory that bears their name."

I glance back at Mary's photograph, the same one that appeared in the program for the piano concert at the Carnegie, but only for an instant. I'm building up to something important, and I don't want to lose my momentum.

"We're all gathered here in Cobh this week to commemorate the sinking of the RMS *Lusitania* one hundred years ago, and you'll be hearing a lot about the voyage, and the cargo of munitions it may or may not have been carrying, and the historical significance of this event in the context of the First World War. But we have to remember the human scale, too. The individual lives that changed course as a result of the disaster. Caroline Hochstetter Talmadge was one of those lives, and the Talmadge Conservatory and all it represents came out of that transformation, and she's the reason I'm here, speaking to you this afternoon. Caroline Talmadge, who emerged from tragedy to reinvent herself as perhaps the greatest arts philanthropist of the twentieth century. Caroline Talmadge, the subject of my new biography, *Caroline's Music: Birth and Rebirth in the Wake of the* Lusitania."

I like to leave plenty of time for audience questions, and this crowd has many of them. When I launched the book in Savannah a week ago, readers wanted to know about Caroline's years in philanthropy, and the unusual methods of musical instruction she pioneered with Mary and then the conservatory as a whole. Here, of course, the focus is strictly *Lusitania*. Why were Caroline and her husband on the ship in the first place? Had I come across any evidence of a conspiracy? What about Robert Langford?

Yes. What *about* Robert Langford?

I answer that one carefully, as I always do, whenever it comes up. "He's a fascinating man, obviously. But the focus of this book is Caroline, not Robert, and I deliberately left the question of his involvement in—or knowledge of—British intelligence operations for other biographers to answer. I will say this: I uncovered absolutely nothing in all my research to conclude that Robert Langford ever betrayed his country, or even considered the possibility. I would say that the evidence suggests the opposite, in fact. And I'm afraid that's all the time we have—"

"Wait."

The voice booms from the back of the room, the very last row of seats. A strong voice from a masculine chest, the kind of voice that makes everybody startle and turn in its direction.

I shade my eyes against the sharp glare of the stage lights. Against the charge of adrenaline shooting through my veins, I can do nothing.

"Sir? I'm afraid we've already run over our allotted time—"

"Just one brief question, if you don't mind."

The man has risen from his seat, and while I can't see his face in the shadows, neither can I mistake the impressive size and shape of his figure.

"I'm afraid it will have to be *very* brief," I say.

"It's just this. I'm curious, Ms. Blake, how you came to interest yourself in the subject of Caroline Talmadge to begin with. Where that initial spark, if I may so call it, was ignited inside you."

I clear my throat and reach for the water glass. "Well. That's a very interesting question, Mr. . . . ?"

"Langford," he says. "John Langford."

A stir of voices. Somebody gasps.

He disregards all this commotion and continues, almost without pause, "I expect a thoroughly interesting answer, Ms. Blake. And I do have a follow-up question, if you don't mind."

He sits down slowly, lankily, like a man whose limbs are too long to fit in his allotted space, and for an instant I remember just how long those limbs are, and how heavy. Under the warm lights—of course it's just the warm lights—my skin starts to flush.

"The truth is," I say, "I was initially drawn to the Langford family as I began my research. There was a previous connection. A very deep, old connection. My great-grandfather was a steward on that ship, and he died that day in May, and I was hoping to learn more about his fate and his connection to the Langfords. Sadly, however, I was unable to win the trust of certain members of the family, and my research took a new direction. But I believe, in the end, that change was for the best. I discovered something else. I discovered Caroline. And while it's possible she may have made some untenable choices on board the *Lusitania*—following her heart, you might say, in a moment of weakness—she faced the consequences of those choices and overcame them, and became—I believe—a better person. They both did. The affair, while passionate, wasn't meant to last. You might say they were better apart than together. They went on to marry other people and lead happy, productive lives." I take a deep breath and another sip of water. "Have I answered the question to your satisfaction, Mr. Langford?"

He rises again, and the room has grown so quiet, so expectant, I can hear the scrape of his shoes against the wooden floor.

"To my satisfaction? I'm afraid not, Ms. Blake. In fact, I find your argument entirely unconvincing. But we'll leave that aside for the moment, if you don't mind addressing my follow-up question."

"Which is?"

"Will you perhaps do me the great honor of having dinner with me tonight, and allow me to apologize for acting like a complete and utter ass two years ago?"

For the first six months or so after my return from England, I refused to think about John Langford at all. I wasn't angry at him, not exactly. After all, I couldn't really blame him for being upset, for jumping to conclusions, for storming off. We're all human, aren't we? We overreact, we assume, we see what—consciously or otherwise—we expect to see. And John Langford had been betrayed by pretty much everyone he'd ever loved in his life, the women especially. As for me, I'd been stupid to meet with Jared Holm in the first place, stupid and maybe even wrong. If I'd been sensible that day, I'd have followed John out that door and forced him to listen to me. I'd have apologized, I'd have explained everything, and he'd have run his hand through his hair and understood, and we'd have made it all up to each other, probably in bed, and to tremendous mutual satisfaction.

But something stopped me. Pride, I told myself, but it wasn't pride at all. Looking back, I think I was grateful John gave me a reason to bolt, back to my mother and my old life, my old worries and neuroses, my old excuses. Where I depended on no one but myself. Where no man could touch me, betray me, leave me, and hurt me. Maybe I even met with Jared as an act of sabotage, knowing—at least unconsciously—what might happen. Whatever it was, this something inside me, it held me fast, and I filled my time instead with my research, with my writing, with my mother and her swift decline. I sent John no emails, no drunken texts, no social media messages to his official Parliamentary accounts.

And yet. He was still there. I found him at Christmas, when my mother unwrapped the present I'd had made for her—a tiny, favorite photograph of the two of us, imprinted into a charm—and said, *What the fuck is this?* and threw it across the room. Naturally I held myself together, picked up the mess and put it in a drawer, tucked her in and gave her water, but then I went into the hallway and cried in huge, shuddering, lonely sobs. Nobody was there because it was Christmas, and even people who don't celebrate Christmas will still take advantage of the holiday and stay home to eat turkey or Chinese takeout with their families. It was dark outside the window, and the hallway was cold and smelled of antiseptic, and I was alone. Just me and my shuddering, so hard and so body-wracking that something broke inside me, some barrier, and there stood John behind it. Large and quiet and reassuring. Stuck in my bones.

Oh, go piss off, I told him. *You're too late.*

But he refused to go away, and eventually I got used to him. We made peace. There were times I couldn't even remember why I'd pushed him away in the first place.

John's waiting for me after the event is over, the real John, flesh and blood, sitting discreetly in the back of the room until the last book is signed, the last reader has departed. My publisher has assigned me a handler for this portion of the book tour, and she stands uncertainly near the signing table, glancing between the two of us.

"That's okay, Joanna," I say. "I can find my own way back to the hotel."

She picks up her coat and bag and bolts toward the door, which John opens for her. I gather my things, my Sharpies and my iPhone, my bookmarks, and place them in my tote with my laptop. Stand slowly, holding the edge of the table with one hand, in case my legs wobble at the sight of him, arms crossed, leaning against the door.

"You said something about an apology," I say.

"Sarah, I—"

"Just kidding. I'm the one who should apologize. You tried to reach out and I ghosted you, and ever since then—"

"Ghosted you? Is that what it's called?"

"I told myself that I couldn't handle your drama on top of my own, and maybe that was true, but I—well, the truth was, I was scared. You scared me."

He uncrosses his arms and steps toward me. "And you scared the very devil out of me, Blake, and you'd every right to—what was it?—every right to ghost me, after I walked out like that, like a bounder, not even asking for your side of the story."

He stops, but he's found the light now. I can see his face, which looks older and plainer than I remember. The lines have settled around his eyes and his mouth. But he's as lean as ever—too lean, maybe—and his hair is a bit longer, flopping onto his forehead. Two years. I know what he's been up to, of course. Don't think I haven't Googled him. I have Googled him, and I have stared at his image on my computer screen, and I have *almost* emailed him about eight dozen times, usually late at night after a glass or two of wine. Just enough wine to be both lucid and reckless.

I think, I could sure use a glass of wine now. Something to bridge the gap between us, the thick, awkward stuffing packed into the three or four yards that still separate the two of us, him and me, John Langford and Sarah Blake.

He reaches inside his jacket and pulls out a manila envelope. "I brought this for you. Something for your research."

"What is it?"

"You're supposed to open it and find out."

I undo the clasp and stick my hand inside. Find the stiff, delicate paper inside and pull it out. "It's a sketch. Oh my God, it's the same portrait, the one of Robert! Where did you find this?"

"In the last stack of papers, the ones we hadn't finished. Look at the signature at the bottom."

I place my finger under the single word "Tess."

"His wife," I whisper. "Your great-grandmother."

"She was a tremendous artist. Those are her landscapes around the house. She was one of the best-known watercolorists of the thirties, until her work fell out of favor after the war."

"Then why haven't I heard of her?"

"She exhibited as Tennessee Fairweather. Everyone assumed she was a man. I did a little research of my own, you see."

I blink at Robert's image, his crinkling eyes that had always seemed to me to contain some naughty secret between himself and the artist. I pass my fingers over the wave of hair on his forehead, and when it begins to blur before me I hastily shove the paper back into its envelope, taking my time with the clasp.

"Thank you for the flowers," I say.

"I'm so sorry, Sarah. So profoundly sorry for your loss. I wanted to come to the service. I nearly did. Then I thought it was best if I didn't."

"You were probably right."

His head turns away slightly. "I see."

"But not for the reason you think. When I saw the flowers—and then the note—the beautiful note you sent with them—"

I break off, because I can't go on. It's all I can do to blink back the dampness in my eyes. Swallow back the sting at the back of my throat. The prickling in my nose.

"We rushed it," he says. "I rushed it. My fault. I thought that just because I knew you were the one, because I was so certain about you, we could simply race past the preliminaries. I wanted—well, it doesn't matter. I didn't want to waste any more time, and it turns out that it's not a waste, that long dance."

"It's just as well. I wouldn't have written this book the way I did. You wouldn't have written that manifesto and won the by-election—"

"Maybe not," he says, "but maybe we would have. Only together."

"No. Everything happens for a reason, Langford. Haven't you learned that by now? You can't change one thing without changing everything. We all exist on this planet, each of us, because of an extraordinary, improbable, random series of coincidences that can't be repeated. And everything you do affects everything that happens after. Look at Robert and Caroline and your great-grandmother. And I'll bet that if I'd called after you in that pub, if you'd turned around and heard me out, I would have written that Robert Langford biography instead of flying to Savannah and moving my mother to the care home there—"

"Where it took me the devil's own time to find you, even with modern technology."

"Ah, so you were *stalking* me."

"Weren't you stalking *me*?"

And there it is, just like that. A smile turns up the corner of his mouth, exactly the way it used to do. The familiarity of him strikes me in the stomach. How can his smile be so familiar? It's been two years since I saw him smile like that, as we lay in bed together. Two dizzying weeks in his company, two years without him. I find myself wondering if he's slept with anybody in the meantime, kissed anybody, gone on dinner dates or dirty weekends. Two years is a long time. In two years, you move on, you change, you grow, you forget.

"The answer to your question," he says softly, "is yes. I tried. But it never took. It was just tedious, and I couldn't sort out why. I began drinking too much. Threw myself into work. And eventually I realized that I wasn't myself. That I felt more *myself* during those two damned weeks in the folly than I ever had in the two years since. I missed you. I missed drinking my morning coffee with you. I missed sharing your breath. I missed your naps on the sofa and the way it felt to look at you and think, that bloody woman will just fall asleep right in front of me, like she belongs there."

Like she belongs there.

I stand without speaking. I'm out of words; I've spoken so many tonight, stood so confidently on that stage, pretending to be an expert. As if I belonged in front of all those people, and yet I don't belong anywhere, do I? No father and no mother remaining to me, no siblings, no home, just a rented apartment in Savannah, Georgia, not far from the Talmadge Conservatory of Music. I am adrift, I am without anchor, I am between ports. Belong to nothing and nowhere and nobody, really. I am just *New York Times* Bestselling Author Sarah Blake, that's all. A face on a book jacket in ten thousand bookstores. *What's your next book about?* someone inevitably asks in every crowd, and my answer is always the same.

I find the best ideas are the ones that come to you. So I'm just waiting for the next one to turn up, and hope I have the good sense to know it when I see it.

John lifts his arm and holds out his hand to me, palm-up.

"If it's any incentive, Walnut's waiting in the car outside."

"*Walnut?*"

"He missed you. Almost as much as I did."

I lift my tote over my shoulder, swing around the corner of the signing table, and take his hand. His warm fingers close around mine, and I catch the scent of his soap as if I last sniffed it yesterday. And dog. He smells, very faintly, of dog. I stare at the hollow of his throat, which is just visible at the junction of his shirt collar, and admire the swift tick of his pulse. The tenderness of his skin.

John whispers, "I love you."

I look up and find his eyes, and for an instant I experience a sense of confusion, of disorientation, as if I'm standing not before John but before his great-grandfather, and I am somebody else. Somebody else cut adrift, who doesn't belong to anyone.

Then the world goes back into focus, and he's John again.

And I am Sarah. Just Sarah.

I lay my hand along the side of his face and say, "I know."

ACKNOWLEDGMENTS

TEAM W WOULD like to thank our amazing editor, Rachel Kahan, and the rest of the team at William Morrow (Tavia and Lauren T., we're looking at you!) for launching *Lusitania* safely onto the Glass Ocean.

To our agents, Amy Berkower and Alexandra Machinist, for believing in the crazy idea that three writers could work together to produce one seamless novel. And then believing in it again.

To our long-suffering spouses, children, and pets, for putting up with our absconding to the writing cave (and periodically to the outlets together) and especially to Oliver, for waiting until the manuscript was in before making his appearance into the world.

Thanks to Alyson Richman for our opening scene at the book club, which was, sadly, drawn from life (just say no to book piracy!). Thanks also to Joan Heflin for the loan of her front porch and backyard for the Team W author photo.

If you're looking for more information about the *Lusitania*, we highly recommend Erik Larson's *Dead Wake*. We are deeply indebted to Mr. Larson for his detailed account of the *Lusitania*'s fateful final voyage.

Last but not least, thank you to all of you who took *The Forgotten Room* into your hearts and made this second collaboration possible. Thank you for your emails, your Instagram posts, your Facebook messages, and your reviews. It means more to us than we can say.

Until we meet again—possibly in Paris . . .

ABOUT THE AUTHORS

Beatriz Williams, Lauren Willig, and Karen White are the coauthors of the beloved *New York Times* bestselling novel *The Forgotten Room*.

Beatriz Williams is the *New York Times* bestselling author of eight novels, including *A Hundred Summers, The Secret Life of Violet Grant*, and *The Summer Wives*. A native of Seattle, she graduated from Stanford University and earned an MBA in finance from Columbia University, then spent several years in New York and London as a corporate strategy consultant before pursuing her passion for historical fiction. She lives with her husband and four children near the Connecticut shore, where she divides her time between writing and laundry.

Lauren Willig is the *New York Times* and *USA Today* bestselling author of *The Ashford Affair*, *That Summer*, *The Other Daughter*, and *The English Wife*, as well as the RITA Award–winning Pink Carnation series. An alumna of Yale University, she has a graduate degree in history from Harvard and a JD from Harvard Law School. She lives in New York City with her husband, preschooler, and baby, and lots and lots of coffee.

Karen White is a *New York Times* and *USA Today* bestselling author and currently writes what she refers to as "grit lit"—Southern women's fiction—and has also expanded her horizons into writing a mystery series set in Charleston, South Carolina. When not writing, she spends her time reading, scrapbooking, playing piano, and avoiding cooking. She has two grown children and currently lives near Atlanta, Georgia, with her husband and two spoiled Havanese dogs.